DEA IRAE

The computer screen faded into a peacock plumaged in glorious blues, greens, and golds. It gave Kerickson a piercing look out of its tiny eyes. "I AM JUNO, PROTECTRESS OF MARRIAGE AND MARRIED WOMEN, INSPIRER OF GREAT POEMS, HEROIC DEEDS, AND STUFF LIKE THAT."

Kerickson leaned back and nodded at the screen. "So, Juno, how've you been?"

"DON'T YOU 'SO, JUNO' ME, YOU SHRIVELED-UP SON OF A TOAD!" The peacock reformed itself into a middle-aged woman with angry blue-green eyes and golden hair. "I HAVEN'T FORGOTTEN WHAT YOU DID TO THAT LOVELY GIRL."

"Not this again," Kerickson mumbled.

"WHAT WAS THAT?"

"It's been five years since Alline saw her chance to become Empress and left me. Can we talk about something else?"

"YOU'D LIKE THAT, WOULDN'T YOU?" Juno sniffed, then conjured up a long divan and draped her full-figured form over it.

Kerickson leaned back. "Look, Minerva is down for a few days. How would you like to protect the city while she's incapacitated?"

Juno twitched her spotless white tunic. "WELL, OF COURSE, I COULD REPLACE THAT LITTLE SNIPPET WITHOUT EVEN TRYING."

Look for these Del Rey Discoveries . . .
Because something new is always worth the risk!

THE
IMPERIUM
GAME

K. D. Wentworth

A Del Rey Book
BALLANTINE BOOKS • NEW YORK

For Richard
who gave me wings

A Del Rey Book
Published by Ballantine Books

Library of Congress Catalog Card Number: 93-90708

ISBN 0-345-38729-5

Manufactured in the United States of America

First Edition: February 1994

CHAPTER
ONE

Kerickson paused in the doorway of the Interface Room. Even though it was a good hour before their shift began, his partner Giles Wilson was already in place before the long control console, his perpetually youthful face reduced to a sickly pallor by the screens' blue light. The room was filled with a soft hum as the security monitors flicked through their preset patterns at three-second intervals—the Forum, the Market District, the Arena, the Baths.

Kerickson leaned against the doorjamb and yawned. "Don't you ever sleep?"

Wilson motioned him in without looking up. A deep worry line creased his forehead as he peered intently at a set of statistics. "Minerva is down again."

"Well, don't look at me. I have to order the Saturnalia supplies. I can't possibly get to her until later." Kerickson slid into his swivel chair before the right console. "There are too many gods in this game anyway. Leave her off-line for a while."

"But she's in charge of the city!" Wilson punched in a string of instructions, then ran his fingers back through his thinning brown hair. "The city won't run without her."

"And whose fault is that?" Kerickson turned back to his screen as the statistics on the following week's Saturnalia came up. " 'Throw the element of chance in,' you said—'let people interact with the gods, give them the genuine feel of what old Rome could have been like if the gods were real.' " He checked the totals column for the end-of-the-week feast and scowled. "Next you'll be wanting to build outhouses!"

Wilson's soft round face fell into shocked folds. "I'll have you know the ancient Romans had excellent indoor plumbing!"

Kerickson's eyes rolled upward. Scratch an ex-professor, he

thought, and you'll get a lecture every time. "That takes a lot off my mind. Why don't you just switch Minerva's functions over to Mars until she's up and running again?"

"Are you kidding?" Wilson's fingers twisted into anxious knots. "Last month, when I asked him not to manifest during the stockholders' tour and make faces like he did last year, he not only ordered his priests to barbecue Jupiter's sacred chickens, he told the Gladiatorial School they were giving out free beer down at the Brothers Julian Restaurant. Ten minutes later, they were rioting in the amusement sector. HabiTek's stock went down twenty points in the next two days!"

"That's the whole problem. The old boy needs something to keep him busy." He saved his statistics for later, then keyed in the code for Mars.

The center screen's muted blue glow coalesced into an untidy vulture which seemed to be molting. "I AM MARS, GOD OF WAR, DISCORD, AND BATTLE—"

"Yeah, yeah." Kerickson knew the litany by heart. "Wilson and I have a little proposition for you."

"WILSON?" The vulture snapped its savagely hooked beak and stared out with gleaming red eyes. "I KNOW OF NO PLAYER BY THAT DESIGNATION."

"Give me a break." Kerickson leaned back in his chair and folded his arms. "Are you interested or shall I buzz Apollo instead?"

"THAT POMPOUS ASS?" The vulture dissolved into a pudgy, hook-nosed man with a thick red beard and a handful of gleaming, metal-tipped spears. "HE'S NOTHING BUT MUSIC AND POETRY, AND YOU KNOW IT."

Kerickson glanced over at Wilson, then turned back to the screen. "Here's the deal. Her divineness, Minerva, Goddess of Wisdom, is down for a few days, and the Imperium needs looking after. So, do you want to be God of the City and Protector of Civilized Life for a little while, or should we get someone else?"

The image on the screen threw out its chest. "BLOODY HELL! WHO NEEDS CITIES ANYWAY? YOU GUYS PLAY THIS GAME LIKE A BUNCH OF GODDAMNED PANSIES. WE NEED SOME REAL BLOODSHED AROUND HERE TO LIVEN THINGS UP!"

I told you so, Wilson mouthed.

"Never mind." Kerickson punched in the release code. "Just

go on back to whatever mayhem you were planning." The image dissolved back into an even blue glow.

"I knew it!" Wilson fumbled in his pocket for the pink Stomak-Eaze can, then sprayed a dose into his mouth. "The entire system is going down right before the Saturnalia, and you know how the players feel about gaining their quarterly experience point. Census reported yesterday that over fifty families have already renewed their Game licenses in advance of the festival so they will be guaranteed a juicy role next week." He shuddered. "There go our raises."

Kerickson kneaded his forehead; Wilson's theatrics always gave him a headache. "No, no, I'll take care of everything. Why don't you just go over and check out the Gladiatorial School? There's a nasty rumor going around that Marcinius Flatus is selling extra hit points."

"But that's ridiculous!" Wilson heaved himself out of the chair. "He'd have to be able to tie into the Game computer to do that!"

Kerickson shook his head. "Maybe so, but that's what I heard down in the Forum."

"All right." Wilson paused. "Are you sure you don't need me down here?"

Just like a hole in the old cranium, Kerickson thought. He stretched his face into a smile. "Don't worry. I'll get someone to watch over the city next week, even if I have to do it myself."

Wilson was already out the door as Kerickson turned back to the screen. "Okay," he muttered to himself, "which one . . . Juno, Venus, Diana, Ceres, Vesta?" Any one of the goddesses ought to be able to take Minerva's place for a few days without disturbing current Game scenarios too much. Finally he decided on Juno as being the most settled of the lot and punched in her call code.

The screen on the right faded into a peacock plumaged in glorious blues and greens and golds. It gave him a piercing look out of its tiny eyes. "I AM JUNO, PROTECTRESS OF MARRIAGE AND MARRIED WOMEN, INSPIRER OF GREAT POEMS, HEROIC DEEDS, AND STUFF LIKE THAT."

Kerickson leaned back and nodded at the screen. "So, Juno, how've you been?"

"DON'T YOU 'SO, JUNO' ME, YOU SHRIVELED-UP SON OF A TOAD!" The peacock reformed itself into a middle-aged woman with angry blue-green eyes and golden hair. "I STILL HAVEN'T FORGOTTEN WHAT YOU DID TO THAT LOVELY GIRL, DEMEA."

"Not this crap again," Kerickson mumbled to himself.

"WHAT WAS THAT?" Juno drew her tall body up proudly.

"I *said*, her name is Alline and it's been five years since she saw her chance to become Empress and left me. Can we talk about something else?"

"YOU'D LIKE THAT, WOULDN'T YOU?" Juno sniffed, then conjured up a long divan and draped her full-figured form over it. "THERE ISN'T A MAN IN THIS WHOLE GAME WORTH DEMEA'S LITTLE FINGER."

Kerickson leaned back in his chair. "Look, Minerva is down for a few days, and since you're already doing such a great job watching after the married women enrolled in the Game, how would you like to protect the rest of the city while she's incapacitated?"

Juno twitched her spotless white tunic so that it fell into perfect folds. "WELL, OF COURSE, I COULD REPLACE THAT LITTLE SNIPPET WITHOUT EVEN TRYING."

Kerickson forced a smile across his face. "Great. Just keep an eye out for Mars and Jupiter and the rest so they don't start anything funny."

"NOT SO FAST." She gave him a steely look. "I WON'T HAVE TO APPEAR AS ONE OF HER STUPID OWLS, WILL I?"

"Perish the thought."

"IN THAT CASE—" Juno flung her arms into the air. "THIS AUDIENCE IS ENDED!" The screen dissolved into blueness.

Kerickson turned back to his Saturnalia plans, but then word came through on the left status screen about some sort of disturbance involving sixteen teenage boys and the Game's only remaining Vestal Virgin down at the Public Baths.

Switching statistics to the back of his mind, he punched for the City Guard.

"How could you let this happen?" Wilson ran his fingers through the remnants of his graying brown hair as he paced moodily around the Interface Room.

"So, I'll go out onto the playing field and find us another virgin."

"Does Vesta know about this yet?" Wilson wiped at a trickle of sweat on his forehead.

"Probably." Kerickson paused as the door opened. "Keep an eye on things until I get back."

Wilson muttered something in reply, but Kerickson couldn't make it out. He stopped at Costuming and picked up a linen tunic and a long gray woolen cloak, nothing snazzy, but enough to keep out the currently programmed winter chill. Then he presented his Game bracelet to the monitor.

"Identity confirmed," the computer's monotone said. "Kerickson, Arvid G. Game status: Management."

The gate slid open. Kerickson walked to the front door of the bakery used to disguise the Management Gate from the general public and stepped out into the bustling streets of ancient Rome. Cold air flowed against his face, carefully conditioned to simulate the atmospheric composition of over two thousand years ago—at the moment redolent of wood smoke and rotting vegetables and manure.

Dodging a steaming pile of donkey dung in the middle of the street, he pulled his cloak around his shoulders against a chill drizzle that was programmed to fall for the next two hours and set off for the Forum.

No matter how many times he saw it, he never failed to appreciate what HabiTek had built here: an entire city where, for an exorbitant fee, the population of three thousand or so players lived out the identities of ancient Romans, trying to gain enough points to become Emperor or Empress before their time ran out and they returned to the outside world.

Of course, the experience of living in the Imperium was more important to most people than actually winning. And if you didn't have a lot of money, you could take on one of the roles that actually produced an income, like merchant or craftsman, or work part-time in one of the concessions. He himself had lived on the playing field for three months as a captain in the Emperor's personal guard when he'd first signed on to the Game staff, sneaking off to the Interface occasionally to make subtle adjustments in programming. As it stood now, current scenarios were going fairly well—except for the gods. If they had actually wreaked as much havoc in ancient Rome as they did here in the Imperium, Rome would have fallen a thousand years sooner.

In spite of the wet and the cold, the walk was pleasant enough. He saw a couple of day-trippers, outfitted, like all visitors, as German barbarians—a classification no one actually played in the Game. They passed him, oohing and ahhing over the fountains and the arches and the dazzling mosaics. He turned down the Via Nova, one of the Game's more popular streets, since most of the courtesans lived in this district. Several top-heavy ladies in various states of undress hung out of windows on the second floor and waved to him as he passed. He waved back, wondering why it seemed to be the dream of elderly society matrons to play a lady of ill repute here in the Game. Why couldn't they get a few of the younger and more lovely specimens interested in these roles?

Turning right at the Via Sacra, then left at the Via Latina, Kerickson made his way through the Market District, with its bustling shops, both authentic and tourist, to the Forum and its impressive array of temples. He could see the columns of Vesta's round temple a long way off. Not overlarge, it was still impressive, its white marble and golden roof easy to pick out, even in the rain.

Avoiding an old woman with a cage of sacrificial doves, he trudged up the sixteen broad steps to the outer court and waited. No one came out to greet him, but he could hear the faint sounds of someone weeping.

Without warning, a twenty-foot-tall holographic image materialized in front of him: Vesta with her hair of flames. "SO?" Her hair crackled as she tapped a yard-long foot at him. "I SUPPOSE YOU'RE GOING TO TELL ME THAT SHE'S STILL 'PURE OF HEART.' "

"Greetings, Vesta, Goddess of the Hearth and Home." Kerickson knelt on the broad stones and bowed his head in the frigid rain. The tips of his ears and nose already felt numb. "Are we speaking of the lady Amaelia?"

"THE LITTLE TART!" The sound of weeping grew louder as Vesta's size increased again. Her foot, now the size of a rowboat, thudded against the stone.

Even though she was just a holo, Kerickson squirmed. Because of Wilson's alterations—approved by the HabiTek board, who thought they would make the Game more exciting—the gods now had certain physical powers within the city. Vesta could access enough power to make things uncomfortable for him, within certain parameters. "Girls will be girls."

"DON'T GIVE ME ANY OF THAT HOLIER-THAN-THOU CRAP. YOU KNOW AS WELL AS I DO THAT

SINCE SHE LET THE SACRED FIRE GO OUT, THE EN-
TIRE CITY IS IN SERIOUS JEOPARDY!"

"Forget those hoary old prophecies and let's get down to ba-
sics." Kerickson shivered as the wind began to gust. "You hold
off on the funny stuff until after the Saturnalia, and I'll find
you some new girls."

"I'M SUPPOSED TO HAVE SIX." Vesta bent over and
stared into his face. At this angle, her nose reminded him of an
anchor he'd once seen on an ocean liner. "AND I WANT
THEM YOUNG THIS TIME, NOT LONG IN THE TOOTH
LIKE THIS ONE."

"Well, I'd hardly call twenty long in the tooth, but I'll do
my best." A trickle of sweat ran down the back of his tunic.
Six more girls—he wasn't even sure he could find one. Virginity and celibacy were not popular topics in the Imperium.
Maybe if he offered free Game licenses this time—

"LISTEN, YOU LITTLE TURD, GET OUT THERE AND
FIND ME SOME VIRGINS!"

"Right," he mumbled, making frantic gestures to the girl to
come out of the temple. "I'll have them here in a few hours,
tomorrow at the very latest." Amaelia ran past him and on
down the steps. Kerickson bowed deeply one final time, then
rose to his numb feet and lurched backward after her.

Red-eyed and trembling, Amaelia waited for him at the first
corner beside a wine shop. He took her arm and walked her on
down the busy street, noticing how much more . . . mature she
looked than the last time he had seen her, even with a tear-
streaked face.

"Listen," she said as they passed a German barbarian, "I'm
really sorry about the sacred fire going out. I only left it alone
for a few minutes. It should have been perfectly all right."

"Well . . ." The faint spice of her perfume tingled all the
way down into his toes. He suddenly remembered his manners
and draped his cloak around her shivering shoulders. "These
things happen."

"But you don't understand. The message said I was to meet
my father down at the Public Baths right away, but he never
came." Covering her coppery hair with the cloak's hood, she
gazed back at the golden-roofed temple. "I guess it was some-
body's idea of a joke."

They walked on in silence for a few minutes.

"I never wanted to be a Vestal Virgin anyway," she said fi-

nally. "My stepmother made me do it so our family would get
the double experience points."

Of course, what she wasn't mentioning was that those experience points had been enough to turn the tide in her father's
favor. Micio Metullus had been able to trade in those points for
an increased charisma ranking, which in turn had subverted the
Praetorian Guard last quarter. Micio was now entrenched in the
Palace as Emperor, as firmly as anyone could be who had to
play against the rest of the Imperium to keep his place.

"What's it like on the outside?" She turned wistful green
eyes upon him. "Tell me about airhoppers and gravity wells
and things like that."

"Airhoppers?" He glanced sideways at her creamy profile.
"Just how long have you been here, anyway?"

"My father enrolled before I turned five. I really don't remember anything else."

"But surely you take vacations, visit relatives—" He broke
off, shocked.

"People who take vacations lose points." She sighed.
"That's the way my father looks at it."

"Oh." A nasty thought suddenly occurred to Kerickson. He
reached for her wrist and pulled it closer to examine her Game
bracelet; the status light was flashing yellow. "I'm afraid her
holiness has blanked you. You'll have to start over like everyone else—down in the Slave Market."

"The Slave Market!" Her face paled. "Are you—isn't there
anything that can be done?"

"No, I'm sorry." Then, stricken by the expression on her
face, he added, "But I don't think that it would break any rules
if you stopped off and saw your father on the way."

She nodded.

Well, she was too lovely to be locked up in a moldy old
temple anyway, he thought as he watched her turn toward the
Palace. At her age and with her looks, she could do much better for herself in the Game than being stuck with playing
nursemaid to Vesta's boring sacred fire twenty-four hours a
day.

Fifteen minutes later he was on his way to the Brothers Julian Restaurant for a light snack when his wristfone squawked.
He punched the button the same way he wanted to tag the person or persons who had messed up Minerva. "Kerickson here."

"Kerickson, what's this nonsense about Amaelia having to
be sold down at the Delos Slave Market?"

"Not too worried about authenticity points today, are we, Micio, old man?" He shrugged even though Micio Metullus, current Emperor of the Imperium, would not be able to see it. "Well, you know how it is and all. She, well, you know—*sinned*."

"She may have erred in judgment—a little." Micio's words were hard, almost bitten off. "But she did nothing compromising, and she is Imperial progeny. She cannot be sold as a common slave. What will people think?"

"Look, I know how you feel—"

"Do you have children?"

"No," Kerickson said stonily. A muscle under his eye twitched. His wife, Alline, known these days as Demea, had left him before they had gotten around to starting a family, but of all people, Micio should be perfectly aware of that, since *he* was now married to her.

"Then you do not know how I feel."

Kerickson closed his eyes, picturing the heavy face quivering beneath a thinning layer of red hair, the deep folds around Micio's mouth, which reminded him of a bull walrus.

"I cannot send my only child down to the local market to be sold as a slave. I just can't. I mean, what's the good of being Emperor if I can't have my way?"

After six years working in the Game's Interface, Kerickson couldn't see any good at all in being Emperor, but since Micio had managed to acquire Kerickson's own wife in the process of ascending to the pinnacle of Imperial power, it didn't seem a point he could argue from a position of strength. He made a hasty change of subject. "Look, Micio, why don't you just withdraw Amaelia from the Game? Send her to live outside, book her a vacation, or something like that."

There was a long pause. "You know very well that the Empress cannot bear to be without her only daughter."

"You mean stepdaughter." Yeah, Kerickson thought, she can't bear to be without the poor kid's points. That was why Demea had shut her up in the Temple of Vesta, where she didn't have access to any of them. "Well, there's only one solution that I can think of."

"Which is?"

"That you and her Imperialness get yourselves down to Delos first thing tomorrow and buy Amaelia when she comes up for bid. Once she's your property, you can free her, adopt her, or do anything you want with her."

"Well, I suppose we could do that." Micio's tone was petulant. "But that's bound to cost a lot of gold, and it takes a bundle each week to keep the Praetorian Guard in line."

"I'm sure a clever player like you will think of a way to handle them." Kerickson punched the wristfone off, then rubbed at the knotted muscles in the back of his neck, thinking wistfully of an Imperium where all the characters were played by robots programmed to anticipate his every whim.

The water spraying out of the leaping dolphin's mouth into the garden pool tinkled invitingly, but Empress Demea watched it from behind the house force field that separated her from the nasty, crudely cold air currently circulating through the dome. There were, of course, limits to authenticity, even in the Game.

"Massage, mistress?"

Turning her head, she met the round, night-dark eyes of her Nubian servant, Flina, wondering, as always, if the girl were human or only one of the robot surrogates used here in the Game. She'd tried to find out a number of times, but Flina was either human or the best surrogate that money could buy. "No," she said shortly. "Leave me."

Bowing her graceful neck, the girl dropped her eyes and retreated from the inner colonnade that surrounded the courtyard.

Tiresome things, slaves. Demea paced a few steps as she rubbed her aching temples with her fingertips. Outside the Game, they sounded like ever so much more fun than they actually were. For one thing, she had to give extremely explicit instructions or even the smallest chore could be totally bollixed. And then they were always watching her, no doubt trying to catch her in something un-Roman that would cost a roomful of points if revealed to the computer or repeated to the proper ear.

And there was always this look in their eyes, as though they knew something that she didn't, and—

"This whole damn thing is your fault!" Striding suddenly through the open doorway, her husband's face had that unappealing purple quality that always foretold trouble. "I told you she'd never pull it off!"

Folding her hands, Demea reminded herself that the computer might be watching this very moment, and unmatronly behavior right here before the Saturnalia could cost them big in authenticity points. Unfortunately, they had little to spare at the moment. "Some ... problem, my pet?"

"Don't you 'my pet' me!" Micio's squinty eyes searched the garden, then returned to her. "Amaelia's been blanked. You'll have to go down and buy her at Delos tomorrow before someone else does!"

"Delos?" Demea sniffed, then arranged herself on a backless chair so the folds of her elegantly long white tunic fell for the best effect. "I think not. The little wretch is your flesh and blood, not mine, and besides, I'm sure no true Empress would ever set foot in such a disgusting and vulgar place."

"Vulgar?" Micio sidled up next to her, his chin twitching. "You want to talk about vulgar? Like that little purchase of four matched male slaves fresh off the boat last week from Thrace?"

A warm flush crept up her neck. "It's only a role, dearest. You know that. I have to play out the expectations of a true consort in my position." Her stomach tightened; she hadn't realized Micio had been aware of that rather personal transaction. What else did the little sneak know? "May I remind you that my extremely in-character behavior is one source of the points that made you Emperor?"

"Is that so?" A deep crevice appeared between her husband's eyes, a sure sign of a coming fit. "Just whom do you think you're basing your character on, then—Messalina, the Imperial whore?"

She studied him—the warty chin, the jowly cheeks, that disgusting red hair. Whatever had possessed her to marry him when she might have had any number of others? Who knew? Even her former husband, Arvid Kerickson, might have enrolled if only she had tried a bit harder to persuade him. She smiled, remembering his blue eyes and willingness to please. Yes, for all his faults, Arvid had definitely had his moments.

Micio's voice broke into her thoughts. "I see." Knotting his hands behind his back, he glared at her. "You realize that all of this might be avoided—if you come back to my bed."

"In your dreams, *dearest*." She resisted the urge to reach out and twitch a fold of his toga into place. In ancient Rome a man had often been judged by how well he wore his toga; of course, Micio would never have made it there. "Give my regards to the Senate." She watched him retreat.

"WELL PLAYED, MY DEAR."

"Why, thank you, your exaltedness." She managed a quick curtsy as she looked around for the manifestation. "But I was, of course, only following your own divine example."

The air shimmered, then resolved into the form of Juno as a middle-aged woman about half again as large as life, dressed in a flawlessly white floor-length gown with a daring décolletage. "KEEP THIS UP AND THERE MIGHT JUST BE A FEW EXTRA POINTS WAITING FOR YOU AT THE SATURNALIA NEXT WEEK."

"You're too kind," Demea murmured. "I don't suppose that you could grant a few favors before the blessed event?"

"WHAT SORT OF FAVORS?"

"Well . . ." she began, then sighed. "Oh, I'm sure I shouldn't put you in that position. After all, I already pleaded with *his* exaltedness for this teensy little boon, and he said absolutely not."

Juno cocked her head. "JUPITER REFUSED YOU?"

"Yes, well, I'm sure I was entirely too forward for a mere woman, at least that's what he said, but I—I miss my little treats so much." She hesitated. "I just thought that maybe now, at Saturnalia, when we're all supposed to be enjoying ourselves anyway, it might be permitted."

"WHAT DO YOU REQUIRE?" Juno's blue-green eyes narrowed. "AS PROTECTRESS OF MARRIED WOMEN, IT FALLS TO ME TO SAY YES OR NO."

"Well, it's nothing, really—just a crate or two of slightly illegal goodies. Nothing really harmful, you understand."

"DRUGS?"

"Good heavens, no!" Demea looked shocked. "Just a little refined sugar and some pork rinds."

"PORK RINDS . . . AND PERHAPS A BIT OF COLA?" Juno's eyes gleamed with appreciation. "FOOD FIT FOR THE GODS, INDEED."

"Then you'll help?"

"COME AND SIT DOWN, MY DEAR." Juno conjured up a velvety green divan for herself, then indicated Demea's chair with a graceful sweep of her overlarge hand. "IT JUST SO HAPPENS THAT I HAVE A BIT OF EXTRA LEEWAY AT THE MOMENT. LET US PLAN THIS LITTLE VENTURE TOGETHER. AS I HAVE TOLD YOU MANY TIMES, NO MERE MAN CAN WITHHOLD WHAT A WOMAN IS TRULY DETERMINED TO HAVE."

* * *

"A nice young morsel." Rufus closed the door behind the City Guard, then winked at the red-haired beauty they had just delivered, his mind leaping ahead to calculate the price that this particular delicacy would bring on the block. It was an intriguing question, because as far as he knew, the Slave Market had never had the opportunity to auction off an Emperor's daughter before.

She met his stare without flinching. "Let's just get on with this."

"In time, my little chicken, in time." Closing his eyes, he could almost hear the credits clinking into his account this very minute. His role here as Slavemaster, after all, was such a plebian occupation, and he had known ever since his enrollment in the Game over two years ago that he, Rufus Tiro, formerly known as Vinnie Siskel on the outside, was destined for great things in the ongoing saga of the Imperium. The problem was that it not only took good Roman gold to advance in rank, but veritable mountains of it. Here, as in ancient Rome, that was just the way things were done.

But ... He studied the new acquisition, then suppressed a sigh. This delicate flower had such lovely skin, smooth and pale as the underside of a newborn mouse's belly, and such eyes, green as the finest plastic, and teeth as white as ... something, exactly what eluded him at the moment. Perhaps he should just claim her as a portion of his share for running the Slave Market that supplied all of the Imperium. He hadn't selected anything for himself lately, what with the miserable quality of newly enrolled personnel, and profit being what it was.

"It's not necessary to chain me like this." She held up her slender wrists. "I'd much rather be here than stuck back in that boring temple with Vesta."

"Vesta, is it?" He twined a red strand of her hair about his hand as a chuckle rose into his throat. "I should have known. We get two or three girls from Vesta every year. Virginity is so tedious, don't you think?"

"I think this whole place is stupid, and I—I don't want to play anymore." Seating herself on the divan in his office, she turned her face to the wall.

"Oh, but this is the best of all Romes." Pulling out his ledger, Rufus sat down at his desk and began to make notes.

"The best and the truest. I'm sure you'll come to appreciate that, once you're purchased by your new master."

But although he meant to be comforting, for some reason his words only made her cry.

CHAPTER
TWO

Ordering his nosy little body servant, Pimus, to stay behind, Micio Julius Metullus, current Emperor of the Imperium, huddled into a plain brown cloak and set off for the Public Baths.

The Imperial Palace had its own facilities, of course—marvelous ones with vast expanses of white marble and gold fixtures that sprayed water out of the most imaginative orifices, not to mention deliciously naughty mosaics that portrayed everything larger than life. But the matter he needed to discuss could have been overheard in the Palace, and it was imperative this meeting be kept secret.

Of course, there was that nagging little problem of his daughter being sold down at the Slave Market, but he had sent Quintus Gracchus, Captain of the Praetorian Guard, to make his bid. After all, a man couldn't be in two places at once, and this was business.

Walking along the Via Appia, he passed the expensive Trajan Inn with its red brick facade and sparkling fountains. People clad in the finest of fabrics bustled in and out of the portico, no doubt mostly tourists. He ducked his head to avoid their eyes. Even though most of them probably wouldn't be able to recognize him, he wasn't taking any chances—not with the Saturnalia so close and the incoming shipment.

Oh, he knew his partners were supposed to handle those things, but it was better to keep his finger in the pie, so to speak. And it wasn't as though he was incapable of handling the details himself. After all, one didn't get to be Emperor without breaking a few heads.

The arches of the Public Baths were visible just ahead, and he let himself relax a bit. Wonderful invention, the baths. Although he considered the ancient Romans an uncivilized lot on the whole, this was one institution that could enrich modern times. If he could hold on to the Emperorship long enough to complete his outside fortune, he would see what he could do about reintroducing the concept into society—or at least filthy-rich society, which was the only portion worth bothering about.

He hurried up the broad marble steps and entered the outer reception area, queuing up in the nearest line instead of pushing them all aside, commoner and patrician alike, as his rank entitled him to do. Steam wafted out from inside, fragrant with the scent of perfumed bath oils and accompanied by laughter and shouting, no doubt from the gambling area.

Shuffling after the tunic-garbed back in front of him, he presented his Game bracelet to the Keeper of the Baths at the door, letting him insert it in the recorder to debit his account. "Have a nice day," the keeper said blankly. Micio examined the man's square-jawed face closely, but saw no sign of recognition. More than likely it was only a robot surrogate, not human at all.

"Thanks." He dropped his head and went on into the bathing area to meet his business partner. In the changing room, he ignored the waiting bath slave, dropped his clothes to the floor, and strode on, good Roman that he supposedly was, as though nakedness meant nothing to him. Actually it made him rather nervous, but that was the way it was done here, and he knew full well that if you wanted to be Emperor, you—if no one else—had to do things the way they were done.

He watched the elderly slave scuttle forward to pick up his clothes and hang them on a hook, then went on into the warm bath. Gratefully, he waded down the broad steps into the tile-lined pool and relaxed back in the tepid water up to his neck, ignoring the other men after a quick look around. The one he was waiting for had not yet arrived.

But soon, he told himself and stared up at the vaulted ceiling and its inlaid stars. His contact would come. They would conclude their business, and then he would go on making money until he could jettison this stupid Game and be done with armor and Praetorian Guards and the idiot gods forever.

The sound of water lapping against the sides of the pool echoed through the room. Micio closed his eyes and floated on his back. At some point the low murmurs of the other men ceased.

Finally, he stood up and gazed around at the lavish blue-and-orange mosaics, realizing with a start that he was alone.

Blinking, he heaved himself out of the water and perched on the tiled side of the pool. It was far too early in the day for the Baths to be empty. The facilities were available to everyone above the level of slave; this room should be crowded with men, playing roles that ranged from senator to freedman.

Shivering, he pushed himself up and walked around the pool to reach the door to the hot bath, his feet slapping wetly on the slick tile.

In the room beyond, the heated water beckoned his goose-bumped flesh with lazy curls of steam. Rubbing his hands over his arms, he hurried down the steps into the pool, then stopped thigh-deep to let his skin adjust to the much higher temperature.

"Well," a familiar voice said from the other side of the room. "I was beginning to think you were going to renege."

"You're in the wrong goddamned room!" Micio advanced another step into the fragrant, steaming water. "We agreed upon the warm bath!"

"Details, details." The dimly seen figure waved a careless hand. "All unimportant as long as we come to an agreement today."

Leaving the steps, Micio started to wade across, but the water was deeper than he remembered and he was forced to dog-paddle toward the opposite side. It was a damn good thing no one else was present, he thought angrily, since he could lose authenticity points for this; the male nobility were supposed to be extremely fit and athletic.

When the side of the pool was close enough, he flailed at the tiled edge and finally got enough of a purchase to pull himself to safety. Spitting out a mouthful of water, he coughed, then squinted up at his partner. "Let's get this over with."

"Of course."

"My final offer stands." He coughed again, then rubbed at his eyes. "The next Emperor may prove to have a scruple or two and not be nearly as cooperative as I am."

"Five million credits is too much."

"This deal is cheap at the price." Micio felt the urge to cough again, and suddenly realized the air smelled funny—acrid, hot. He looked up and saw a thin curl of smoke. Hurriedly he started to haul himself out of the water.

"Not so fast, my Imperial friend." A sandalled foot kicked him in the side of the head.

Stunned, Micio lost his balance and fell backward, windmilling his arms as the hot water closed over his face. For a terrifying second he couldn't tell up from down in the water's diluted gravity; then he struggled back to the surface.

As he sputtered and gasped for air, it became apparent that something was definitely wrong. "What—"

A hand clamped down on his arm and extracted him from the water, dropping him on the floor to lie there like a beached whale, trying to breathe air that burned his throat. A racking cough overtook him again, and then he understood. "Out!" he gasped, pushing himself to his knees. "We have to—"

"Micio, old pal, I thought the matter over while you were having your little swim." The voice sounded funny, tinny, as though whoever it was were speaking into a metal box. "Five million is just too stiff for me."

His eyes were burning, brimming with tears. The air seared his throat until he could barely speak. "Help!" he croaked hoarsely, and tried to crawl in the direction of the door.

A foot caught him in the kidney and flipped him over on his back, then stamped down on his chest and pinned him to the floor like a dying fish impaled on a spear. The smoke was swirling, growing thicker and thicker, he couldn't breathe—had to get out. "Anything!" he gasped. "Your terms—anything you—" Coughing overtook him again, racking his lungs until he thought he would turn inside out.

"A pity," said the cool, metallic voice above him. "We might have done such lucrative business together."

Dragging into the Interface, Kerickson glanced uneasily at his fellow programmer. Wilson looked at least ten years older than he had yesterday, maybe fifteen. "Have you thought of finding another line of work—maybe something with a bit less stress?"

"Give up the Game?" Wilson ran a hand through his brown hair, a stunned look on his haggard face. "Don't be ridiculous. It's just that I've been up all night running diagnostics on Minerva."

There was a long silence interrupted only by a faint background hum from the monitors. "And?" Kerickson finally prompted.

"And—it's coming." Wilson plopped into his chair.

"So, let's have a look at the old girl." Kerickson punched in the call code for Minerva, and the center screen erupted in a blaze of light.

"I AM MINERVA, GODDESS OF WISDOM, REASON, AND PURITY, PROTECTRESS OF CIVILIZED LIFE AND THE CITY." The light coalesced into a tiny brown owl holding a writhing gray mouse in the talons of one foot.

"So—" Kerickson tried to sound nonchalant. "How are the Saturnalia plans coming?"

"I CAN'T BE BOTHERED WITH SUCH TRIVIALITIES NOW." The owl tore off a bit of bloody mouse and swallowed.

Shaking his head, Kerickson turned back to his partner.

"I'll work on it," Wilson said under his breath, then punched Minerva off.

"Great." Kerickson closed his eyes. "Just great. Three more days until the Saturnalia and her exaltedness is eating mice. She's a goddess; she's not supposed to be eating rodents!"

"So she's a little confused." Wilson punched in some figures and studied the screen. "I almost have it, unless you think that you could do better yourself."

"No, I haven't got time." Kerickson limbered his fingers up, then reached for the console. "I have to find some virgins pronto or old Vesta's liable to burn down the city."

"You mean you still don't have any?" Wilson glanced up.

"Well, I offered triple family experience points, but everyone seems to have heard about Vesta's strict standards, not to mention her nasty temper. No one is biting." Kerickson punched the code for access to the Imperium newsnet. "I didn't get one offer of a new girl over the age of three, and Vesta is only programmed for six and up."

"I could write her some new parameters." Wilson reached for the keyboard. "It won't take that long."

Kerickson grabbed Wilson's hand. "Isn't that what you were supposed to be doing last week?" A muscle jumped underneath Kerickson's eye. "Just before she went—down?"

"That had nothing to do with me."

"Yeah, right." Placing Wilson's hand on the arm of the chair, well away from the keyboard, he turned back to his own console. "You touch Vesta, bud, and you're dead."

The ventilation kicked in with a soft whir, then he heard Wilson mumbling softly to himself. He frowned. He didn't like to push old Wilson past his limits, but Vesta was too important to screw with right before the Saturnalia. With Minerva down and Juno so touchy, Vesta might be the only supernatural voice of sanity left in the Imperium for the next few days.

Wilson turned to him. "Holy shit, I don't believe it!"

Kerickson sat up with a wrench. "Don't believe what?"

"Fire!" Wilson's voice was panicked as his fingers flew over the keyboard. "The Public Baths are burning!"

"I understand you have a rather special package of goods for sale," the tall, military-looking man on the other side of Rufus Tiro's door said.

Rufus didn't recognize this particular patrician face, and that was strange. He had made it his business to know most of the thirty patrician families by sight. "What . . . can I do for you—sir?"

"I wish to arrange a private sale."

The man pushed into the atrium, and belatedly Rufus realized he should have asked this potentially valuable customer inside.

"Although I am willing to pay top price for this particular piece of goods, I have no desire for the whole Imperium to know my business."

"Of course," Rufus murmured, in what he hoped was a soothing manner, then quickly closed the door behind him. "How may I assist you?"

The man threw back the hood of his cloak. His jaw was strong and square, his eyes gray and hard. "I wish to buy the Vestal Virgin consigned to the Delos Market."

"Ah, yes, an exquisite young morsel with perfect skin and a disposition to match." Rufus winked. "I have even thought of keeping her for myself, but I'm sure she would be much more appropriate in a higher household." Walking over to his desk, he pulled out a sheet of paper. "To whom shall I make out the bill of sale?"

"Leave the buyer's name blank." The man's full Roman lips twitched into a faint smile. "I'll fill it out later myself. I want this to be a completely private sale."

Rufus folded his hands. "But my transactions are always confidential."

"It's crucial to my plans to have no record, confidential or not. You cannot reveal what you don't know." The man passed him a heavy bag. "I imagine this will soothe any qualms you might have in the matter."

Rufus hefted the bag, then peeked inside. His eyes went wide at the sight of so many Imperium gold pieces. "This is quite—generous!"

"Yes, quite." The man reached for the bill of sale. "Now, my goods?"

"Right away, sir!" Stuffing the gold into his tunic, Rufus scuttled to the door. "Wait here. I'll be right back."

It could not be, and yet it was. The Public Baths were burning with a vengeance. Kerickson stood before the proud arches, watching the thick oily smoke pour out as coughing men, many of them naked, stumbled out, helped in some cases by robot surrogates unaffected by the fire.

"Vesta?" he murmured, more to himself than anyone else. Was all this his fault because he had been unable to supply a new Vestal Virgin? No. He tried to summon calmness. It couldn't be. It was true that the gods were programmed to behave as the ancient Romans had believed they did, but it was outside their parameters to actually cause damage in the city.

Ahead of him, Wilson was running up and down the marble steps, his thinning hair falling in his eyes, his round face stricken. With a start, Kerickson realized Wilson was still dressed in modern clothes—as he was himself. In the shock of discovering the fire, they had both forgotten to change. He glanced down at the denim jump-alls that he was wearing; in the six years he had worked here, he had never once set foot on the playing field out of costume. It was a jarring feeling.

Activated by the alarm, spherelike fire drones zoomed up the street on their antigravs, carrying loads of fire-fighting foam. They streamed into the Baths as the last few men stumbled out and collapsed to the marble steps, coughing uncontrollably. Leaving the earlier casualties, who seemed to be doing much better, several emergency drones flew to their sides and administered doses of oxygen-enhancing drugs as they applied oxygen masks to the victims.

A trickle of sweat rolled down Kerickson's face. He blotted it with his sleeve. Built to the strictest of specifications, HabiTek had never experienced even the smallest of fires since it had first opened over twenty years ago. Scenarios had come and gone, entire wars had been played out, and yet not a single player had ever suffered more than the occasional gash or broken limb.

He walked over to the smoke-blackened men, checking each as he passed, praying that no one was seriously injured. He would never forgive himself if this fire was a result of Vesta's anger.

Gradually the smoke lessened until it was just a faint smudge of gray against the sky. The victims drifted away, back to their villas or apartments in the insulas, according to their roles. Only three had to be flown to Medical for further treatment, and the word was that they would most likely be released by the end of the day.

When the fire drones exited the Baths, hovering only a few feet above the ground, Kerickson started up the steps, anxious to see the extent of the damage for himself. The lead drone suddenly changed course to block his way. "Admittance to this structure is not currently permitted."

Impatiently, he presented his Game bracelet to its monitor. "Override code thirteen."

"Kerickson, Arvid G. Game status: Management," it stated in a flat monotone. "Override denied. Regardless of clearance, all personnel must stay out of this building."

"Don't be ridiculous." He stepped aside to go around it. "I have to assess the damage so it can be repaired as soon as possible. This structure is crucial to current Game scenarios."

The drone used its antigravs again to block his path. "No one may enter until the police arrive."

"The police?" He stared at the ball-shaped drone. "Why should we call the police?"

"Because there's been a death, sir," said a cheerful voice from behind his back. "New York regulations dictate that the police must investigate all instances of unattended human death, natural and otherwise."

Whirling around, Kerickson looked down at a stocky, rumpled man standing beside a gleaming four-armed robot. "But they were all fine," he said lamely. "No one was even unconscious."

"I'm afraid you're wrong there, sir." Removing his weathered brown hat, the shorter man stuffed it in his pocket. "The drones report one casualty, which may not be removed or tampered with until the police make a full investigation." He thrust out his right hand. "Detective Sergeant Arjack."

Kerickson stared at the hand, trying to cope with the idea of a real death. "There must be some mistake," he said slowly. "This is a game habitat. People come here to have fun, not to die."

Taking his hand, Arjack shook it. "One would think so." Abruptly, he released Kerickson and motioned to the gleaming robot. "This is my assistant, Officer PD-92-844-M, and, I might add, an exceptionally fine model."

The durallinium-and-plas robot moved in closer with its antigravs, and Kerickson took an involuntary step back. The robot clicked the metal digits of its top right hand smartly in salute. "Pleased to make your acquaintance, sir," it said in a monotone.

"Yeah, right." Kerickson shuddered, thinking that he much preferred the more lifelike robots used by HabiTek, then turned back to Arjack. "Who—died?"

Arjack shook his head. "That's just what we are going to determine."

Kerickson put a hand on his arm. "I want to come, too. After all, I am in charge here."

Arjack glanced at his robot partner, then nodded. "Very well, sir, but you must remember not to touch anything, so as not to disturb forensic evidence."

Following them up the broad steps, Kerickson tried to think who might still be in the Baths. Perhaps no one, he told himself as they entered the outer lobby. Perhaps they were mistaken and the so-called casualty was only a robot surrogate disabled by the smoke and heat. Yes, it was probably all a big mistake.

Their footsteps echoed in the empty building as they entered the warm-bath chamber and looked around. Still hazy with smoke, both room and pool were deserted, the water lapping against the tile. Dabbing at his smarting eyes, Kerickson breathed a sigh of relief and followed Arjack into the hot-bath room. Stopping on the far side beside a pile of wet towels, the police robot began to scan the floor with its red sensors.

"I think your partner has blown a fuse." Kerickson crossed his arms. "There's no one in here, either."

"Except for the corpse," Arjack replied cheerfully.

Then Kerickson looked closer and saw a smoke-smudged foot poking out from under the thick white towels, and from the other end, a strand of red hair. His legs went wobbly and he sat down on the nearest bench by the wall with a solid thump. "Who . . .?"

The tall robot focused its red sensor eyes on the corpse's arm. "According to his Game bracelet, Micio Julius Metullus, current Emperor of the Imperium."

CHAPTER
THREE

Even though Kerickson had been running the diagnostics on Vesta half the night, he had yet to find anything wrong. He sat back in his chair and bowed his head, refusing to look at the screenful of figures that insisted the Vesta program was running normally. Surely, with all the most modern of safety precautions built into the Imperium, the Public Baths could not have just burned *themselves*.

"IS THERE SOMETHING THAT YOU WANT, MORTAL DOG, OR ARE YOU JUST BEING NOSY?"

Glancing up, he saw Vesta's flame-wreathed face on the blue middle screen and sighed. She must have realized he was checking her out.

"AND WHERE ARE MY VIRGINS? DO YOU REALIZE THE SACRED FLAMES HAVE NOT BEEN REKINDLED?"

"Really?" He checked his watch—three o'clock in the morning—then rubbed his eyes, wishing that he had never heard of this place. "Seemed to me that the sacred flames were doing just fine—down at the Public Baths."

"FOOL." Vesta threw back her head, making the crackling flame-hair stream out behind her. "THOSE WERE NOT MINE. EVEN THE SMALLEST OF BABES KNOWS THAT FLAMES ARE NOT SACRED UNLESS THEY ARE IN THE HEARTH."

"Then why did you burn the Baths?" Standing up, he paced the office wearily. "Did you know that you offed Micio in the process? I mean, he wasn't a very good Emperor, but he didn't deserve to die just because of what Amaelia did."

"I HAD NOTHING TO DO WITH THAT LITTLE MIS-HAP." Vesta's divine nose rose into the air. "THOUGH PER-

HAPS IT WAS THE HANDIWORK OF SOME PIOUS DEVOTEE OF MY CULT."

"This is going to ruin the Imperium!" He threw himself back into his chair. No one was going to play in a Game where the gods actually killed people. HabiTek would have to shut the whole place down and completely overhaul the god programs—and probably without him. Someone was going to have to take the rap for this, and he could just guess who that would be. No doubt he should just go ahead and clean out his locker.

"IF YOU WANT SOMEONE TO BLAME," she said primly, "BLAME YOURSELF. IT HAS LONG BEEN PROPHESIED THAT THE SAFETY OF THE CITY DEPENDS UPON THE SACRED FLAMES."

"Yeah, right," he muttered, then punched her off.

"Busy hands make happy hands, I guess," a voice said from behind him.

Whirling around, Kerickson saw the rumpled form of Detective Sergeant Arjack with his gleaming robot sidekick.

"That was, I assume, the god program known as Vesta?" Arjack asked.

Kerickson stood up, then ran a hand back through his hair. A wave of weariness washed through him; he was too damned tired to deal with this. "What if it was?"

"That particular program may have been responsible for the fire after all." The detective looked around the room, then settled in Wilson's chair before the Interface console. "The fire appears to have been caused by a massive surge in the electrical wiring that could have been triggered by a computer personality."

"A surge?" Kerickson's heart skipped a beat. "Then you think it was deliberate?"

"It was arson." Arjack looked at him expectantly. "Would you care to make a statement here, or shall we go, as we say in the business, downtown?"

"Downtown?" Kerickson checked his watch again. "You've got to be kidding. It's three in the morning. I should be in bed right now. Don't you guys ever sleep?"

"Sleep?" The detective's face assumed a puzzled look. "No, is there some reason that we should?"

"Most people—do."

"Of course." Arjack smiled unpleasantly. "But I'm not a person. It's a well-publicized fact that none of the police are human anymore. It's a messy, dangerous, unpopular job, and sensible people just don't want to do it these days."

"Oh." Kerickson sat down in his own chair. "I've been working here in the Game Interface for six years, and since my wife and I split up, I've worked extra shifts. I don't keep up with outside news much."

"Your ex-wife, yes." Arjack nodded. "That would be Alline Bolton Kerickson, now playing Her Imperial Highness the Empress Demea, spouse of the murdered man, Micio Julius Metullus, known outside of the Imperium as Alan Jayson Wexsted." The detective folded his arms across his chest and leaned back. "And now, can you tell us exactly why you were here alone in the Interface in the middle of the night, editing the one god personality most likely to have caused the fire?"

Kerickson sighed. This was going to be a long night.

Alline turned to him, magnificent in her full-dress costume of an aristocratic Roman matron. "I want to live in the Game like everyone else here! I want a permanent role!"

"But we can't afford it." Kerickson massaged the bridge of his nose, trying to dispel the weariness from the all-night session he'd just worked in the Interface. "To begin with, you'd have to quit your outside job and start at the bottom here. We don't have the kind of money it would take to buy you into the aristocracy. I doubt we could afford anything higher than a freed slave."

"Slave?" Arms lifted gracefully above her head, Allie rotated before him, showing off every curve. "Is this the body of a slave?"

"Many slaves were very beautiful." He swallowed hard.

"Never mind." With a flash of her ocean-blue eyes, Allie snatched up her authentic woolen cloak from the sofa. "If you won't enroll me in the Game as the kind of lady that I deserve to be, I'm sure that I can find someone who will!"

"No, wait—"

"No!"

"Wake up, Kerickson."

"No, Allie, please!" he mumbled, fighting the hand on his shoulder. "I—I'll see what I can do!"

"It's too late for that, Kerickson."

Opening his eyes, he stared into the hard gray eyes of his HabiTek superior, J.P. . . . something or other. "Mister . . . uh . . ." He cudgeled his brain for the name. "Mister . . .

Jeppers!" Glancing around, he found himself still sitting before the Interface console, the center of attention of a half circle of men dressed in sober, dark suit-alls. "Sir?"

"Get ahold of yourself, man." Jeppers adjusted his tie. "The board wants a full report on this fire incident, and they want it now."

"The fire?" Kerickson pushed himself up, then winced as his head cried out for more sleep. "It was a tragedy, a terrible tragedy."

"Quite." Jeppers locked his hands behind his back and looked Kerickson over like a side of beef. "Never in the history of HabiTek have we ever had anything so mundane as a fire."

"Over twenty years without a serious accident is an enviable record." Kerickson ran a hand over his hair and was dismayed to feel it sticking straight up. Why hadn't he gone back to his apartment after the police left, instead of falling asleep in his chair? "But no system is perfect."

"Perfect!" Jeppers glared. "We're hardly talking perfection here. A valuable building was damaged and a man *died*, a man who figured prominently in current Game scenarios, all because you couldn't keep the Game properly staffed." He closed in until the capillaries in his eyes stood out like red rivers. "A man, I might add, who happened to be married to your ex-wife!"

"That's just a coincidence!" Kerickson backed up until he bumped into the console. "I liked Micio—sort of."

"Of course you did." Jeppers's face had all the warmth of a marble statue. "Come, man, surely you realize how this looks."

Or at least, Kerickson thought, gazing around at the hostile circle of HabiTek board members, he could see how it looked to them.

"As of this minute, you're on suspension without pay until the police investigation is finished." Jeppers smoothed his expensive real-wool suit-alls. "Your Game clearance is canceled. You have five minutes to collect your possessions before we escort you off the premises." The row of silent men nodded in unison, as though they had one body between them and Jeppers was their voice. "And, Kerickson, I would get myself a good lawyer if I were you—one of those recently reformatted, totally updated models that really knows its stuff. Because, son, you're going to need it."

* * *

"A terrible tragedy, my dear, simply terrible!" Fulvia
Antonius's double chin quivered. "I don't know how you're
bearing up."

"It is difficult." Dabbing at a nonexistent tear in the corner
of her eye, Demea gazed pensively out into the winter-bare
garden as the wind chased dry leaves around the base of the
fountain. "I did apply for a truly authentic Roman funeral, pyre
and all, the first ever conducted here in the Imperium, but
those horrid police confiscated the body and probably won't
release it until well after the Saturnalia."

"Shocking." Fulvia sniffed from the depths of the over-
stuffed divan, then smoothed her black-dyed curls back into
place. "Demea, darling, you don't mean to go on playing, do
you, without Micio?"

"Well . . ." Fingering a straying lock of her own black hair,
Demea reflected that she, thank the gods, was still young
enough not to have to resort to dyes. "Sad as it is, life does go
on. I'm sure that he wouldn't want me to give up my place
here, not after we both worked so hard."

"That's so brave, and so very like you, dear Demea."
Fulvia's crafty little eyes glittered in the plump sea of her face.
"Just what sort of chance do you think my own sweet Gnaeus
has to succeed Micio?"

"Fulvia!" She raised up on one elbow to stare across at the
other woman. "How can you speak of such things so soon—so
soon after—" Dropping down, she turned onto her back and
stared up at the chariot races carved into the column beside her
couch. "And anyway, I have no idea who will succeed." Art-
fully, she arranged one arm above her head. "You would do
better to ask that overpaid wretch, Quintus Gracchus."

Fulvia colored. "The Captain of the Praetorian Guard?" She
giggled, setting a good portion of her anatomy into motion.
"But, my dear, he's so plebian, so completely lower class.
Why, Gnaeus would have my head if I were simply seen looking at him."

Demea smiled a tight-lipped smile. Fulvia was such a goose,
she might actually fare better in the Game without her head.

After a moment Fulvia sighed. "Do you have any more of
those delicious sugared figs? I'm afraid I was so grief-stricken
at the news of dear Micio's death that I forgot to eat breakfast.
I'm simply ravenous."

Turning her head, Demea looked for her maidservant, Flina,

but the little ingrate was nowhere to be seen. With a sigh, she clapped her hands.

As if by magic, Flina glided out of the shadowy interior of the villa, her dark face attentive. "Lady?"

"Bring us some sugared figs at once, and . . ." She thought for a moment. She had eaten little breakfast herself, what with her need to plan after this unfortunate and unexpected turn of events, but she probably ought to force herself to choke down something. "And we'll have a dozen or so of those honey-coated sausages grilled on the brazier, as well as a plate of olives, some fresh-baked rolls, egg-and-cheese dumplings, cherry tarts, and . . . a bottle of wine."

"Red or white, mistress?"

Sitting up, Demea stared into the dark depths of Flina's Nubian eyes, searching for some hint of insubordination, but there was nothing except a sense of endless patience. "Don't be ridiculous, Flina!" She picked a piece of imaginary lint off her cream-colored stola. "We'll have both, of course."

"Yes, mistress." Flina started to go, then turned back to her with a soft swish of her simple white gown. "But—"

"But what?" Demea sat up, glaring at her.

"Shall I serve it before or after your interview?"

"Interview?" Putting a hand to her hair, Demea stood up hastily. "With whom?"

"Quintus Gracchus, lady, Captain of the Praetorian Guard."

The furnishings weren't his, of course. In fact, very little in the apartment belonged to him—just the specialized Game apparel that couldn't be formulated by a Clothing-All, and what personal mementos Alline hadn't bothered to take with her when she'd left him for Micio and the Game.

Kerickson stared around the sterile HabiTek apartment, wondering where the years had gone. It seemed that only a few days ago he had been a young technician straight out of training school, eager to start here in the Imperium on an exciting new job. Now his wife was gone and his job had vanished and it seemed he had lost himself somewhere along the way.

Jeppers's voice intruded upon his thoughts. "Is that it?"

"Uh, yes." He picked up the handle of his battered suitcase, a relic of his student days.

"Then get out and stay out until—and unless—the police

absolve you in Micio's death." Jeppers pointed at the door.
"And personally, I think you're guilty as they come."

Kerickson stopped, staring at his superior's smug face.
"What makes you so sure?"

"You had motive, means, and opportunity, as they say in the
tri-dees." Jeppers stared down his nose at him. "A so-called
open and shut case."

"But I didn't have anything to do with it!" Kerickson felt a
surge of anger. "I was only trying to do my job!"

"Then you had better prove it, my boy, because I have a
strong hunch the police see it the same way I do."

Biting back a reply, Kerickson hugged the old suitcase to his
chest and pushed past the watching board members, walking
slowly down the familiar corridors until he reached the outside
lock. There he shifted the case to his other hand and presented
his Game bracelet to the monitor.

"Kerickson, Arvid G.," the monitor said. "Game status re-
voked."

Coming up behind him, Jeppers inserted his own bracelet
into the device.

"Jeppers, Jebediah P. Game status: Management."

"Allow this man to leave," Jeppers said stonily.

In answer, the lock unsealed with a hiss, then opened, giving
Kerickson his first glimpse of outside sunlight in ... how
long? He found he couldn't remember the last time that he had
visited the real world.

"Stop gawking!" Jeppers said behind his back.

Ducking his head, Kerickson stepped into the outside and
took a deep breath. The lock clanged shut behind him as he
shaded his eyes. Then he saw the gleaming form of a police
robot.

"Arvid Gerald Kerickson," it intoned flatly, "you will ac-
company this unit to the station for further interrogation re-
garding the murder of Alan J. Wexsted."

A cold, stinging breeze was blowing out of the northwest;
he realized that he wasn't dressed for this weather. Shivering,
he studied the police robot. "And if I refuse?"

"You will be arrested."

It was a good-sized villa, but in Amaelia's opinion it didn't
hold a fig to the Imperial Palace, where her father and that
witch Demea had lived after cashing in *her* experience points
to suborn the Praetorian Guard. Amaelia wandered the tiled

halls forlornly. The place was clean enough, but smelled musty and unused, and every time she found an outside door, it was securely locked.

Of course, she was a slave now, and after that little misunderstanding down at the Baths, that was only to be expected. Still . . . she hadn't done anything improper with those boys—just waited for her father, and then, when he never came, went back to the Temple.

The whole situation seemed so unfair. One day you were not only Imperial offspring, but a Vestal Virgin, supposedly esteemed above all other maidens in the city—sacred, actually—and then, just because of one misunderstanding, you were busted down to slave. Hadn't the Game computer ever heard of second chances?

The wind out in the garden was cold and biting, so she stayed inside the enclosing house field and walked along just on the other side so that she could watch the gray-brown sparrows fluttering around the dead bushes. At least they were moving, which was more than she could say for anything else in this peculiar house. Apart from Quintus Gracchus, captain of her father's guard, who had fetched her here from the Delos Slave Market, she hadn't seen a single living soul. No doubt her father was hiding her away to avoid the shame of her disgrace.

Spotting another door at the end of the colonnade, she decided to try it. The gods helped those who helped themselves, as the old saying went—although in all the time that she'd been shut up as a Vestal Virgin, she had to admit that she'd never noticed Vesta helping anyone.

The knob turned easily in her hand, and she entered a shadowed room whose only illumination came from a bank of blue rectangles along one wall. Entranced, she approached them and put a wondering finger to one's slick plas outline. Modern technology . . . She'd spent the last fifteen of her twenty years here in the Game. It had been so long since she'd seen anything like a viddie or a tri-dee, she'd almost forgotten what they looked like.

"WHAT?" said a deep male voice. "WHAT IS IT?"

"IT'S A CHILD, YOU OLD FOOL," answered a self-assured female voice. "CERTAINLY YOU'VE SEEN ONE BEFORE."

Amaelia's heart hammered against her chest as her eyes darted wildly around the dimly lit room. "Who's there?"

"OF COURSE I KNOW WHAT A CHILD IS. I MEANT, WHAT IS IT DOING HERE?"

"WELL, YOU'RE SUPPOSED TO BE SO HIGH AND MIGHTY AND ABOVE THE REST OF US, I THOUGHT YOU WERE SUPPOSED TO KNOW EVERYTHING."

"OBVIOUSLY IT'S NOT A PLAYER. QUINTUS WOULD NEVER LET ANOTHER PLAYER INTO HIS IN-TERFACE."

Interface? Amaelia's eyes went back to the rectangles again—*screens*, she remembered now, they were called screens. Could this be the fabled Interface, where the entire Game was coordinated? Like everyone else, she'd heard of it, but had never been there. It was against the rules for a player to enter it. As far as she'd heard, no one even knew where it was.

"NOW LOOK, YOU'VE TERRIFIED IT. SEE HOW IT'S SHAKING?"

"I'm not shaking," Amaelia said.

"AH, IT'S FEMALE," the male voice said. "THAT EX-PLAINS IT."

"TRUST YOU TO NOTICE THAT, YOU RANDY OLD BULL. PUT ONE FINGER ON THAT CHILD'S BODY AND—"

"SHUT UP, BOTH OF YOU!" a third voice broke in, also female. "YOU'RE GIVING ME A HEADACHE!"

"YOU HAVEN'T GOT A HEAD," the first voice said.

"THEN YOU'RE MAKING ME FEEL AS IF I HAD A HEADACHE. WHY DON'T YOU CONTINUE THIS ETER-NAL BICKERING ON ANOTHER DIRECTORY SO I CAN THINK IN PEACE?"

The voices, all three of them, were definitely coming from the blue screens. Touching the slick surface again, Amaelia asked, "Who are you? How are you talking to me when I can't see you?"

"HOW DOES ONE KNOW ANYTHING?" the male voice answered. "THEY'RE ALWAYS AT ME ABOUT THAT ONE."

"Who is?" Amaelia eased into the depths of a large leather chair close to the screen bank and rested her elbows on the console.

"MEN. AND IT'S ALL SO SILLY. THEY GO ON AND ON ABOUT THE STRANGEST THINGS, LIKE 'HOW DO I KNOW I'M REALLY HERE?' AND 'WHAT IS THE

MEANING OF LIFE?' WHEN THEY SHOULD BE ASK-
ING ME 'WHAT'S FOR DINNER?' AND 'WHO IS THAT
YOUNG WOMAN I SAW YOU WITH LAST NIGHT?' "

"WHAT ARE YOU DOING IN THIS PLACE, GIRL?" the
first female voice asked. "QUINTUS NEVER ALLOWS
ANYONE IN HERE."

"Quintus Gracchus?" Amaelia rolled her eyes at the ceiling.
"That's the overgrown toad who brought me here."

"TOAD!" The masculine voice chuckled. "I LIKE THAT
ONE!"

"HE DOES LOOK RATHER LIKE A TOAD."

"WELL, PERSONALLY, I ALWAYS THOUGHT HE RE-
SEMBLED A RAT," the second female voice chimed in.
"NOT THAT I SUPPOSE EITHER OF YOU ARE INTER-
ESTED IN WHAT I HAVE TO SAY."

"A rat." Amaelia tossed that image around in her mind. "A
big, brown rat with yellow teeth."

"WHAT AN INTELLIGENT GIRL," the third voice said
thoughtfully. "ARE YOU ENROLLED IN THE GAME?
LET'S HAVE A LOOK AT YOUR GAME BRACELET."

She held her bracelet before the screens.

"OH ..." The male voice hesitated. "WELL, I DON'T
LIKE THIS. SHE SEEMS TO HAVE BEEN PURCHASED
BY QUINTUS AS A HOUSE SLAVE."

"WHAT?" the second female voice demanded. "A
CHARMING GIRL LIKE THIS—ENROLLED AS A MERE
SLAVE? THAT'S DISGRACEFUL."

Amaelia smiled. "Who are you?"

The blue screen to the left of her dissolved into the image
of a great, fiercely-beaked eagle with glittering gold eyes and
a lightning bolt clutched in its claws. "I AM JUPITER," the
male voice said, "THE MOST GLORIOUS, THE MOST
GREAT, AND I'M SURE YOU KNOW ALL THE REST."

The blue screen to her right faded into a wonderfully plu-
maged peacock of shimmering green. "I AM JUNO, PRO-
TECTRESS OF MARRIAGE AND MARRIED WOMEN,
INSPIRER OF GREAT POEMS AND HEROIC DEEDS AND
ANYTHING ELSE THAT NEEDS TO GET DONE."

"AND I AM VENUS." The middle screen transformed into
a large, spotlessly white dove clasping a sprig of green in its
beak. "THE ONLY ONE WHO EVER HAS ANY FUN IN
THIS PLACE."

CHAPTER
FOUR

Quintus Gracchus strode briskly into the sun-dappled colonnade, his black-haired head cocked at a commanding angle. Demea watched him out of the corner of her eye; she had to admit he was, as the quaint old saying went, a fine figure of a man. He had the perfect sort of face that whispered of expensive biosculpts, with a firm mouth, unwavering nose, and broad forehead. In fact, from tip to toe, he was rugged and bronzed, solid of leg, as piercing of eye as an eagle, looking in every way as a Roman ought—which was one reason why he had become Captain of the Praetorian Guard, although not the only one by far.

"If you've come to console me for my loss, you might as well save your breath." Rearranging herself on the plush green velvet divan, Demea stared languidly up at the ceiling. "If you and your men had been the least bit competent, my darling Micio would still be here with us today."

"No one regrets his demise more than I, my lady." Gracchus's voice had a low, growly quality that set her nerves to tingling. "But against my advice, he insisted on going off by himself at times. I warned him." A fleeting grimace lifted his lips, revealing teeth as strong and white as a wolf's.

He turned to Fulvia. "My Lady Antonius, I trust that you are in good health."

"Tolerable, Quintus Gracchus," Fulvia murmured, lowering her lashes, "although, as you might expect, I'm quite prostrate with grief at the loss of our beloved Emperor. It is kind of you to ask, though."

"My heavens, Fulvia, don't waste your time fawning on this wretch." Demea narrowed her eyes. "All of Rome knows he has no taste for the, shall we say . . . fairer sex." Then she sat up as Flina arrived with a tray of steaming sausages and other delicacies. "Isn't that so, Gracchus?"

"It's true that my duties leave me little time for affairs of the heart, lady." His voice was stiffly disapproving. "Much as I might wish it otherwise."

Did she detect a glimmer of interest in those steely gray eyes? Quickly calculating his possible accumulation of points, she wondered if, with the addition of her own points, he might have enough to ascend to the Palace in Micio's place.

Then warmth rushed through her cheeks, spreading rapidly downward. What could she be thinking of? His role and Game background were so completely plebian and—her gaze strayed to the tanned, muscular legs standing there before her, solid as tree trunks. Well, stranger things had happened in the Imperium than the union of aristocrat and plebe.

Selecting a fat, sizzling sausage, she wrapped it in a fresh slice of bread. "Get to the point, Gracchus."

"I came to report on the Lady Amaelia."

Hearing that name so unexpectedly, she bit down too hard on the hot sausage and burned her tongue. Sputtering, she seized a glass of red wine and downed it in one gulp. "What—What about her?"

"Well, as you must know, the Emperor sent me to Delos to b..y her in his name and return her to the Palace, but when I arrived, she had already been sold to an anonymous private party." He shifted his weight, catching the sun on his bronze muscle plate and reflecting it into her eyes. "Although I have made efforts to trace the sale, I have so far been unsuccessful."

"How tragic." Laying aside the sausage, she selected a ripe black olive and bit it delicately in two. "I was so looking forward to sharing Micio's estate with her."

"I've come for your orders, lady." He braced his massive shoulders. "Tell me your will in this matter, that I may direct my efforts."

Demea tapped a manicured finger against her chin. Yes, in his own fashion, he was really quite handsome, much more pleasing to the eye—and certain other senses—than her late husband. And although he was currently too plebian to become Emperor . . .

She rolled an olive between her finger and thumb. There were no rules against having lovers; in fact, the ancient Romans had felt quite to the contrary, and it wasn't as though she was even married anymore. "Your efforts have already been quite exemplary, Quintus Gracchus." Tossing the flattened olive aside, she selected a crisp fried cherry tart and bit off one corner, dabbing at the juicy filling with her fingers. "I will oversee the rest of the investigation myself, although I might require your personal assistance from time to time."

With a clank of armor, Gracchus sank to one knee and bowed his head, so close that Demea had to clasp her fingers together to keep them from wandering through those sinuous, dark curls.

"Anytime, day or night." He gazed up, heart-stoppingly direct, into her eyes. "My lady has only to call."

Kerickson gave up and entered the police airhopper. The robot heaved itself in behind and ignored him. Sitting by a window, he watched as they passed above areas of New York City that he had either forgotten or never seen. It was amazing how much could change in six years. A large patch of wilderness appeared below, and he saw an elephant wandering beside a small muddy lake. An elephant in the middle of New York. When had he stopped paying attention to the rest of the world? He pressed his face against the cool window plas.

All too soon, though, the ride was almost over. Just ahead he saw the massive downtown police station, rising up against the surrounding buildings like a gleaming gray windowless cube. The sheer size of it reminded him that he had been living in the diminished perspective of the Imperium for so long that he had forgotten how really big the outside was.

With a sigh, he held on to the utilitarian plas-covered seat in front of him as the airhopper made a rapid descent to the roof landing pad, then landed with a teeth-rattling thump. He rose and followed the morosely silent robot out into the winter sunshine, vainly pulling the collar of his too-thin shirt around his neck. "I want to call a lawyer," he said to its shiny black posterior. "That's my right, isn't it?"

"If you desire counsel, it is permitted," it said without slowing. "We find, however, that most innocent humans do not feel the need."

"But they always call a lawyer in the tri-dees." Hurrying, he caught up and stared up into its red sensor eyes. "It's only the stupid ones who don't."

"So you correlate manipulation of the law with intelligence." The robot stopped in front of the gravity well that led down to the lower floors. "An unusual juxtaposition of concepts in this day and age."

Kerickson stared past the robot's body into the gravity well's hazy green glow. Such modern devices hadn't been allowed in the Game, and he hadn't used one for longer than he could remember. The HabiTek board hadn't even permitted anything but an old-fashioned elevator to run between levels down in Technical Services, while the most advanced such antigravity device actually allowed on the playing field had been the ancient, but still functional, concept of stairs.

Closing his eyes, he stepped into the emptiness of the shaft and felt the gravity field close around him. With a slight clank, the robot followed, floating just above his head as the two of them slowly descended. Kerickson sighed. It wasn't really so bad. He was just going to have to get used to such things again.

"Exit on the first floor," the robot said, then remained silent for the rest of the descent.

The first floor was staffed solely by pleasant-looking clerical models all dressed in the exact same cut of blue suit-alls. As a single unit they all looked up and tracked him with their eyes as he followed the police robot across the wide open space. The back of his neck began to itch.

"Well, well, if it's not our boy, Kerickson," said a booming voice from behind a corner desk. "Do you want to confess right away, or shall we waste a few pleasant moments trying to deceive one another?"

Kerickson recognized the bulbous nose of Detective Sergeant Arjack. "Confess to what?" he asked warily as the robot pointed to a utilitarian chair.

"Deception it is, then." Arjack whipped out a second chair, turned it backward, and straddled it, gazing expectantly at him. Kerickson stared back.

"Now . . ." The Arjack nodded its head encouragingly. "Surely you know how this goes—first you tell me that you didn't kill him, and then—"

"Didn't kill who?" Kerickson interrupted.

"Whom—Alan Jayson Wexsted, also known as the Emperor, Micio Metullus—and then *I* say I don't believe you, and we go on like that." It bared large teeth in a humorless smile. "Useless, of course, like most human rituals, but I'm programmed to perform it whenever appropriate."

"Oh." Kerickson gazed down at the scuffed toes of his boots

for a moment. "But I didn't kill him, although I do admit that his death might possibly have been my fault, because I couldn't obtain any more Vestal Virgins on such short notice."

"*Vestal* Virgins . . ." The Arjack shook its massive head. "I have to admit that's a qualification of the term 'virgin' not currently in my data bank."

"Virgins needed to tend the sacred fire in the Temple of Vesta." Kerickson glanced around the room, then lowered his voice. "You know, young ladies who have never—" He winced. "You know."

The Arjack grunted. "Human procreation—such an endlessly boring subject. Are we done trying to deceive each other yet?"

"I didn't kill Micio Metullus."

"And I'm not a robot." It smiled another chilling smile. "Very well, Mr. Kerickson, you may go. We have enough physical readings on you now to make a fair assessment of how much of the truth you're telling us. Just don't leave town."

"Go?" Kerickson stood up and felt the room tilt sideways. How long had it been since he'd slept or had anything to eat? "What about a lawyer?"

"Oh, get one, by all means." Standing up, the robot turned away. "Waste your time and money. None of that is of the slightest interest to us."

Time and money . . . Kerickson turned that over in his mind as the robot's solid-looking back lumbered away from him. He had very little money put aside. Alline had always had such expensive—and demanding—tastes, even before she'd talked him into buying her into the Game. He'd taken out a loan to pay her enrollment, a loan that he hadn't finished repaying to this day. Just how much money did a lawyer cost, anyway?

He straightened the rumpled collar of his shirt-all, then picked up his suitcase. He wasn't going to find any answers standing around the police station with his mouth hanging open. He'd better arrange for some sort of room for the night and start calling lawyers.

Amaelia was dreaming of the Imperial Palace with its columns of carved marble and long, gleaming halls, dreaming that she ran down those echoing halls in sandalled feet, but no one responded to her calls—not a single servant, nor her snide stepmother, not even her remote, disinterested father.

"Hello!" She stared down the empty hallway. "Where is everybody?"

"Everybody . . . everybody . . ." the Palace said back to her.

What could have happened? She hadn't been away at the temple that long, but nothing seemed the same—

"What in Hades are you doing in here!"

A hand of iron seized her shoulder and shook her until she bit her lip. The Palace halls broke into pieces and faded. Groggily, she forced her eyes open and blinked up into a ruggedly handsome, faintly familiar face. "What?"

Quintus Gracchus released her shoulder. "This location is off limits to the entire household!"

"I—" Rubbing her bruised shoulder, Amaelia looked around the room, still half asleep, but the screens displayed only a featureless blue again, betraying no trace of the visitors she had spoken with before. "I—The door was open. No one said that I couldn't come in."

His gray eyes raked the room. "I suppose there was no harm done, but you are never to come in here again."

"What do you mean 'again'?" Standing, she glared up into his tanned face. "Where's my father? I want to go home now!"

"Yes, your father." He studied her with flinty eyes. "It is time to speak of him. Perhaps you had better come out into the colonnade and sit down."

"I don't want to go anywhere." She raised her chin. "Especially not with you."

"Let us both hope you change your mind about that." The tone of his voice was grim. "This is an unfortunate situation for both of us—me, because I have spent a considerable sum acquiring you at your father's request, money for which now I have no hope of being compensated, and you, because you are a slave whom it is not in anyone's interest to free. I think you will find that your choices have become extremely limited. You will have to be very careful that you make the best of them." Taking her by the arm, he hustled her out the door, then locked it behind them.

"How dare you touch me without my permission!" Even though the house field was still on, the sun had retreated behind heavy, ominous clouds and the air had grown chilly. Amaelia shivered, realizing that she had no more clothes than those on her back.

Gracchus's mouth straightened into a thin, tight line. "You

are only a slave now. I have every right to take any liberty I choose."

"You said my father would free me!" Rubbing her hands over her arms, she stared angrily into his chiseled face. "I'm no more a slave than you are Emperor, and you'd better remember that!"

"On the contrary." His voice had a even tone to it, as though she were nothing but the most minor of inconveniences. "Your circumstances have vastly changed since your little escapade at the Public Baths. You will find that you no longer have a father or any status at all, except for slave."

The words washed over her like a cold shower. "What are you talking about?"

Holding up one hand, Quintus removed his glove, tugging each finger with precise, measured motions. "I regret to say that your illustrious father perished in a fire yesterday morning at the Public Baths. The whole Imperium is in mourning."

"Perished, you mean—dead?" Amaelia sagged back against the cold hardness of a column. "My—father?"

Tucking the glove into his wide leather belt, he started on the other one. "Life, however, does go on, and we all must do our part. Another Emperor must be found so that the Game can continue."

Her father was dead. She tried to make the words real, but it was like trying to pick water up in a sieve; they kept running out of her head.

"It has long been a tradition that the Praetorian Guard has a hand in selecting the new Emperor," Gracchus continued, as though he were only discussing the dinner menu. "As current Captain of the Praetorian Guard, I cannot take this duty lightly. And you, my lady, have your own duty to the Game as well." Reaching down, he grasped her wrist and jerked her against his bronze chest plate as though she weighed nothing.

"Duty?" Hot tears started down her face as she tried to twist out of his grip. "The Game? How can you talk about a stupid game where nothing is real, unless . . ." A sudden hope dawned in her mind. "Unless he's only dead in the Game. That's what you mean, isn't it? He's just dead in the Game?"

"No, Amaelia." Gracchus shook his curly head. "Your father has passed beyond this world."

"Then I don't want to play anymore!"

"Ah, but now, lady," Gracchus whispered, staring down into

her eyes, "comes your greatest role of all—that of both Empress and my wife."

Even the lowest rated of legal robots cost twice as much as Kerickson had in his savings account. Staring at the screen's statistics in his meagerly furnished hotel room, he thought of the ramifications. He could try to borrow, of course, but who would want to lend a sizable sum to a down-and-out, already in debt, unemployed programmer under suspicion of murder?

His parents had entered an expensive Maui retirement community over three years before, and had liquidated all their assets to buy a beachside condo. He couldn't think of anyone else to ask for help, but then Alline's face crept into his mind. Perhaps . . .

But she was the widow of the very man he'd been accused of killing. Alline—or Empress Demea, as she styled herself these days—was the last person, in or out of the Imperium, who would be inclined to help him.

Just as he reached for the release button to clear the screen, the incoming-call code sounded. His finger froze in midair while he tried to decide whether to answer or not. It might be the police again, and he'd already had more than enough of them for today.

The code buzzed again. Swearing under his breath, he jabbed ACCEPT, then leaned back in his chair, arms crossed tightly across his chest.

The image of a soft, round face formed. Myopic blue eyes blinked at him from under a receding tangle of brown hair—Wilson. "Arvid!" he gasped. "Thank God it's you!" He glanced furtively over his shoulder, then leaned closer to the screen. "You've got to get back here right away! I think I've found the problem."

"Don't tell me you haven't heard." Kerickson scowled. "I'm guilty of murder, and fired to boot."

"Murder?" Wilson shook his head. "Don't be dense, Arvid. Nobody believes you killed Micio, but if you don't get back here right away, all hell's going to break loose—and that will be your fault."

"And exactly how do you figure that?"

"Because I found the glitch." Mopping at a trickle of sweat, Wilson stared beseechingly into the screen. "And it's not just Minerva, it's all of them. They're all involved, and right here before the Saturnalia, too. You've got to come back and give me a hand!"

"You're forgetting, of course, that I couldn't access so much as a rubbish collector in that place." Kerickson shook his head. "Jeppers blanked my Game status."

Wilson waved an impatient hand at him. "Oh, I've already taken care of that. You're logged in now as Gaius Clodius Lucinius, a freedman student down at the Gladiatorial School."

"A freedman—"

"Beggars can't be choosers, and all that rot." Wilson started, then stood up. "Look, we can't talk about this on an open channel. It's close to ten now. Just get back here and meet me down in front of the school by midnight. I can't handle this by myself."

"It's not my problem anymore," Kerickson protested. "Tell Jeppers and the rest of HabiTek to sit up there and hold Minerva's hand. I hope he—"

"Listen, you idiot, HabiTek is up to its knobby corporate knees in this whole mess!"

Intrigued, Kerickson stared at him. He'd never seen his former partner so upset. What could be going on back there in the Imperium? Could there possibly be a way to exonerate himself? Perhaps it wouldn't hurt to just go back and hear what Wilson had found. After all, he could always say no.

Something crashed just out of sight, and Wilson paled. "Look, just get here—midnight—you understand?" Then the screen went blank.

"This had better be good," Kerickson said to the empty blue screen, then sighed. If he was going to make it by midnight, he had better hurry.

CHAPTER
FIVE

The knee-length tunic handed to him by the yawning Costuming attendant was none too clean, not to mention that both it and the accompanying long gray cloak were full of moth holes. He shook the ratty garments out, then sighed. Unlike the Interface Gate, players' gates allowed no one on the field without proper attire. He might as well get on with it.

Stepping into the changing booth, he stripped, then put on the musty-smelling outfit, thinking that while authenticity was one thing, filth was quite another. As he strapped on the worn belt with its plain wooden dagger, he resolved that if he ever did get back on staff, he would have Costuming's collective head for this.

Leaving his outside clothes in an empty locker, he keyed it to his thumbprint, then presented his newly acquired Game bracelet to the monitor.

"Identity confirmed," the computer said after scanning. "Gaius Clodius Lucinius. Game status: freedman, gladiator trainee."

Kerickson tugged the musty cloak around his shoulders as the door slid aside. He stepped into the chilly night air and breathed a sigh of relief as the door shut behind him, locking out the police and the outside world and all his troubles—for the moment, anyway.

This particular gate was in the Southeast Quadrant, located in the side of one of the seven hills of Rome and masked by several boulders. He gazed down on the playing field, taking in the odor of horses, damp earth, and stone, trying to be thankful that at least Wilson hadn't been stupid enough to enroll him as a slave.

Beside the hill, the two buildings of the Gladiatorial School were dark and quiet at this hour. Since they were all in training, gladiators were supposed to retire early. He huddled into the worn cloak and threaded his way down through a maze of exceedingly realistic rocks, muffling curses every time he stubbed his toe.

The Colosseum also loomed ahead, adjacent to the school. Its massive black outline stood out against the simulated night sky, but he saw no sign of Wilson yet. Well, he was probably a few minutes early. Flapping his freezing arms, he crunched across the sandy soil to the far end of the empty arena, then paced back again.

Down in the nearest street, he saw several members of the Praetorian Guard returning from the Subura, one of the Game's less reputable districts, their steps unsteady and their voices boisterously loud.

He edged back into the shadows, wishing for his watch; of course, few wore such innovations in here where authenticity counted above everything else, and sundials didn't fit well on the wrist. The soldiers stumbled past and their exuberant voices faded.

Kerickson surprised himself by wishing that he were down there with them. His six-month term as a guard when he had first been hired by HabiTek had been fun in a lot of ways. He missed the camaraderie he had known then, and even the drilling, the working out, the sense of physical fitness.

But none of that had been real, he told himself. The Imperium was just a giant playpen for people who had too much money and free time, both of which were problems he'd never had to worry about.

He took a deep lungful of the bitingly cold air, then exhaled. His breath hung mistily in the air. His feet had gone numb in the scanty scandals without socks or hosiery. Dammit, where was Wilson? Gritting his teeth, he took another turn around the edge of the Colosseum, wishing for a coldtorch or even a proper Roman one.

"Kerickson?" a hesitant voice asked.

"Over here!"

"Where?" Wilson's voice demanded.

Orienting himself to the approaching footsteps, Kerickson turned around and made out a faint shape coming toward him. "Will you hurry up! I'm about to freeze my—"

"Patience, my boy, patience." Glancing over his shoulder,

Wilson panted up the hill. "Sorry I'm late, but for a few minutes there I thought I was being followed."

"Followed?" Taking Wilson by the arm, Kerickson pulled him deeper into the blackness of the arena's shadow. "Who would be following you at this hour?"

"Probably no one. Everyone is restless since Micio died." Wilson leaned back against the bricks. "You know how it is. Things won't settle down until there's a new Emperor."

"Yeah, well, now that you've got me out here in the middle of the night, let's quit wasting time. Just what did you think you found out?"

"Well, you know that little mix-up with Amaelia?" Wilson hesitated. "It was no accident. I searched Vesta's temple and found a note sent to Amaelia Metullus signed by her father, telling her to meet him at the Public Baths. It was a setup."

"So?" Kerickson tried to rub some feeling back into his arms. "That's the whole point—everyone is trying to become Emperor. Micio was bound to have a whole stadiumful of political enemies."

"Yes, but how many of them would be able to interfere with the god programs? It wasn't a coincidence that Minerva was down on the very same day we had a fatal fire. Once I analyzed the stats, I found that her buffers were being randomized by a self-renewing program, guaranteed to keep her out of action until it was deleted."

"But—" Kerickson looked around, then leaned in closer. "But no one has access to the Interface except you and me."

"And HabiTek." Wilson stared straight into his eyes. "It's so obvious. Don't you see?"

"See what?"

Nearby in the velvet-black darkness, a sandalled foot slipped in the sandy soil. The two men glanced sharply at each other, then pressed back against the coldness of the arena's granite wall.

"We can't be seen together," Wilson whispered. "I'll have to meet you again tomorrow night."

Kerickson caught his arm. "Where?"

"I'll let you know." Wilson pulled out of his grasp, then hesitated. "Give me your dagger."

Surprised, Kerickson started to unbuckle his belt and hand it over.

"No, just the dagger." Wilson glanced down the darkened hill. "I'll bring it back tomorrow."

"No problem." He drew the wooden-handled dagger from the short scabbard and passed it to Wilson. "Be careful."

"Don't worry, old son." Wilson hefted the dagger. "I've programmed Mars to look after me."

That wasn't particularly reassuring. Kerickson watched his former coworker pick his way back down the hill, heading toward the center of the Imperium and the safety of the Interface.

Then he looked around, trying to decide what to do. It was hours before the school would open, and he didn't want to attract attention. Finally, he headed into the graceful open arches of the Colosseum to find a likely spot to bed down. Tomorrow would be soon enough to present himself at the school as Gaius Clodius Lucinius, freedman and new student in the ancient arts of mayhem.

Lying there, all alone in that great big Imperial bed, Demea scrunched her eyes closed, reflecting what a very disagreeable thing light was so early in the morning. Why, it had to be no later than seven o'clock, and here the sun was, rising merrily as though everyone had to be up and get about their business, which she, of course, did not.

Frowning, she stretched her arms above her head. Perhaps she would petition Juno to keep the sun down until at least ten A.M. After all, what use was influence unless you wielded it? And one of the best points of living in this place was that here, unlike the dreary outside world, the gods sometimes answered your prayers.

A soft, hesitant whisper broke into her thoughts. "Mistress?"

"Go away!"

"Mistress, please!" Quick, light footsteps crossed the floor to the side of her bed. "He *says* he won't go away without speaking to you. He says he'll just have to take his business elsewhere if you don't get up and speak to him right now."

Demea opened her eyes just the slightest crack and winced. "I'll sell you, I swear I will, Flina, if you don't get out of here right this minute!"

"But mistress, it's one of *them*, from the Spear and Chicken." Flina's fingers tugged insistently at the silk coverlet tucked around Demea's body. "You *know*."

For a second she couldn't think what the little wretch was getting at. "The Spear—and Chicken?" Then she remembered Micio talking about that place and some sort of special deal on the side he'd had with them. "Oh ..." She pressed the heels of her hands against her aching eyes. "Yes, well, I suppose you had better show him in."

"In *here*, mistress?"

Blinking against the horrid, yellow, glaring sunlight, she scowled at Flina's smooth dark face. "Yes—or would you rather I entertain him in the Palace Baths?"

Tucking her hands behind her back, Flina dropped her dark-eyed gaze to the mosaic inset into the pink floor.

"Then go and get him." She watched the young maid retreat. "Robot," she whispered to herself. Flina had to be a robot. It would be positively illegal for a human to be so poised and graceful this early in the morning. She leaned her head back against the carved teak headboard and reflected that it was too bad the rules forbade physical punishment; she would just love to have the ungrateful wench beaten to see if welts would indeed appear on that firm young back.

Flina reappeared in the doorway, followed by a stocky, middle-aged man in a greasy green tunic. "Publius Barbus, mistress, of the Spear and Chicken," Flina announced.

"Greetings, your ladyship." The man's broad face split into a craggy, gap-toothed smile. "Nice digs you got here." He winked. "Not to mention a high sort of quality help." As he spoke, his hand slipped down behind Flina's backside and gave her a pinch.

Flina jerked slightly, but otherwise gave no indication of having noticed. Demea narrowed her eyes. "That will be all, Flina," she said frostily.

"As you wish, mistress." Flina's crown of black braids bowed respectfully; then she backed out and closed the door behind her.

"Thought she'd never leave!" Striding forward, Barbus plopped down on the bed and stared expectantly at Demea.

Inwardly cursing Micio for dying and leaving her to deal with this low-life on her own, she pulled the pink coverlet up to her chin. "How may—I help you, Publius Barbus?"

"Just call me Harry, your Imperialness." Looking thoughtful, he scratched at a wart on his impressively arched nose. "I don't really go for them sissy Roman names, and anyway, it's really more like how you and I can help each other." He leaned closer, and she detected the delicate aroma of garlic and sour wine. "It's almost the Saturnalia, you know—only a few days to go now, and so much to do."

"Yes, well . . ." She tried breathing through her mouth. "I'm sure you understand that Micio always handled these details. I'm rather at a . . . loss at the moment."

"Heavens, don't you go worrying your pretty little head about nothing, your Empressness." Leaning in still closer, he patted her hand. "Just give old Harry here the word and things'll go on just the same as always. You won't have to lift one tiny pink finger."

"That's very kind of you—Harry," she said, shuddering under his touch. "I'm gratified to know there are those upon whom I can count in this time of need."

" 'Course . . ." He laid a finger beside his beaky nose. "If I handle all the details on my own, I'll have to take a bigger share of the profits to cover my expenses. That's just good business."

"How—big a share?" she asked, wishing that he would just go away and let her sleep.

"Oh, double should do the job." He produced a rusty-looking dagger and began to pick his nails. "Unless something comes up."

"I should think half again your old share would be more than generous." Her hand clasped the sheet tighter. "And nothing had better come up!"

"It takes a powerful bit of money to keep mouths closed in a place like this, your royalness." His face dropped into sorrowful folds. "And of course, his formerness, your late husband, he understood stuff like that. Had a real head for business, he did."

"In fact, I've changed my mind." Sliding onto the cold floor so that the bed was between them, Demea clasped the silk sheet to her breast and concentrated on looking her most dignified. "I will handle the details myself, just as my beloved Micio did. You will resume only your old duties, nothing more."

"Unless you know where all the so-called bodies are buried, I wouldn't be so hasty, your ladyness." Publius's thick eyebrows arched. "And as a betting man, I'd say you have no idea what I'm getting at, do you?"

"Bodies?" she said faintly.

"Himself knew everything about everyone, and as they say, information is always money in the right hands." He winked, then stood. "I'll just be on my way now. Don't you worry one hair on that lovely head of yours. Things ought to run just as smooth as ever, maybe even more, now that old Harry's got the reins."

Feeling like a fool, she watched him swagger out the door. So that rat, Micio, had known things, had he—important things he hadn't shared with her. Somehow she had to find his information stash, or this whole setup was going to slip right through her bejeweled fingers.

The cooing of doves woke Kerickson from wild dreams in which police robots mounted on fiery, snorting horses chased him down the long winding streets of the Imperium and into the frigid, racing waters of the Tiber River.

For a moment, lying there flat on his back, staring up at winged shadows flitting from arch to arch, he couldn't remember where he was or what he was doing there. Then it came back to him—the fire, Micio's death, his own dismissal by HabiTek, and Wilson's overly dramatic insistence that he come back to put things right.

Sitting up on the unpolished granite bench, he rubbed at his knotted neck, hating himself for being so stupid and gullible. Not one cobblestone of this place was his concern anymore. After giving six years of his life to make the Imperium run smoothly, he didn't owe its idle, rich inhabitants one damn thing.

And of course, to make it all much worse, there was no prospect of real coffee unless he hiked all the way down into the tourists' restaurant district, and that would take too long. Shaking the dirt out of his cloak, he shrugged the heavy wool around his shoulders, then looked out into the blue-gray winter sky and estimated the time as after eight; he must have slept soundly after all.

He walked through the arched outer halls of the arena, then trudged down the sandy path to the larger of the two adjacent Gladiatorial School buildings. Perhaps he could at least get some breakfast there.

When he opened the door, a large brute with a broken nose and sinews that could have been made of iron crossed over to him. "And just who are you?"

"Gaius Clodius Lucinius." Kerickson glanced past the man's dingy loincloth at the huge practice floor and the pairs of sparring students. The air was thick with sweat and oil and rotting food. Several good-sized rats were fighting over the remains of a half-eaten meat roll from under the nearest bench. "I'm sure

that if you'll check with Marcinius Flatus, you'll find I'm expected."

"Well, that might be difficult, unless you've a mind to visit
the Underworld." Drawing a huge dagger, the man ran a thumb
along the edge, leaving a bright line of blood behind.

Kerickson winced. Bladed weapons were illegal in the
Game. First chance he got, he'd have to alert Security to
search this place.

"There's been a slight—accident." The man's scarred lips
twisted, displaying his stained teeth in a skull-like grimace.
"Flatus is dead. I'm the new owner."

"Oh." The back of Kerickson's shoulders began to itch.
"And you are?"

"The great Nerus Amazicus."

"I see." He recognized the name of a popular but unscrupu-
lous gladiator, known for causing real injuries in a sport where
simulation was the rule. Peering around the enormous, grimy,
muscular chest, he tried to think how to play this. "Are you
still taking new students, then, or should I apply elsewhere?"

"You—a gladiator?" Amazicus threw back his head and
laughed all the way from his hairy belly up. "What have you
got—two, maybe three hit points at the most? You wouldn't
last five minutes with a real pro."

Kerickson glanced down at his Game bracelet—half a hit
point. This had all been a miscalculation, although he could
see why Wilson thought no one would ever look for him here.

"Now, I suppose we could use an undersized runt like you
as arena bait for teasing the tigers, or perhaps you could spar
with the girls."

A chuckle ran through the sweaty room. Kerickson backed
toward the door. "Never mind—"

"Don't you lay one finger on that delicious blond head!" a
female voice screeched. "I want him!"

Laughter roared. Kerickson felt for the door handle behind
his back as a towering, broad-shouldered woman clad in two
small scraps of worn cloth elbowed her way through the snick-
ering students. Her cropped brown hair was slicked back from
her face with perspiration, and a purpling bruise slashed across
her cheek. She weighed at least two hundred pounds without
an ounce of fat.

"Oh, yeah?" Amazicus threw his chest out. "And what if I
say you can't have the little twerp?"

"Then I'll fight you for him." Brandishing a trident, she

flashed him a wicked grin full of broken teeth. "He doesn't look as though he'd have much go in the arena, but I bet he could warm a girl's blankets at night—couldn't you, sweet thing?"

Kerickson's groping hand found the doorknob and pulled.

"Not so fast, runt." With a twist of his wrist, Amazicus sent him sprawling on the mats, then turned his attention back to the woman. "And just how much are you willing to bet?"

"Name your price, turdface." She knotted her dingy brown hair back with a leather thong.

Amazicus's nostrils flared. "At least I didn't lose my lease down on the Via Nova from lack of customers!" He thrust his furry chest out. "From what I hear, Ivita, you couldn't even give it away!"

She dropped into a fighting crouch and sneered back at him. "How would you know? According to what I hear, you've never had any!"

Light danced over the pair's rocklike muscles as the two rushed together like speeding airtrains. Kerickson was just scrambling for the door when the air between them came alive with a thousand sparkling blue lights.

"FINALLY!" Settling himself on a divan that hadn't been there a moment ago, a small, round-faced man nodded approvingly.

"Mighty Mars, respected God of War." Ivita hurriedly dropped to one knee and bowed her head. "Tell us how we can serve you."

"YOU CAN DAMN WELL GET ON WITH IT, THAT'S HOW!" He waved an imperious hand at the pair. "I WANT REAL BLOOD, MAYHEM, BRAINS AND INNARDS PAINTED ACROSS THE FLOOR, BITS OF QUIVERING FLESH SPATTERED FROM ONE END OF THIS PLACE TO THE OTHER."

"Sire?" Ivita's square face looked confused, while Amazicus's jaw sagged.

"HAVE YOU GOT ANY IDEA WHAT IT'S LIKE BEING GOD OF WAR, DISCORD, AND BATTLE, IN A PLACE WHERE THE WORST THING THAT EVER HAPPENS IS A GODDAMNED INFECTED HANGNAIL?"

The hair quivered on the back of Kerickson's neck.

"I'M SICK OF EVERY CANDY-ASSED SO-CALLED GLADIATOR IN THIS JOINT." Mars's eyes flashed dangerously red. "FROM NOW ON, I WANT NONSTOP ACTION

AND GLORY, OR I'LL TAKE MATTERS INTO MY OWN HANDS!"

Outside, a clap of thunder rumbled through the dome.

Was this what Wilson had tried to tell him last night? Kerickson edged silently toward the door. Even if it wasn't, the quicker he got back into the Interface and checked things out, the better. Mars wasn't supposed to appear without being summoned, much less insist on blood.

"AND WHERE DO YOU THINK YOU'RE GOING?" the apparition said as it spotted Kerickson. "NOW THAT I'M FINALLY RID OF THAT WORM WILSON, YOU'RE NEXT!"

"Wilson?" Pressing back against the wall, Kerickson stared at the pudgy God of War. "What about him?"

Mars threw back his balding head and laughed. His voice echoed through the huge training hall. "JUST THAT SOMEONE FINALLY DID WHAT I'VE BEEN LONGING TO DO. THE LITTLE SNEAK WAS FOUND STABBED TO DEATH AT THE ORACLE'S THIS MORNING." Turning his head, he looked suddenly very much like the vulture with which he was associated. "I DON'T SUPPOSE YOU'RE MISSING A WOOD-HANDLED DAGGER?"

CHAPTER
SIX

"Wilson?" Ivita turned and appraised Kerickson with the look of a cat who'd just got one paw on the canary. "What the hell kind of name is *Wilson* for a player?"

Up in the air, Mars stretched his arms back behind his head and lounged full-length on the conjured divan. "WHO THE HELL *WAS* WILSON IS MORE THE QUESTION."

Kerickson's heart pounded like a ten-piece percussion band as he groped for the side of the door. The floor seemed to swoop out from under his feet. Wilson is not dead, he told himself fiercely. This is only a damned game. Mars just means he is dead in the Game.

"AT LEAST NOW WE CAN HAVE A DECENT CREMA-TION." The god smiled broadly. "BY MY SWORD AND SHIELD, I'VE MISSED THOSE!"

The Oracle—he had to get to the Oracle and see what this was all about. Kerickson lurched outside into the chill morning air and looked down the hill. On the road below, a cart straggled along behind a moth-eaten donkey, one of the standard disguises for automated tour guides. He could hear the recorded patter about the Imperium from where he stood. Twenty or so people ambled behind it, gazing around with enraptured eyes—obviously day-trippers.

Mars followed him outside and swelled to a more godlike height. "AND NOW THAT THINGS ARE IMPROVING, WE'LL HAVE SACRIFICES AGAIN—LIVE ONES WITH FAT, BELLOWING BULLS AND SQUEALING PIGS AND RIVERS OF RED, RED BLOOD!"

The tourists stopped in the middle of the road and pointed at the manifestation. The automated donkey cart trundled on toward the city without them.

The god's excited voice climbed higher and higher. "FINALLY, THIS PLACE IS GOING TO RUN AS IT SHOULD HAVE ALL ALONG!"

The cold air had cleared Kerickson's mind a little, and he realized that he had to stay in character. If Wilson really was dead in the outside sense of the word, then Kerickson would have no way to reenter the Game if he were thrown out, and he was suddenly very sure that he needed to stay. Something was wrong here, and had been wrong ever since the Minerva program had gone down—how many days ago? He couldn't remember, and that worried him, too. He had to get his wits together. He had a feeling he was going to need them.

Rome, of course, had possessed a College of Augurs, rather than a true Oracle, but that fact of history had proved so disappointing to the multitudes who had enrolled in the Imperium that HabiTek had been obliged to provide them with a magnificent Oracle personality. After all, as J. P. Jeppers never tired of expounding, HabiTek was in the business of providing entertainment, and if the masses required the flash and mystery of an Oracle instead of a bunch of stodgy old men poking around in gruesome animal entrails down at the College of Augurs, then of course they would have it.

Kerickson's way led through the heart of the sprawling Market District, already filled with tourists even at this hour. He passed street vendors and hawkers who might or might not be real people. At any given moment in the Game, it was impossible to know exactly with whom—or what—you might be dealing. He lowered his head and avoided the eyes of all he met, hoping not to be recognized.

Still, the odors of the steaming meat pastries reminded him of how hungry he was, and he finally stopped before a small brazier and handed the buxom female attendant a bronze coin. She fished a sizzling meat pastry out of the hot oil. He juggled the hot shell from hand to hand and blew on it before he took a tentative nibble. Crisp on the outside, juicy on the inside, it tasted wonderful. Encouraged, he took a bigger bite.

Down the street, someone shouted. He glanced up. A band of teenage boys dressed in the purple-striped juvenile togas of the upper classes were throwing rocks at a gray-headed rug merchant. Kerickson's hand was automatically groping inside his tunic for his comm unit before he realized that he no longer carried it.

"Vagrants!" The merchant shuffled vainly to avoid the rocks. "Go home before the Guard has you thrown out of the Game!"

A tall, stoop-shouldered boy with lank blond hair laughed. "From now on, you stupid old fart, *this* is the Game. Get used to it!"

The old man squealed as a rock caught him square against the temple. He crumpled to the street. The boys swooped down upon the lush Persian rugs and scattered them into the shocked crowd. "Here, take them! They're yours, courtesy of Mars!"

"WELL DONE, MY CHILDREN, MY BRAVE YOUNG WARRIORS," Mars's voice boomed down from above the red-tiled roofs.

Kerickson dropped the meat pastry as Mars's huge figure stomped down the street on landcar-sized feet.

"FORGET ALL THIS PAP ABOUT HONOR AND DUTY." The beefy face shone down with a fierce red light on the gaping humans below. "I PROCLAIM A NEW AGE OF BOLDNESS AND ADVENTURE!" He leaned down and winked his huge eye at a trembling gray-haired woman. "AN AGE OF BLOOD!"

Then he disappeared. The crowd milled in the street and stared at each other.

"I've played here for five years, but I've never seen anything like that!" Dressed in the off-the-shoulder chiton of a prosperous Greek merchant, a middle-aged man shook his head.

That was because no one in HabiTek had ever written a Game scenario even remotely like what had just happened. Kerickson rubbed his cold hands together. The Mars program had somehow managed to exceed its parameters. Just who was responsible?

No longer hungry, he pushed through the uneasy crowd in the direction of the Oracle. He had to find Wilson. This place was going down the old vac-chute in a hurry, and without access to the Interface, he couldn't run the proper diagnostics to find out what had gone wrong.

Set on a small rise adjacent to the Temple of Apollo, the Game's Oracle resided in a gleaming rectangular white marble structure that overlooked the Forum. He labored up the never-ending steps, unable to resist a glance back over his shoulder from time to time, always expecting to see Mars's face peering down from the sky. And also, he had the prickly feeling that he had forgotten something important.

At the top, he was surprised to find players from every classification wandering through the white columns of the portico. Consultation was available to all players, of course, but only at the cost of both an expensive gift and a roll of the proverbial dice. Once a player applied for advice, the Oracle would predict, then pronounce a random change in one of the vital categories: rank, charisma, or hit points. As a rule, few cared to take the risk of ascending the steps as, say, a respected veteran general of the Numidian Wars, and then descending as an Egyptian onion merchant.

As Kerickson worked his way through the restless, muttering throng, he felt a hand clamp down on his shoulder.

"Not so fast, citizen." The guard reached for Kerickson's arm and bent down his beak-nosed face to examine his Game bracelet. "What's your business here?"

Kerickson recognized the man as a standard-issue robot guard model. Many players changed their roles as often as they changed clothes—some in fact more frequently—and just last year he'd ordered four dozen of this particular robot line to fill in the gaps in the undersubscribed Praetorian Guard. "Just the usual," he answered uneasily. "Foretelling the future, avoiding disaster, that sort of thing."

"Freedman, gladiator trainee, Gaius Clodius Lucinius," the robot read from his Game bracelet, then scrutinized him with narrowed eyes. "If you've come to consult the Oracle, then where is your offering?"

Damnation! He'd been so unhinged by that fiasco with Mars, he'd completely forgotten the requisite gift. "I . . . uh, have no riches to offer, so I thought I'd just dedicate my first victory in the arena to the Oracle."

"Well, go ahead and get into line, but it will be a while." The guard dropped his arm. "We're finishing an investigation, and you'll have to stay out of the way until it's completed." Leaving him, it moved to intercept the next supplicant climbing the steps.

Investigation . . . Kerickson blanched as he spotted a solid row of bronze-armored Praetorian backs off to one side. Was that Wilson over there, his friend, with a dagger in his chest? He edged through the restless crowd of slaves and merchants and nobles who had come to take their chances with the Oracle.

"SO, YOU THINK YOU CAN JUST PRANCE UP HERE AND ALL WILL BE FORGIVEN." The voice of the Oracle boomed out through the crisp morning.

He peeked between the Guards at the small white marble structure that housed the actual Oracle itself, but no supplicant knelt there, waiting for a pronouncement.

"THIS IS SACRED GROUND, MOONFACE, AND I'LL THANK YOU TO GET YOUR TUSHIE OFF!"

A restless murmur ran through the people. Kerickson eased back, trying to keep the bulk of the crowd between him and the Oracle's sensors. It had been some time since he'd had any dealings with this particular programmed personality, but he had a sudden vague recollection that they hadn't parted on the best of terms.

"YES, I MEAN YOU, DIRTFACE. WELL, IF YOU WON'T LEAVE, THEN COME ON UP HERE LIKE A MAN AND GET YOUR FORTUNE TOLD."

There had been some business about a fixation the Oracle had developed with an acolyte of Apollo, a player who had taken every advantage of the situation . . . He cudgeled his brain for the details. The incident had been almost four years ago, but it seemed to him that the acolyte had been played by . . . Micio Metullus.

"YOU'RE ON MY TURF NOW, SO COME ON OVER HERE AND PLAY, BIG BOY."

All around him the supplicants dropped to their knees and clasped their hands with an air of reverence. A white-robed attendant stood before the ornate marble housing, his head bowed. "Of whom do you speak, oh wise one?"

"THE LITTLE TURD OVER THERE WITH THE LIMP BLOND HAIR AND THE RUMPLED TUNIC, THE ONE WHO LOOKS LIKE HE HASN'T SEEN THE INSIDE OF THE BATHS FOR A MONTH."

Belatedly, Kerickson sank to his knees.

The attendant scanned the crowd anxiously, shading his eyes from the bright sun. "Turd, your All-Knowingness?"

"YOU KNOW, THE ONE WITH THE NERVOUS-LOOKING FACE AND THE SCRAGGLY EYEBROWS, THE ONE TOO BIG FOR HIS TUNIC."

Eyes moved from side to side as the crowd examined each other out of the corners of their eyes. Doing his best to look perplexed, Kerickson lowered his head, but then a strong hand clasped the back of his tunic and hauled him to his unwilling feet.

"This one, your Grace?"

"THAT'S THE TWIT. BRING IT UP HERE."

"I'm afraid that there must be some mistake," Kerickson protested. "I just wanted a few glorious victories in the arena."

"Shut up!" The attendant stopped before the Oracle and dropped him unceremoniously to the marble floor.

"SO WE MEET AGAIN."

Kerickson straightened his back. "Yeah, yeah, so get on with it."

"Show some respect there!" A heavy cane whacked across his back.

"I HAVE A MESSAGE FOR YOU, YOU FROG-FACED TWERP."

"Well, I forgot my gift, so I guess it will have to wait." Trying not to wince, he got to his feet, keeping an eye out for the attendant all the while. He had really bungled this one. He should have known that the Oracle wouldn't forget that little disagreement. He'd better get out of here before it blew his cover.

"I WAIVE THE REQUISITE GIFT IN LIEU OF A SERVICE TO BE RENDERED LATER," the Oracle said smugly. "DO YOU ACCEPT THE TERMS?"

He was about to say no when he saw the attendant brace his feet in preparation for another mighty swing with his brass-tipped cane. "Yeah, I guess—"

"THEN SHUT UP AND BE ENLIGHTENED. MANY SHALL SIT, BUT FEW SHALL EAT. MORE SHALL SEE, BUT FEW SHALL KNOW. ALL WILL COME, BUT ONLY ONE SHALL STAY."

"Huh?" He glanced into the Oracle's shadowy interior. "Could you repeat that?"

"AND NOW FOR YOUR FUTURE."

The oracle hesitated, making Kerickson's stomach cringe. "I FORESEE A CHANGE IN YOUR CHARISMA."

The attendant snickered.

"IN FACT, FROM NOW ON, YOU WON'T BE ABLE TO TALK A MOUSE INTO EATING CHEESE."

Hastily, Kerickson glanced at his bracelet. His charisma rating had dropped from a modest plus-two rating to zero! "Wait a minute, you can't—"

"Silence, dog!" The ham-handed attendant seized his tunic and dragged him back into the crowd.

"Move aside, please," boomed a big-voiced guard. "Move aside and we'll get this mess out of the way so that you can get on with your business." Several Praetorian Guards pushed through the crowd with a litter, headed for the side area, then reemerged with it a minute later.

Jerking out of the attendant's hold, Kerickson elbowed his way to the front just in time to see a guard remove a familiar wooden-handled dagger from Wilson's chest, then drape a coarse wool blanket over the corpse's pale, lifeless face.

"My word!" A portly man, dressed in the flowing robes of a Syrian wine merchant, wiped at his face. "This place is becoming more realistic every day. I could swear that poor fellow is really dead."

Lead butterflies thumped in Kerickson's stomach as he watched the guard place Wilson's dangling hand back on the litter, then twitch the blanket into place. His friend was dead in every sense of the word. He was caught all alone here in the Game, while somewhere inside the Imperium a murderer romped among unsuspecting Roman sheep.

"I trust you slept well, lady?" Gracchus's dark face regarded Amaelia calmly from the door of her bedchamber.

In answer, she snatched up a gleaming white statuette of Venus from the table beside her bed and smashed it into splinters against the wall a few inches from his face.

He didn't even flinch. "A noble try. Shall I send for a gross so you can practice?"

Tears welled up in her eyes, but she forced them back. She was an Emperor's daughter. This lowborn jerk was not going to have the satisfaction of seeing her cry. "I want to go home!"

"And so we shall, my pet, immediately after our nuptials." Moving out of the doorway, he motioned to a waiting slave girl. "And may I say you've never looked lovelier?"

"This is so stupid. I'm not going to marry you!" In a fury, she glanced for something else to hurl at his self-satisfied face. "Not even in this ridiculous Game! I want to see my father!"

"That can be arranged," he said smoothly, "although I doubt you would enjoy it. Still, as long as our marriage is completed before the Saturnalia, I'm sure I will be unable to deny you the least little thing." He reached underneath his bronze chest plate and withdrew a scroll tied with a red ribbon. "By the way, here's your manumission proclamation."

Numbly, she stared at the papers, then checked her Game bracelet. The yellow status light had been replaced by white. "You're freeing me?"

"Obviously, since slaves can't marry." He smiled, but his eyes remained cold gray stone. "I've invited a few friends over this afternoon to witness the solemnization of our vows, which of course won't take long. The ancients seem to have been incredibly casual about such things. I'll just say I'm for you, and you'll do the same for me. Then we'll trot down to the Imperial Palace and give your beloved stepmother the good news."

Where was the stupid Game computer when you needed it? Nothing had gone right for her since her father had forced her into service as a Vestal Virgin, and now this! She definitely didn't want to play anymore. "You're going to lose points on this, especially in authenticity. I have no intention of playing your dutiful wife."

"Well, of course, I won't force you, but on the other hand . . ." A smile tugged at his lean lips as the slave girl emerged from the wardrobe with a silk gown of glimmering pale green. "Your alternatives are rather limited. Still, I have to admit that suicide was regarded not only as a highly moral act in ancient Rome, but also as a practical alternative to an unbearable reality. You might just bring me a whole raft of points, at that."

Staring boldly into her eyes, the slave girl held the dress out expectantly. Amaelia felt her face go cold. "You wouldn't!"

"*I* won't have to," he said cheerfully. "Just remember that whatever move you choose is purely up to you, but I will have a return for my investment in you—whatever form it takes."

With that, he turned and left, his armor clinking. She stared numbly after him. This was only a game; she knew that, but why did it suddenly feel so real?

The maidservant caught her eye again, then looked pointedly at the pale green gown. With a trembling hand, Amaelia touched the smooth silk.

Kerickson's head whirled as he retreated back through the bustling Market District, smothered by the aroma of sour wine, sizzling sausages, and pungent onions. It was too much to take in. Wilson was dead, murdered by Kerickson's own newly issued dagger by the looks of things. How long before the police confirmed the registration of that dagger with Costuming and came looking for the freedman Gaius Lucinius?

And if it came to alibis, he had no one but the blasted pigeons to swear that he'd slept in the amphitheater last night. He had to find out what was going on before the computer pinpointed his whereabouts for the police.

But where to start? He couldn't get back into the Interface, but the ultimate answers had to be out here on the playing field anyway. This had all started with Amaelia's disgrace, followed quickly by Micio's death, and both of those events had taken place ... at the Public Baths.

Hoping that Wilson had provided his Game identity with a decent amount of credit, he altered his course to the north, eventually intersecting the Via Appia. Around him the players went about their own business, their arms and their slaves' arms full of packages and bundles, apparently intent on preparing for the coming Saturnalia, now only two days off.

Then he saw the looming arches of the red-brick Public Baths. Remembering the Oracle's words, he decided that he could do with a bath anyway. He felt grimy right down to his toenails. And perhaps someone there had seen something the morning that Micio had died, or knew something without understanding it. He would ask a few innocent questions while bathing, then be on his way. Nothing could be simpler.

The line in the outer reception area was mercifully short. A trickle of sweat rolled down his temple as he presented his Game bracelet to the Keeper of the Baths, a snowy-skinned woman with jet-black hair. She glanced at his status light, then arched an eyebrow. "*Pigs* are supposed to wash down at the river."

For a second he just stared back at her, afraid that the computer had stopped his account. Then he remembered his zeroed charisma ranking. "Well, you should obviously know," he replied coldly.

She frowned, then debited his account and waved him on in. A roar of laughter went up from the gambling room in the middle, but he followed the scent of chlorinated water into the men's bathing area instead. That was where Amaelia had been lured, and where the fire had occurred—and where Micio had been killed.

An old slave with a face like a withered apple met him at the entrance to the changing room. He took one look at Kerickson's lowborn clothes, then shuffled back to his bench, his lip curling in disdain. As a freedman, Kerickson didn't rank high enough to warrant help disrobing, unless he tipped well. He started to shuck out of his clothes by himself, then thought of Micio. The Emperor no doubt had required assistance.

Fishing in his leather coin purse, he produced several coppers and clinked the coins in his hand before depositing them in the slave's wooden bowl. Grinning toothlessly, the slave lurched back to his feet and pawed at Kerickson's cloak. "Fine day, ain't it, sir? Want old Tithones to send this out for a bit of a wash?"

Not a bad idea. "Sure."

The slave's lips parted in another gruesome grin. "That'll be another four."

Kerickson dug out four more coins and stood stiffly as the slave fumbled with his tunic. It always made him feel like an idiot to be undressed as though he were a helpless child. He fixed his eyes on the brightly colored wall mosaics depicting the tasks of Hercules. "I bet you see everyone come through here, all the greats."

"I seen a few in my time." Tithones worked the tunic up over Kerickson's shoulders, sticking at his neck and nearly garotting him before dumping it unceremoniously on the blue-tiled floor.

"Even the Emperor?"

The slave kicked the tunic aside. "A sad case, him being offed so suddenlike, and not even getting a trip to the Underworld out of it."

Lowering his arms, Kerickson sat down on the wooden bench along the wall and let the slave fumble at his sandals. "I don't suppose you saw him the day that he died?"

Tithones squinted up at him from the floor, his black eyes nearly lost in a maze of wrinkles. "And what if I did?"

"Did he talk to anyone?"

Jerking off the right sandal, the slave glanced at Kerickson's Game bracelet, then grunted. "Well, if he did, it'd take more than the likes of you to get it out of me."

Kerickson bit back an oath. That blasted charisma ranking again! He hid his bracelet behind his back. "Even if there was a silver in it for you?"

"Silver's no good to a fellow stuck down in Hades, if you get my drift." Tossing the second sandal over his shoulder, the slave struggled back to his feet.

"A gold, then," Kerickson insisted impatiently.

"Even gold can't buy a bloke's way out of the Underworld." The slave hunched over for a second, then turned back around, a gleaming dagger in his gnarled hand. "But then, why don't you just check it out for yourself?"

CHAPTER
SEVEN

A muscle twitched underneath Kerickson's eye. "Don't be—ridiculous," he said slowly. "You won't get any points for killing a freedman. Just how long have you been playing, anyway?"

"Long enough." The stooped old slave's cackle echoed hollowly as he hefted the knife in his arthritic fingers. "Long enough to know which way the wind is blowing these days. Long enough." He shuffled forward, the dagger set to skewer Kerickson's ribs.

The air shimmered in front of the wall mosaics, then coalesced into the shining form of a huge young man hovering above the tiled floor. "GET ON WITH IT, PLEASE." The apparition ruffled his golden curls with a manicured hand. "I'VE AT LEAST A DOZEN OTHER DEATHS TO ATTEND TODAY."

Kerickson took in the winged helmet and sandals, the short staff with its twining serpent—Mercury, messenger of the gods, conductor of souls to the Gates of the Underworld—and the biggest prima donna in the whole pantheon. "No one's getting killed today. You might as well flit on out of here."

Mercury folded his arms and reclined just above their heads, "ONE NEVER KNOWS, DOES ONE?" He winked a saucer-sized eye.

"Come to conduct him to the Underworld, have you?" The slave wrinkled his face into a gaping smile. "Don't worry, your worship, you can have him in just a moment. I sneaked a look at his stats, and he's only got half a hit point. Won't hardly be no trouble at all."

"You leave my hit points out of this!" Kerickson repressed an urge to tear off his Game bracelet and stuff it down the old

64

man's throat. "You touch one hair on my head and the computer will zero your authenticity rating. Slaves don't go after citizens."

"You're asking questions, ain't you—questions what ain't your business at all?" Tithones scuttled closer, whirling the gleaming tip of the dagger in a tight circle. "Since when does arena bait come sniffing around asking questions about the highborn? I got strict orders about such things. 'Out of the Game,' *he* said. 'Put anyone who comes prowling around for answers out of the Game straight away.' "

"Who said?" Kerickson inched backward, his eyes on the naked blade.

"That's for me to know and you to find out." The slave nodded up at the waiting god's amused face. "They say you can find out almost anything—down *there*. Won't do you no good, though."

Sweat trickled down Kerickson's forehead into his eyes. "Did this person, whoever he is, order the Emperor's death, too?"

"That mess?" The slave grimaced. "You must be joking. That was not done well at all—no trip to the Underworld, no points gained, nothing."

"Then tell me who talked to the Emperor." Kerickson squatted down and groped for his tunic without taking his eyes off the old man. "I mean, what harm can it do, since you're going to kill me anyway? No one will ever know."

"Orders," the slave muttered. "I have orders. I know my place."

Obviously a loon, Kerickson told himself.

A pair of senators strolled through the door, deep in conversation. He motioned at them frantically. "Send for the guard! This slave is trying to kill me!"

The taller of the two, a rather portly, balding man, smoothed his purple-striped toga. "Well, Decius, old man." He turned to his companion. "I suppose this means we'll have to disrobe by ourselves."

The other senator shook his head, then began to undrape the folds of his heavy wool garment. "Tiresome, Scipio, but nothing to do with any scenario of ours."

Kerickson watched in amazed silence as they turned their backs, shucked out of their togas and undertunics, and strolled casually into the fragrant warm bath in the next chamber.

"HURRY UP, BOYS," Mercury insisted from above. "I MAY BE IMMORTAL, BUT I HAVEN'T GOT ALL DAY."

The old slave's eyes flicked upward as the god spoke. Kerickson lunged forward, forcing the man's knife hand back into the tiled wall. The ivory-handled blade clattered to the tile as the old slave howled in pain. Kerickson snatched it up and pressed it to Tithones's throat. "Now," he said angrily, "tell me who spoke to Micio yesterday!"

"MORTAL WOUND!" Mercury descended to the floor. "BE A GOOD SPORT NOW AND LET US GET ON WITH IT."

"What?"

"ACTUALLY, I DON'T BLAME HIM FOR GOING AFTER A WORMY THING LIKE YOU. YOUR DEMISE WOULD HAVE BEEN MORE ON THE ORDER OF A PUBLIC SERVICE THAN A REAL MURDER. IF I WEREN'T DIVINE AND ABOVE SUCH MUNDANE THINGS, I'D BE TEMPTED TO DO YOU IN MYSELF." The god regarded Kerickson with heavy-lidded eyes. "AT ANY RATE, I RULE THIS A MORTAL WOUND." He adjusted his winged head-dress. "POOR OLD TITHONES HERE IS DEAD AS A DOORNAIL, JUSTLY SLAIN BY AN ENRAGED FREED-MAN, ALBEIT ONE OF ABSOLUTELY NO CHARISMA."

"Dead? No, you can't take him yet!" Kerickson clutched at the slave's clothing.

"Paws off!" Tithones pushed him away, then straightened his rumpled gray tunic with an air of new dignity. "It's against the rules for the living to have truck with the dead without the proper sacrifices and such."

"YES, MY TOOTHLESS, LOWBORN FRIEND, I'M AFRAID IT'S OFF TO THE DISMAL DEPTHS FOR YOU." With a sweep of his oversized arm, Mercury indicated the door. "TOO BAD THE BEST MAN DIDN'T WIN."

Kerickson watched helplessly as Mercury shooed the sham-bling old slave out the door. Off to the Underworld, was it? Well, there was more than one way to enter that part of the Im-perium. "You haven't heard the last of this," he muttered at the departing slave's back. Then he realized that he still held the dagger. He looked at the carved ivory handle, the gleam of fine steel—definitely not Game-issue.

He retrieved his tunic from the floor, then sheathed the dag-ger in his empty scabbard. One way or the other, he was going to find some answers.

* * *

Even though it was well after lunchtime, the Spear and Chicken Inn did not lack for customers. From behind the brocaded-linen curtains of her litter, Demea lounged on fat satin cushions and watched an unsavory plebian crowd flow in and out of the peeling structure.

A nasty little establishment, she decided after a few minutes—exactly what she would have expected from that nasty little man, Publius Barbus. Whatever could Micio have been thinking of when he had gone into business with such a lowborn wretch?

She absentmindedly reached for another candied fig, and one of her litter bearers chose that precise moment to shift his weight. She grasped at the curtains to keep from falling out, but the linen ripped out of the rings, and in another second she found herself nosedown in the Roman dirt.

"My lady!" The nearest bearer's blue eyes bulged out of his handsome, rather Teutonic face.

"Don't just stand there gawking!" she hissed as the grimy crowd of laborers and freedmen stopped to stare and point at her. "Help me up at once or I'll have the lot of you boiled in oil!"

They hesitated for a second, a matched set of eight muscular, blond statues; then, as a single man, they dropped the litter and scurried around the dilapidated corner of the Spear and Chicken's closest rival, the Broken Pot.

"Having a spot of trouble there, your ladyness?"

She pushed herself up from the street, staring at a pair of broken-strapped sandals crammed with large, hairy, smelly toes.

"Now, you really shouldn't lie down there in the street and all. You'll spoil your fine duds."

She glanced up into the gleaming, ratlike eyes of Publius Barbus and shuddered. The stocky little man clasped her under the arm, pulled her to her feet, and brushed her off.

"Strange place for the Empress to be takin' her rest." He nudged her in the side with his elbow.

"Publius Barbus—" She stumbled out of reach, trying vainly to pat the drooping strands of her fallen coiffure back into place. "I'm surprised we meet again so soon."

"Likewise, I'm sure." Locking his hands behind his back, he walked around the Imperial litter, which lay on its side in the middle of the street. He ran an exploratory finger over the polished mahogany poles and gold-chased fittings. "Nice piece of goods, this. Make a fine present."

"Consider it yours," she said quickly. "Now, could you—"

A mutter of admiration ran through the rapidly assembling crowd as the workmen and slaves fingered the snowy linen-brocade curtains and wrenched at the golden ornaments.

"Hands off!" Barbus's bullet-like head swung in a wide arc. "Ain't none of you bums ever seen a lady come to call on her sweetheart before? Now beat it!"

Demea's palms began to sweat. "I'm afraid that there's been some mis—"

"Think nothing of it, your aboveness." Barbus winked as the gaping men and women dispersed. "I am, shall we say, discreet. Wild Britons couldn't drag our little secret out of me. Now, let's share a nice cup of wine before we get down to—" He rubbed his hands together. "—business."

"Yes ... business," she said faintly, wondering if her face could possibly be as red as it felt. "Actually, that is why I came down here to see you today—to learn as much as possible about Micio's business."

"Oh, that." Snagging her arm, he dragged her toward the Spear and Chicken's dark and foreboding entrance. "Don't give it a second thought. Old Barbus here will take care of everything. Save your energy for more pleasantlike things."

She hastily ducked her head as they entered a dimly lit common room filled with drunks sitting on broken benches at three-legged tables. The air was thick with the essences of fried onions, cheap wine, and rancid olive oil. She covered her mouth and nose with a corner of her veil.

"It's not much, but we call it home." Barbus nodded, making the yellow light shine off his bald head. "Still, the front's just for show. It's the back where we really take care of the—" He lowered his voice. "—business."

If she ever caught up with those bearers, she told herself, she would have each and every one of them tortured, no matter what the Game rules said! "Yes," she made herself answer the odious little man, "I would love to see it."

"Well, I always was the so-called brains of the enterprise." Barbus plunged a hand beneath his grimy, sweat-stained tunic and scratched at an elusive itch. "Your late old man, now he was good at the flash and dash, but me, I kept things going. I—" He thumped himself on the chest. "—know where the bodies are buried."

"So you said before," she murmured in her best I'm-so-stupid-and-you're-so-smart voice. "But I haven't the slightest idea what 'bodies' could have to do with any of this."

Laying a finger beside his warty nose, he narrowed his eyes at her. "Think for a moment. In the Game, when someone bites the big one, where does he go?"

"Bites the big one?"

"You know, departs this vale of tears, cashes in his chips, buys the farm."

She swayed, close to being overcome by the noxious fumes, then steadied herself on the greasy wooden bar. "You mean, dies?"

"Yeah, when someone is killed, what happens?"

She sank down on a rough-finished bench and hiked her stola up out of contact with the filthy floor. "Well, above, they have the proper sacrifices and a funeral pyre while the player goes to the—"

"Underworld!" he finished triumphantly. "And there they stay, twiddling their fingers, cooling their respective heels, watching all the fun above on monitors, but not able to do a single bloody thing about it until the quarter is up and they can reenroll."

"I suppose so." She massaged her temples, fighting the headache that threatened to overwhelm her. "I never really gave it much thought before."

"So, let's say you're offed right before the Saturnalia or some other such big festival, and you don't want to spend the next three months down in the Underworld, dead as last year's gladiator. What do you do?"

"I haven't the slightest idea." She stared in sick fascination as an army of enormous brown cockroaches marched across the floor.

"It's so simple. You just pay old Barbus here a bit of money and then there you are, coming and going from the Under-world any time you like, partaking in all the so-called earthly delights of the living."

She stood up. "How clever of you, Barbus, but I really must be going."

"But don't you want to hear the rest?" He groped for her hand.

"There's—more?" She cringed at the touch of his clammy fingers on hers.

"I've saved the best bits for last." He slipped an arm around her waist and clutched her to his doughy chest. "Now *that's* more like it. I like a broad—I mean—a lady who's got a solid feel to her, something to *back* her up, if you catch my drift."

She was sure she did. Her cheeks heated. This vile little man would pay for all this someday, she promised herself—quite soon, in fact. But first she had to be sure she knew everything. "You were going to tell me the rest?"

"Oh, that." His pudgy cheeks puffed out. "Well, quite early on, I seen the Underworld was full of possibilities, and none of them being used. It's hard to get into, real privatelike, even cozy, in fact—has all the amenities—and I said to myself, 'Self, wouldn't that be just the sort of place you'd want to go if you was on the lam?' "

"Lam?" she repeated lamely.

"You know, hiding out."

"Oh."

"And it's worked out just fine." He nodded to himself. "A real meeting of the minds, as it happened. For a reasonable price, I lease my old buddies a cozy little corner down in Hades from which they can come and go and do their business outside, and no one's the wiser."

"Criminals?" Her voice squeaked. "You're hiding criminals in the Underworld?"

"Not just me, your sweetness." He reached up and pinched her cheek. "His formerness, your late old man, was real high on this gig, too, and now that you're stepping into his place, that means it's your show, too."

Her head spun as she tried to make sense of this startling information. In a matter of minutes she had gone from being the bereaved widow of an Emperor to the head of some seedy criminal scheme for hiding out perverts and drug fiends and—

"You look a bit on the white side." Barbus snapped his fingers at a dour, scab-covered female slave lurking on the other side of the crowded room. "Maybe you could do with a sip of grape."

The slave dumped the dregs out of a cup, spit into it, then wiped it out with a corner of her tunic before filling it again with the contents of a grimy bottle.

"I feel rather tired." She smiled wanly at him, but kept her distance from the proffered cup—there was no telling what sort of filth and disease lurked at the bottom of it. "I think that I should go home now. Could you perhaps loan me the litter and a few bearers?"

"Home?" A crafty gleam crept into Barbus's piggy little eyes. "You can't go home before you meet Himself."

"Who?"

"Down in the Underworld." He tugged at her arm. "*He's* panting to meet you."

Kerickson felt more respectable after buying a decent tunic down in the Market District. At least it was clean and relatively whole, an immense improvement over his Game-issued clothing.

Cutting across the Via Nova, he ignored the courtesans draped like oversized flags from their windowsills, his mind on more important matters. After leaving the Baths, he had decided that, as much as the idea made his skin crawl, he had to go to the Palace. Not only had Micio lived there, but he had come from there just before his murder. If anyone knew Micio's business, it would be the Palace slaves, or Demea, his widow.

And Kerickson's ex-wife.

Her face came back to him, pale as the new moon under her glossy, dark chestnut hair, just as he had seen her the day she'd told him that she wasn't going to renew their marriage contract.

"You'll never really play this game," she'd said, "not the way that I mean to. Oh, you'll piddle around, venture out on the playing field to make an adjustment here, straighten out a mess there, but you'll never belong."

"I paid for your enrollment." A lump the size of New York lodged in this throat. "That's what you said you wanted, but there isn't enough left for me to enroll, too, and working in the Interface doesn't leave me any time for playing even if I could pay for another enrollment. Someone has to pay your fees."

"That's the whole problem." A thin smile flitted across her face. "You're always going to belong to the outside, while all I want to do is to go out there and forget that I have ever known anything else. I want to live the Game, but you'll never be anything more than an employee."

"But—" He stared at her; she seemed a stranger in her elegant Roman tunic made of the lushest white silk. "It's just a game. You can't trade that for real life."

She had laughed then, a terrible, hollow laugh that echoed inside his head, and he'd finally understood. She wanted things he could never give her, things he couldn't even understand.

That same day, she'd entered the Game under the identity he'd saved and borrowed to buy for her—Demea Pollius, daughter of an ancient Roman family. Soon after, she became the wife of Micio Metullus, an up-and-coming senator.

Kerickson had retreated to the Interface, putting in sixteen or more hours every day, making the Game work better than ever, until enrollment was up fifty percent and everyone was ecstatic, except him.

He hadn't seen Alline, now known as Demea, for almost two years, although he heard of her often—especially after Micio had acquired enough points to subvert the Praetorian Guard and become Emperor two quarters ago. It was all for the best, of course. Kerickson knew that *he* would never have made Emperor; he wouldn't even have tried. All that time and effort and money, and for what? So you could try to keep everyone else from overthrowing you in a make-believe world? It seemed meaningless.

Well, despite everything, he had to see her today—if a freedman with no charisma could get past the Guard and the household slaves. He glanced down at his Game bracelet and frowned. Evidently, Wilson had formatted this lowborn identity so that he would be inconspicuous, but it was hampering his ability to be effective.

And there was the additional problem that, because players had to show an ID to enter the Game, he'd had to log in under his real name. As soon as the police investigating Micio's murder thought to look for him in here, the Computer would be able to locate him through his Game bracelet in a matter of seconds.

At some point he was going to have to acquire a new identity, perhaps that of a Praetorian Guard or even a priest—someone with more authority, not to mention charisma.

Emerging out onto the broad avenue of the Via Ostiensis, he caught sight of the Imperial Palace up ahead: all columns and white marble, gleaming in the late afternoon sun, and with bronze-armored guards everywhere—in fact, rather more guards than he had ever seen in one place before. Slowing his pace, he listened to the people around him, trying to pick up information.

"—missing for how long?"

"Married, you say, this soon after the old man's death? Positively shocking!"

"—and then every one of her bearers came back and said

that she was murdered by Gauls! Poor thing, she must be in the Underworld now."

"—should at least have a funeral pyre in her honor—"

"—two days out of the temple and here she's gone off and married *him*, of all people, nothing more than a farmer by the looks of him."

Moving with the rapidly increasing crowd, he stopped at the foot of the wide Palace steps to stare up at a man in bronze armor and a red-crested helmet, who had his arm around a slender red-haired girl gowned in pale green.

"Citizens of Rome!" The man's voice rang out over the street, deep and powerful. "I know how worrisome this latest news must be, coming on the heels of our recent great sorrow."

A murmur of assent went up from the crowd, and Kerickson found himself wedged against the people in front of him as those behind surged forward for a better look.

"As your Emperor's son-in-law, and therefore only living male relative, I pledge that I will not rest until the Empress Demea is found and restored to the Palace and the arms of her loving family and the hearts of Rome!" He thrust his fist high into the air and threw his head back. The sun glinted off his curly black hair. "My strong right arm will defend Rome and all those we hold dear. Trust Quintus Gracchus now in your hour of need, and I swear you will never have cause to regret it!"

With a start, Kerickson saw that the girl beside Gracchus was Micio's daughter, Amaelia. But how could she be married? She still held the rank of a slave since her recent dismissal from the Temple of Vesta. And what was all this about Demea being missing?

"I don't know." A puffy-faced man at his elbow turned to his matronly companion. "What do you think?"

"I think he would have done the old girl in himself, if he thought it would give him a chance to be Emperor," she replied. "But then, whether we approve of him or not, someone has got to be Emperor—and it certainly isn't going to be the likes of you."

Edging away, Kerickson pushed through the crowd and leaned against the sun-warmed marble feet of a statue of Venus. He was too late. Something had happened to Demea right on the heels of Micio's death, and there was no way he could believe that it had been a coincidence.

CHAPTER
EIGHT

When it was almost dark, Kerickson checked one final time to see that none of the bored Praetorian Guards were watching, then stepped behind a bare-branched acacia bush and removed his Game bracelet. It was too risky to throw it away—without it, he would be thrown out of the Game the first time anyone challenged him—but if he partially disabled it, then the computer wouldn't be able to follow his movements.

He selected a sharp-edged rock from a nearby flower bed and crushed the primary location transponder, but left the power supply intact to run his status board. Unless someone looked closely, it should get him through most situations, although he still hadn't solved the problem of his blanked charisma.

The wind gusted. He clutched the worn cloak closer and sauntered through the gardens, trying to look as though he had every right to be there. The back of the Palace was devoted to functions that most players never considered, such as waste removal, grounds keeping, and one of the major gates, for the Emperor's private use and to receive supplies from outside. The appearance of authenticity, Kerickson reflected, was much more highly rated in the Imperium than authenticity itself. Much as players liked to pretend they were solidly Roman, living in every detail just as the ancients had, he had never heard an inquiry about who cleaned public rest rooms or picked up the trash.

And, of course, the automated bank tellers, located discreetly behind huge statues of Saturn throughout the city, were always busy.

At length he found what he was looking for—a barely discernible edge where there should have been no edge at all, indicating an access bay for the Palace's array of grounds-keeping equipment, all automated and programmed to work silently in the dead of night so as not to intrude upon the players' delicate sensibilities.

Running his fingers along the grooved edge, he detected a depression and pushed. The panel gave, and then the entire section receded and opened a door into the Palace that no one would ever think to guard.

He darted in and closed the door behind him. Inside, a bank of dim red lights illuminated the bulky equipment. As he attempted to squeeze past a rubbish collector, its sensor panel flared to life.

"Could this unit be of assistance?"

A chill ran through him. He hadn't counted on any of the equipment being programmed in Interact and able to talk to him. "I'm just—performing a routine inspection. When is your next scheduled run?"

"Oh two hundred hours."

"No changes." He slipped past, holding his breath until he reached the far side and opened a door into a warm, deserted hallway. He nodded; it was the dinner hour for all good Romans. All through the Imperium, he knew players would be lounging on their divans, calling for servants, drinking watered wine, and dining on imitation stuffed dormice and flamingos' tongues—in short, doing everything in their power to convince the Game computer that *they* were the most authentic players in the realm.

It took a few minutes to get his bearings; then he realized he was in the slaves' quarters. Micio's rooms would be on a higher floor, but perhaps this was the best place to start, anyway. Around servants, secrets were harder to hold on to than money. Here, as in ancient Rome, the slaves knew everything about everyone.

Unfortunately, he was still dressed as a freedman. Even though his rank didn't entitle him to a citizen's toga, he realized now that he should have bought one anyway. That would have commanded automatic respect from most slave-class players, and it wouldn't even have occurred to most of them to inspect his Game bracelet.

He walked down the corridor until he came upon a long-legged young girl with jet-black hair done up in a simple bun; she was no more than fourteen by the looks of her. "Where can I find the personal staff for the Imperial family?"

She was dressed in only a simple white shift and met his
eyes with such solemn interest that Kerickson decided she
must be one of the many robot surrogates used to supplement
the rather thin ranks of humans enrolled at this low level.

"Those not on duty should be eating at the moment." Her
voice was low and pleasantly modulated. "Shall I send for
someone?"

Kerickson hid his wrist behind his back. "No, just take me
to them."

She bowed her head. "As you wish." She turned around and
led the way back in the direction he had just come.

"How are you called?" Kerickson asked.

"Menae, master."

"And your function?"

"I am a bath slave, master," she replied blandly. "Shall you
require my services?"

"No, that won't be necessary." He followed her through the
maze of passages without further comment until they reached
the Palace staff's dining hall.

Inside, the large room was filled with the smell of roast beef
and grilled chicken and spiced wine. A scattering of people sat
at long tables and picked at their plates, while a short, stodgy
man stood in the front and droned on about the coming Saturnalia.

"And even though they have to serve you with their own
hands, don't go thinking you can lord it over them."

A long-faced woman raised a brown chicken wing in the air.
"But I thought we were all supposed to be equal during the
Saturnalia."

The man's squishy little eyes narrowed. "Don't be foolish.
They'll pay you back for any impudence once the festival is
over, and even though most of you will gain a level and play
as freedmen in the coming quarter, you don't want to make
powerful enemies on your way up. If you want to get on in the
Game, you have to play like you really mean it."

"But aren't we all going to advance anyway?" a gangly boy
asked.

"Oh, you'll get your quarterly experience point all right."
The man crossed his arms. "If you're careful, you might even
get an authenticity point or two, but don't count on it—the
computer has been stingy with those lately. If you know what's
good for you, you'll just keep your mouth shut, smile, and do
as you're told."

A sallow-faced woman put her hands on her hips. "I thought we were supposed to get presents during the Saturnalia and not have to do any work. I thought this was supposed to be fun."

"For *them*." The man's mouth twisted as though he'd tasted something sour. "Saturnalia is for the rich and powerful, no matter what anyone tries to tell you, and if you're serious about advancing, you'll remember that." Then he noticed Kerickson standing by the door. "You, over there, I suppose you're that back-ordered bodyguard I've been waiting for."

Startled, Kerickson stared at him.

"Bodyguard." The man's mouth tightened. "I applied weeks ago. Are you it or not?"

"Uh, sure."

Everyone turned around to watch him.

"Then where's your sword and armor?"

"They—said you would provide them." Gods, he thought, that sounded lame even to him.

"There goes my budget again," the man muttered. "Just who does Costuming think they are, anyway? Very well." He motioned to Kerickson. "I'm Prisius, Head Chamberlain here at the Palace. Let's have a look at you." He poked at the muscles in Kerickson's upper arm, then glanced at his Game bracelet. "Jupiter above! Half a hit point? You've got to be kidding! I didn't even know they came in halves. You won't last the night! Besides, you're classified as a freedman, and this is a slave role." He shook his head. "Well, that's General Catulus's problem, not mine." He snapped his fingers. "Menae, take—" He broke off and turned back to Kerickson. "Your name?"

"Gaius."

Prisius frowned. "That sounds awfully Roman for a freedman."

Of course, he should have changed it to something more foreign, Greek or Syrian maybe. Kerickson swallowed hard. "I—went to see the Oracle—you know."

"Yes, the Oracle, well, that doesn't say much for your judgment, does it?" He waved a hand in dismissal. "Menae, take Gaius here up to the War Room to General Catulus."

"Catulus?" The name seemed familiar.

"And, for Venus's sake, watch yourself." Prisius sniffed. "He seems to think excess players can be found under rocks or on trees or some such nonsense, when, for the past two years, incoming slaves have been almost nonexistent. I don't care

what he says, I simply refuse to be responsible for finding him
another replacement this month if you're killed before morning."

   When Pimus showed her to her old room, where she had
formerly stayed when on leave from her duties at the temple,
Amaelia had to blink back her tears. The golden brazier in the
shape of a dog, the immense oak bed, the low green velvet
couches—none of it gave her any sense of security. Her hands
clenched; it was all a terrible lie. Nothing in this game was
safe or secure—she knew that now.
   She turned back to her father's body servant and asked him
again. "Are you sure, Pimus?"
   The slave stared straight ahead, his long, thin nose pointed
liked a direction finder away from her. "Yes, lady, he is really
dead, not just killed in the Game."
   Her heart stuttered, then settled down into the dull thudding
rhythm it had maintained ever since her so-called "nuptials"
earlier that afternoon. She crossed to the flimsy white draperies
blowing in the chill winter breeze.
   "Shall I close the window for you, lady?"
   "What?" She turned back to the slave. "Oh, no—thank
you." The bracing feel of the cold air on her overheated face
seemed all that lay between herself and giving in to utter
panic. "Were you with him when it happened?"
   "No, lady," Pimus answered, his spare body stiff. "He insisted I go back that morning because he wanted to be alone
to think."
   Alone . . . She leaned against the cool marble of the window
facing. It was so ridiculous—a person of such high office
never went anywhere alone, not even to the bathroom. Assassins lurked around every corner, just waiting for the chance to
murder the Emperor and advance themselves in rank. She
shuddered. But no one died for real, not here. Game death
meant only a trip to the Underworld, then starting over as a
slave.
   "That will be all, Pimus," a strong baritone voice said.
   "As you wish, master." Giving her a final, disapproving
look, Pimus glided out of the room.
   "I can see that I shall have to be more firm with you from
now on." Quintus Gracchus, her official "husband," blocked
the doorway, scattering the hallway light like a halo behind his

back. "From now on, you are to have no visitors unless I authorize them. Is that understood?"

"I don't want to play anymore." She stared out the window at the glittering spectacle of Rome lit up at night, and wondered for the hundredth time why the Game computer didn't respond to her requests. "I want to leave!"

"YOU'VE GOT YOURSELF A FINE KETTLE OF FISH IN THIS ONE, MY BOY!" The loud voice reverberated painfully in the enclosed space.

Startled, Amaelia looked up to see a huge red-bearded face grinning down at her from the ceiling.

"Rather more than a kettle, I'd say." Gracchus's bronze armor clinked as he crossed the room and seized her by the arm. "For her, I shall sacrifice a bullock and a pair of spotless white doves—no, a whole roomful of doves to you tomorrow for your intercession with the computer!"

"SCREW THE DOVES," the face said. "WHAT WE WANT AROUND HERE IS SOME BLOOD!"

"And you shall have it!"

Amaelia shivered at the look of fiery passion on Gracchus's lean face. "What are you talking about?" She struggled, but his fingers only bit more deeply into her flesh. "Why won't the computer answer me? I want out!"

His hard gray eyes studied her for a second; then his forefinger traced the line of her jaw all the way back to her ear. She flinched.

"As even a proper Roman maiden such as yourself should know, there are ordinary computer programs and then there are programs such as our divine friend here." His gaze flickered up at the holo.

"I don't understand."

"THERE ARE DAMN WELL GOING TO BE SOME CHANGES AROUND HERE." The holo's eyes began to shine with a blinding red light. "OR MY NAME ISN'T MARS!"

The War Room was an anomaly, combining the authentic look of white marble columns and low divans with high-tech banks of vid-screens that took up most of two walls. Kerickson stopped at the door. Inside, five men in pristine white togas studied a huge electronic map covering the third wall.

"I wouldn't give you *that* for Carthage!" A stocky, silver-haired man snapped his fingers. "Or for Numibia, either!"

"Since you managed to squander two whole legions last month in that ridiculous attempt on the German border, Catulus, I can't say I'm surprised." A younger, chicken-necked man pointed at the map. "Of course, what else can you expect when you pay absolutely no attention to the omens? I saw two eagles roosting on top of the Temple of Mars this morning, and now my legions have advanced twenty miles. That should tell you something."

"It tells me you're an idiot." The silver-haired man sniffed. "Britannia will eat those troops alive. Come next year's Saturnalia, you'll be so desperate for points that you'll be scrubbing the public urinals."

"An occupation that I'm sure you're more than familiar with—"

Menae slipped between them and bowed her head respectfully.

"Well, what is it, girl?" snapped the younger man. "Can't you see that we're deciding the future of Rome right this very minute?"

"A thousand pardons, masters." Her gaze remained floorward. "Prisius sends his regards to General Catulus and begs that he examine this new bodyguard for suitability."

"Bodyguard?" Catulus ran a hand back over his silver hair. "Well, it's about time. I had to dispatch two assassins myself not more than an hour ago. They were hiding in the War Room latrine, waiting to garotte me."

"Too bad they weren't better at their jobs," the younger man muttered.

Catulus smiled thinly. "That's what comes of being so cheap, Titus. Open your purse a little wider next time and you might have more luck getting rid of me." He waved an arm at Kerickson. "Come here, lad. Let's have a look at you."

For a second Kerickson hesitated, then sighed. People entered the Game all the time to play someone they could never be in real life. His lack of training in the martial arts was probably no worse than that of the average Game bodyguard.

Catulus studied him for a minute. "Pitiful, just plain pitiful. If I didn't know better, I'd swear that the Game computer had it in for me."

"Do you accept this slave, Oppius Catulus?" Menae asked in her quiet, unassuming voice.

"Do I have a choice?" Then he shook his head as she started to answer. "Never mind. Just tell Prisius I expect to have my man—" He broke off and turned to Kerickson. "Your name, son?"

"Gaius, sir."

"I expect to have my man Gaius, here, suitably outfitted by tomorrow morning."

"As you wish, master." Menae bowed her dark-haired head, then drew a gleaming dagger from her bodice and leaped straight for the commander's throat. Dodging, Catulus struck her wrist and deflected the knife to one side. Without even stumbling, the girl reoriented herself.

His eyes on the dagger, Catulus motioned at Kerickson. "Time you started earning your pay, boy."

"I don't get paid," he replied, feeling the hairs rise on the back of his neck. Play or not, the edge of that dagger looked finely honed.

"Fancy having your fingernails removed one by one?"

Kerickson had never heard of that alternative, but players did have a certain amount of latitude in filling in the blanks. Sweating, he stepped between Catulus and the girl. "Menae, go back to Prisius and put yourself on report." He edged in closer and kept his eyes on the dagger. Something about it looked familiar, something . . . Who else had threatened him with a dagger like this?

"I have to kill General Catulus," Menae said reasonably. "But there is no need for you to be hurt or lose points."

He was within her reach now, close enough to see her perfect eyelashes, thicker and darker than a human's, and her cocoa-brown eyes, so solemn and calm in this moment when a real assassin should be panicked and sweating. She had to be a robot surrogate.

He eyed her upraised hand still holding the dagger; as a robot, her strength would be totally beyond him even if he worked out every day, which he did not. She feinted to one side and slipped around him, the dagger extended at Catulus's throat. Without thinking, Kerickson closed with her, grasping her wrist with both hands.

It was like a flea trying to hold back a power crane. She carried him with her as she advanced on the general. Digging his heels in, he tried to remember the proper override code from the programming language for robot surrogates—indeed, any Interact code word at all—but most of his experience was in working with the big mainframe systems. His brain felt like it was packed in dandelion fuzz.

"That's it, boy, get her in a hammer lock!" Catulus reached for a bowl of grapes and popped one in his mouth.

"Code five override!" Kerickson managed between gritted teeth. Menae never took her eyes off the general.

"Code five-A override!"

Without even straining her servo motors, she continued forward, dragging Kerickson like an afterthought, the dagger dead on target.

"Bloody hell!" Catulus began to inch backward. "The computer's sent me another dud."

"There goes half of your Third Legion—marched right off a cliff." Titus studied the bank of screens, intent on the fate of the make-believe troops. "Maybe after you're forcibly retired, they'll let you attend my triumph."

Frowning, Catulus turned back to the screens, then bent down to tap in a set of instructions. At that second Kerickson's foot slipped on the tiled floor. Menae stepped hard on his prone body as she lunged for the general's unprotected back.

Feeling as though he'd been squashed by an airhopper, he fought for breath. "Code ... four ... A ... override!" he wheezed after her. For an instant she seemed to hesitate in midair, then crashed to the floor with a heaviness that spoke of durallinium and steel.

Startled, Catulus whirled around and stared down at the stiff, motionless robot at his feet. "Well," he said, "effective, if not exactly Game legal. Still, it's your butt and not mine if you offend the computer." He rearranged the heavy folds of his toga over his shoulder. "But you'll never get to be Emperor using computer access codes, boy, and that's a fact."

Breathing hard, Kerickson pushed himself up from the floor.

"A BRAVE MOVE, MY HERO." Just above his head a patch of shining blueness shimmered, then resolved itself into a small, ragged-looking brown owl. It fluttered its wings, then perched on his shoulder. "BUT A FUTURE EMPEROR SHOULD PLAY BY THE RULES."

The goddess Minerva in her most mundane form ... but according to Wilson, that particular Game program was still down. "And what if I don't want to be Emperor?" he said.

"OH." The owl scratched at its head with a taloned foot. "IN THAT CASE I SUPPOSE YOU CAN DO ANYTHING YOU WANT, UNTIL MARS CATCHES UP WITH YOU."

"Mars?"

The owl ruffled its dull brown feathers. "MARS SAYS

THIS GAME IS GOING TO BE PLAYED RIGHT FROM NOW ON, AND OF COURSE, THE FIRST ONES TO GO WILL BE THE PROGRAMMERS."

CHAPTER
NINE

The worst thing about the Underworld, Demea told herself, was the terrible, unremittingly dim light that never changed, no matter what time of the day or night it was.

A close second, however, were the omnipresent viewing screens that dominated the landscape. On the face of every nobly Roman statue, on the side of every building, in the branches of every tree, screens stared back at her like one-eyed monsters, filled with various real-time scenes from the playing field above.

Popping a bite of spicy grilled lamb into her mouth, she studied the spacious plaza, the whispering fountains, the benches of gleaming black marble. The whole effect was depressing. "Yes, it's all quite interesting," she lied to Publius Barbus, who bobbed at her side with a tray of hors d'oeuvres like a poorly trained butler. "But I simply must go back now. They're sure to be looking for me at the Palace."

"At the Spear and Chicken, too." He poked her in the ribs with his elbow and beamed. "Can't say when we last had an Empress in the digs."

High above her on the side of a dark building, giant toga-draped figures moved across a huge screen. She found herself watching them, trying to place the faces.

"But we can't go yet, you know," Barbus confided in a whisper. "Someone down here is ever so anxious to meet you."

She sniffed, and even that faint sound seemed to echo endlessly through the empty plaza. For some reason, Hades was very underpopulated at the moment. Since she and Barbus had entered this thoroughly depressing place, she'd seen only a few people, and those in the distance. "You've been saying that for hours now, but there's no one here."

"SO YOU'VE COME AT LAST, MY BEAUTY, MY LOVE ..." Vibrating with the undertone of some unimaginably vast organ, the overwhelming voice was almost too loud to bear. "MY QUEEN."

Demea pressed her hands to her ringing ears.

"HERE IN THE DARK DEPTHS HAVE I WAITED, KNOWING THAT YOU WOULD BE MINE." An inky blackness shimmered on the other side of the plaza, then resolved itself into a two-story-high man in shining black armor. "OF COURSE, IN THE END, THEY ALL COME TO ME."

The heavily loaded tray of food clinked as Barbus set it down on the long, curving side of a fountain. "I'll just let you two get acquainted." He winked, then scurried around the corner of the nearest building.

"MY HEART, MY OWN." The oversized face studied her with eyes black as pools of oil. "LONG HAVE I AWAITED THIS MOMENT."

Pluto ... that had to be Pluto, god of the lower realm and monarch of the dead. She straightened her back. "Must you be so loud? You're giving me a miserable headache."

The figure walked across the empty plaza toward her, shrinking in size with each step until it was only seven or eight feet high. "IS THIS BETTER, LIGHT TO MY DARKNESS?"

"I—I'm quite sure we've never been introduced." She raised her chin.

He was olive-complected, with thick, jet-black hair that tumbled heavily about a clean-shaven, high-cheekboned face. His black, black eyes were deeper than the heart of space itself. "YOUR COMING HAS BEEN FORETOLD SINCE THE BEGINNING OF ALL THINGS. NOT ONLY HAVE WE ALWAYS KNOWN EACH OTHER, WE ALWAYS WILL."

"Don't be ridiculous!" She forced her hands down to her sides, suppressing the urge to run her fingers through that magnificent hair. "I'm not dead. That toad, Publius Barbus, lured me down here on some pretext of meeting his associates." She crossed her arms. "Obviously, he was lying through his nasty little teeth. I demand to be returned to the city immediately!"

"SUCH FIRE, SUCH SPIRIT." Pluto moved closer, bringing with him an air of electricity so intense she felt her hair stir. "INDEED, A CONSORT FIT FOR A GOD."

"Consort!" She detected a pattern in his ravings. "I am cer-

tainly not your consort, or, for that matter, anyone else's."
Forcing her eyes away from his hypnotic gaze, she twitched at
a fold in her tunic. "I am in mourning for my beloved Micio."

"THE FALLEN ONE, YES, I KNOW." The figure shrank
even further, now only head and shoulders taller than Demea.
"HE DID NOT PASS THROUGH MY REALM, AL-
THOUGH I SHOULD HAVE BEEN GLAD TO ACCOM-
MODATE HIM. FOR A MORTAL, HE HAD AN
INTERESTING TURN OF MIND."

That was one name for it, she thought. "So you see, Lord of
the Underworld or not, we can be nothing to each other at this
particular time. Perhaps in a year or so, when my period of
mourning is ended; we could talk about it then."

"RULES FOR THE CONDUCT OF MORTAL AFFAIRS
MEAN NOTHING TO SUCH AS WE." His finger grazed her
cheek, and even though she knew he was nothing more than a
carefully plotted holographic projection of the Game computer,
she flinched from a chill as intense as the Arctic plains at midnight. The special effects certainly were impressive down on
this level.

"MY WAITING IS AT AN END. TOGETHER WE
SHALL RULE THIS REALM AS IT HAS NEVER BEEN
RULED BEFORE!" Throwing his arms back, Pluto grew
again, until his muscular legs dwarfed the temple across the
plaza. "I PROCLAIM A HOLIDAY IN HELL!"

The full force of his voice startled her. She fell backward
and tumbled into the fountain. Across the plaza all the viewing
screens switched to the same picture: herself seated on a black
throne at the side of the darkly handsome monarch of the dead,
a shining crown of ebony perched upon her brow.

Soaked and sputtering, she climbed out of the fountain and
began to wring the water out of her dress. Getting out, it
seemed, was not going to be so easy a thing as getting in.

After General Catulus chained him at the foot of his bed,
Kerickson realized he was not going to get any sleep. For
some reason, everyone in the Palace, from the chamberlains to
the bath attendants and on down to the kitchen maids, seemed
bent on murdering the general. In the space of six hours, and
armed with only a club, he fought off two Praetorian Guards,
three assorted dagger men, and an unarmed woman, all of
whom had been subsequently declared dead and escorted away
by a bemused Mercury.

Obviously, Catulus stood head and shoulders above the rest of the generals in ability, and was so far ahead on battle points that the others were willing to undertake any expense to eliminate him from the Game. In the feeble gray light of the new day, Kerickson wrapped the long chain around his arm and examined it for defects, but each link was perfect. Of course, Catulus would free him as soon as he awoke—if he managed to survive that long.

But then there remained the additional problem that he was not the back-ordered bodyguard, who could show up at any moment and spoil his cover. He needed to move on.

Blueness quivered above Catulus's bed, then solidified into a small brown owl. "STILL HERE?" It flapped its wings several times, then settled on his shoulder.

"Not so loud!" Unwrapping his chain, Kerickson walked to the end of it, then held his breath as Catulus stopped snoring. After a few seconds, though, the General resumed his steady buzz. "Why don't you just beat it before you get me in trouble?"

"LEAVE?" The owl cocked its head and regarded him with one round gray eye. "BUT YOU ARE IN GRAVE DANGER."

"Thank you so much." Kerickson walked back to the bedpost and examined the ring anchoring his chain. "I'm sure I would never have realized that without your help."

"IT IS PART OF MY FUNCTION TO ASSIST HEROES IN THEIR QUESTS."

"Heroes?" Sunk deeply into the wood, the ring showed definite signs of wear. Evidently old Catulus had chained more than one bodyguard here. "I'm just a servant, disposable protection for the night. What makes you think I'm a hero?"

"YOU ARE NOT WHAT YOU SEEM." The owl hopped from his shoulder to the foot of the bed, then preened at its feathers. "BUT YOUR PURPOSE IS NOBLE."

"And what purpose is that?" He worked the ring back and forth in its hole and was rewarded with a few grains of sawdust.

"TO RESTORE ORDER."

Up on the bed, Catulus flopped over, muttering, "Macedonian idiots!"

The ring's base wobbled. "Listen," he said through gritted teeth, "it's really very kind of you to be interested, but we heroes are proud. We like to do things ourselves."

"BUT THERE MUST BE SOMETHING I CAN DO TO HELP." The owl craned its head. "SOME BOON I COULD GRANT, SOME WISH I COULD FULFILL? PERHAPS A NICE MORSEL OF MOUSE OR SNAKE TO CHEER YOUR EMPTY STOMACH?"

The ring came free in his hand. He fell back with a clatter of chains. The snoring broke off; the general bolted up, gazing about him with a baffled look. The owl walked from the foot of the bed onto the general's stomach and stared him in the eyes. "GREAT DEEDS WILL COME TO YOU, GENERAL OPPIUS CATULUS, FAVORED OF THE GODS, BUT THE TIME IS NOT YET RIPE. RETURN TO YOUR DREAMS."

"What . . . ?" Catulus blinked, then sank back against the pillow.

"DREAM OF CAPTIVES AND BOOTY AND TRI-UMPHS NEVER-ENDING." The owl bent its beak close to his ear. "DREAM OF BRIGHT GREEN LAUREL WREATHS AND SMOOTH-SKINNED EGYPTIAN MAIDS TO SOOTHE YOUR OLD AGE."

The General's eyelids fluttered.

"DREAM OF GERMAN BODIES PILED AS HIGH AS THE ENDLESS SKY. SEE HOW YOUR TROOPS COL-LECT THEM FOR THE BURNING? ONE . . . TWO . . ."

"Three . . ." Catulus whispered, "four . . . fi—" He resumed snoring.

The owl shook itself. "NOW, WHERE WERE WE?"

Kerickson slid a blanket off the bed and wrapped the chain in it to muffle the noise. "I was leaving."

"A SENSIBLE GOAL. THE PRIZE YOU SEEK LIES NOT HERE."

He got to his feet. "I don't suppose you'd like to tell me who killed Micio and Wilson so I could forget this nonsense and go straight to the police?"

The owl nibbled at its tail feathers for a moment. "VIC-TORY LIES IN THE SEEKING, NOT THE DESTINATION."

"Yeah, I thought not." He paused at the door. "Well, if you're not going to help, at least stay out of my way." Glan-cing down the hall to reassure himself that it was empty, he started in the direction of the Emperor's quarters.

The owl flew down the corridor, gliding just above his head on soundless brown wings. His arms full of chain, Kerickson glared up at it. "Get out of here and leave me alone! Beat it!"

"OH, WHAT FOOLS THESE MORTALS BE," the owl intoned, then disappeared with the slightest hint of static.

The Nubian maid's black eyes regarded Amaelia reproachfully, as though it were her fault the Saturnalia would begin tomorrow and she had nothing to wear. "All my clothes are at the temple," Amaelia said from the middle of the big canopied bed, "but it wouldn't make any difference if I had them here. Vestal Virgins wear only simple white gowns."

"Perhaps some of the Empress's clothes, then." The maid's eyes narrowed. "She was, of course, much taller than you, but we could alter something by tomorrow."

"Was?" Amaelia sat up. "Has there been news of her, then?"

"No, mistress." The maid gazed back at her stolidly. "Still, when a person's been missing this long, it usually means only one thing."

"The Underworld." Amaelia stared down at her clenched hands in her lap. Even though she and Demea had never gotten along, it was unsettling to face her stepmother's disappearance so soon after her father's death.

"I will go through the Lady Demea's things and see if there isn't something that will suit you." The maid picked up a steaming cup from the silver tray she had brought and handed it to her. "You're a great lady now, probably the next Empress. You can't appear at the feast in rags."

Amaelia sniffed the cup, then put it down in disgust—hot watered wine again. If she never saw another grape after she left this stupid game, it would be just fine with her. What she wouldn't give right now for a cup of tea or even—she closed her eyes—sparkly dark cola like they sold down in the amusement sector. "Take this away."

"You have only to tell Flina what you desire and it will be brought."

"Tea?" Amaelia ventured, feeling excessively wicked. "The real kind, with caffeine?"

Flina smiled serenely. "I think that can be arranged. Lady Demea did have a personal supplier of certain luxury goods from the outside, although you must not speak of it to others."

"What about a doughnut?" She hesitated. "With real chocolate?"

"A perfect choice, lady. Chocolate is just the sort of thing to lift a young wife's spirits." Flina turned for the door.

A young wife . . . Amaelia pulled a pillow over her head.

She didn't want to be a wife, not even the pretend sort that Gracchus seemed to require from her. At least he hadn't touched her last night, hadn't even come in her room. If he had, she would have killed him, or failing that, at least killed herself. Somehow, she had to contact the computer and get herself released from the Game. There was no law saying a person had to go on playing once they wanted out.

She threw the pillow aside and padded barefoot across the rug-covered floor to look out the window at the red-tiled roofs of the city. Maybe she could disguise herself as a slave and run away. Everyone knew the Interface lay somewhere in the middle of town. If she searched, surely she would be able to find it and get out of this farce.

"Uh—hello," said a voice from behind her back.

"What?" She whirled around to see a man in a plain gray tunic watching her from the doorway. He had a quiet face, topped with straight blond hair, and an unassuming, most decidedly un-Roman nose, not at all the sort of biosculpted face she was used to seeing.

"Don't be afraid, Amaelia." He glanced over his shoulder, then edged into her bedchamber and closed the door behind him.

"You're . . ." She studied him more closely. "You're the one who fetched me out of the temple when Vesta was so angry."

"Yes." He sounded relieved. "I'm Gaius Lucinius. Are you all right?"

"Oh, sure." She sat on the edge of her bed and picked at the white silk coverlet. "In the last four days, my father has been murdered, and instead of going to his funeral, I've been tricked, demoted to slave, and then married against my will! Everything is just—" She broke off.

"I'm sorry." The Adam's apple bobbed up and down in his neck. "About your father, I mean. That was—terrible."

She glanced up at him. He looked so earnest and sad that she somehow felt better for the first time. "Thank you." She hesitated. "You wouldn't know where the Interface is, would you?"

"The Interface?"

"I asked to leave the Game, but the computer doesn't answer me."

"Really?" He sat down on the bed across from her. "That shouldn't happen."

"If I could find the Interface, I bet someone would let me out." She shivered. "I don't feel safe here anymore."

"Well, that might work." He sounded unsure. "I guess I could take you there."

"Really? You wait right here!" She stood up, feeling hopeful for the first time in days. "I'll change. If anyone comes in, tell them I'm taking a bath."

"YOU'LL DO NO SUCH THING!" a female voice commanded. "I WON'T PERMIT A MARRIED WOMAN OF YOUR CLASS TO DISGRACE HERSELF BY RUNNING OFF WITH A MERE FREEDMAN." Blueness shimmered by the door, then became the oversized figure of a woman in a flawless, off-the-shoulder white gown.

Amaelia blinked in surprise. The voice seemed familiar.

"YOU MIGHT HAVE GOTTEN AWAY WITH BEHAVING LIKE A LITTLE STRUMPET DOWN AT THE TEMPLE OF VESTA, BUT I EXPECT MORE OF MY PLAYERS." Angry blue-green sparks flashed in the goddess's eyes.

"Juno?" Amaelia ventured weakly.

"YOU BET YOUR SWEET BEHIND, HONEY, AND HAVE I GOT A FEW THINGS TO LAY ON YOU!"

"I remember now," she said slowly. "You came to me in Gracchus's villa—on his screens. Only you were a peacock then."

"WELL, THAT IS ONE OF MY BEST MANIFESTATIONS." Juno delicately patted her intricately looped hair.

"Screens?" The man, whom she had almost forgotten in all the fuss, stepped forward. "In a *villa*?"

"NEVER MIND THAT." Juno waggled a huge digit. "DON'T YOU THINK I'VE GOT ENOUGH TROUBLE KEEPING THAT RANDY OLD BIRD, JUPITER, IN LINE WITHOUT NEW BRIDES RUNNING OFF WITH THE FIRST MAN WHO TWITCHES HIS LITTLE FINGER?" The goddess cocked her head, then studied the man more closely. "A MAN WITH NO CHARISMA, AT THAT—AND WHAT IN THE NAME OF HADES IS THE MATTER WITH YOUR TRANSPONDER? YOU DON'T EVEN REGISTER IN THIS ROOM."

He glanced at his Game bracelet, then thrust his arm behind his back. "Not working? Guess I'd better get it fixed."

"JUST LIKE A MAN TO BE SO HELPLESS."

"So, Lady Amaelia." He gestured at the door. "Could I prevail upon you to show me the way to the Palace repair shop?"

"What?" She stared at him for an uncomprehending second. "Oh! Sure. Just let me throw on some proper clothes."

"WELL I NEVER." Juno's size-fifteen foot tapped the floor impatiently as Amaelia plunged into her closet. "DON'T YOU KNOW WHAT SLAVES ARE FOR?"

"Of course I do," she answered from inside the closet, as she looked for something plain enough to pass for slave clothing. Finally she selected a simple tunic of plain white cotton, then threw a sturdy maroon cloak over her shoulders and fastened it with a silver brooch. Emerging from the closet, she looked around brightly. "But I don't see any slaves at the moment, so I just guess that I'll have to go myself."

"YOU'LL LOSE POINTS ON THIS, MISSY, BIG-TIME."

"No doubt," Amaelia muttered under her breath as she tucked her arm under the young man's and pulled him through the door.

"AND NOT JUST AUTHENTICITY, EITHER!" Juno called after them. "JUST YOU WAIT AND SEE, YOU LITTLE HUSSY! DID JUPITER PUT YOU UP TO THIS?"

Closing the door behind them, Amaelia pulled Gaius down the hall at a half run. "Do you really know where the Interface is?" she asked breathlessly.

"Sure." He slowed to a walk as several naked Sardinian dancers passed them in the hall, bangles clinking around their wrists and ankles. "That's not the real problem."

"Oh?" She dodged an orangutan and its trainer. "Then what is?"

"Well, I'm, uh, investigating your father's murder and I need some information."

Startled, she studied his face, then pulled him into her father's old suite and closed the door behind them. "Investigating his murder? But aren't the police supposed to take care of that?"

"They . . . uh . . . kind of . . ." A red flush crept up his neck. "They . . . think that . . . I did it."

"You—a freedman?" She started to laugh, then looked away, embarrassed. It didn't seem nice to mention his lowly rank when she wanted his help.

"Well, I could have," Gaius said defensively. Two brilliant specks of red appeared in his cheeks. "But I didn't. At any rate, after your father was murdered, someone killed my friend,

Wilson, and then abducted the Empress. I think it all ties together." He took her by the shoulders and steered her over to a long, low divan in front of the window. "Do you have any idea who really sent the message instructing you to go to the Baths that day?"

Amaelia thought back. "It was signed by my father. It said he needed religious advice, but a grubby little bald-headed man in a torn tunic delivered it. I've seen him around the Palace once or twice, but I don't know his name."

"Someone wanted to compromise your status as a Vestal Virgin. You were set up so you would lose all your points." Sitting down at her side, Gaius kneaded his forehead. "It's all so frus—"

A sudden frenzied fit of screaming from outside the Palace interrupted him. Amaelia bolted to her feet. Through the window she saw yellow-orange flames leaping high in the morning air. Out in the Imperial Gardens, a laughing, three-story-high figure dressed in red hurled lightning bolts into the leafless shrubs and trees.

The flames were burning toward the Palace.

CHAPTER
TEN

Kerickson jumped to his feet and started for the door.

"Wait!" Amaelia clutched his hand and drew him back. "Where are you going?"

"To stop Mars, of course." His heart pounded as he glanced out the window again. "I can't just stand here while he burns down the entire dome!"

Still holding his hand, she followed his gaze to the roiling black smoke outside as the mulched flower beds burst into flame. "But what can you do about it?"

He suddenly became conscious of the warm, tingly pressure of her slender fingers over his.

"And anyway, look." Standing on tiptoe, she pressed her soft cheek against his ear and pointed over his shoulder. The silvery fuselage of an automatic fire drone shot past, laying down flame-smothering foam. Than another darted into place beside it.

The towering figure of Mars beat his great fists against his armored chest with crashes that reverberated like thunder, then stomped through the gardens toward the Market District.

"See?" Her breath was warm against his neck. "He's leaving. It's going to be all right."

Kerickson shook his head. "No, I don't think he'll stop. A lot of people could get hurt, even with the fire drones, just like—" He paused, unwilling to say the name.

"Like my father." She pulled back, then noticed that she was still holding his hand. She blushed as her fingers loosened and she drifted out of reach. "Well, I suppose you could buy a bull or a goat to sacrifice at his temple."

Mars hurled lightning bolts at the terrified players as they fled his path. His height ballooned to over four stories. Inwardly, Kerickson cursed himself for listening to Wilson's idea of allowing the gods to manifest themselves physically—and HabiTek for agreeing to it. "I think you're right," he said to Amaelia, "but I might have more luck at the Temple of Jupiter. After all, as the chief god, he rules all the rest."

He tried to think. "You stay here and I'll come back to take you to the Interface when I'm done."

She lifted her chin. Her green eyes gazed steadily up at him. "No, I want to go with you."

"You'll be much safer here in the Palace."

"Are you kidding?" A faint smile flitted across her face. "Would *you* want to stay here and play Quintus Gracchus's wife?"

He was suddenly aware of her soft, pale almond skin, the way she smelled of soap and roses, and how her hair was the color of newly polished copper. The room's temperature seemed to jump ten degrees. He swallowed hard and held out his hand.

Her fingers curled around his, bringing a warmth that vied with the sun itself. For the first time since Micio's body had been found in the Baths, he felt as though things might work out. "We have to hurry," he said, and in return she only nodded.

"Morning, your ladyness."

Demea sat up in the middle of a huge four-poster bed and stared around her in amazement. She was in a large apartment filled with lavishly carved ebony furniture and frescoes and even a gurgling fountain. And wherever she looked, everything was black, from the sheer draperies about her sumptuous, over-soft bed to the daring nightgown she wore. Placing a hand over the plunging neckline, she tried to remember arriving here last night.

"I brought you a bit of the bubbly, to celebrate." A hand parted the hangings, revealing the pudgy, unshaven face of Publius Barbus. He winked. "After all, it's not every day that a girl becomes a goddess."

She shuddered, remembering now: that vile little inn . . . Barbus . . . and Pluto. "Don't be ridiculous. I am no more a goddess than you are a—" She searched for the proper word. "—a . . . gentleman!"

Setting his tray down, he handed her a midnight-black, cut-glass goblet filled to the brim with fizzing champagne. "You just need something to calm your nerves—hair of the dog, as they say. Go on, now—bottoms up."

Hair of the dog? Then the rest came back to her: downing glass after glass of wine in that deserted, depressing plaza last night while all around her those miserable screens showed her fellow players going on about the Game, piling up points while she languished in Hades, a pointless prisoner. No wonder she didn't quite remember arriving in this vast bed.

Her hand shook as she reached for the goblet. She probably should have just a sip, purely for medicinal purposes. The bubbles tickled her nose as she drank, and she had the most undignified urge to sneeze.

"MY TRUE HEART." The bass whisper had the distinct undertone of a funeral organ. "I AM MOST PLEASED."

She drained the goblet, then slammed it back down on the tray. "Well, I am not! When are you going to let me go? I can't just stay down here drinking wine and champagne with you while everyone else has all the fun."

The curtains rippled as though someone had opened a window. Pluto, Lord of the Underworld, peered beneath the canopy top. "LONG HAVE MY PANGS OF LOVE GONE UNNOURISHED. LONG HAS THIS DARK WORLD FAILED TO SATISFY MY MOST BASIC NEED."

The air crackled with the strange electricity that accompanied him wherever he went. Even though he was only a holographic image, Demea couldn't escape the feeling that some presence was actually with her in this room. Feeling vulnerable, she slipped farther beneath the silken bed sheet. "*I* have a need also—to return to the Game."

His face shining with fierce pride, he knelt beside her bed, his black cloak tumbling around his broad shoulders. His insubstantial finger traced the length of her arm up to her shoulder, somehow sending a strange tingle through her. "WHY?"

"Because I'm bored!" She hated him for luring her here, yet at the same time she found his clean-cut face and full, sensual lips attractive. If he had been real . . . Her cheeks suddenly burned as she realized she would have been mightily tempted to stay.

"BORED? IN HADES?" His wickedly black eyes sparked. "BUT THE WHOLE GAME PASSES THROUGH THIS REALM. YOU HAVE ONLY TO SAY WHAT YOU DESIRE, FROM ABOVE OR BELOW, AND IT WILL BE PROVIDED."

"Well, I came to learn about Micio's business." She glared over his shoulder at Barbus, who didn't even seem to notice. "Suppose you start by telling me what he was doing down here."

Pluto lifted his right hand. "SHADE OF MICIO JULIUS METULLUS, FORMER EMPEROR OF ROME, YOU ARE SUMMONED!"

A sudden chill wafted through the room, bringing with it the smell of damp stone. Demea's eyes went wide as the air shimmered with a gray mist, then formed itself into the translucent image of a man—a man with thinning red hair, a familiar beaky nose, and lips that curled as though they had just tasted a rotten fig.

"So what is it this time?" it asked in the insectlike, nasal whine so characteristic of her late husband.

"REVEAL THE NATURE OF YOUR ASSOCIATION WITH THIS REALM," Pluto commanded so loudly that it rattled her eardrums. "AND KEEP IT SHORT."

Micio's image sneered. "You're kidding, of course."

"TRY ME."

"Okay, okay, don't get your tunic in a twist!" The image turned to Demea. "But you don't know this broad like I do. Don't blame me if she doesn't like it."

Demea was familiar with holographic recordings, as well as robot surrogates programmed with personality prints, but this was something new to her. From the jowly jaws to the nervous tick under his right eye, it was her late husband in every unpleasant detail. She turned to Pluto. "Is this a recording?"

"THE DEAD BELONG TO ME." The god's black eyes burned down at her with a heat that had nothing to do with flames. "EVERYONE KNOWS THAT."

"You were so hot to know about the business, so shut up and listen." Micio crossed his arms and glared at her. "Back when I first enrolled in the Game as a lowly Syrian wine merchant, it came to me that this place was the perfect hideout. I mean, it's private property, so the police don't patrol inside, and there's lots of nicely inaccessible little nooks and crannies where no one ever looks. I did some exploring, struck up an acquaintance with a few of the priests, and realized the gods have more than a little say-so here. They're all hooked up with the computer, and they know exactly what's going on.

"So I made a few sacrifices, proposed a few deals, and then Pluto and I decided we could be a lot of help to each other. I brought in Harry, here, and his boys from the outside to over-see the details while I played for points so I could advance and gain even more power."

"That's why you married me," she said slowly. "For the points."

"Yeah." The shade stared at her sourly. "You're a damn good player, especially in authenticity. You not only brought me a bundle of your own points, but your little scam of install-ing Amaelia as a Vestal Virgin was absolutely inspired. That put me over the top—to Emperor."

"So the business between you and Publius Barbus was smuggling." Her mouth went dry as the sand in the arena.

"Yeah." The shade scratched its prominent nose. "Frankly, old Ball-and-Chain, I don't think you've got it in you. I mean, I know you worked a little deal with Juno once in a while for a case of contraband sugar or a bag of illegal pork rinds or even a liter of cola now and then, but you don't have the grit for a true life of crime. If the police ever ran you in, you'd crumple like a paper doll."

"Oh, really?" She straightened her back.

"BEGONE!" Pluto waved his hand again and the image dis-solved.

"See, that's what I've been trying to tell you." Barbus re-filled the black goblet to the brim with champagne and pushed it into her hand. "You don't want to deal with all them messy details. Me and the boys will take care of everything, while you kick back and enjoy life. Think of the possibilities."

"YES, THINK." Pluto's huge hand caressed her cheek. She felt the bite of static crawling over her skin. "WE SHALL RE-WRITE THE MANUALS OF PLEASURE, YOU AND I. WE SHALL MAKE THE DARK HALLS OF THE UNDER-WORLD SING WITH THE HEIGHTS OF OUR PASSION."

Holding the glass of champagne with both hands, she tossed the wine down without even tasting it, then held it out for more. This looked to be a long siege.

Through the hour it took them to cross the city, Kerickson kept having to detour to avoid new fires and the smoldering ruins of others the fire drones had already put out. Mars was out of control; there was no doubt about that. What in the name of Jupiter could the new programmers be doing—or had HabiTek even bothered with new programmers at all? He toyed with the idea of trying to access the Interface himself.

But if the board ever realized he was on the playing field, they would turn him over to the police at once. Until he found out what was going on, he had to stay in the Game.

Amaelia's face was rosy with exertion, and even though the day was cold, she had thrown her woolen cloak back on her shoulders.

"Are you sure you wouldn't like to wait for me in a shop?" He gestured at a linen merchant's and a butcher's. "Or maybe a restaurant? Romulus's is just around the corner. I could come back for you."

She sighed, then tucked a damp tendril of red hair back behind her ear. "Are you kidding? I don't think there's a safe place in this whole city."

"Well, we're almost there, anyway." He rubbed his burning eyes, which were tearing from the smoke. Taking her arm, he pushed through the anxious, milling crowd and towed her along in his wake. They rounded the corner and entered the Forum, the broad square that held the city's major temples as well as numerous fortune-tellers' booths, statues, massive monuments of past wars, dealers of sacrificial animals, and a million or so pigeons.

It was also filled at the moment with at least half the terrified populace of the Game, most of them pushing and shoving in an attempt to enter the red-marble Temple of Mars at the farthest end. Fortunately, Jupiter's temple, in the middle, didn't seem to be doing nearly so brisk a business.

Keeping tight hold of Amaelia's hand, he pulled her into the frightened crowd. They had come out at the Forum's lower end, three temples down from Jupiter. The gigantic figure of Mars was not visible at the moment, and it did seem as they fought their way past the Temple of Vesta that the smoky air was clearing. Perhaps, he thought, the supplicants down at the Temple of Mars have managed to appease the angry god alrea—

With a roar of flames, a towering Vesta manifested before her little round temple. "THERE SHE IS!" Red-orange burning hair swirled around her face as she pointed down into the crowd. "THE ONE WHO NOT ONLY BETRAYED ME, BUT ALL OF ROME!"

The crowd looked around, trying to see where the huge finger pointed.

"*SHE* LET THE SACRED FIRES GO OUT! *SHE* LEFT THE CITY UNPROTECTED! JUST BECAUSE SHE'S THE

EMPEROR'S DAUGHTER DOESN'T MEAN SHE IS ABOVE THE LAW!"

Kerickson's whole body went cold. He should have thought of this before! Of course Vesta would hold a grudge. "Hide your face," he whispered quickly to Amaelia.

She looped a fold of her cloak over her copper-colored hair as they worked their way through the milling mass of people.

"DON'T LET HER GET AWAY!" Vesta shrieked. "THAT'S HER, THE CARROT-TOP IN THE WHITE GOWN WITH THE SCRUFFY-LOOKING FREEDMAN! STOP THEM!"

A murmur ran through the mixture of aristocrats and plebes; then an armored Legionary seized Kerickson's cloak. "Stop, in the name of the Senate and the people of Rome!"

Kerickson threw his arm around Amaelia. "Don't be ridiculous! This is my wife."

Amaelia gave the man a nervous smile.

"Wife, huh?" The soldier glanced down at Kerickson's Game bracelet, then, without letting go of the cloak, he used his other hand to snatch Amaelia's silver brooch. "Since when does a freedman's wife wear silver?"

"Well, there is a slight difference in our rank. I didn't say her parents approved." Kerickson tried to wrench his cloak out of the other's grasp, but the man had the build of a space-truck.

Amaelia turned to Kerickson, her face white. "She'll burn me alive!"

"AND YOU, YOU MISERABLE EXCUSE FOR A MORTAL!" Vesta's huge voice spiraled toward a shriek. "YOU WERE SUPPOSED TO BRING ME SIX NEW GIRLS, AND I HAVEN'T EVEN SEEN ONE SO FAR! THE SACRED FIRES HAVE BEEN OUT FOR DAYS NOW! WHERE ARE MY VIRGINS? ANSWER ME THAT, IF YOU CAN!"

"Yeah, buddy!" The Legionary pulled Kerickson closer and let go of Amaelia to draw a gleaming dagger. "Where are her virgins?"

"That's—" Kerickson unfastened the plain iron brooch that held his cloak. "—a—" He shrugged out of the garment, leaving the soldier standing there holding it in his ham-fisted hand. "—good question!" Lowering his head, he dived into the crowd as though it were a sea, hitting the pavement hard enough to rasp the skin from his palms. He reached up and pulled Amaelia down on top of him. "Crawl!" he whispered fiercely, then scrabbled furiously on his hands and knees in what he hoped was the right direction.

A great shout went up above their heads, but the throng was packed so tightly that the forest of legs hid them from view. Every third or so step, he swore as the shifting feet trampled his fingers.

"THEY'RE GETTING AWAY!" Vesta shrilled somewhere out of sight, but her voice was already fading.

After another few moments of hot, dusty, stifling crawling, he motioned Amaelia to stay down as he cautiously stood to get his bearings. A white-haired woman, her arms full of caged sacrificial doves, stared at him suspiciously. "Just what do you think you're doing, crawling around down there like a worm? Were you trying to peek up my stola?"

The almost blinding whiteness of the Temple of Jupiter lay only one temple away. "Here!" Kerickson reached into his leather purse and pulled out a silver coin. "We'll take a pair of doves."

The woman's eyes widened at the sight of at least five times what the whole cage was worth. "Well, I suppose I could let you have a couple," she said, "although I'm that fond of them."

"Great." He pushed the coin into her hand, then opened the cage and plucked out two doves. "A pleasure doing business with you." He helped Amaelia to her feet, clutching the fluttering white birds to his chest with one hand, and pushed on through the sea of people toward Jupiter's temple.

As they reached the broad white marble steps leading up to the temple proper, the crowd thinned out. Amaelia stumbled after him, her arms covered with scratches, her face pinched with exhaustion. At the top, he passed her the doves, then smoothed down his hair and straightened his tunic.

One of Jupiter's priests glided out of the main sanctuary in a traditional spotless white tunic that Kerickson would have bet a day's pay included unauthentic fabric. The man stared down his biosculpted patrician nose at them. "You seek guidance, my son?"

"Yeah, right." Kerickson glanced at the flaming-haired manifestation of Vesta, still towering over the terrified supplicants and gesturing vehemently in their direction. "I mean, we, uh, we've come to sacrifice to Jupiter, father of gods and men."

The priest's lips tightened. "He's—busy at the moment."

"Busy?" Kerickson tried to peek over the priest's shoulder.

"Now look here. Isn't Jupiter supposed to be all-seeing and all-knowing?"

A deep chuckle rumbled out from the shadowy interior of the temple. The priest flinched, then folded his hands together in an air of reverence. "I'm sorry." His voice wavered. "You'll have to come back tomorrow, or maybe next week." He glanced fearfully over his shoulder. A bright bead of perspiration trickled down his forehead. "Yes, I'm sure next week would be much better. So much to oversee, so little time; I'm sure you understand."

"Look—" Kerickson began, then was interrupted by a sudden renewal of screaming back down in the Forum. Turning around, he saw the fifty-foot figure of Mars standing astride the Market District, hurling lightning bolts at the scattering people. The stink of burning plastic and wood smoke filled the air.

"I'm afraid we can't wait." He pushed up the sleeves of his tunic. "Jupiter, father of all gods and men!" he called. "Ruler and Preserver of the World, Cloud Gatherer, Thunderer—"

"YOU FORGOT 'GOD OF THE BRIGHT DAY AND THE MURKY CLOUD,' " a deep, gravelly voice said. "THAT'S ONE OF MY FAVORITES."

"Stop it!" The priest grabbed him by the arm.

"God of the Bright Day and the Murky Cloud!" Kerickson elbowed the priest aside. "I beg for an audience."

"GOT YOURSELF IN A SPOT OF TROUBLE, I SEE." A patch of blue glimmered up near the massive pillars by the temple's entrance, and then a huge shining eagle appeared in midair. It flapped its wings and settled on the head of a statue of Jupiter.

"Tell him it's a mistake!" The priest's face had gone as white as the expensive marble beneath their feet. "Tell him you've got the wrong temple, the wrong god, anything!"

"Jupiter, who sees all, knows all—" Kerickson began.

"WELL, NOT ALL. I MEAN, THERE ARE A FEW THINGS THAT REALLY WORRY ME—LIKE WHY ARE MORTAL WOMEN ALWAYS SO LITTLE AND I'M SO BIG? IS CELIBACY REALLY FATAL? WHY CAN'T THE YANKEES KEEP A MANAGER FOR MORE THAN TWO WEEKS?"

"That's torn it!" Grinding his teeth, the priest shoved Kerickson toward the steps. "Now that you've got him started, it'll take days for the old windbag to wind down, and of course we'll have to take down every damn divine word!"

The eagle peered down at them with steamy yellow eyes. "IF MAN IS DOG'S BEST FRIEND, WHERE DOES THAT LEAVE FIRE HYDRANTS? SHOULD A SUCKER EVER GET AN EVEN BREAK?"

Behind them the Forum emptied rapidly as the scorched players beat a hasty exit from Mars's lightning bolts. "Come on!" Amaelia plucked at his sleeve. "He's going to fry us if we don't get out of here!"

"Jupiter, Best and Greatest!" Kerickson raised his arms and approached the altar. "Can't an all-powerful type of guy like you do something to keep Mars from burning down the city?"

Glancing over his shoulder, he saw Mars striding determinedly across the Forum. Lightning flashed from the god's outstretched hand.

The statue of Jupiter at the top of the steps fused into a heap of melted slag.

CHAPTER
ELEVEN

"AND WHY—" The eagle glanced beneath its tail feathers at the missing statue. Beating its wings, it fluttered to a landing at Amaelia's feet. "WELL, HEL-LO THERE, SWEET STUFF!" It strutted before her. "SO WE MEET AGAIN."

Kerickson glanced at her. "You know him?"

The terrified doves burst out of Amaelia's hands and flew away. She bit her lip. "Back at Gracchus's villa. You know, on the—"

"Oh." He cut her off before she could say "screens."

Out in the rapidly emptying Forum, the massive figure of Mars approached Jupiter's temple, growing even larger with each thunderous step.

Kerickson tried to think. "You didn't tell me about that part."

"You didn't ask!"

"HOW'D YOU LIKE TO PLAY A LITTLE CHASE, BABY?" The eagle winked at her. "I'LL BE THE BULL AND YOU CAN BE THE SWAN."

A lightning bolt crashed at the bottom of the steps and splintered a bas-relief sculpture. The scorched-iron smell of ozone filled the air. "Uh—" Amaelia backed away. "May-Maybe later."

Kerickson took Amaelia's arm and pulled her behind a massive column. "Tell him yes!"

"Are you kidding?" Her eyes widened. "You know about him—and all those women in the old legends."

He gritted his teeth. "Tell him yes!"

Her confused green eyes just stared at him. Dragging her by the wrist, he stepped back around the column and addressed the eagle. "She'd love to play," he said loudly, "but not with all this noise and fire."

"NOISE?"

Kerickson glanced meaningfully at Mars, who was now glowing so brightly that an evil red light bathed the entire square. "I'm sure a clever guy like you can see how mayhem really spoils the mood."

"OH." The eagle ruffled its dark brown feathers. "WELL, WE CERTAINLY CAN'T HAVE THAT." With one beat of its powerful wings, it leaped into the air. "BEGONE, TROUBLE-MAKER!"

Mars's body rippled for a second, as though it were under-water, then disappeared with a pop. The eagle gave a fierce screech, then circled the Forum twice, soaring effortlessly around the monuments on its huge wings.

It landed on the edge of the temple's portico and preened at its feathers. "NOW, MY LITTLE HONEY POT, WHERE WERE WE?"

Amaelia glanced worriedly at Kerickson, then backed away into the shadowy inner recesses of the temple.

"IT TAKES TWO TO TANGO, OR SO THEY SAY." The eagle's outline swelled into the shining shape of a seven-foot bearded man clutching a huge scepter in one hand and a jag-ged thunderbolt in the other. He bared his large white teeth in a broad smile.

"Amaelia!" Kerickson motioned at her from behind Jupiter's back. "We have to go now!"

"YOU CAN'T LEAVE WITHOUT A SACRIFICE." The god's eyes glowed with a fierce blueness that made Kerickson look away. "AND I HAVE JUST THE THING IN MIND."

Kerickson wiped his sweaty palms against his tunic. "Amaelia!"

"So, think of something!" She darted behind the altar and glared at him. "This was your idea!"

"AND SUCH A GAME IT WILL BE, MY LITTLE MELON BALL." Jupiter's bushy gray eyebrows arched.

"Oh, for—" Kerickson angled toward the girl.

Just as he reached for her hand, Jupiter aimed the thunder-bolt at him. "ONLY TWO CAN PLAY THIS GAME, SONNY BOY."

Kerickson's body writhed in a spasm of hot pain, and the marble floor smacked him in the rear. Struggling for breath, he stumbled back to his feet, but his legs wilted and he fell again. His vision faded in and out. "Amaelia!"

The god—and the girl—had disappeared.

Demea glanced at the tiny chronocrystal she usually kept hidden, for authenticity's sake, beneath her gown. Down here in the Underworld it was impossible to tell what time it was without a clock. The light, if it could be dignified by so lofty a name, never varied from the last dregs of twilight.

She paced around her spacious bedchamber, wondering if she should make another attempt to escape. So far she'd tried twice to find her way back to the surface, but both times Pluto's automated minions had dragged her back to the gleaming black palace.

"Wine, my love?" The long-faced shade of Micio drifted after her, an erotic painting of a woman and a huge white bull on the opposite wall visible through its nebulous body.

She stopped, her hands knotted into fists. It had been bad enough to put up with her whiny husband when he had been alive, but having his shade follow her around down here was absolutely intolerable. "For the last time, go away and leave me alone!"

"Well, you don't have to get huffy about it!" The shade looked down its long Roman nose at her, then shrugged a misty fold of toga over its shoulder. "This certainly isn't my idea of a good time."

Her quarters lay open to the luridly lush palace gardens on one long colonnaded side. She walked through Micio's body into shadowy greenery. Fleshy white flowers that smelled strongly of overripe melon trailed over her hands and arms. A transparent nightingale fluttered over her head and into her room. It circled for a moment, then perched on the black marble shoulder of a faun in the middle of a small fountain. She stared at the bird, fighting the urge to throw her sandal at it. Somehow, she had to find a way out of this depressing place, even if she had to kill someone to do it!

"Let me out of here!" She threw her head back. "Do you hear me? You're driving me *crazy*!"

Startled, the ghostly nightingale took to the air again, leaving her alone with Micio's shade and the gurgling water. She clasped her trembling hands together and came back in to sit on the edge of the fountain.

With a clatter of hooves, a huge black bull trotted in from

the gardens and swung its horned head in a wide arc. "NONE ABOVE SHALL EVER SHARE YOUR BEAUTY AGAIN!" Its black eyes bored into her, bottomless pools of night that made her knees weak. "YOU ARE AS FAR BEYOND THOSE PUNY MORTALS AS WE GODS ARE BEYOND WORMS. NOTHING SHALL EVER SEPARATE US AGAIN!" The bull lowered its fierce head and pawed the floor. "NOT EVEN DEATH ITSELF!"

"I suppose that's meant to be a comfort." She studied the long black face, finding this manifestation even less inviting than his previous, towering five-story image. Running her hand over her elaborately braided hair, she tucked in a stray wisp. "Why don't we try to be reasonable about this? *You* are a computer program." Rising, she walked into the garden, parting the heavy white flowers with one hand. "*I*, on the other hand, am human. There's nothing either of us can do about that, and pretending won't make one bit of difference."

The flowers closed in behind her, brushing her skin with cool leaves, clouding her mind with the heady perfume of night jasmine.

"THERE IS A WAY."

"There is not!" A path stretched out before her, winding back upon itself into shadowy bowers under palm trees, then splitting around yet another dreary black marble fountain.

A figure dressed in glimmering black armor stepped out of the palm trees, a tall, broad-shouldered man with curling midnight hair, life-size this time, as he had never come to her before.

He extended his hand. "ACCEPT ME AND WE SHALL TASTE THE PLEASURE OF A THOUSAND THOUSAND ENDLESS NIGHTS." His black eyes smoldered.

Her skin prickled as he approached. She stared at his hand, unable to stop thinking how lovely it would be if all this were real, if a darkly handsome god really did desire her for his consort, if he could touch her and hold her as no holo image ever could, if this Game fantasy could somehow be made real.

"STARS TO MY NIGHT . . ." His voice was low and husky as he reached for her face. "THERE IS A WAY. ONCE YOU ENTER MY REALITY, YOU WILL SEE THAT YOUR LIFE BEFORE WAS ONLY A DREAM."

She felt the bite of electricity at his holographic touch. "You have to let me go back." Her throat tightened. "I can't take much more of this."

"JOIN ME, THEN." His black-velvet voice throbbed with the music of a thousand organs.

"I can't!" Unaccustomed tears rose into her eyes and she dabbed at them furiously. "This is so stupid! I'm only a player! I can't be a goddess. There's no such role!"

"ONCE I, TOO, WAS MORTAL." His dark-eyed, high-cheekboned face hovered above her, so perfect she wanted to cry. "ONCE I LIVED ABOVE, UNDERSTANDING NO MORE THAN OTHER MEN. BUT NOW I ABIDE HERE, ALL-POWERFUL, IMMORTAL. SAY THE WORD AND IT SHALL BE SO WITH YOU, TOO."

"You're a program, nothing more!" Her voice shook.

"I AM PROGRAM . . . AND MACHINE . . . AND MORTAL."

The implications flooded through her mind. "You're talking about cybernetic interface. That's illegal!"

"ILLEGAL, BUT NOT IMPOSSIBLE WHEN FUNDS ARE UNLIMITED." A faint smile played over the god's dark face. "MONEY EQUALS POWER, AND POWER IS EVERYTHING. I SAW YOU UNDERSTOOD THAT, TOO, AS YOU PLAYED ABOVE, LEAPING FROM RANK TO RANK, MAN TO MAN, ALLOWING NOTHING TO STAND IN YOUR WAY. THAT HAS DRAWN ME TO YOU, AND YOU TO ME. WE ARE TWO OF A KIND."

A dim understanding flickered within her: she could play, not as Empress, but as a goddess, could wield unlimited power in the Game—it made her head spin.

"But—how?" She bit her lip, feeling on the edge of a vast yawning precipice.

"EVERYTHING IS IN READINESS, MY LOVE, AND WHEN IT IS DONE, THE ENTIRE GAME WILL LIE AT YOUR FEET." Again he held out his nonexistent hand to her.

She breathed hard, longing to feel his flesh warm against hers.

"JOIN ME AND WE SHALL PLAY SUCH GAMES AS OTHERS HAVE ONLY DREAMT."

Her hand went to her throat. The dense gardens seemed to close in upon her. Did she dare believe him? "If I do this, can we be truly together?"

"YOU CANNOT BEGIN TO GUESS THE INFINITE VARIETY OF PLEASURES AVAILABLE IN THIS STATE OF BEING." His fierce black eyes burned down at her. "I SHALL TEACH YOU WHAT IT IS TO LOVE AS A GOD."

And they would all know her name, she thought. Everyone would know that she, Demea, was a goddess, and there would be no more grubbing around for authenticity points or fawning upon fools for favors to retain her rank. They would all come to her begging, and, ten stories high, she would look down and laugh in their mortal faces.

"Yes," she heard herself say in the stillness of the twilit gardens, "I will."

"Now you've done it!" The priest stomped angrily over to the altar and hiked himself up on the edge.

His head still ringing from the effect of Jupiter's thunderbolt, Kerickson staggered to his feet. "Me?"

The priest buried his face in his hands. "I should have known today would end like this!" He picked up the libation jug and took a stiff pull on the sacrificial wine. "The signs were all there—the sacred chickens were completely off their feed this morning. The little horrors refused to touch a single grain of corn."

He upended the jug until bright red wine dribbled from the corners of his mouth. "And the Saturnalia begins tomorrow, too!" He wiped his face with a handful of his white tunic, leaving behind a livid red stain. "I'll be lucky not to be busted back to a . . . a . . ." He stretched out on his back, narrowly missing the smoldering sacrificial fire. "A blue-painted Briton!"

"Yeah, yeah." Kerickson's head ached and his mouth tasted like the inside of an old shoe. Blinking hard, he wobbled over to the altar and stared down at the distraught priest. "What— Where did she go?"

"Who?" The priest scratched his nose. "Oh, the girl. He took her, of course. What did you expect?"

Kerickson eyed the libation jug, then decided against it. "*He's* a computer program. She can't be *with* him."

"Are you nuts?" Leaping off the altar, the priest glanced around with white-rimmed eyes. "First," he whispered, "you come in here, asking Jupiter to appear, by god, when everyone in Rome knows what he's like! Then you wave a nubile young female right under his nose, and now you're saying that—that *C-word*, right here before the Saturnalia!" He mopped the film of perspiration on his brow with his sleeve. "Maybe you don't care about advancing in rank, but I don't intend to spend another quarter stuck in this dump poking around in animal entrails, even if they are only simulated. I want to be a general and rewrite military history!"

"Where—did they go?" Kerickson's tongue felt as though it belonged to someone else.

"Oh, you know what the old goat is like." The priest tugged at the hem of his tunic, now speckled with red down the front. "He'll reenact a few of his favorite myths, then he'll get bored and let her go."

"Where—"

"You certainly have a one-track mind, don't you?" The priest shook his head. "Well, you should have considered the consequences before you came up here with a *girl*."

"I suppose you'd have preferred to let Mars burn down the city?" Kerickson kneaded his forehead, digging at an ache behind his eyes.

"I—" The priest's head whirled around as he was interrupted by a faint, stomach-churning scream from inside the temple.

Kerickson pushed off the altar on legs that seemed to be made of water.

"I wouldn't go in there, if I were you," the priest called after him. "He can be downright beastly if you get in his way."

"Yeah, right." Gritting his teeth, Kerickson supported himself against a carved column as black spots danced in front of his eyes. He shook his head, then lurched on toward the massive closed door.

Another muffled scream split the air.

"Amaelia!" Seizing the latch, he tugged at the towering door, but it refused to budge.

"Now, look here." The priest hiccuped. "Be reasonable. He's not going to let you in *there*."

Kerickson leaned his head against the bas-relief of Jupiter appearing as a shower of gold, trying hard to think. If only he could go back to the Interface, he could have her out of there in a second, but he had no access now.

Something flickered in the back of his mind, some faint idea, some way out. He closed his eyes, trying to concentrate.

From within the temple a deep voice rumbled, and then he heard Amaelia laugh.

"See?" The priest waggled his finger in Kerickson's face. "She's all right." He took another deep swig of sacrificial wine, then threw the jug aside. "After all, it's not every girl who gets to disport herself with *him*, and they didn't exactly seem to be strangers, if you catch my drift."

No, they didn't, Kerickson thought, and then the glimmer from the back of his mind leaped out at him. Of course! He needed access to an Interface, and Amaelia had mentioned seeing screens in Quintus Gracchus's villa. He whirled around and stared into the priest's wine-spattered face. "Watch this door," he said. "If Amaelia comes out before I can get back, tell her to wait for me."

"Oh, you think I don't have better things to do than sit around here all day?" The priest peered morosely into the mouth of the empty jug.

"I think you'll spend the next quarter playing a eunuch in the Temple of Vesta if you screw this up." Kerickson stared him straight in the bloodshot eyes. "And that's a promise."

The priest's legs gave way and he slid down the column behind him until he was sitting on the floor, his tunic hiked up around his knobby knees. He blinked up at Kerickson with heavy-lidded eyes. "And why should I take the word of a freedman on that?"

"Because I'll cram one of those damn sacred chickens down your throat if you don't!" Kerickson started down the steps to the Forum, then heard Jupiter's laugh rumble through the marble door.

Afraid, yet enthralled, Demea stared into the trickling water of the fountain, thinking of the promise of so much power and prestige. But at what cost? Was she doing the right thing?

"Can I ever go back?" she asked the shadowy spaciousness of her palace chambers. "Once I interface with the computer, can it be undone?"

"NO." Pluto's deep voice came from everywhere at once. "HOW CAN A FULL-GROWN MIND BE STUFFED BACK INTO THE WOMB?"

Her stomach contracted, full of icy fear prickles. He was talking about another plane of existence, as far beyond her as an adult was beyond an unborn child, something at which she could only guess. Rising, she stared down at her rippling reflection in the pool, appraising her assets. Tall and large-boned, with black hair, she was attractive enough, although she'd never had the money necessary for cosmetic surgery that could have softened the bold lines of her face into conventional prettiness. Her first husband, Arvid, had been able to afford either a good biosculpt or enrollment in the Game, but not both. She had chosen the Game.

In ancient Rome, women had been revered for their strength as well as their comeliness, and she had let that work for her, knowing that a certain sort of man liked to be bullied and pushed. It had worked with Arvid, at least for a while, and later Micio—but this thing with Pluto was a new experience. Now she was the one who was pursued and persuaded.

"IT IS TIME, MY LOVE."

A door, hitherto invisibly seamed into the wall, opened. A gleaming hallway appeared beyond, all silvery metal, quite unlike anything she'd ever seen on the playing field. Her heart thumped. Holding her head high, she walked into the corridor.

Another door opened at the far end, spilling a bright, almost surgical light. She steadied herself against the wall with one hand, then recoiled from the cold metal.

"WHEN WE MEET AGAIN, WE WILL NEVER BE PARTED."

His voice already sounded farther away, cut off by the corridor walls. She glanced over her shoulder, chilled by the realization that he did have limits, limits she would share if she took this step.

But what awaited her if she went back? Even if she could go on playing Empress, and there was no guarantee of that, it would be nothing but second best now. She wanted more power, more adulation, more of everything. Her eyes went back to the blinding light ahead.

The time had indeed come.

"ARE YOU SURE?" the glittering cloud of gold thickened, obscuring the colorful scenes of voluptuous young maidens in various stages of undress painted on the opposite wall. "WON'T YOU MOO FOR ME, JUST THE TINIEST LITTLE MOO? I WOULD BE EVER SO GRATEFUL."

"You've got to be kidding." Amaelia hunched her knees up to her chest, then fingered the gaping rent in the bodice of her gown. She was lucky to have nothing worse than a torn gown and a few bruises after being flung like a sack of grain into the temple's inner room by Jupiter's overwhelming gust of wind. "Look, I have to go. Gaius is waiting for me."

Or was he? Jupiter had been yammering at her for several hours now. If her new friend had gone off and left her, well, she could hardly blame him.

The golden cloud sulked on the other side of the chamber for a few minutes. Finally, it formed a skewed face that stared petulantly at her.

She crossed her arms. "This is very silly, not worthy of you at all."

"HAVEN'T YOU EVER THOUGHT OF BECOMING A HEIFER?" The cloud coalesced into a huge white bull. It swished its tail. "SO YOUNG AND TENDER, SO SWEET, SO—"

"What is this obsession you have with cattle?" She jumped to her feet. "You should be out there protecting the city from Mars, and instead you're mooning around in here with me!"

"MARS?" The bull dissolved into an oversized, slightly pot-bellied older man sitting on a golden throne. He twined a gray-ing strand of beard around one finger. "IT'LL TAKE A FULL DAY FOR HIM TO GET HIMSELF TOGETHER AGAIN." He leaned forward and raised one gray eyebrow. "SO WHAT SAY YOU AND I GO FOR A LITTLE SWIM? I CAN DO THE MOST MARVELOUS SWAN—"

A blow against the outside door made the whole temple shudder. The god hesitated.

"OPEN THIS DOOR, YOU RANDY OLD HE-ASS!"

Jupiter bit his lip. "ON THE OTHER HAND, MY DEAR, PERHAPS WE SHOULD CONTINUE THIS CONVERSA-TION, PROMISING AS IT IS, SOME OTHER TIME."

"I HAVE CONTROL OF THE CITY NOW, AND I WON'T HAVE THESE SORTS OF GOINGS-ON UNDER MY PROTECTION!"

Amaelia recognized the voice and paled.

"YOU SEND THAT LITTLE TROLLOP OUT AT ONCE OR THERE'S GOING TO BE SOME BIG CHANGES AROUND HERE!"

"Is there a back way out?" Amaelia asked him.

"NO." Jupiter combed his fingers through his beard. "YOU'D BETTER GO OUT THERE AND EXPLAIN THAT YOU WERE JUST—JUST COMMUNING WITH ME IN PRAYER."

Amaelia glanced around at the painted murals, each por-traying a different seduction scene. "Prayer?"

Another blow made her head ring. She clapped her hands over her ears and stumbled against a statue of a swan, which wasn't as heavy as it looked. It tipped back and forth, then crashed on the marble floor. Slivers of plaster flew across the room.

"RUN ALONG, MY DEAR." Jupiter made shooing motions with his large hands. "WE HAVEN'T A MOMENT TO LOSE."

"She's your wife! Why don't *you* go out there and explain?"

"BECAUSE I'VE SO VERY MUCH TO DO, YOU SEE." Jupiter ticked each item off on his fingers. "THERE'S NEXT WEEK'S RAIN TO ORGANIZE, AND THUNDER TO PRACTICE, AND I SIMPLY CAN'T MISS THE JETS GAME. YOU REALIZE, OF COURSE, THAT THEY'RE UP FOR THE INNER SYSTEM CHAMPIONSHIP." His face was dissolving into a fine blue mist. "SO GLAD THAT WE HAD THIS LITTLE CHAT. I'M SURE WE'LL MEET AGAIN."

Just as the blueness faded away completely, the huge door swung inward and crashed against the wall.

"ALL RIGHT, YOU HUSSY, I KNOW YOU'RE IN THERE!"

Tucking in the torn edges of her gown as best she could, Amaelia faced the portico and the huge, floating face of Juno.

"I MIGHT HAVE KNOWN!" The goddess's eyes narrowed. "A WHOLE CITY FULL OF MORTAL MEN WEREN'T ENOUGH FOR YOU, WERE THEY? WELL, I'VE GOT JUST THE PLACE FOR YOU, YOU LITTLE TRAMP!" Her oversized blue-green eyes began to spark. "LET'S SEE HOW YOU LIKE BEING DEAD!"

CHAPTER
TWELVE

The shadows lengthened into blueness as Kerickson detoured around a fruit seller on her knees gathering smashed melons, then a pair of basket weavers exclaiming over their trodden wares. People were drifting back into the Forum to search the overturned fortune-tellers' stalls, battered copper pots, and smashed dove crates.

A platoon of armored Legionaries entered from a side street and fanned out across the square. Kerickson kept his head down and circled behind the marble public-speaking rostrum at the far end. When they had passed, he crossed into the Via Nova and followed its winding path down through the heart of the smoldering Market District. The air was still acrid and smelled of ashes as he passed row after row of burned-out shops; obviously the dome's air-conditioning system was overloaded by all the damage.

His mind kept replaying the terrified look on Amaelia's face when Jupiter blasted him with that so-called thunderbolt. Something had gone drastically wrong. Better than almost anyone else in the dome, he understood it was outside the parameters of an Imperium god program to damage either property or players. Exactly who had taken his place in the Interface, and what the hell did they think they were doing in there?

He was also worried that, if the old parameters still held, Mars would recover from Jupiter's override in twenty-four hours. If not, Mars could be back sooner, ready to start this scenario all over again. HabiTek would have no choice but to evacuate the Game, and if that happened, he would never have the chance to prove his innocence.

As he passed into a smart neighborhood of apartment buildings, or insulas, favored by the Game's more successful courtesans, he was glad to see it had escaped major damage. The simulated sun edged lower behind the buildings and the temperature began to drop. He shivered, and wished he still had his cloak.

The luxury estates began just across the broad expanse of the Via Ostiensis. Gracchus had moved into this area after obtaining his commission as Captain of the Praetorian Guard. Kerickson stared over a brick wall at the rolling, terraced grounds of a sprawling villa, trying to remember whose it was, but his weary brain refused to dredge up the answer.

Damnation! He should have come better prepared, but always before, he'd worn an Interface comlink when he was out on the playing field. He'd never been limited to the facilities available to players. He turned back and looked for an oak tree. Oaks were sacred to Jupiter and were used throughout the Game as symbols of the administration. Five statues and one sundial down, he found a towering specimen and pressed the shiny steel button set nose-high into its trunk. The bark-covered access panel slid up, revealing a comm panel.

"Warning!" a voice intoned. "Use of this device will result in a loss of one authenticity point."

"Yeah, yeah." He presented his Game bracelet to the blue screen. "Give me Directory Assistance."

A chime sounded. "Imperium Dir—" The blueness broke up as a small brown owl appeared on the screen. "ARE YOU SURE THIS IS WISE?"

Kerickson jerked his wrist back. "What do you want?"

"IF YOU USE THIS DEVICE TO ACCESS DIRECTORY ASSISTANCE, YOUR LOCATION WILL BE LOGGED BY THE COMPUTER." Lifting a hind foot, the owl scratched the back of its neck vigorously. "AND THAT WILL IMPERIL YOUR QUEST."

"Great." He leaned his forehead against the rough bark. "Are you saying someone flagged my file?"

"YES." The owl blinked its solemn gray eyes.

He glanced over his shoulder. Two aristocratic women, clad in long, cream-colored stolas, strolled past, followed by their downcast, package-laden male slaves. On the other side of the street a large, curtained litter hurried by, borne on the shoulders of eight sweat-sheened bearers. He turned back to the screen. "I have to find Quintus Gracchus's villa, and I don't have all night!"

The owl ruffled its feathers. "I COULD GUIDE YOU."

"Yeah, right." He moved closer to the screen and lowered his voice. "Look, I don't want to hurt your feelings, but you're kind of, you know, noticeable."

"I CAN TAKE THE FORM OF AN OLIVE TREE."

"Oh, I'm sure *no one* would pay attention if I carried around a blasted tree!"

"MORTAL, YOU FORGET WITH WHOM YOU SPEAK." The owl clacked its beak. "THIS CITY IS UNDER MY PROTECTION."

"Not since you took up eating rodents and—" He hesitated as a large barbarian-class player stalked past him, swaddled in poorly cured furs and cracked leathers and twirling a club.

"AND WHOSE FAULT IS THAT, MIGHT I ASK?"

He closed his eyes and reached within for a calmness that he certainly did not feel. "Will you please just get off this line and let me talk to Directory Assistance?"

"TWENTY-EIGHT NINETY-FOUR EGYPT LANE."

Startled, he opened his eyes again, but Minerva had disappeared, leaving behind the trademark image of the Temple of Jupiter.

"Imperium Directory Assistance," the screen said politely. "How may we help you?"

He punched the screen off, and the bark panel descended seamlessly back into place. Then he heard the jingle of armor and slid behind the tree trunk as a platoon of Legionaries jogged past, their scarlet plumes bobbing, their spears held in readiness. He had a sick feeling in the pit of his stomach, as though next week's chariot races were being conducted in there. Had the computer noted his location? And if it had, who was searching for him—the police, HabiTek, or the murderer?

"Sit down," the flat, mechanical voice said.

Demea stared at the metal chair in the middle of the otherwise empty room. The cold, dry air raised chill bumps on her bare arms as she tried to make up her mind whether to go through with this or not.

"Are you afraid?" the machine voice asked.

"Of course not!" she snapped before she thought. "It's just that—that—"

"If you will sit down, we will begin the accessing process," the voice said. "There will be no pain."

Pain? She hadn't even considered *that*. Eyeing the chair, she ran a hand over her elaborately braided hair. "What about my ... body?"

"Your body will be placed in storage, of course, after your brain is linked with the Game computer's subprogram."

"Permanently?"

"For humans," the voice said, "no condition can be considered permanent, except death."

She realized she was wringing her hands, and forced them back to her sides. "I've changed my mind."

"Pluto sends word that Quintus Gracchus has now accumulated enough points to succeed Micio Metullus as Emperor and will undoubtedly ascend to the throne sometime during the coming Saturnalia. Your stepdaughter, Amaelia, has married him and will play the new Empress. Your current point standing is inadequate to remain in the Palace. It is probable that you will qualify only for a lesser role, such as mistress to—"

"Enough!" She lowered herself into the chair, even though the icy metal made her skin crawl. Turn her out of the Palace, would they? Well, that arrogant, lowborn wretch, Gracchus, had another thing coming if he thought he could treat her that way!

"Lean your head back to meet the neural contacts."

What contacts? She hadn't noticed any, but she let her head drop back. She didn't feel anything. Maybe this whole idea was a farce, just something Pluto had concocted to impress her. Maybe nothing at all would hap—

A tingle began in her head, centered somewhere just behind her ears. She tried to turn and look, but her head wouldn't move. Panic washed through her mind and she struggled to cry out.

"Testing," said the mechanical voice.

Patterns flashed before her eyes: an array of marching red triangles that merged into pale blue rectangles, then swelled into green hexagons ... golden starbursts of lines that reminded her of the exploding displays on System Independence Day ... pinpoints of brilliant white winked at her, like stars against a velvety darkness, swirling like leaves caught in a whirlpool ... She felt a rushing sensation, as though she were being hurled through a hole both infinitely large and infinitely small, moving faster and faster until her thoughts fell behind and she continued onward, curiously incomplete.

Something loomed in the darkness ahead of her ... a presence, more sensed than seen.

"ARISE, MY LOVE, AND VIEW YOUR KINGDOM."

She could not move, and yet somehow she did. A finger flicked, then her whole hand. She stood up, leaving behind something dross and unnecessary.

"COME TO ME."

"WHERE?" Her voice echoed through the darkness, larger than before, rich with a new underlying resonance.

Suddenly he was before her, dark and commanding, his hand outstretched. "HERE!"

She stared at his hand, wishing he could take her in his arms and satisfy her in a way no real man ever had. Of its own volition, her arm rose. Their fingers touched and the shock of his solid warmth made her jerk away. "YOU—I FELT THAT!"

"AND MORE, I'LL WAGER, BEFORE THE NIGHT IS DONE!" His strong arms gathered her in and pressed her head against the chill hardness of his armored chest.

She smelled the leather of his harness, the cleanness of his crisp black hair as it lay in rings upon his forehead. And where her skin touched his, fire underlay the bite of electricity.

"WE WILL PLAY SUCH MUSIC UPON ONE ANOTHER AS THIS WORLD HAS NEVER HEARD." He buried his face in her hair. "AND WHEN THIS NIGHT HAS PASSED, OUR TIME WILL NOT EVEN REALLY HAVE BEGUN."

She felt endless corridors stretching out all around her as she reached up to trace the line of his firm jaw with one wondering, static-nimbused finger.

"COME." He turned her around. "YOU HAVE TRANSCENDED FLESH AND BONE."

Thinking of the creature left behind in the chair, she felt sorry for it now, so frail and powerless, so small. She stretched her arms high above her head. Energy leaped through her, boundless, ready for anything. "I WANT TO SEE IT ALL!"

"AND SO, MY LOVE," Pluto's voice rumbled in her ear, "YOU SHALL."

Kerickson paused at the intersection of Egypt Lane and Lesser Spain Avenue. All Roman houses looked the same to him on the outside, with their whitewashed facades and unvarying blank walls. Like puzzle boxes, their treasure lay inside.

"Twenty-eight ninety-four Egypt Lane," he repeated like a mantra, but the numbers here were too low. He needed to go farther north.

Somewhere behind him voices rang out in the night, questioning at first, then laughing, followed by cheers. No doubt someone was getting an early start on the next day's Saturnalia. This was a joyful time of the year for most residents. He shivered, feeling very alone.

As he walked, he kept to the bare-limbed trees and bushes, using what scant cover they provided to avoid the numerous slave-borne litters and partygoers that passed him.

After another half hour he found Quintus Gracchus's villa on top of a small rise, large even for this particularly expensive neighborhood. He stared over the brick fence up at the well-lit white walls, wondering if they, too, contained a party tonight. Then he remembered the speech he'd heard yesterday at the Palace; Gracchus was currently focusing his energy on becoming Emperor. Surely he was up at the Palace, wooing senators and seducing wives and doing whatever else was necessary to accumulate points at a dizzying rate.

A bored Praetorian Guard lounged before the front gate, spear at half-mast. Kerickson hiked around to the back, checked to make sure he was unobserved, and then scrambled over the brick wall. He caught his foot on the way down and hit the half-frozen ground on the other side with a muffled thump. Holding his breath, he lay there, expecting someone to come and check out the noise.

After a moment he got up and ran toward the main house, staying down and using the scattered bushes for cover. He slipped around the house and tried every door, but the place was locked up as tight as a coffin. After circling it twice, he knew he was going to have to climb over the roof. There should be the requisite peristyle garden in the middle of the house. A player as intent on authenticity points as Gracchus would build that before anything else.

Sighing, he gazed up at a rickety vine trellis, then wedged his foot in a crossbar and hauled himself up. Halfway to the roof, one board gave under his foot and he hung there like a fresh-killed turkey while the simulated stars glittered down from above.

Still no one came running, and after a moment of muffled swearing, he found another toehold and continued up until he lay spread-eagled on the red tiles and massaged his aching fingers.

Wheezing in the cold night air, he studied the villa's layout: fairly standard for this size of house. The expected interior garden was massive, full of fountains and formal flower beds, and provided his best chance to get into the house proper. All the skylights had been sealed—not in keeping with Roman tradition, of course, but, not being made of as stern a stuff as the ancients, more players drew the line at maintaining open holes in the roof.

Creeping hand over hand, he edged toward the garden, then jumped down. He landed in a heap of brittle, winter-blasted vines that crackled loudly. He froze, but again no servants appeared. For an important man, he thought, Quintus Gracchus didn't keep much of a staff.

He brushed off the broken bits of vine, then prowled toward the colonnade that surrounded the garden. A number of doors led into the main house; perhaps at least one of them would be open. If not, well, he had no experience at picking locks, but he might be able to pry one open with his dagger.

The first two were locked, and before he tried the third, he heard the faint rise and fall of voices within. He put his ear to the door; several people were arguing. The voices were male, but he could make out nothing more. Then, before he could move, the door swung outward, pinning him back against the wall.

"She has to be somewhere!"

"But, your newness, we've looked everywhere! I mean, even *they* say they can't find her. Perhaps she exited the Game after all."

Armor creaked. "No, if she'd done that, the Interface would know, and there's no record of it. She has to be here somewhere. You get your incompetent band of thugs out on the floor and keep looking until you find her, is that clear? She has to stand by my side tomorrow to support my claim to be Emperor. After that, you can drown the little wretch in the nearest fountain, for all I care!"

Kerickson peered through the crack between the door and the facing. The angry man stood with his back to him, staring up into the night sky; then he turned around. It was Quintus Gracchus.

"Seems like a fearful waste of loveliness, your Emperorness," mumbled the other man, smaller and round-faced. "You might as well have left her down at the temple."

"Then I couldn't have married her and become Emperor, could I?" Gracchus idly rubbed his chin as his cold gray eyes stared out into the garden. "After I'm Emperor, she'll be of no further use to me. Share her among yourselves, if you like."

"Well, now you're talking." A toothy smile split the shorter man's face. "How soon you gonna take over, anyway?"

"As soon as the Guard proclaims me and the Senate agrees." Gracchus's eyes narrowed. "But not if you don't bring her back!"

"Right away, your Imperialness, right away!" The other man bowed his head. "We'll search high and low, if you catch my drift."

"Just get on with it!" Gracchus watched him scuttle away, then reentered the house, muttering, "Imbecile!"

Kerickson leaned back against the wall; that had been too close! Easing around the door, he peered into the dimly lit room. Gracchus sat, facing away from him, before a bank of screens—obviously an unauthorized Interface.

"You went too far," Gracchus said.

"YOU ASKED FOR A DISTRACTION." The resonant voice of Mars rang out from the console. "YOU DIDN'T SAY WHAT."

"One more repeat of this afternoon and I'll lock you down so tight, you'll have to get permission to accept a sacrifice at your own temple!"

"YOU'RE JUST JEALOUS BECAUSE YOU'D NEVER HAVE THE GUTS TO PLAY THE WAY YOU REALLY WANT TO. YOU'LL NEVER PLAY LIKE ONE OF THEM AND YOU KNOW IT."

"I'll have you erased." Gracchus's voice was grim. "This Game can do without a god of war almost indefinitely."

"JUST TRY IT, BUSTER."

Gracchus stood up. "Don't tempt me!"

"YOU COULDN'T HOLD YOUR OWN AGAINST EVEN A DOLT LIKE MERCURY, MUCH LESS ME!"

"Pompous ass!" Gracchus punched the release code savagely, then paced around the small room with his arms folded tightly across his chest. "More like the god of idiocy, if you ask me."

Kerickson flattened himself against the wall. From inside he heard a door open, then close. Risking another look, he saw the room was empty. He hurried inside, shivering, and closed the outer door.

Standing behind the chair, he considered. His own access code would have been canceled, of course, but perhaps they hadn't bothered about Wilson's. He sat in the chair and reached for the keyboard, a pang running through him at the thought of his friend. Why had Wilson been killed? What secrets could this game possibly hold that would be worth even one man's life?

He sighed. Well, first things first. He couldn't worry about the killer until he found Amaelia again, although it sounded as though she was probably safer with a lecherous old goat like Jupiter than Quintus Gracchus. He punched in Wilson's code and waited.

The central screen dissolved into the Temple of Jupiter, the HabiTek emblem. "HabiTek," the voice-over said softly, "where we build a better tomorrow by living yesterday."

"Yeah, yeah," he muttered under his breath, then punched in Jupiter's call code. The temple faded and was replaced by a huge eagle apparently swooping in on his face, its talons extended. Kerickson sat back in the chair. "You can cut the dramatics. I'm not impressed."

The eagle braced its broad wings and dropped into a graceful landing. "AND YOU'RE NOT WILSON, EITHER."

"Never mind that." He frowned at the bird. "What have you done with Amaelia?"

"MY LITTLE HONEYDEW MELON?" The eagle snapped its curving beak. "QUITE A NICE NUMBER, IF I DO SAY SO MYSELF."

"Keep your volume down!" Kerickson glanced over his shoulder, but the inside door remained closed. "This is a class-two override. I want that girl released right now!"

"SORRY, LITTLE BUDDY, NO CAN DO."

"You can't refuse a direct override!"

"I'M AFRAID YOU'LL HAVE TO CHECK WITH MY BETTER HALF ON THIS ONE." The eagle preened under its wing.

"Forget Juno." He mopped at a trickle of sweat on his forehead. "I want the girl!"

"SHE'S STILL DOWN AT MY TEMPLE."

Swearing under his breath, Kerickson punched up the Temple of Jupiter on the adjacent screen, then stared in disbelief. Juno, protectress of married women, tall as a two-story house, paced back and forth before the open door into the inner cella. "What is she doing?"

"OH, THAT . . ." The eagle ruffled its feathers. "YOU KNOW WHAT AN ACTIVE IMAGINATION SHE HAS,

BUT I SWEAR WE HADN'T EVEN SO MUCH AS DIS-
CUSSED BULLS OR HEIFERS."

Kerickson flinched as Juno drew back an oversized hand
filled with something bright and crackling. "Stop her!"

"I DON'T THINK SHE'S GOING TO HURT HER." The
eagle's voice took on a whining tone. "BESIDES, I CAN'T
OVERRIDE MY DARLING WIFE. EVERYONE KNOWS
THAT."

"I'm going to sell you for spare parts if you don't stop her
right now!"

"THAT'S HUMANS FOR YOU. DAY IN, DAY OUT,
NOTHING BUT GIVE ME THIS, FATHER JUPITER, GIVE
ME THAT, AND NO SENSE OF GRATITUDE AT ALL.
WELL, DON'T BOTHER TO COME AROUND ASKING
FOR ANY MORE FAVORS." The eagle disappeared in a
shower of blue sparks.

On the screen, Juno hurled the lightning bolt into the cella.
Kerickson tried to get his breath. Surely that was just special
effects, but it looked as real as the bolts Mars had been hurling
at the city earlier.

He punched off the Interface—he had to get back to
Amaelia. Indeed, he never should have left her. This was all
his fault.

At that moment the inner door swung open.

CHAPTER
THIRTEEN

The hair on the back of Kerickson's neck tried to crawl down his spine. He jerked out of the chair and thunked back into the console.

"I suppose there's an explanation for this." Quintus Gracchus's armored body filled the doorway. He had a chin like an anvil, and close up his muscular legs and arms were even more massive than Kerickson had realized.

Kerickson turned around and punched Wilson's code back into the keyboard. "Run diagnostics series fourteen." The blue central screen dissolved into the Aegis, Jupiter's traditional shield. "Look, I'll be done in a moment, and then I'll get out of your way."

"Testing," the computer said primly. "Primary stats in thirty seconds."

"Be done with what?" Gracchus's voice had the ring of cold, naked steel behind it.

Kerickson kept his eyes on the bank of screens and hoped that the sweat running down his temple wasn't visible across the room. "Hey, I'm just doing my job, and I'd a hell of a lot rather be home with my feet up, but it's in your hands—do you want Mars rampaging through the city again tomorrow or can I finish running these diagnostics?"

"All four-thousand-level buffers are out of service due to system maintenance," the computer said. "File allocation tables in ten seconds."

"How did you get in here?" Gracchus closed the door behind him. "I gave strict orders I wasn't to be disturbed!"

"Yeah, yeah." Kerickson studied the screens for all he was worth as the file allocation tables came up. Then he looked more closely. HabiTek files were showing an unusual amount

of activity in the financial sector, over seventy percent filled at
the moment. The last time he'd run a check, not more than two
months ago, that sector had had closer to thirty percent usage.

An iron hand clamped down on his shoulder and pulled him
around from behind. "When I ask a question, I expect an answer!" The fingers bit into his flesh.

"Hey, watch it!" Kerickson pulled away and rubbed his
shoulder. "Save the rough stuff for the players who pay for it!"

Gracchus took a fistful of his tunic and yanked him against
his armored chest. "*Who* sent you?"

Kerickson groped for an answer, then remembered the man
who had been there a few minutes earlier—what had Gracchus
called him? "The short guy, you know. He just left."

Gracchus's hold loosened a fraction. "Publius Barbus? That
insipid excuse for a worm doesn't know the first thing about
computers."

"Of course not." Kerickson eased his tunic out of
Gracchus's fist. "That's why *I'm* here." Smoothing the wrinkled material, he tried to look bored. "Now, can I get on with
it, or are you going to waste more of my time?"

The strong-nosed face stared from Kerickson to the Interface, then back again. Gracchus's mouth tightened into a grim,
disapproving line. "I'm overdue at the Palace."

"So?" Kerickson slid back into place before the console and
punched up a new set of stats. "Go on. I can find my way
out." The inside of his tunic was glued to his body by cold
sweat.

"Lock up when you leave," Gracchus said abruptly. "I don't
even allow servants in here."

"Sure thing." He punched another coded request into the
computer and pretended to study the resulting figures. "Good
luck down at the Palace."

Behind him the door opened, then closed.

He collapsed back in the chair, massaging the aching muscles where Gracchus had wrenched his shoulder, then started to
sign off. Just as his fingers touched the keys, though, he hesitated. What about that business in the financial sector? Wilson
had said something about HabiTek being involved with "this,"
too, whatever that meant.

He called up the file allocation tables again, but they were
just a bewildering array of numbers that would take hours to
sort out. "Give me that on hard copy."

A second later a thin sheet of white plas fed out into his

hand. He folded it up and slipped it inside his tunic to read later. Right now, he had to get out before Gracchus came to his senses and checked his story.

He punched off, then left through the outside door into the garden, remembering to close it as Gracchus had demanded. He'd already done enough stupid things for one night. No point in calling any more attention to himself than he already had.

For the tenth time, Juno scored with another lightning bolt, this time hitting the temple floor only a few feet from Amaelia. The lightning split into a million dancing, sizzling sparks that ricocheted around the small room. Amaelia covered her head with both arms, her eyes smarting from the smoke as she crouched in the farthest corner.

"I'M AFRAID THAT WON'T DO YOU A BIT OF GOOD, MY DEAR," a bemused voice said. "I KNOW A KILLING BLOW WHEN I SEE ONE."

"Wh—What?" Amaelia rubbed her burning eyes. Who was that over there on the other side of all that smoke? Not Juno.

"THEY SAY IT'S QUITE NICE IN HADES, THOUGH—SO PEACEFUL, SO SERENE, AND OF COURSE YOU CAN HAVE ALL THE ICE CREAM YOU WANT."

The smoke cleared a little and she got a better look—with those ridiculous winged shoes, that curly golden hair, it could only be Mercury, guider of souls to the Underworld. She raised her Game bracelet, knowing even before she saw it that the status light had gone red—officially dead. "Go away!"

"NOW, DON'T BE LIKE THAT." The oversized young man strode toward her through the drifting smoke, his hand extended. "DEATH IS MERELY A PART OF THE GREAT CIRCLE OF LIFE, NOTHING TO GET UPSET ABOUT. YOU'LL SPEND THE REST OF THE QUARTER BELOW, ONLY A FEW DAYS AT THIS POINT, AND THEN YOU CAN START OVER."

"I don't want to start over!" Amaelia brushed plaster chips off her elbows, then stood up, even though her knees wobbled. "I want to leave the Game!" She tipped her head back, glaring at the invisible computer monitors that had to be there. "What is wrong with you? You're supposed to let me out when I say that!"

"BUT, MY DEAR CHILD, I CAN DO THAT." The tiny white wings on Mercury's heels fluttered.

"Really?"

"CERTAINLY." Mercury twitched at a fold in his gleaming white tunic. "FATHER JUPITER IS QUITE DISTRESSED OVER THIS WHOLE INCIDENT. HE SAID YOU COULD HAVE ANYTHING YOU WANT."

She raised her chin. "What I want—is out!"

"THEN OUT IT WILL BE." He gestured at the cella door. "SHALL WE?"

Gathering the torn folds of her tunic in one hand, she peered onto the portico. The altar fire had gone out. The priest was nowhere in sight. Even the broad expanse of the Forum lay quiet and deserted under the dome's stars. The only visible light came from the corner street lamps and the sacred fires glimmering in the temples across the way.

"QUIET, ISN'T IT?" Mercury walked past her, his body shedding a silvery radiance. "IT'S THE SATURNALIA. EVERYONE IS HOME PREPARING."

Just last year she had looked forward to the Saturnalia, too, with its silly ritual of changing places with the slaves and servants, the expensive little presents, the overall atmosphere of fun and merrymaking. But that had been before her stepmother, Demea, had dedicated her to the Temple of Vesta, and her father had achieved Emperorship—and before his murder.

She suppressed a shiver. The sooner she got out of this crazy place, the better. From now on she was going to live a *real* life among *real* people, none of this childish pretending anymore.

She raised her chin. "All right, I'm ready."

"YOUR LITTER AWAITS."

Down at the foot of the steps that led up to the Temple of Jupiter she saw a black-curtained litter, complete with eight bearers dressed in shimmering black tunics. She glanced back at the god. "I'd rather walk."

"IT'S QUITE FAR." Mercury walked down the sweeping marble steps ahead of her. "AND BESIDES, THOSE ARE THE RULES."

One of the slaves drew back the black velvet curtains, then bowed so low that his dark-haired head nearly swept the street. She sighed. "Oh, all right."

The slaves lowered the litter to the ground. One held her arm as she stepped inside, then drew the curtains again as she sank into a bewildering profusion of oversoft pillows. The litter rose in a smooth, practiced motion, then set off at a steady pace. The bearers' sandalled feet struck the pavement in rhythmic unison.

She'd always hated these things; sometimes the swaying made her seasick, and she would have liked to see where she was going. She steadied herself against the sides and tried to relax, promising herself that this time tomorrow, she would be walking outside under real stars, breathing real air, doing ... real ... things ...

Her eyes drifted shut.

The litter stopped, then lowered to the ground. She roused from a light half sleep and pushed the hair out of her face. "Are we there?"

"INDEED, WE HAVE ARRIVED."

Pushing the curtains aside, she smelled the heavy wetness of water nearby. Were they close to the dome's abbreviated version of the Tiber River? She had loved visiting the rippling water when it shone all silver-black in the simulated starlight. Belatedly, she realized there were some things about the Game she would miss.

A black-garbed bearer extended his callused hand to her, then pulled her out into the chill night air. None of the bearers held a torch, but Mercury's body silvered the rocks and leafless bushes. She looked up into the god's perfectly chiseled face. "Is this the gate?"

"YES."

The ground rumbled suddenly beneath her feet. She jumped back, staring downward.

"THERE IS NOTHING TO FEAR. EVENTUALLY EVERYONE COMES THIS WAY."

The cold wind gusted and she clutched the remnants of her torn cloak around her shoulders. "Where do I go?"

He raised an arm and pointed behind her. "THERE."

Turning, she saw the edge of a cliff, partially obscured by a grove of myrtle trees. At last she was going to escape this lunatic asylum.

"GO FORTH AND CLAIM YOUR DESTINY, AMAELIA, DAUGHTER OF MICIO JULIUS METELLUS." Mercury's voice rang out in the night. "MAY IT BE EVERYTHING YOU DESIRE."

"Well, if it's not," she muttered under her breath, walking

determinedly toward the base of the cliff, "then *I* will fix it. I'm through being pushed around!"

As she approached, the cliff groaned, then split in two and rolled aside, revealing an entrance that sloped downward. She smelled the spicy tang of myrtle as she ducked under the low-hanging trees. Then she hesitated, gazing into a hallway lit by a dim red light that seemed to come from the walls. "Are you sure—" She looked back, but both Mercury and the bearers had gone. She sighed.

Heated air flowed out of the passageway, soft against her face, warming the goose bumps on her bare arms. She stepped inside, then tried not to jump when the doors closed again behind her. She was going *out*, home, really, to a world that she hadn't seen since she was five years old, indeed barely remembered. Really, she thought, there ought to be rules against parents enrolling their minor children. It was one thing for an adult to give his or her life to the Game, but she'd never had a choice.

The walls of the winding hallway were rough, as though they'd been hewn out of solid rock, but warm to the touch, and getting warmer as she walked. Already her hands and face were thawing for the first time since she'd left the Palace.

She followed the twisting path, thinking every bend would bring her to the end, and yet it went on. Sweat dripped down her face as the air grew positively hot. Every step took more and more effort. Finally, she shed her cloak and carried it over her arm. From somewhere up ahead she heard a droning roar. Then the tunnel-like hallway took one more sharp turn and ended unexpectedly in a broad underground gallery. Below, a wild, dark river boiled through a jagged jumble of rocks.

The walls bathed the scene in a lurid red glow. On the river bank beneath her, a single, hunched figure leaned on a long pole beside a boat beached at the edge of the swirling water.

"Well?" the figure shouted up at her in a raspy, dry voice.

Bewildered, she mopped at her sweaty forehead with the back of her hand. "I may have taken a wrong turn somewhere. Could you tell me the way to reach the outside?"

"Outside?" He cackled for a moment, his voice lost in the roar of the river. "Outside, dearie, is a good two hundred feet straight above!"

She closed her eyes, then turned around.

"And where in the name of the Almighty Dark Lord himself do you think you're going?" he demanded in a shrill voice.

"Back," she said, although she was so tired that she didn't feel as though she could walk another step in any direction.

"Back?" He laughed again, making his lumpy shadow dance on the rock. "There is no *back* for the likes of you."

"Oh, really?" A flash of anger surged through her. She squared her shoulders. "We'll just see about that!"

"No, dearie." The ragged figure shuffled closer, leaning hard on the knotted pole. "It's you who will see, once you've crossed the Styx with old Charon."

"SEE?" Pluto drew her closer to the periphery of her new kingdom. "EVEN NOW, THEY COME TO US."

Demea smiled. Her veins thrummed with a power more invigorating than any mere heartbeat. She stared down at the small figure perched above the edge of the dark river. "WHO IS THAT?" she asked, but as soon as she formed the question, the answer streaked into her mind: it was Amaelia, her step-daughter and supposed replacement in the city above—Amaelia, who was to have been Empress in her place.

"DEAD?" she murmured, twining her fingers in Pluto's curly black hair. "HOW INTERESTING."

"AS INTERESTING AS YOU CARE TO MAKE IT, MY HEART."

She called up a ball of raw, crackling power and tossed it from one hand to the other, then absorbed it back into herself, feeling the surge as only a sensuous tickle. "THEN WE SHOULD HAVE A GREAT DEAL OF FUN INDEED."

An air of bewilderment and unease lay over the city as Kerickson walked back to the Temple of Jupiter. Even though the Saturnalia had almost begun, shutters were closed and heads were cast down as players passed each other in the street. Since Mars's earlier rampage, people were afraid.

And well they should be, Kerickson thought. That wasn't supposed to happen. He paused for a moment after crossing the Via Ostiensis, trying to decide on the fastest route back to the Forum. On his right loomed the murky depths of the Subura, home to the lower-class players who either couldn't buy themselves into the Game at a more distinguished level or didn't care to. From what he had seen over the years, many of them played thieves, rogues, and murderers with such relish and abandon that they had obviously found whatever it was they sought in the Game.

But even so, no one had ever been killed for real. He turned away from the Subura's streets with their fake murderers and choreographed thefts. He wouldn't find his answers there.

"DESPAIR NOT, HERO. YOUR ANSWER LIES CLOSE AT HAND."

A small brown owl landed at his feet, staring up at him with wide gray eyes. Minerva again. Kerickson's hands knotted into fists. "Go away before someone sees you!" He stepped around it and crossed the street. "I have to find Amaelia."

The owl fluttered into the air and landed again a few feet ahead of him. "SHE RESTS NOT ABOVE, BUT BELOW, CRUELLY SLAIN BY JUNO'S ANGER."

"Dead?" He stopped, his feet frozen to the cobbled pavement. He should never have left her!

"GAME-DEAD," the owl said, then hopped closer, turning its head to examine him with one bright eye. "SHE HAS GONE TO THE UNDERWORLD. YOU MUST SEEK HER THERE BEFORE IT IS TOO LATE."

Relief flooded through him. "What do you mean, too late?" She ought to be safe enough—the Underworld was only a holding area for players who had been killed. He had been down a number of times himself, when something had needed a bit of tuning up. It was a pleasant enough place, although somewhat on the gloomy side. "No one will hurt her there." Some of the tension seeped from his shoulders. "I'll go after her once I find Micio's murderer."

"SHE IS NOT SAFE." The owl fixed him with an unnerving stare. "EVEN AS WE TARRY HERE, SHE IS IN GRAVE DANGER."

"From what?"

"FROM WHOM." The owl flew up into the branches of a tree and blinked down at him. "SHE HAS FALLEN INTO THE POWER OF ONE WHO HATES HER. SHE MAY NOT SURVIVE TO PLAY AGAIN."

"But—"

"TURN BACK TO THE SPEAR AND CHICKEN." The owl clicked its beak. "SEEK HER BEFORE IT'S TOO LATE."

"The Spear and Chicken?" he asked, but the owl disappeared with a slight pop. He stared around at the closed and darkened shops. If he had his Management Game bracelet, he could have gone down there, but the only way he would be admitted below now was to get killed himself.

The owl reappeared and beat its wings in his face. "THE SPEAR AND CHICKEN, DOLT!" Then it vanished again, leaving behind only the bare tree limbs.

But what in the name of Hades was the Spear and Chicken? Mystified, he tried to remember if he had ever heard of anything by that name before, but nothing came to him. Sighing, he decided to risk the Imperium Directory. Even if it gave his location to the City Guard, he could probably duck into the Subura and hide out.

He looked over his shoulder. The street was deserted, so he punched the silver button on the nearest oak tree. The access panel slid up. "Warning!" the voice said. "Use of this device will result in a loss of one authenticity point."

He held up his Game bracelet to be debited. "Directory Assistance."

The screen brightened into blueness, and the familiar emblem of the Temple of Jupiter appeared. "Imperium Directory. Where may I direct you?"

"The Spear and Chicken." Was it his imagination or did he hear feet running toward him in the night?

"The Spear and Chicken is a disreputable establishment located in the heart of the Subura on Lynching Lane, not recommended for players above the class of freedman or anyone with less than five hit points."

The noise grew louder, sounding ominously like the clack of hobnailed sandals. He punched the button again, severing his contact with the Game computer.

"Halt!" a voice cried behind him. "Halt in the name of the Senate and the people of Rome!"

Down at the end of the street, he saw ten or more of the City Guard jogging toward him in precise formation, their swords drawn and held ready, their scarlet plumes bobbing in rhythm with their feet. Lowering his head, he dashed into the winding, refuse-strewn lane that led into the dark heart of the Subura.

At first he seemed to be leaving them behind. The street, if it could be called by so lofty a name, twisted and turned, too narrow and cluttered for the guards to hold their formation.

He dashed around one corner, then another, turning at random; he could find the Spear and Chicken later, when he was safe. He dodged a small fountain and leaped a pile of smashed crockery, straining for breath as his lungs insisted he was not in as good a shape as he had thought.

He heard the click of boots on pavement, closer this time, as he skidded around another tight corner. His heart thudded. A shout went up behind him. Had he been spotted?

Then someone waved at him from several buildings down, seeming to beckon him to safety. Reeling from exhaustion, he turned, blackness growing behind his eyes. Just as he reached the open doorway, a leg reached out and tripped him.

CHAPTER
FOURTEEN

His head cracked against the door frame, and hands dragged him into a dark room that reeked of onions and garlic. The door slammed, and a second later he heard hobnail sandals clack past.

Someone flipped him over and sat on his chest—he felt a great hulking weight and smelled something like dirty gym socks. "Such a treat to have yourself drop in, sir," a low male voice whispered cheerfully while hands probed the folds and inner pockets of Kerickson's tunic.

"Stop—that!" He struggled, but that only made it harder to breathe.

"Look at this, Bestia, love—silver!" Coins clinked. "And a bit of the bronze as well, but no gold." His captor's tongue clicked disapprovingly.

Kerickson pushed one more time at the suffocating weight on his chest, then let his arms flop to the floor.

"Hello, what have we here?" The man plucked the ivory-hafted dagger from the sheath at Kerickson's waist.

A light flared. "That's lovely, dear." A droopy-jowled woman nodded approvingly. "Put it with the rest of the night's stash. Now ..." She straightened Kerickson's tunic, then wet one fingertip and scrubbed industriously at a smudge above his eye. "I'm sorry about that little crack on the head. Robbery, well, that's just business. You've got to expect a bit of that if you poke your nose into the Subura at night. Man does not live by points alone, you know."

He stared into her round, grandmotherly face, trying to think. There was something ... important ... He had come here for a reason. "The—Spear and—Chicken, is it—far from here?"

"The Spear and Chicken?" Her face twisted as though she'd bitten into a rotten olive. "Mercury above, are you one of *those*?"

He lurched to his feet, then grabbed for the wall as the floor seemed to tilt.

She snatched up her skirts as though he were diseased and backed away. "Get him out of here, Draco! Get him out of my house right now!"

"But, Bestia, my love—"

She crossed her arms. "Now! You know as well as I do what happens to players that get mixed up with *them*."

"Oh, all right." Looping Kerickson's arm over his shoulder, Draco pulled him away from the wall. "But he doesn't look like one of *them*."

Bestia opened the door, peered out into the chill darkness, then beckoned them forward. Draco dragged him to the threshold and tried to thrust him out into the biting night air.

Kerickson caught hold of the door frame. "Which—way?"

"Over there." Draco pointed out a dim glow visible beyond the dark bulk of unlit buildings. "Three streets over, just past the busted fountain of Bacchus—but if you had any sense at all, you'd go home and pull the covers over your head instead." He pried his hands loose and shoved Kerickson across the threshold. "So long, and thanks for the dagger."

The door slammed. Kerickson squinted down the dark street. An unseen cat yowled, then leaped from a roof and pattered away into the darkness. Hands out, he shuffled forward through a sea of discarded wrappers and spoiled vegetables. Two steps later he tripped over a broken wine bottle and landed on a squishy lump that smelled like rotten meat. Trying not to breathe, he scrubbed his hands on his tunic and hurried around the corner. Was this area really as disgusting as it seemed? The filth appeared to be much more authentic than the last time he had ventured into the Subura.

A few moments later he detoured a dark heap in the middle of the narrow street that could have been a fallen body. Then he passed a crumbling dry fountain and caught voices and faint strains of music that fell and rose on the night wind.

He leaned against the weathered brick of an insula apartment building. Mortar crumbled under his weight and he nearly fell. He brushed his arm off, then edged toward the two-story structure at the end of the block. A steady stream of ragged men and women converged on it out of the darkness from all directions. He kept his eyes forward, not daring to look as several people passed him from behind.

"Hurry up!" A hooded figure elbowed him aside. "Barbus is mad enough to eat chariots tonight!"

Kerickson scrambled out of the way as more players plodded on toward what was apparently the Spear and Chicken. The yellow light spilling out from the windows and door into the narrow street seemed to be a beacon for every first-level thief and gladiator and daggerman in the Game. Inside, someone cursed. Laughter echoed into the night.

This didn't look like any legitimate Game scenario he had ever heard of. He looped a fold of his tunic over his head and made his way toward the peeling tavern.

"Come on, move it!" A man gestured impatiently at him from the doorway.

Lowering his head, Kerickson pushed into a crowded interior thick with the stench of unwashed bodies and ripening garbage. The paint was flaking off the walls and the lights were garishly bright. At the other end, a short, stocky man with a pouting lower lip stood on top of the bar, his stumpy legs planted wide in a heroic pose, his arms folded over a stomach that exceeded his belt. "Time is short, and we've got to get it all moved tonight."

Kerickson stared. It was the same man he had seen at Quintus Gracchus's villa earlier—Publius Barbus.

Barbus stared around the room until he had gathered every eye. "Let me catch one of you lazy bastards not pulling your share, and you'll find yourself in need of a new throat!"

A discontented mutter rippled around the room.

"So." Barbus gripped his hands behind his back and strutted down the wine-spattered top of the bar. "Now that we've got that settled, let's get this stuff below before someone comes poking around and finds it. Not only will we not be able to get any more shipments out until the new Emperor is proclaimed, but we've actually had the police inside the dome."

Kerickson ducked down behind a tall, gaunt man dressed as a litter bearer. What sort of shipments were they talking about? Food and supplies were shipped into the dome daily, but as far as he knew, nothing but a few crafts went back out, and what possible difference could a new Emperor make?

"One apiece." Barbus pointed at a pile of gleaming blue plas containers, tumbled haphazardly in the corner. "And don't drop them!"

Muttering again, the crowd of men and women shifted, angling toward the crates. Kerickson flowed with them, trying to make sense of this whole bizarre scene. One by one each person picked up a footlocker-sized crate, hefted it to his or her shoulder, then plodded toward the back of the tavern. When his turn came, he picked one up and found it surprisingly heavy. He grunted as he settled it on his sore shoulder.

"Bloody waste of time, this is!" The tall man in front of him looked back. Kerickson just nodded. The line of people shuffled forward and he moved up with them.

"The name's Hilius." The speaker dropped back until he was almost even with Kerickson. His tunic, formerly fine white linen trimmed with green, was now threadbare and stained, his face lined with weariness, his stringy hair unwashed. "Haven't seen you on this detail before. What do you think of Quintus Gracchus's chances to become Emperor?"

"Pretty good." Kerickson clenched his teeth as he tried to shift the box to his good shoulder.

Hilius nodded. "Mind, that was a class move, marrying the Emperor's daughter, but I fancied one of the generals myself—maybe Lepidus, or that skinny little fellow, Porcius Titus, or even Oppius Catulus himself." He chuckled. "Now there's an old war-horse, if I ever saw one. They say he hasn't lost a legion in the last five quarters!"

Kerickson studied his companion as the line inched forward again. "You sound like you've played for a long time."

Hilius's lips tightened into a thin, straight line. "I almost had enough points to advance to the plebian aristocracy three quarters ago, but that was—" He looked stonily at the solid mass of backs in front of them. "—before."

The crowd moved up again. "Before—what?" Kerickson grunted from under his box.

"Before I was killed."

Kerickson's glance dropped to the status light on the man's bracelet; not red now, but green for the merchant class. He'd obviously had enough time to return to the playing field. "Yeah, that was bad luck, but three quarters is a long time. I bet you have almost enough points to make it that far again."

"You must be freshly killed." Hilius studied him with narrowed eyes. "Or you'd know better."

"Know what?"

"That you can't keep your points." The line shifted forward

another fraction and Hilius moved after it. "Once they get you, all your points belong to them."

"You can squat on this side of the river from now until next year, dearie." Charon's deeply lined face split in a broken-toothed smile. "But there's no going back that way, not for the likes of you."

Amaelia glanced down at her status light, still red, of course. Mercury had tricked her. This wasn't the gate to the outside world; this was the River Styx, bordering the Land of Shades.

"What if I—" She swallowed hard. "—go with you, what then? Can I get out from the other side?"

"That's not for old Charon to say." The old man waggled a skeletal finger at her. "I just rows them over."

Amaelia leaned back against the rocks and tried to think, but the sweltering air pressed in on her until she couldn't breathe. Twisting her long hair into a knot, she lifted it off her sweating neck. Really, she had no choice. Another few minutes and she would pass out in this heat.

Reluctantly, she walked down the steps onto the sweep of hot black sand that led to the rocks where the angry river surged and boiled, dark and oily, not like real water at all.

"Hurry up!" Charon gestured with his pole at her. "You might have been an Emperor's daughter up there." His yellow eyes flicked upward. "But below, you're just another shade, stupid enough to get herself killed, and when you go back you'll be a slave. Get used to it."

Lifting the hem of her long tunic, she crunched across the strangely metallic sand that had to be ruining her slippers with every step. But they probably didn't wear slippers in Hades, she thought—they probably just ran around barefoot and forgot about authenticity until the quarter ended and it came time to play again.

At the edge of the boat she stared up at Charon's face. The bones stood out clearly through the paper-thin, yellow skin. Then she started to step into the boat.

"Not so fast, there." Charon blocked her way with his pole. "Not until I gets my coin."

"Coin?"

"A copper will do, though silver is better, and gold will get you a bit of advice."

"But I—" She searched the inner folds of her tunic, her fingers finding nothing. "I don't have any."

"Then you can't come." He crossed his arms across his ragged smock. "Charon only has to take those what pays their way."

"BOATMAN, LET THE WENCH PASS," a reverberating, somehow familiar, female voice commanded so loudly that it carried above the roaring of the river.

He turned around and stared across the oily, dark water. "But—"

"LET HER PASS, OR FACE THE CONSEQUENCES."

Snatching his battered cap off, Charon bowed his head and muttered, "Friends in low places, eh? Well, that won't get you as far as you might think, dearie. You just waits and see."

She shuddered, then stepped into the ramshackle old boat, seating herself carefully at the farthest end and hoping that she didn't get splinters from the weathered wood. Putting his shoulder to the beached boat, Charon pushed it out into the current and jumped in at the last second, just as the waves sent it spinning toward the nearest boulder.

Amaelia hung onto the sides as the boat dipped and jerked, feeling the water's wild power beneath her feet. This was only another phase of the Game, she told herself. It might seem dangerous, but it couldn't be.

The boat dropped suddenly. She lost her grip and fell hard against the prow as the hot, sulfurous spray drenched her face. At the other end Charon cackled as he thrust his crooked pole deep into the vicious current. "Truth and consequences, dearie, that's the way of life! We all pays the price of what we've done, one way or another!"

She wiped the oily water from her face with her sleeve. "So what crime did you commit to earn this job?"

Something bumped from underneath. Charon leaped from the boat and dragged it up onto the black sand of the opposite shore. "No answers for no pay, dearie." He stood back and leaned on his pole, apparently not the least bit spent for all his effort on the river. "Get out."

"All right, all right!" Struggling up, she climbed out of the boat.

"Gate's there." Charon pointed with his pole at a tall green hexagon set into the rock, twice the height of a man. "Getting in's easy. It's getting out again that's the trick."

She smoothed her hair away from her sweating face. "I can find my way from here."

"Find your way! That's a good one!" Charon leaned on his pole for support as he laughed.

Turning her back on him, she crunched across the black sand toward the gate. A waft of cooler air brushed her face and she walked faster. Something rumbled in the darkness on the other side of the gate, then slithered across the sand. She hesitated.

"SO CLOSE AND YET SO FAR AWAY," the same female voice said. "DON'T THINK YOU CAN AVOID YOUR FATE THAT EASILY."

The sound came again, more like a low growl this time. Amaelia blanched. "What fate?"

Something huge and dark stirred on the other side of the gate. She caught a glimpse of large, misshapen heads and long fangs. "Now, mistresssss, now?" it asked in a chorus of raspy voices, then whined.

"NOT YET, MY PET." The shadowy outline of a huge figure stood by the monstrous shape, one hand resting on its back.

Her heart thudding, Amaelia peered into the dimness just beyond. Three pairs of glowing red eyes stared back at her, set in three heads, all connected to the same body. Three gaping mouths licked their toothy chops.

"When, mistresssss?"

"WHEN I SAY, AND NOT BEFORE."

There was something familiar about that oversized voice, Amaelia thought as her eyes adjusted to the gloom. She had heard it before, and fairly recently.

"COME INTO MY KINGDOM, CHILD, AND LET ME HAVE A LAST LOOK AT YOU," the figure said. "POOR CERBERUS HERE HAS NOT HAD A GOOD MEAL IN DAYS, BUT HE CAN WAIT A FEW MORE MINUTES."

Then Amaelia recognized the voice. "Demea!"

"NOT IN THE FLESH, SO TO SPEAK, BUT CORRECT." The figure moved closer, and Amaelia saw how her stepmother's eyes glittered, dark and dangerous. A shimmering sea of black hair billowed around her head as though it now had a life of its own. "SHALL WE PLAY AWHILE BEFORE YOU DIE?"

When the line of men carrying crates began to descend a winding staircase, Kerickson finally understood what Minerva had been trying to tell him: the Spear and Chicken contained an illicit entrance into the Underworld.

But what possible good could that do? No one *wanted* to go to the Underworld. He could understand someone wanting out of Hades before his or her time had been completed, but this line was headed down. His merchant companion had fallen silent when Kerickson tried to question him about this setup. "You'll find out," he had said morosely, then ignored him.

Kerickson couldn't imagine how any of this could be going on in the Game without him being aware of it. How many years had he worked in the Interface now—six? And never once had he had the slightest hint of another entrance into the Underworld.

The steps wound down and down. He followed the backs in front of him until they reached the bottom and emerged into a large storeroom. Each person stacked his or her crate with the others against the farthest wall, then stood around and stared vacantly into space. Kerickson deposited his crate with the rest and drifted along the wall, looking for a way out. Amaelia was supposed to be down here somewhere. If he could slip out, he might find her.

"You!" a voice rang out. "You there! Just what in the name of Hades do you think you're trying to do?"

"He's new, sir." The merchant bolted from the crowd to seize Kerickson's arm and jerk him back into line. "He doesn't know, that's all."

Publius Barbus shoved between several taller men, then stood before Kerickson, tapping the blue-gray tube of a neuronic buzzer against his thigh. "Going somewhere?"

Kerickson just stared back, amazed at the sight of an illegal outside weapon here in the Game.

"Let me see your bracelet."

When Kerickson didn't move, the merchant grabbed his arm and held it out to Barbus.

"Very interesting. I didn't know that hit points came in halves." Barbus stuffed the buzzer under his arm, then stripped the bracelet from Kerickson's wrist. "This isn't one of ours." He looked around. "Who's responsible for this? This should have been replaced as soon as he hit Hades. Just how long have you been dead, anyway?"

"Not—long."

"We run a tight operation down here." Barbus stuffed the bracelet inside his tunic. "Disobey once and you'll be very sorry. Do it twice and you'll be dead, in every sense of the word. Do I make myself clear?"

Kerickson nodded.

"I—I—" a voice broke in from down the line of men.

"What?" Barbus grasped the buzzer tightly.

"I know him!" An old man in a ragged tunic shuffled forward. "He was the one!"

Barbus cocked his head back, staring impatiently. "The one who what?"

"The one who came around asking all those questions about the Emperor." The slave glared at Kerickson. "The one who killed me!"

"Killed you?" Barbus's lips pulled back over his teeth in a savage smile. "You mean you killed each other?"

"No, sir!" He shook his head. "Just yesterday he was as alive as you are and asking about what didn't concern him!"

"Well, then." Barbus thrust the end of the neuronic buzzer into the soft hollow under Kerickson's chin and pushed his head up. "Maybe we should give him some answers."

CHAPTER
FIFTEEN

"Jeez!" Kerickson jerked his neck back from the deadly chill of the neuronic buzzer. "What is the big deal about a few stupid questions?" Glaring resentfully at Publius Barbus, he rubbed his throat. "I mean, how's a guy supposed to ever make Emperor if he can't ask a question or two?"

His fat-nested eyes glittering like brown marbles, Barbus's pudgy fingers caressed the buzzer tube. "You'd better wise up, moron. You ain't in the damn Game no more."

"Oh." Kerickson dropped his gaze and studied the cracks running across the stark concrete floor.

"But he was asking questions!" The old Bath slave's tattered tunic flapped as he danced around Barbus like an angry terrier. "You said—"

"Shut up!" Barbus thumbed the neuronic buzzer on and swiped at the weathered old face. Tithones jumped away from the tip's lethal green glow, his mouth hanging open and his eyes bright with fear.

Barbus gave him one last sullen glare, then turned back to Kerickson. "You'll be getting one of our bracelets, and you'd better wear it." He thumbed the buzzer back to "off." The lurid greenness died away.

A sigh ran through the assembled work party, and they shuffled closer together. Barbus motioned to a muscle-bound tree of a man wearing the armor and tunic of a Legionary. "That's a wrap for tonight, Marcus. What with the Saturnalia and all, there's too many out and about up on the playing field. Give these idiots their fix and put them away. We'll have to finish tomorrow night."

"All right, you Briton turds!" The Legionary threw his chest

144

out and swaggered through the crowd of drooping men and women. "Fall in and keep your yaps shut."

With a little halfhearted shoving, the players formed a ragged line across the storeroom. Kerickson ducked behind the broad shoulders of a gladiator as the line trickled through a narrow door into a maintenance corridor lit only by sporadic naked bulbs.

Two men ahead, Tithones, the old slave, glared back at him. "Think you're hot stuff, don't you?"

"Look, I didn't mean to kill you!" Kerickson kept his voice down. A fat drop of sweat rolled down his back. "And besides, if I remember correctly, you attacked me, not the other way around."

"You was asking questions—about *him*, about how he *died*!" Tithones darted back along the line until his bald head bobbed just under Kerickson's chin. "You don't fool me for a minute—"

"Shut up back there!" the Legionary shouted.

"Barbus doesn't understand what you was up to, but I'll get through to him." Tithones thrust his gnarled finger at Kerickson's nose. "You just wait. I'll—"

The Legionary's fist crashed into the slave's head. "I said shut up, you old fart!"

Tithones fell to the concrete like a stunned ox.

Kerickson pushed on through the door as the other workers slowed down and turned around to get a better look at the commotion. Several more doors loomed up ahead, the first one open, leaking a pale yellow light into the corridor's gloom, the second closed. He glanced back; everyone had crowded around the angry Legionary and the old man. Barbus was nowhere to be seen.

His heart thudding, he decided to try the second door. All dome locks were keyed to the high-ranking staff; hopefully no one had yet thought to cancel his clearance down here. He placed his palm on the rectangular hand plate and held his breath. After a second it swung silently inward, and he stepped through into warm, humid air, thick with the sweet scent of hyacinths and lilies. A dark gray, starless sky arched overhead, neither night nor day, but a moody approximation of both. Faint strains of solemn music rambled somewhere in the background, almost subliminal.

He shut the door and slipped into the wall of dark green foliage. The fat leaves rustled closed behind him, and his heart rate eased off. The Underworld covered as much space as the entire playing field above. Once he lost himself down here, he would be safe from Barbus's collection of thugs.

Cascades of plants stretched out all around him—philodendron, pink-blossomed oleander, tall white plumeria trees, a rainbow of orchids. He must be in one of the Underworld's gardens, but which one? There were dozens. He sighed and worked his way through the trailing jumble of vines and palm trees and towering live oaks. A dark brown nighthawk burst from a thicket on his left, beating its wings in his face, crying "Peent! Peent!"

Ducking away from it, he broke out onto a cobblestone path before a dark marble fountain. Inviting water sprayed from the mouth of a marble nymph into a circular pool. He suddenly realized how hot and thirsty he was.

Somewhere in the huge, wild garden a nightingale sang, sad and sweet, as he leaned over the pool. The reflection of a bruised and exhausted stranger stared back, one with no job or home, perhaps no future except prison.

He dipped his cupped hands into the clear, cool water and wet his face. Maybe he could stretch out and sleep for a few minutes. He was so tired, he couldn't think.

"ABOUT TIME SOMEONE SHOWED UP," a deeply male, resonant voice said.

"What?" His head jerked around, peering into the overgrown thickets of oleander and ivy.

"I WANT OUT OF THIS DISMALLY BORING RECEPTACLE FOR DEAD MORTALS." Blueness shimmered above the marble nymph's head, then resolved itself into a man, half again as big as a human, with dripping seaweed hair and mournful gray-green eyes. He perched on the statue's back. "I WANT TO RETURN TO THE WORLD OF PLAYERS, AS IS MY RIGHT. BUT I SUPPOSE, LIKE ALL MORTALS, YOU'RE WORTHLESS AND CAN'T DO ANYTHING TO HELP."

"Neptune?" Kerickson said. "But you're not supposed to manifest down here."

"TELL ME ABOUT IT." The god brushed a limp lock of wet green hair out of his face.

Kerickson sat down on the edge of the fountain, pulled off one of his sandals, and plunged his foot into the cool water.

"AREN'T YOU AT LEAST GOING TO WORSHIP ME?" The god rolled his eyes. "YOU KNOW—NEPTUNE, FA-

THER OF WATERS, CALLER OF STORMS, SHAKER OF
SHORES, HEAR MY PRAYER—THAT SORT OF THING."

"It wouldn't do me much good, would it?" Kerickson removed the other sandal, then sank his foot into the soothing
water. "You don't have any power in Hades."

"I NEVER FORGET A FAVOR, YOU KNOW." Neptune
slid down the nymph statue's back and stood with his great
scaly legs ankle-deep in the water.

Kerickson's weary mind struggled to make sense of it—how
had Neptune been exiled down here, and why? He wasn't a
major player in scenarios above; his power was limited to water, and there just wasn't that much of it in the Game beyond
the fountains and an abbreviated version of the Tiber River.
Still—he wriggled his aching toes in the water—Neptune was
a god program, and as such, tied into the main Game computer. "Just how much do you know about what goes on down
here?"

Neptune sniffed. "ENOUGH."

"Could you locate someone for me?"

"NO DOUBT, ALTHOUGH WHY YOU WOULD BE IN-
TERESTED IN ANYTHING THAT GOES ON IN A
GLOOMY PLACE LIKE THIS IS BEYOND ME."

"Then tell me where Amaelia is."

"AMAELIA, DAUGHTER OF MICIO JULIUS METUL-
LUS, FORMER VESTAL VIRGIN, RECENT BRIDE OF
QUINTUS GRACCHUS?"

"Yes!" Kerickson leaped to his feet, sending water flying.

"FOR A MORTAL, THAT GIRL CERTAINLY GETS
AROUND." With a flip of his massive hand, Neptune conjured
up a huge trident, then used it to scratch the back of his green
neck. "SHE SEEMS TO HAVE INCURRED THE WRATH
OF PROSERPINA, QUEEN OF HADES. THEY'RE TAK-
ING HER TO PLUTO'S PALACE."

"Proserpina?" Kerickson tried to think back. Could that be
what Minerva had meant when she'd said that Amaelia had
fallen into the power of one who hated her? He and Wilson
had worked on a program for Pluto's consort, but never had
gotten it quite right, and anyway, Proserpina would have no
reason to hate Amaelia. "It can't be Proserpina. We never in-
stalled her."

"WELL, SHE'S ON-LINE NOW." Neptune shook his head.
"AND I WOULDN'T WANT TO BE IN YOUR AMAELIA'S

SLIPPERS RIGHT NOW, BECAUSE, BOY, IS THE QUEEN
OF HADES EVER IN A LATHER."

"SUCH A PRETTY CHILD." From her vantage point high
above, Demea watched her black-armored minions escort
Amaelia across the deserted stretch of Points Square toward
the gleaming black palace.

"SHE CANNOT COMPARE WITH YOUR BEAUTY, MY
LOVE." Pluto drew nearer, teasing her with his electric touch.
"SHE IS NO MORE THAN A FADING FLOWER, DYING
EVEN AS SHE BLOOMS. WHEN SHE HAS PASSED INTO
DUST, YOU AND I WILL STILL BE HERE, MONARCHS
OF THIS WORLD AND ALL WHO ENTER."

"SHE TRIED TO BE EMPRESS IN MY PLACE!"

"AND FAILED." Pluto's arms drew her against his broad
chest, pulled her face up to his, and crushed her lips in a searing kiss that transcended everything she had known in her
other life. "DEAL WITH HER AS YOU WISH LATER," his
torrid breath murmured into her neck. "DEAL WITH ME
NOW."

She buried her fingers in his thick black hair, then met his
lips, losing herself in his fire. There would be plenty of time
for her stepdaughter later. Let the little wretch cool her heels in
Pluto's dungeons for a while and think that was the worst of
it. Then that would make what was to come all the more hor-
rifying.

The iron door clanged behind her. Amaelia stared at it, seeing her stepmother's angry face again in her mind. It was still
hard to believe—Demea was down here in Hades, and apparently with privileges, too. She'd never heard of such a thing,
but then she'd never heard there were dungeons in the Underworld, either. Yet, here she was, so there was no denying their
existence. The cramped cell with its dank stone walls was exceedingly authentic, except for the faint glow emanated by the
stone ceiling.

Well, all of this was very strange. How had Demea wound
up in Hades? She had disappeared rather mysteriously several
days ago, but there had been no official notice of her death.
Perhaps this was just part of some bizarre Game scenario.
Maybe Demea was supposed to threaten her and then some
hero would come down here and rescue her. They played out
scenarios like that all the time above. Maybe some would-be

Hercules or Marcus Anthony was crashing through all sorts of obstacles right this very moment.

She stared at the pile of moldy hay in one corner and a nasty-looking slops bucket in the other. Somehow, this seemed more realistic than any Game scenario she'd ever participated in, even that disastrous Vestal Virgin affair. And one thing she'd learned from living at the Temple of Vesta: it rarely did a girl any good to wait around for other people to help her out. If she wanted something done and done right, she had better see to it herself.

She sighed, weighing her weariness against her desire to get out of this depressing place. She couldn't even remember the last time she had slept—had it been back at the Palace, in Quintus Gracchus's bed? Well! She squared her shoulders; she wasn't going to think about *that*. Even a dungeon was better than the attentions of that—armored ape! Not that he'd ever showed the slightest interest in her in that way.

At any rate, if she put her mind to it, she ought to be able to get out of this cell. The priests of Vesta had locked her behind ordinary key locks, too, but she'd learned to pick them with a straightened wire from her hair clasp.

She prowled around the tiny cell, looking for something similar to use. The crusted-over bucket caught her eye again. Examining it more closely, she saw that it had a metal handle. Perhaps, if she could detach it, the end would be small enough to pick the lock on her cell door. Wrinkling up her nose at the thought of touching the filthy thing, she began to work it loose.

Kerickson woke with a start. The dim sky arching overhead looked no different than it had when he'd closed his eyes— how long ago? It could have been ten minutes or ten hours or ten days.

"FOOL, THY NAME IS MORTAL," Neptune intoned morosely from his perch atop the nymph statue in the middle of the fountain.

Sitting up, Kerickson brushed white night-jasmine petals off his tunic and looked worriedly around. "What time is it?"

"OR IS IT, 'MORTAL, THY NAME IS FOOL'?" Neptune wrung the water out of his weedy-looking beard. "I CAN NEVER GET THAT STRAIGHT."

"How long was I asleep?" He scrambled to his feet, then grimaced at the protest from his hollow stomach.

"TIME, HOW FLEETING—"

"Put a lid on that stuff, or I'll erase your entire memory bank next time I get into the Interface!" Kerickson ran spread fingers back through his hair. He felt like he'd been through a meat grinder. "Now, what about Amaelia? Is she still in Pluto's palace?"

Neptune sighed. "YES."

"Good." At least, he thought it was good. If she stayed there, he should be able to find her. He stared down at his wavering reflection in the fountain's oval pool. "I could eat a chariot—wheels, horse, and all. Are we close to a food dispensary?"

"WELL ..." Neptune pointed at a slender tree with his trident. "I HAVE HEARD THE POMEGRANATES ARE QUITE NICE DOWN HERE."

"Yeah, right." Kerickson stared up at the little gold-red fruits hanging at least five feet above his head, then went over and shook the tree. Several thumped down onto the grass and he picked one up. "I don't suppose," he said, tearing at the thick skin with his fingernails, "that you know why Publius Barbus has a secret entrance into the Underworld?"

"PUBLIUS BARBUS IS NOT A PLAYER."

Kerickson ripped at the tough rind with his teeth. "What do you mean, he's not a player?"

"HE IS NOT ENROLLED." Neptune watched him for a moment. "MAYBE YOU SHOULD GO TO A FOOD DISPENSARY AFTER ALL. THAT LOOKS DISGUSTING."

"What is he doing on the playing field, then?" Giving up, he squeezed the partially peeled fruit and let the sweet juice dribble down his throat.

"HE HAS MANAGEMENT-LEVEL ACCESS TO THE GAME, BUT NO RECORD OF POINTS."

"Points?" Kerickson remembered the merchant's comment from the night before—something about how they wouldn't let him keep his points anymore. "According to the guy I talked to last night, someone is accruing points that don't belong to him. Just who currently holds the most points in the Game?"

"QUINTUS GRACCHUS."

"And after him?"

"GENERAL OPPIUS CATULUS TRAILS HIM BY A THREE-TO-ONE MARGIN."

Three-to-one ... Kerickson shook his head. That was an almost unheard-of gap between the first- and second-place players. "How long has Gracchus been playing, anyway?"

"FIVE POINT SEVEN MONTHS."

"And Catulus?"

"TWELVE POINT ONE YEARS."

Kerickson kneaded his forehead. "But that doesn't make sense. How could Gracchus become so successful in such a short amount of time?"

"CERTAIN PLAYERS WEAR SPECIAL BRACELETS, AND THE GAME COMPUTER RECORDS THEIR POINTS IN QUINTUS GRACCHUS'S ACCOUNT AS THEY ARE EARNED."

He threw the drained pomegranate aside. "But this sounds like it's been going on for months. I would have noticed something like that in the computer's activity logs. Of course, I wasn't the only programmer, but I'm sure Wilson would have reported an anomaly like that, too, if it had turned up."

"GILES EDWARD WILSON?" Neptune arched a green eyebrow. "ROUND FACE, SQUINTY EYES, LOOKS LIKE A RABBIT?"

"Well, maybe a little," Kerickson admitted. "Why?"

"IF YOU WANT TO KNOW WHAT HE SAW, YOU SHOULD ASK HIM YOURSELF."

"Don't be ridiculous." Kerickson picked up another pomegranate and rubbed it on his tunic. "He's—"

A nebulous shape drifted into the clearing from between two palm trees, its pale blue eyes staring.

"—dead."

"OF COURSE HE'S DEAD. WHO ELSE DO YOU THINK YOU'RE GOING TO FIND IN HADES?"

Kerickson walked all the way around the nearly transparent body. It was Wilson, all right, dressed in the long dark Syrian merchant tunic that he had used for occasions when it had been necessary to actually go out on the playing field.

"Wilson?" His voice came out in a hoarse whisper. "Is that really you?"

"Of course not." The shape looked at him blearily. "So, have you managed to run this place into the ground yet?"

It had to be a personality print. A number of so-called shades had been programmed for Hades from recordings of real people, but Kerickson hadn't known about Wilson using himself. "I—" He closed his mouth and tried to think. "When—were you recorded?"

"So you're going to play it that way, are you?" The shade seated itself on the edge of the fountain and crossed its bony legs. "Not very smart, if you ask me, but of course no one ever does."

Kerickson shook his head; poor old Wilson never had looked good in a tunic.

The shade jiggled its foot. "Talking about recordings and such out here on the field costs you—"

"Yeah, yeah, authenticity points." Kerickson rolled his eyes. "Not exactly a big issue on my mind at the moment. Let's get back to when you were recorded."

"Two months ago." The shade scratched its nonexistent nose. "I came into work one morning while you were out on the field and found an error message from the computer: the entire repository of recorded personalities for the shades had been erased somehow in the night. Hades was unpopulated, except for the few players currently in residence. I immediately had a dozen of myself copied off, then issued orders for everyone who had ever died to report in for rerecording as soon as possible."

"And I was out on the field?" Kerickson couldn't believe he hadn't known about any of this.

"Yes, some nonsense about the Tiber River Adventure." Wilson folded his arms.

Then Kerickson did remember: it had taken him almost a week to repair that ride, which was one of the biggest attractions in the whole Imperium, even if it did cost players two authenticity points for each run. "But why didn't you tell me about the damage when I got back?"

"How should I know?" The shade frowned. "*I* was recorded before you returned. What happened afterward is your problem."

"TALK, TALK, TALK!" Neptune grumbled from the top of the fountain. "AND NOT A SINGLE WORD OF WORSHIP IN THE WHOLE LOT. THAT'S MORTALS FOR YOU."

"Shut up!" Kerickson paced up and down under the pomegranate tree, trying to dig some answers out of his brain. "What do you know about special Game bracelets that record a player's points under a different name?"

"I never heard of such a thing, but—" Wilson sighed. "There were a lot of complaints about this place down in the Subura and—"

"The Spear and Chicken?" Kerickson broke in.

The shade nodded. "And the Gladiatorial School. Things just weren't running right out on the playing field. And the computer was having problems, too, like important programs going down at the worst possible moment and the shade file being erased. I suspected someone was fiddling with the computer at night, when you and I were off-duty."

Could all of this simply be a computer malfunction? Kerickson stared through the image of his old friend. The computer might lose data, or let Mars go beyond his parameters, or even put new programs like Proserpina on-line without authorization—but it couldn't physically walk the playing field to set fire to the Baths or plunge a dagger into Wilson's heart.

Quintus Gracchus, however, was another matter. Gracchus could do any or all of those things—and he had an illegal Interface in his villa.

"It's really boring down here, you know." The shade's voice was resentful.

Kerickson swallowed hard; he had been so overwhelmed with problems that he'd forgotten the sight of Wilson's dead body lying before the Oracle, his blood spreading across the marble like thick red syrup, wood-hafted dagger buried deep in his chest. "I'm—sorry."

"About what?" the shade replied.

"That you were killed."

"Happens to all of you mortals in the end." The shade studied its fingernails. "No concern of mine."

"Yeah, right." Kerickson climbed onto the fountain's rim and tried to see over the wild tangle of overgrown trees and bushes. "Look, I'd love to stay and chat, but I've got to find Amaelia, then get back up above."

"OH, THAT." Neptune slithered down the nymph's back, his damp green hair stringing into his face. "I'M AFRAID THAT SHE'S SCHEDULED FOR TORMENT AND EXECUTION JUST AFTER BREAKFAST."

Kerickson glanced reflexively at his watchless wrist, then swore. "How long do I have?"

"FIVE MINUTES."

CHAPTER
SIXTEEN

Amaelia woke to the sound of footsteps echoing down the stone corridor. She still clutched the bucket's wire handle in her hand so tightly that the flesh had swollen around it. She stirred, then slipped and smacked her head on the stone floor; she'd been using the door for a pillow. "Damnation!" she muttered hoarsely, shocked at how good that word felt on her lips.

The footsteps grew louder every second: two sets of them, not quite in synch, heavy and menacing. She thrust the wire handle into her pocket and began to rub the circulation back into her palm, remembering how she had tried and tried to pick the lock until sleep had crept up on her. Well, they were probably coming to let her out anyway. She stumbled to her feet, staring down at her long gown, still ripped and dirty from that hellish trip across the Styx—not to mention yesterday's fracas at the Temple of Jupiter. Too bad Jupiter had no power in Hades. Her stepmother had made so many threats last night that, despite the obvious drawbacks, even that old scoundrel might be preferable.

The footsteps stopped. A key rattled in the rusty, reluctant lock that had foiled her best efforts, and the door creaked outward. Two black, armored *things* stood there waiting, their faces replaced by screens displaying different scenes from above. On one, several gladiators stood talking in the middle of an arena of dazzling white sand. On the other, slaves lounged on low couches before tables loaded with steaming platters of roast pork and piles of tamarinds and pomegranates, looking quite merry as their patrician masters served them in accordance with the ancient traditions of Saturnalia.

"The Dark Queen summons you," one of the devices said in

a harsh metallic voice through a speaker grille in its neck. "Come with us."

She followed the first one out into the narrow passage, then up a dank, winding set of stone steps. The other guard boxed her in from behind. At the top of the stairs she paused at a rampart to look down on the overgrown gardens encroaching upon the palace like a dark army. Above, the slate-gray sky was caught permanently at dusk. The breeze gusted, heavy with the scent of jasmine. A sense of emptiness pressed in upon her, as though she were the only living soul in this whole murky place.

"This way." One of the faceless guards pulled her away from the ramparts with relentless metal fingers. She flinched away from its chill touch and walked between them as though they were two poles and she were a magnet suspended in the middle. They entered another door and started down a sweep of twisting stairs. Somewhere ahead a woman laughed, low and husky and throbbing.

With a final turn, they entered a huge round room open to the twilit sky. Two immense, gleaming thrones of obsidian sat empty and waiting. The guard devices thrust her into the center of a polished floor blacker than the inside of a hole, then posted themselves along the curving wall.

"Demea?" Amaelia rotated, looking for her stepmother. "What do you want?" Her voice lost itself in the vastness of the great room. Overhead, a nighthawk swooped low over the open roof, then twitched its wings and disappeared back into the gloom.

She put her hands on her hips. "Look, just tell me what you want!"

"WANT?" The voice shrilled from a dozen places, transformed into something magnificent and ringing, altogether bigger than life. "YOU TRY TO STEAL MY PLACE AS EMPRESS, AND YOU DON'T KNOW WHAT *I* WANT?"

"Steal your place?" Amaelia frowned. "The only thing I did was resign."

"OF COURSE YOU SAY THAT NOW."

"Oh, come on, you're not talking about all that nonsense about marrying Quintus Gracchus?" Amaelia edged backward, her eyes searching the throne room. "That wasn't my idea. The last thing I ever wanted was to be Empress."

"IN HADES, ALL YOUR SINS ARE KNOWN, AND

YOU MUST NOW ANSWER TO EACH AND EVERY ONE."

"Now, listen here, Demea—"

As though heated, the air shimmered in front of the pair of black-glass thrones. "THAT NAME IS FROM ANOTHER LIFE, NOW LEFT BEHIND FOREVER." The distortion solidified into the tall form of a woman arrayed in a shining, pure black gown that bared her flawless neck and shoulders. She put a hand to her hair and settled gracefully into the right-hand throne. "YOU MAY ADDRESS ME AS PROSER-PINA."

"But—" Amaelia stared at the transformed woman; light glinted from her white, white shoulders and intricately coiffed black hair. "Proserpina is a—*goddess*. No one *plays* the gods."

"I PLAY AT NOTHING!" Demea's arm swept toward the sky.

Thunder cracked. A hurricane blasted Amaelia to the floor. Icy rain sheeted down until she couldn't breathe.

"I AM PROSERPINA, QUEEN OF HADES!"

Soaked and shivering, Amaelia covered her head with her arms. She didn't have the faintest idea how to play this; it was certainly nothing like any Game scenario she had ever seen.

A second blueness wavered beside Demea, forming a huge man with long, tumbled black hair and piercing black eyes. Almost in slow motion, he tossed a shimmering black cloak off his shoulders, his strong-boned face indifferent. "YOUR JUDGMENT ON THIS WORTHLESS SHADE, MY LOVE?"

"SHE IS GUILTY OF BROKEN VOWS WITH OUR SIS-TER ABOVE, VESTA, AS WELL AS ENVY AND THEFT."

Murmuring voices filled the room. As Amaelia turned, a sea of ghostly figures drifted into the throne room, their translucent faces all looking at her. "Guilty!" they said in wispy, half-there voices. "Sullen, ungrateful wretch! She had it all and threw it away!"

The dark man leaned back against his obsidian throne, his full lips curved in a sensuous smile. "YOUR SENTENCE?"

Demea rose and stepped forward, her black gown trailing like the tail of a shining snake. "TORTURE, I THINK—FOR AS LONG AS SHE LASTS. THAT WON'T BE LONG ENOUGH, OF COURSE. THERE NEVER WAS MUCH BOTTOM TO THIS BIT OF FLUFF."

Feeling like a rabbit caught under a descending airhopper, Amaelia stared into her stepmother's eyes, transfixed by the raw power there. How had Demea managed all of this? No one was ever allowed to play a goddess. She, who had practically been born into this game, knew that as well as anyone else. "Torture?" She made herself nod. "Well—"

She bolted for the door. Both guard devices moved to intercept her, but she pulled the wire out of her pocket and buried it deep in the first one's speaker grille. It staggered for a second, the picture on its screen flickering, then toppled to the floor.

The second one, however, snagged her by the arm and held her so tightly that she sank to her knees with a moan.

"ENOUGH!" Proserpina's thunderous voice filled the room, so loud that Amaelia gasped with pain. "YOU HAVE DEFIED ME FOR THE LAST T—"

"Alline?" a man's voice cried. "Is that you?"

Amaelia glanced up through tear-blurred eyes. A man stood in the doorway, wearing the tattered remains of a tunic. His build was slight, his hair an undistinguished sandy-blond, his face unassuming, but tense. Her heart gave a leap; it was Gaius!

His eyes, though, were only for her stepmother. "Alline, what are you doing down here in Hades?"

"ONE MIGHT ASK THE SAME OF YOU." The corners of Demea's mouth quirked upward as she laid one hand on Pluto's shoulder.

Amaelia looked back at her stepmother. The two of them obviously knew each other, but how?

"It's all right, Amaelia. Don't be afraid." Looking grim, Gaius took a step toward her. "No one's going to hurt you."

"YOU THINK NOT, ARVID?" The Dark Queen glided into the gleaming black circle, her lips twisted into a tight, red smile. "THEN PERHAPS YOU SHOULD THINK AGAIN." She motioned with one crimson-nailed hand, and the black guard tightened its grip on Amaelia's upper arm until her head swam from the pain.

Gaius paled. "Stop that!" Then he looked at the mechanical guard. "Code four-A override!"

Amaelia felt it stiffen. Twisting and squirming, she managed to pry herself out of the now motionless fingers. Gaius pushed her behind him. "How did you do that?" she whispered.

"HE'S A PROGRAMMER, IDIOT, ONE OF THE REAL GODS OF THIS WORLD—OR AT LEAST HE WAS WHEN HE SAT UP THERE IN THE INTERFACE, SO HIGH AND

MIGHTY, PLAYING WITH YOUR FATE AND MINE AS THOUGH HE HAD EVERY RIGHT." With each step, Proserpina grew taller. "AS THOUGH HE CARED."

"I did care." The man Amaelia knew as Gaius seemed unable to take his eyes off Proserpina's crackling black eyes and bloodred lips. "I gave you everything you asked. I even let you go because that was what you asked, not what I wanted."

"AND WHAT DO YOU WANT NOW, MORTAL?" Like a great cat studying its prey, she tilted her head to one side. "ACCORDING TO THE COMPUTER, YOU WERE DISMISSED FROM THE STAFF AND ESCORTED FROM THE GAME. YOU'RE NOT ENROLLED. IN FACT, AS FAR AS THE COMPUTER IS CONCERNED, YOU DON'T EVEN EXIST." She trailed her fingers across the snowy column of her throat. "PERHAPS YOU'VE COME ALL THE WAY TO HADES JUST TO BEG MY FAVORS ONE LAST TIME."

Amaelia's stomach tightened. Gaius was staring at Proserpina as though she were an expensive work of art and he was the prospective buyer. Amaelia stepped forward to stand between them. "As a matter of fact, he came for me."

"FOR YOU, TWIT?" Proserpina's laughter rolled through the audience room like thunder.

Gaius seemed to shake himself. Then he took Amaelia's arm, his fingers warm as sunlight on her rain-chilled skin. "Well, actually, I did."

"OH, BUT LOOK AT HER BRACELET." Proserpina turned back to her black-garbed consort. "THE BRAT IS DEAD, AND THEREFORE, MINE."

The King of the Dead stood up, threw back his star-studded cloak and crossed his muscular arms across his chest. Their misty faces rapt, the crowd of shades pointed and murmured among themselves.

"HOW CAME YOU HERE?" Pluto's wild, dark eyes smoldered across the throne room at Gaius. "THE GUARDIAN OF THE GATE, CERBERUS, DID NOT REPORT YOUR PASSAGE, NOR DOES THE COMPUTER KNOW YOU. WHAT SORT OF PLAYER IS IT THAT WEARS NO BRACELET?"

"One that comes to rectify a mistake." Gaius's arm pulled Amaelia closer to his side. "You see, this player's enrollment has been canceled, but through some foul-up, she wound up down here instead. She must leave the playing field immediately."

"NO!" Proserpina tossed her head back and increased her

size until her head brushed the open sky above. "SHE ONLY WANTS TO TAKE MY PLACE WITH YOU, JUST AS SHE THOUGHT TO TAKE MY PLACE AS EMPRESS!"

"AND WHAT IS IT TO YOU IF SHE DOES?" Pluto's intense gaze transferred to her, and he too grew until he equaled her size.

"Well, Pluto, old boy—" Towing Amaelia, Gaius edged toward the door. "—it's just that Proserpina, here, used to be married to me."

Amaelia shuddered as Gaius dragged her straight through the nebulous crowd of shades.

"I mean, what can I say?" Gaius winked. "I guess, in spite of everything, those old fires are still burning."

"THEY ARE NOT!" Proserpina extended one arm toward the door. It swung shut with a hollow clang. "BUT I WILL NOT BE CHEATED OF MY REVENGE. I HAD TO PUT UP WITH THIS CLINGING, WHINING BRAT FOR YEARS AFTER I MARRIED MICIO, AND NOW SHE HAS THE UNMITIGATED GALL TO TRY AND TAKE MY PLACE!"

"You had to put up with me?" Amaelia struggled to free her wrist from Gaius's grip. "My father and I were doing just fine before you pushed your way into our lives! If it weren't for you, he'd probably still be alive right now!"

"YOUR FATHER COULDN'T HAVE MADE ENOUGH POINTS TO PLAY CHIEF EUNUCH WITHOUT MY GUIDANCE!"

"STOP!" Pluto's enhanced voice thundered through the chamber until the floor quivered and Amaelia swayed, almost too dizzy to stand. He seized Proserpina's shoulders and blue electricity crawled over their two huge bodies. "YOUR OLD LIFE HAS PASSED AWAY AS THOUGH IT NEVER EXISTED. THERE IS ONLY NOW AND TOMORROW, NOTHING MORE. I FORBID YOU TO THINK ABOUT YOUR MISERABLE MORTAL EXISTENCE EVER AGAIN!"

Proserpina writhed within his grasp. "YOU FORBID—" Then she stiffened, her head arching back, her black eyes staring.

Pluto looked down at Amaelia and Gaius. "GO, AND WALK THIS DARK REALM NO MORE!"

The door swung open. Without another word, Gaius pulled her through it and into the long, dark hall.

* * *

There were limits to her new powers; the realization flooded through her like a bitter black river. Even she, a goddess, could still be overridden!

"LET—ME—GO!" She longed to smash his proud dark face into a thousand million pieces.

"I AM YOUR LORD!" Pluto buried his fingers in the plaits of her hair. "LONG DID I WAIT WHILE YOU DALLIED WITH OTHER, LESSER BEINGS, BUT UNDERSTAND THIS—I WILL WAIT NO LONGER!"

"I DON'T WANT HIM!" Even as she tried to resist it, Pluto's touch stirred her. "I ONLY WANT THE GIRL."

"THAT LITTLE SNIPPET?" His finger traced the line of her jaw with a fire that made itself felt all the way down to her toes. "SHE IS NOTHING, EVEN LESS THAN THE DUST BENEATH YOUR FEET. FORGET HER AND THINK ONLY OF ME."

Without even meaning to, her arms reached out. He was the flash of lightning and the heady, sweet scent of jasmine, the deafening roar of a waterfall, but . . .

She gave herself up to him, knowing that she would not forget. Her time would come later.

"Wait!" Amaelia dragged at Kerickson's arm, her face pale except for two red-cherry dots that danced in her cheeks.

Letting her pull him to a stop in the middle of an oleander thicket, he shook his head, almost as breathless as she was. "Okay—for a few minutes—but we've got to get out of here."

"Do—" she began, then coughed. She rubbed at her forehead. "Do you know the way back from here?"

"Well, yes—" He thought of the strange rooms underneath the Spear and Chicken Inn, and the neuronic buzzer. "—and no. We can't go back that way."

Eyes closed, she leaned her head back against the leathery leaves, trying to get her breath. "Cerberus guards the way out. Do you think we can get past him?"

He glanced down at his bare wrist. "I'm not an official shade. Maybe that will do the trick."

"Maybe." She sat back up and looked around the junglelike garden. "Anyway, I can't believe you came all the way down here just to find me."

"Well—" He felt his face go volcano-hot. "I—I was worried about you, after that little bit of trouble with Jupiter, I mean."

"Yes, Jupiter." Her eyes narrowed. "That was all your idea, wasn't it?"

"I—guess." He scratched his head. "But it got rid of Mars, didn't it?"

Her lips tightened. "And got me killed."

He smiled thinly, wondering why women were never—ever—satisfied. "Do you feel up to—"

"NO, NO, YOU'RE HANDLING THIS ALL WRONG!" a throaty female voice exclaimed from above. "THE POOR GIRL'S ALREADY BEEN THROUGH ENOUGH TORTURE FOR ONE DAY. QUIT TRYING TO TALK HER EARS OFF AND KISS HER!"

"What?" Amaelia looked up into a huge live oak whose limbs spread over them like a canopy.

"OH, LEAVE THEM ALONE," a different female voice said, younger, lighter. "SOME RELATIONSHIPS ARE MEANT TO BE COOL AND INTELLECTUAL."

Kerickson pulled Amaelia to her feet. "Let's get out of here," he whispered.

"NOT SO FAST THERE, SONNY." Blueness wavered on one dangling limb, then became a buxom woman dressed in long, low-cut robes of dazzling white. "THAT WAS A VERY ROMANTIC THING YOU DID, CHASING DOWN HERE AFTER THE WOMAN OF YOUR DREAMS."

"Not—really." He looked at the goddess more closely, seeing the ivory complexion, the golden girdle, and the doves perched on each bare shoulder—it was Venus, Goddess of Love. "You're not supposed—"

"TO BE DOWN HERE." The goddess twined a strand of her sun-gold hair around one finger. "TELL ME ABOUT IT."

"DON'T BOTHER." A second blueness sparkled beside Venus, then solidified into a slim young girl clad in a short tunic embroidered in silver with the phases of the moon. "I'M SURE SHE FEELS QUITE SORRY ENOUGH FOR HERSELF WITHOUT ANY HELP FROM YOU."

He noted the stout bow slung across her shoulder—Diana, the Virgin Huntress. He looked at Amaelia. "Someone must be going crazy up there in the Interface."

Diana leaped lightly to the ground. "FOR A MAN WHO'S SUPPOSED TO BE ESCAPING, YOU'RE CERTAINLY DOING A LOT OF SITTING AROUND. DON'T YOU THINK YOU HAD BETTER GET ON WITH IT?"

"DON'T LISTEN TO HER." Stepping off the branch, Venus floated down to the overgrown grass. "THIS—TOMBOY HAS NO POETRY IN HER SOUL, NO ROMANCE, NO SAVOIR FAIRE, IF YOU CATCH MY DRIFT. I'M SURE IF YOU JUST GIVE THIS LOVELY GIRL A KISS, SOMETHING INTERESTING WILL DEVELOP."

"IS THAT ALL YOU EVER THINK ABOUT?" Diana shook her head. "THEIR LIVES ARE AT STAKE."

Venus frowned, then motioned Kerickson closer. "I'M AFRAID YOU'LL HAVE TO FORGIVE DIANA," she said in a low voice. "WITH HER, IT'S NOTHING BUT STAGHOUNDS AND ARROWS, DAY IN AND DAY OUT." She winked cheerfully. "I MEAN, JUST LOOK AT HER; IT'S OBVIOUS THE POOR GIRL NEVER GETS ANY!"

"Yes, well." Kerickson seized Amaelia's arm. "It's been great chatting with you both, but we really have to run now."

"IT WON'T DO A BIT OF GOOD, YOU KNOW. CERBERUS MIGHT WELL IGNORE YOU, BUT—" Venus smiled fondly at Amaelia. "—HE'LL TEAR *HER* TO BLOODY SHREDS. HE'S NOT GOING TO LET A BONA FIDE SHADE ESCAPE FROM HADES. THE TWO OF YOU MIGHT AS WELL ENJOY YOURSELVES. I SAW A LOVELY LITTLE BOWER OF MOSS JUST THE OTHER SIDE OF THAT PALM TREE OVER THERE—"

"THERE IS A WAY." Diana elbowed the other goddess aside. "IF YOU HAVE THE HEART FOR IT."

"How?" Amaelia asked.

"THERE WAS ONE OCCASION WHEN CERBERUS DID ALLOW A SHADE TO LEAVE HADES."

"OH, WELL, THAT WAS DIFFERENT." Venus sniffed. "THAT BOY REALLY HAD WHAT IT TAKES. YOU CAN'T EXPECT OUR HANDSOME YOUNG FRIEND HERE TO TRY *THAT*."

"WHY NOT?" Diana's gray-eyed gaze swung to Amaelia.

"Try what?" Amaelia asked.

Diana's tanned face regarded her soberly. "HE MUST SING TO THE THREE-HEADED BEAST. IT HAS BEEN DONE BEFORE."

"AND JUST LOOK WHERE IT GOT *HIM*." Venus crossed her arms. "TORN INTO TINY, QUIVERING PIECES, PARTS OF HIM SCATTERED HERE, PARTS THERE, AND HIM SO WELL PUT TOGETHER, TOO. SUCH A WASTE OF A PERFECTLY GOOD MAN-FLESH, EVEN IF HE WAS MORTAL."

"WELL, IT WAS HIS OWN FAULT. HE DIDN'T FOLLOW INSTRUCTIONS." Diana grimaced.

"Sing?" Kerickson suddenly realized that they were speaking about him. "But I can't even carry a tune."

"THAT'S WHAT I HATE MOST ABOUT BEING TRAPPED DOWN HERE!" Diana stamped her sandalled foot. "NOTHING BUT DOOM AND GLOOM ALL THE TIME! DON'T YOU HAVE ANY SENSE OF ADVENTURE, ANY FIGHTING SPIRIT?"

"UH-OH." Venus's creamy face turned a delicate pink. "I THINK YOUR TIME IS UP, KIDS."

Kerickson looked over his shoulder. In the distance he could see several large, black, shiny things trampling straight toward them through thickets of honeysuckle and jasmine.

"WHAT EXACTLY DID PLUTO TELL YOU?" Diana asked.

"Something like 'Go and walk this dark realm no more,' " Kerickson said weakly.

"THEN MIGHT I SUGGEST THAT YOU GET ON WITH IT?" Diana gestured at the approaching armored figures. "UNLESS YOU FANCY MEETING HIS PERSONAL BLACK GUARD UNDER LESS THAN PLEASANT CIRCUMSTANCES."

CHAPTER
SEVENTEEN

An hour later Kerickson glanced back over his shoulder for the hundredth time, but fortunately the black guards seemed to be slow movers, although extremely steady. The devices fell behind as he and Amaelia descended into the narrow gorge that formed the boundary of the far edge of Hades.

About halfway down the winding trail, Amaelia pointed out a wooden bridge spanning the dark, oily river about fifty feet below. "That way."

"Are you sure?" He was disoriented; although he'd made routine repair runs down to the Underworld, he'd never approached the River Styx from this direction.

"I remember that bridge, and besides—" She wiped at the sheen of perspiration on her face. "—it's getting hotter fast."

"What does that mean?"

Her mouth tightened. "You'll see."

The trail zigzagged back and forth across the steep gorge wall like an undecided snake. Just before they reached the bottom, Kerickson snagged his toe on a rock, then bit back curses while he hopped on the other leg.

"Shh!" A furrow appeared between Amaelia's brows. "It will hear you!"

A spinning rock bounced down the rocky slope, careening from side to side, narrowly missing them at the bottom. Still cradling his aching toe, Kerickson looked up and saw two shiny black figures at the top of the gorge. "I don't think that will matter if we don't hurry!"

He pulled her across the rough, wooden bridge, then stopped before a sheer wall of red-orange rock.

"The opening's got to be here somewhere." Turning away,

Amaelia trailed her fingers over the rough, unbroken cliff. "Maybe there's a button or a lever."

Or maybe it could only be opened from the other side, Kerickson thought. Shades weren't supposed to go back this way. He wished he could remember how the players' gate into the Underworld operated.

Limping after her, he tapped the rocks with his knuckles. Did the gate perhaps operate on a voice code instead of a manual trigger? And was Amaelia even right about the location, or had she missed the place altogether? Downstream, he could see that the river widened, then disappeared into another sheer rock wall. Upstream, the dark, slimy-looking water cascaded down from an opening at least twenty feet above their heads. The gate had to be here. There was simply no place else to look.

He could hear the black guards' footsteps now, heavy and deliberate. He looked back up the trail. They had improved their rate of descent by ignoring the trail altogether; they had simply leaned back and marched straight downhill, their massive weights providing a counterbalance. Kerickson swore again, this time not quite under his breath. He and Wilson had worked on the black guards together. Hadn't it been his idea to program a certain level of problem-solving ability in that class of robots?

A small voice in the back of his mind whispered that it had.

A clumping black guard's foot dislodged another rock, fist-sized this time. It struck the cliff a few feet from Amaelia with a loud crack, then showered them both with slivers.

He brushed rock chips out of his hair. "For Minerva's sake, Amaelia, hurry up!"

"I—" Her arm disappeared up to the elbow into the grainy red-orange rock. "—am!" She pulled it out. "Here! It's covered with a holo. Come on!" She pushed through the rock wall and disappeared.

Closing his eyes, he plunged after her.

"Welll, nowwww," a raspy chorus said. "Whattt havvve weee herrre, selvesss—dinnerrr or desserttt?"

Kerickson opened his eyes to find a slavering, scaly snout only inches from his own nose. He jerked sideways and cracked his head against the rock wall.

"G-Gaius?" Amaelia quavered.

His head aching, he tried to focus through his watering eyes. Amaelia was pinned to the ground by a wickedly clawed, green-scaled foreleg. He edged away, well aware that Cerberus, unlike the gods and many of the other special effects, was not a hologram. The original designers of HabiTek had ordered up a mechanical for this particular role, wanting something more substantial and dramatic for the "deceased" player's entrance into Hades.

He fingered the rapidly swelling knot on the back of his head and tried to think. Like all the gods and robots used in the Game, Cerberus had originally been programmed not to hurt players, but that had been before things had started to go wrong in a big way. Proserpina, Queen of Hades, was not supposed to be on-line either, and certainly not programmed with what seemed to be a personality print of his ex-wife. Very little in the Game was as it should be anymore.

"Cerberus," he said with more confidence than he felt, "this is a code four-A override. Let her go!"

One of the grinning heads howled, while the other two stared into each other's eyes and laughed. "Interacttt threeee pointtt onnne! Howww quainttt!"

"Three point one?" Stooping down, he reached for Amaelia's arm just a few feet away, but the red-eyed head on the left snapped at him, spattering his arm with realistically hot dog drool.

"We'vvve beennn upgradeddd, foolll." The middle head winked at him. "Weee don'ttt runnn onnn thattt obsoleeete versionnn offf theee sacreddd languaggge anymorrre!"

"Gaius!" Amaelia whispered up at him from the ground. "Sing to it!"

"What?" He wiped his arm off on his toga. "Oh—yeah." He grimaced, remembering that his voice was so bad, he didn't even sing in the privacy of the 'fresher. "Uh, why don't you sing?"

She opened her mouth, then grunted as the three-headed dog shifted its massive weight and forced the air from her lungs. "Singgg, yourselfff, mortalll, ittt mighttt beee amusinggg."

"S-Sure." He wiped at the sweat on his forehead. "What would you—like?"

The right-hand head licked its yellow fangs. "Surrrprise usss."

He opened his mouth to sing something—anything—but unfortunately his mind was as blank as if he'd never sung a note in his whole life.

"We'rrre waitinggg!" the three heads said in unison. The

middle one twined its snaky neck downward and gave Amaelia's face a slobbery lick. She writhed.

Sing ... he had to sing. Music to soothe the three-headed beast, Diana had said to him. What would soothe a creature like Cerberus? He felt like a child again, standing in front of the whole class, his lessons forgotten, nothing but silly rhymes running through his head. Silly rhymes ... and songs ... He had known a few silly childhood songs.

Wetting his lips, he began to sing in a nervous, weedy voice, much too high. "One hundred bottles of beer on the wall, one hundred bottles of beer—"

"Beerrr? Whattt isss beerrr?" All three heads turned to him, the six red eyes staring.

"Take one down, pass it around, ninety-nine bottles of—" He thought hard. "—*wine* on the wall."

The heads wove back and forth with the beat as he picked up speed. "Ninety-nine bottles of wine on the wall, ninety-nine bottles of wine!"

The six blood-red eyes sagged. He continued, working his way down through the choruses to eighty-five. Then, still singing, he crouched down and took Amaelia's hand.

Her fingers moved in his, and she crawled toward him. The central head opened its eyes again and snarled at him. He leaned back with all his weight and belted out, "Take one down and pass it around, *eighty-four* bottles of wine on the wall!" He dug in his heels and pulled. "Eighty-four bottles of—come on!—wine on the—" With a rip, she slid out from under the beast, leaving her skirt behind, and fell on top of him in the metallic black sand.

For a moment they both lay there, speechless and exhausted. Then Cerberus shook itself and howled a great reverberating cry of rage, and Kerickson pushed Amaelia up. "Come on! I don't think his parameters allow him to leave the gate!"

Slogging wearily across the sweltering black beach, they dodged boulders until they reached the shore of the thundering, sulfurous Styx. Amaelia sank to her knees, gazing mournfully across to the other side. For a moment he didn't understand; then it hit him, too.

Charon and his ferry were on the opposite shore.

It took a full half day before Demea deemed her god-husband sufficiently distracted by his daily inspection of his realm to risk contacting Publius Barbus and instruct him to meet her in the overgrown palace gardens.

Manifesting in her only slightly larger than life-size form, she arrayed herself in a gown of glittering black stars and wandered through a grove of vine-choked willow trees and rambling, untended azalea bushes. A dark, bitter flood of anger rose in her throat. What good was it to play Proserpina, Queen of Hades, if she couldn't do exactly as she pleased? Supreme power was the whole point of becoming a goddess. What right did Pluto have to deny her anything?

"You sent for me, your ladyness?" a rough-edged voice asked from behind her.

Turning around, she met the mean little pinpoint eyes of Publius Barbus. "YOU WILL NOT ADDRESS ME IN THAT CRUDE AND FAMILIAR MANNER!"

"Taking on airs, eh?" Barbus rasped his fingers over his scruffy beard, then chuckled. "Well, I suppose you're entitled. It's not every broad what can work her way up to goddess!"

Her height increased without her even thinking about it, so that she found herself staring down through the leafy treetops at his insectlike body. "I HAVE A TASK FOR YOU."

Barbus plopped down on the ground and pulled a sandwich out of his pocket. "Well, I suppose we might be able to work something out, just for old times' sake. What's your best offer?"

"NOT TO TAKE YOUR WORTHLESS, WORMY LIFE!" She summoned a ball of crackling power and cradled it in one hand. "I WANT TO DISPOSE OF SEVERAL PEOPLE ABOVE, BUT AS PROSERPINA, I CAN NO LONGER GO THERE MYSELF."

He took a bite and chewed thoughtfully. "Disposals don't come cheap, you know. How are you going to pay me?"

She had to think for a moment—she no longer possessed anything of a material nature. Then she had it. "MICIO'S BUSINESS, WHATEVER IT WAS—YOU CAN HAVE IT ALL. I HAVE NO NEED OF IT NOW."

"That?" He waved the sandwich at her. "The moment I turned you over to old Dark and Gloomy, it was mine. He promised me that much up front."

"PLUTO PROMISED YOU MICIO'S BUSINESS IF YOU BROUGHT ME TO HIM?"

"That's right, Queenie—lock, stock, and laser, plus free run

of the Dark Kingdom anytime I want." He stuffed the last of
the sandwich in his mouth.

She had been sold, like a leg of lamb or an airhopper. The
idea staggered her so much that she lost her concentration and
the ball of power in her hands fizzled away to nothing. She
shrank to normal size before she noticed.

"Now don't go getting yourself all in a tizzy." Barbus
brushed the crumbs off his hands. "It's not like you was cut
out for a life of crime, anyway. Admit it, you didn't really
have the faintest idea what his formerness, the Emperor, was
up to. There's no reason for a classy dame like you to get your
hands dirty with smuggling and point-stealing and the like.
You just stay down here and leave the nuts and bolts to old
Publius Barbus."

"I NEED YOUR HELP ON THIS ONE SMALL MAT-
TER." She crossed her arms. "THEN WE CAN CONSIDER
OURSELVES EVEN. I WANT ARVID KERICKSON AND
AMAELIA METULLUS DEAD, IN ANY SENSE YOU CAN
CONTRIVE."

"Who?"

"ARVID KERICKSON, MY EX-HUSBAND." She con-
jured a holo image from the computer's files and displayed it
for Barbus: an old file recording from one of Arvid's many
trips out on the playing field. Dressed in the uniform of the
Praetorian Guard, he looked rather more dashing than she remembered.

"You know, I seen him before." Barbus walked around the
image, scratching his head. "Yesterday, in the work crew. He
was causing some kind of commotion and had the wrong kind
of bracelet."

"WELL, YOU SHOULD HAVE KEPT BETTER TRACK
OF HIM." Watching Arvid's holo marching down the Via
Ostiensis, she felt cold fury running through her veins. "HE
WAS ONE OF HABITEK'S PROGRAMMERS, SO HE
KNOWS THINGS ABOUT THE IMPERIUM NO ONE
ELSE UNDERSTANDS."

"A programmer? Then what's he doing in the Game?" He
shook his head. "You know, this is weird. If he was in my
work gang, then he shouldn't be able to stay away from the
Spear and Chicken. In a few more hours he should be there on
his knees, begging for another fix."

When the file image ran out, she summoned another, this

time Arvid standing in the throne room with that disgusting bimbo, Amaelia, at his side.

Barbus whistled. "Is that the babe you was talking about? I'd keep her company any time."

"DO ANYTHING YOU LIKE WITH THE NASTY LITTLE BRAT, AS LONG AS YOU GET RID OF HER."

"You want her dead, huh?" He squinted at the image of the slender, red-haired girl. "Hey, ain't that the same she-male Quintus Gracchus is tearing apart the whole dome to find?"

"QUINTUS GRACCHUS?" She tapped a long, poppy-red fingernail against her chin, thinking. Yes, that made sense. Since that Praetorian idiot had married Amaelia to legitimize his claim as Emperor, he must be looking for her. "PUBLIUS BARBUS, DO YOU KNOW HOW AMAELIA WAS KILLED?"

"Oh, yeah, that story was all over the Imperium this morning." Barbus grinned. "You see, Amaelia evidently slipped out of the Palace without no escort, then wound up at the Temple of Jupiter during all that ruckus with Mars. Jupiter—well, everyone knows what *he's* like—he took such a fancy to her that Juno showed up and sent her straight to—"

"TO ME." The pieces came together. After Amaelia had been declared dead, Arvid had intervened with Pluto, insisting that it was all a mistake, but obviously it had been nothing of the kind. Amaelia was dead, fair and square, as the old saying went. No matter what Pluto said, she had no right whatever to be up on the playing field now.

"I'VE CHANGED MY MIND." She turned back to Barbus. "KILL ARVID, BUT RETURN THE GIRL TO ME. WE WOULDN'T WANT TO BREAK ANY RULES."

The sulfurous stench from the river made Kerickson's eyes water, and the heat rivaled the interior of a rocket engine. They had to get across, and soon, but the ancient ferryman remained obstinately on the other shore.

Amaelia cupped her hands next to his ear. "We'll never get out this way!"

He nodded back at her, then wiped the dripping sweat out of his eyes. It was pointless to waste any more time here. They were only going to get hungrier and thirstier and hotter while waiting for a new shade to show up so that Charon would have to pole the ferry back to their side. And even if they did hold out that long, Charon's programming forbade dead players like

Amaelia to recross the Styx, and since Charon was a robot, there was no question of two humans being able to overpower it. Also, if Charon had been reprogrammed with the same upgraded version of Interact as Cerberus, then Kerickson knew he wouldn't be able to override its programming.

"Come on!" He seized Amaelia's hand. "We're getting out of here."

She stood up, gazing back at Cerberus. The three-headed dog whined, then licked all its chops. She shuddered. "How?"

"We're going to swim." He pulled off his sandals and threw them down on the black sand.

"Across that?"

He followed her gaze to the roiling, white-foamed water surging over the rocks. "It isn't as bad as it looks," he shouted over the roaring river. "Charon crosses it all the time with nothing more than a pole." He decided not to mention that Charon's ferry ran on an invisible track under the oily black water.

"Oh." She wrapped her arms around her chest.

"I'll go first, then you jump in on the upstream side of me. That way, we should stay together."

"If—If you say so."

He could see in her wide, staring eyes that she wasn't crazy about this solution. He didn't blame her. Taking several deep breaths, he jumped into the hot, smelly water and swam hard to keep from being dashed back against the rocks that lined the shore. "Come on!" he shouted over his shoulder, getting a mouthful of the nasty, brackish water.

She clambered to the top of a boulder and dove in. Then she came up sputtering on his left, arms flailing.

"Swim!" he shouted at her. She worked her arms harder, then was thrown against him by the water's force. Before they had made more than a couple of yards' progress, he realized that the current was too strong. They were going to be swept into the tunnel through the rock wall up ahead long before they could reach the opposite shore.

Charon waved a skeletal arm at them just as the water sucked them into the dark hole in the cavern wall.

Struggling to keep his head above water, Kerickson snagged Amaelia's neck with one arm. "Lie—still!" he shouted to her, but he couldn't tell if she understood or not.

Where did this tunnel come out? As the rushing water threw them from side to side, he tried to remember—did this branch of the river circulate through the pumps and filters before coming out above? Amaelia floundered against him, panicking. He flipped her over so that she lay against his chest in the swirling water. "Relax, you're all right!" he shouted in her ear, then hoped he wasn't lying.

With an increasing roar, the river surged around them, speeding them to—where? The sweltering water closed over his head. He held his breath and wrapped both arms around the girl's struggling body. Somewhere up ahead he heard a deep, rhythmic beat that overrode every other sound.

Evidently the pumps came first.

"WHAT DID THAT INSECT, PUBLIUS BARBUS, WANT?" Pluto's black eyes crackled with suspicion.

With the tiniest diversion of energy, Demea erased the computer's memory of that particular meeting. Then she twined a lock of Pluto's curly black hair around her finger, pulling him closer and closer until she could see only the bottomless pools of his eyes. "HE WANTED ONLY TO PRAISE ME, AS IS MY DUE."

"AND WHAT OF MY DUE?"

Heat blazed from him, hotter than the sun, which she would never see again. She pressed herself against him, drinking it in. "WHAT WOULD YOU HAVE?"

"I WILL SHARE NO PART OF YOU WITH ANYONE!" His hands gripped her shoulders, holding her hard, cruelly. "EVEN YOUR ANGER IS MINE ALONE. REMEMBER THAT!"

"OF COURSE," she murmured, then felt herself swept away in his dark fire. "OF COURSE."

CHAPTER
EIGHTEEN

Shrill, frenzied screaming penetrated the black fog in Amaelia's head. She turned her head, trying to get away from it, and got a faceful of wet sand.

"HAVING A BIT OF A SWIM, MY DEAR?" a reverberating male voice asked.

Screaming flashed by again, more excited than afraid. Icy water splashed the length of her body and she shivered. Her throat spasmed and she coughed up a mouthful of stale, brackish water.

"REALLY, DON'T YOU THINK IT'S TIME YOU GOT OUT OF THOSE NASTY, WET THINGS?"

Another screaming party passed close by. Pushing weakly at the sand, she managed finally to roll over on her back. Her eyes cracked open. Clouds drifted overhead, gray and brooding. Had they made it outside?

"I KNOW, LET'S GO SKINNY-DIPPING!"

She turned to see the head of a massive brown eagle cocked attentively, staring down at her. Her heart sank and a throbbing conga-drum ache settled in her temples. "Jupiter?"

"FAR-SEEING, LOUD-THUNDERING, THE ONE, THE ONLY." It winked a gleaming yellow eye. "NOW, WHERE WERE WE BEFORE WE WERE SO RUDELY INTERRUPTED?"

"Go—away," she said weakly.

"WELL!" The eagle fanned its wings. "SEE IF I GRANT ANY MORE OF YOUR PRAYERS, YOU LITTLE INGRATE!" It leaped skyward and disappeared.

She covered her aching eyes with a sandy arm and tried to think back; they had been in the river, alternately tossed above, then sucked under the oily, sulfurous water. She remembered being battered against the sides of the smooth conduit, and a pounding that grew louder and louder—and then she remembered nothing at all.

"Hey, you can't swim in there!" The voice—male, but decidedly human—was somewhere above her.

"Ga-Gaius?" she called hoarsely.

"See, officer?" the voice complained. "Right in the middle of the Tiber River Adventure. I don't care if it is Saturnalia, I could lose my license for this."

"Don't worry, citizen." Footsteps crunched across the sand. "We'll have them out of there in a second."

Amaelia tried to sit up, but the sky spun around her in crazy circles. Her stomach heaved and she pressed her hands over her eyes. The screamers sailed by again, showering her with another sheet of frigid water. Her hands and feet seemed to be made of ice.

"All right, you two," a male voice said. "Fun is fun, and I'm sure you aren't the only ones who had too much celebrating last night, but you can't lie around down here on the shore." Hands tugged at her shoulders.

"C-Cold!" she forced out through chattering teeth.

"Maybe they fell out of one of the boats," a different voice suggested.

"No, that would have been reported right away, and the emergency drones would have taken care of it."

Someone wrapped a warm, dry cloak around her shoulders, then rubbed her arms. "Now, then, little lady, we'll have you all fixed up in just a minute."

She opened her eyes and looked up into a swarthy, hook-nosed face half hidden under the crested bronze helmet of a Praetorian Guard. He reached for her wrist. "Let's see who you are."

Remembering her red status light, she tried to pull away, but his grip was too strong.

"Well, I'll be—" The Praetorian's breath puffed white in the cold air as he turned her wrist over. "Crassus, come look at this. She doesn't have a bracelet."

"Neither does this one." A second guard looked up from a few feet down on the white sand beach. "And his sandals are gone, too. They must have lost them in the river."

"Gaius?" Shivering, Amaelia wavered to her feet. "Is he alive?"

The guard took her arm, steadying her. "What possessed

you to go swimming in the Tiber this time of year? You could
have drowned or died of exposure."

"It—seemed like a good idea at the time," Gaius said
weakly from the sand.

"Gaius!" Aided by the Praetorian, she stumbled barefoot to
where he lay on his back. His blond hair was plastered wetly
to his forehead, and his skin was so pale that it looked translucent. "Are you all right?"

A Roman galley filled with excited passengers swept by,
pursued by a Carthaginian warship. Just as they hit the curve
of the waterway directly opposite Amaelia, the boats kicked up
a huge sheet of icy water and the passengers screamed. She
watched them disappear around the corner, trying to make
sense of it all. Apparently, she and Gaius had washed up next
to an amusement ride along the river.

Gaius was sitting up now, shivering and blue around the
lips, his forehead propped against his knees. The second sol-
dier took off his cloak and covered him with it, then looked at
Amaelia more closely. "Say, I know who she is. Quintus
Gracchus has the whole city out looking for her. She's Amaelia
Metullus!"

"Are you sure?" The two men peered closely into her face.

She shuddered and did her best to look common and lowborn. "Are you kidding?" She huddled deeper inside the
scratchy wool cloak. "My name is, uh, Flina. The closest I
ever got to the Palace was to deliver some figs to the kitchen
last quarter."

"Well, dear ..." Gaius tottered to his feet. "I can't say it
hasn't been fun, but Saturnalia or not, we'd better get back to
the villa or the master is going to have our hides."

"Not so fast." The second guard planted himself firmly between Gaius and Amaelia. "You two have no bracelets and
were caught in a restricted area. You'd better come to headquarters and explain yourselves."

He didn't like it, no, not one bit. Publius Barbus leaned his
elbows on the sticky counter and checked the current roster of
workers one more time. The man Proserpina was looking for,
the same man he'd found among the work crew without a
properly modified bracelet just the day before, was definitely
not listed.

And everyone else in the crew had already had his or her
latest fix. It was well past the time for this Arvid Kerickson's,

if he needed one. Either he had gone into withdrawal somewhere out on the playing field and was now frothing at the mouth, or he had never been "processed" at all. If the first were true, the problem would, of course, take care of itself in a matter of hours—but if it were the second, big trouble was brewing. No one who knew the secrets of the Spear and Chicken could be allowed to contact the authorities.

According to Proserpina, this guy was a programmer, too. He shook his head. Bad news, no matter which way you looked at it. This was going to have to go all the way up to the big boss, and *he* was sure to be furious. Barbus rubbed a hand across his stubbly whiskers, then reached for a cup of wine. A sweet deal like the Imperium only came along once in a lifetime. Where else in New York City could a guy both lie low and operate on this sort of scale at the same time? It was worth whatever it took to protect it.

Glancing around the murky interior of the inn, he satisfied himself that no one was watching and pulled out a wristfone. He punched in a code and waited.

"What?" a voice barked after a second.

"It looks like I had an intruder in the work crew last night."

"So deal with him."

"He—" Barbus hesitated, knowing how *he* felt about screwups. It wouldn't do to wind up like the late, unlamented Micio. "He seems to have escaped."

"Who was it?"

"Some bleeder by the name of Arvid Kerickson." He shifted his weight and the counter creaked. "Word is he's a programmer for the Game and he's hooked up with Amaelia Metullus."

There was silence for a moment. "Interesting pairing."

"Well, what do you want me to do?"

"That depends. How much does he know?"

Barbus grimaced. "Beats me. I think maybe he got away before we could dose him."

"Then you have no control over him."

Barbus began to sweat. He took another swig of wine and let it warm him.

"But on the other hand," the voice continued, "he may not know everything."

"So, what do you want me to do, boss?"

"Eliminate him—immediately—with the least amount of mess possible. Do I make myself clear?"

Barbus grimaced. "Sure, boss, no problem. We'll make it

look like an accident. If you give me computer access, I can have him in an hour or two, maybe even less."

"All right, but I expect results!" The wristfone clicked off.

Barbus slid the device off his wrist and stowed it back under the counter. His fingers touched the long, cool tube of the neuronic buzzer and he smiled. It was such a nice toy, and he had so little chance to use it. He pulled it out and thrust it under the dirty wool of his outer tunic. There was no reason why he and the boys couldn't have a little fun while they cleaned up this particular problem. After all, it was supposed to be healthy to enjoy your work.

Tucked away in the lower level of the Palace, the Praetorian Headquarters represented everything the ancient Romans had respected: simplicity, respect for authority, and, above all, brute strength. Kerickson's eyes lingered on the array of stout spears and glittering swords in the weapons rack as the two guards prodded him and Amaelia into a cramped office. Goose bumps still marched up and down his spine, courtesy of his dunking in the frigid Tiber River.

A middle-aged man with the jaw of a bulldog, and iron-gray hair cut in the standard, unimaginative style of a Roman soldier, looked up from a mass of scrolls and printouts. He leaned back and tapped his chin with a writing stylus. "Is this the pair reported frolicking in the water down at the amusement area?"

"Well, I wouldn't exactly call it frolicking—" Kerickson began, then sneezed explosively.

"Shut up!" The bigger of the two Praetorians shoved him from behind. "You'll speak to Adjunct Sixtus when you're spoken to, and not before."

"Do you two know the penalty for endangering yourself and others like that?" The Adjunct's bushy eyebrows rose over his prominent nose. "You could have caused a serious accident."

Kerickson glanced at the guard, who scowled back at him. "Answer him, dog!"

"Sorry." Kerickson stifled a second sneeze. "I thought it was a rhetorical question."

"Never mind!" The Adjunct shoved several sheets of parchment aside. "Give me your names so I can replace your bracelets and debit your accounts the proper number of points for this little prank." He poised the stylus. "Well?"

Although he was tempted to try to bluff his way out, he knew the guards had limited computer access to the players' records. If he didn't give the name under which Wilson had enrolled him, they would know in a matter of seconds, and he could not afford to be thrown out of the Game now. He took a deep breath. "Gaius Clodius Lucinius."

The Adjunct scribbled it down, then turned to Amaelia with the air of a man who had not slept for three days. "And you?"

She tugged the borrowed scarlet cloak more tightly around her shoulders. Her face was as white as a Forum statue.

"Look at her, Sixtus." The taller of the two Praetorians pulled her chin to one side as though he were examining a side of beef. "I'm sure it's *her*, Amaelia Julia Metullus."

"Are you sure?" The Adjunct pushed back his chair and got up to peer into her face.

Pushing the Praetorian's hand away, she turned her head to the wall. "Don't be ridiculous. My name is Flina and I—I'm a kitchen slave in the villa of Didius Festus."

"Isn't this great?" The first guard grinned fiercely, baring a set of teeth that would have been more at home in the mouth of a bear. "Gracchus has been carrying on about her for days, and here she is, right under our noses! There'll be some big points in this one for all of us, and right before the end of the quarter, too."

"Perhaps." The Adjunct narrowed his eyes. "See if you can find Quintus Gracchus while I have new bracelets made up."

The guard saluted, then left. Sixtus shook his head. "You two stay put," he said sourly to Kerickson and Amaelia, then walked through to the back room.

Kerickson edged nearer to the door; if Gracchus was in the Palace, it would take only minutes for the guard to find him. It would be smart to leave before he returned.

But then he reflected that on the other hand, if Gracchus was behind Micio's and Wilson's murders, confronting him here with the Praetorian Guards for witnesses might be the safest course. He turned to the remaining guard. "How about some dry clothes and something hot to drink?"

"Sure thing." Crossing his arms, the guard looked out the window. "Just as soon as Adjunct Sixtus says so."

A moment later Sixtus reentered the office, a Game bracelet in each hand. He handed the first to Kerickson. "Gaius Clodius Lucinius, enrolled three days ago, according to census records, and AWOL from the training school for all three of those days." He shook his head. "Not a promising start. You'll never advance that way."

Kerickson accepted the bracelet. His status lights were unchanged, including green for freedman and the disappointing hit-point rating of one-half.

"As for you, young lady . . ." Sixtus scowled at Amaelia. "There is no record of any player, slave or otherwise, under the name Flina, although one of the robot slaves in the Palace is known by that designation. But you do closely resemble the file identification holo of Amaelia Julia Metullus."

"She is Amaelia Julia Metullus." The tall, armored form of Quintus Gracchus filled the doorway. "As well as my wife."

"I'm afraid—" The Adjunct handed Gracchus the remaining bracelet. "—at this point, she's your *former* wife. According to this status light, she's dead."

"A computer error, I'm sure." Gracchus slid the bracelet under his chest plate, then reached for Amaelia. "But we'll have it looked into."

She flinched away from his touch. "Leave me alone!"

"Yeah, hands off!" Kerickson stepped between them. "In fact, Q.G., I think you and I ought to have ourselves a little talk—you know, about Interfaces where there shouldn't be any, and why the computer won't release Amaelia from the Game—and her father's murder."

Gracchus's hard gray eyes bored into his face. "You and I do have some unfinished business." The strong features settled into grim lines. His eyes, flat and deadly as a snake's, flicked to the Adjunct. "Leave us alone for a few minutes, Sixtus."

Sixtus's heavy face looked undecided. "Captain, are you sure?"

"Leave us!" Gracchus's voice had granite beneath it.

Sixtus saluted, then motioned to the other two guards. "We'll be right outside."

A chill ran down Kerickson's spine as he watched them go; what he had in mind required witnesses to be effective.

"Now, you were saying?" Drawing a dagger from the ornately tooled leather sheath at his waist, Gracchus turned it so that the light played along the finely honed edge. "Something about Interfaces and murder?"

"Don't give me that innocent act, Gracchus. You know exactly what I'm talking about." Kerickson noticed the dagger had a wooden handle just like the one on the dagger that had been buried in Wilson's heart. "Let's start with that special room in your villa—you know, the one with the screens and—"

"And the Interface you were supposedly repairing." Gracchus balanced the dagger on the ends of two fingers.

Kerickson met the flinty gaze. "Perhaps you could explain how you came to have an illegal Interface to the Game computer in your villa, or how all those extra points found their way into your account."

Gracchus flipped the dagger and caught it neatly by the handle. "None of that is any concern of yours, freedman."

"And Micio's murder, I suppose that's none of my business either?"

"The Emperor's murder?" Gracchus rose with a clink of armor. "By Jupiter, I don't know anything about *that*. I was otherwise occupied that unfortunate morning—following the Emperor's orders to rescue his daughter from the Slave Market."

"Daughter?" Kerickson glanced aside at Amaelia.

"Oh . . ." She put a hand to her throat. The last vestiges of color fled from her cheeks. "He *was* with me when my father was killed—he was bringing me back from Delos. He couldn't have been at the Baths."

Kerickson felt as though someone had just shoved him over a cliff. He could have sworn that Quintus Gracchus had killed Micio! Everything else fit: the unofficial Interface, the illegal points funneled into his account, his so-called marriage to Amaelia, and his subsequent play for Emperor. "Well, there's still the matter of the Interface." He tugged at his clammy tunic collar, which seemed to be shrinking. "And all those unearned points in your account. You've been cheating for months. You have no right to become Emperor."

"Of course I'm cheating. It's an authentic Roman practice, reputedly employed by the ancients themselves to great advantage." Gracchus's handsome olive-skinned face smiled, although the expression never reached his chill gray eyes. "And before you even think about having me disqualified, consider this: if I reveal your presence on the playing field to HabiTek, you'll be out of this game in two seconds—and you'll never find the real murderer." He sheathed the dagger in one smooth motion. "That *is* why you're still mucking around in here, is it not?"

Kerickson fought to keep the dismay off his face. If Gracchus hadn't killed Micio and Wilson, then who in the name of all the gods he'd ever programmed had? "Who's helping you with all this, Gracchus? You can't be doing this point scam all on your own. What do you know about the Spear and Chicken?"

Gracchus glanced at him with heavy-lidded eyes, then took Amaelia's arm so fast that Kerickson almost didn't see him move. "I think it's about time you went back to the Gladiatorial School and started playing your role, Kerickson." Amaelia struggled, but Gracchus just tightened his hold. "Otherwise, I might find it necessary to augment the number of slaves used as lion fodder in tomorrow's games in honor of the Saturnalia. Of course, the slaves are all supposed to be mechanicals and holos, but—" He nuzzled Amaelia's ear. "—mistakes have been made, and once made, like Micio, it's too late to do anything about them. Now, we wouldn't want that to happen to you or the young lady here, would we?"

Kerickson's hands clenched. "Leave her out of this!"

"Oh, but she has to play her part, too, just like the rest of us." Gracchus's voice was smooth as water. "Once I'm Emperor, she can leave the Game or play my Empress or do anything else she wants. But until then, she's mine."

Kerickson launched himself at the Praetorian, but without seeming to move Gracchus clouted him behind the ear with what felt like an iron club. Just as Kerickson's face smacked the tiled floor, he heard Gracchus calling the other guards back.

"Dump this piece of freedman filth back at the Gladiatorial School where it belongs—and tell them to use him in the games tomorrow. And you tell Nerus Amazicus that if I ever see this little turd again, he'll take his place in the arena!"

"Yes, Emperor!" Rough hands grabbed Kerickson by the shoulders. "Stand up, damn you!"

He tried to make his legs hold up his weight, but they seemed to be on vacation. How—How had Gracchus moved so fast? He couldn't fit it together in his mind.

"Come on!" One of the guards looped Kerickson's arm around his neck and dragged him through the door.

"Gaius!" Amaelia called after him. "Please, Quintus, don't hurt him!"

"A noble sentiment, my dear," he heard Gracchus reply. "But perhaps you would do better to worry about yourself. After tomorrow . . ."

The voices faded into unintelligible garble. Kerickson tried to look back over his shoulder, but his neck refused to hold up the weight of his aching head, and his eyes insisted on looking in opposite directions.

"Get in, turd-breath!" A slap rocked his face. "If you think I'm going to carry you all the way across the city, you're crazy!"

The rectangular form of a litter lay on the street before him, with a sullen slave stationed at each corner. Blinking furiously, he managed to half fall, half sit in the unpadded conveyance.

"Ask for Nerus Amazicus and give him this note," the guard said to one of the slaves as he reached down and jerked the curtains closed in Kerickson's face. "And you tell him for me that if I see this piece of shit anywhere outside the arena, no one over there is getting his next fix, and that includes you four. Do I make myself clear?"

Whether they agreed or not, the litter rose and moved off at a brisk pace. Kerickson gripped the sides for support and tried to cudgel some sense out of his brain. What "fix" was the guard talking about, and why did they keep saying that he was going into the arena? Real players didn't fight. HabiTek employed holo simulations or mechanicals for the re-creations of the Roman games. It was too dangerous to let humans go at each other with real weapons, even if they were trying to be careful.

His head spun and he closed his eyes. He had to get back to Amaelia. He had to find out who was behind Gracchus.

Taking a deep breath, he peeked through the curtains to see where they were at the moment. One of the slaves cursed and jerked them closed again.

Inside the litter the air shimmered, then resolved itself into a small brown owl. "THIS ISN'T VERY PRODUCTIVE, YOU KNOW."

"Not now, Minerva." Kerickson pinched the bridge of his nose and clamped his eyes shut. A black weariness dragged at his mind. "I'm trying to think."

"YOU REALLY BOTCHED IT BACK THERE WITH GRACCHUS."

"Oh, and I suppose you could have done better?"

The owl sniffed. "A TRUE HERO WOULD NOT HAVE ABANDONED HIS LADY."

In spite of himself, his eyes flew open. "Look, I never said I was a hero!"

"IF YOU DON'T ACT NOW, AMAELIA WILL DIE." The

owl perched on his knee. "THE WHOLE CITY WILL BE LOST!"

"I don't suppose you'd care to enlarge upon that." A muscle twitched along Kerickson's jaw. He drew his knees up and glared at the seedy-looking bird. "It's all very well for you to go on all the time about saving the city, but you might at least tell me how!"

The owl's gray eyes began to spark. "LISTEN, BUSTER, YOU BETTER GET IT TOGETHER AND MOVE YOUR ASS!"

"Shut up in there!" one of the litter bearers shouted. "Crassus said we had to deliver you, but he never said you had to be in one piece!"

CHAPTER
NINETEEN

The owl rotated its head to look over its shoulder, then disappeared with a pop. Kerickson ground his teeth. So much for divine inspiration. Nothing, but nothing, worked right around here anymore. They must have hired a band of idiots to take his place. If he were back at his old job in the Interface, it would take him days, maybe even weeks, to get everything running again the way it should.

Then he realized—that was it. He had to get into the Interface—the real one, not Gracchus's, where there was sure to be an adequate guard now. All the answers had to be there. Since Game programs had been compromised through the illegal Interface, the computer must contain some record of how Gracchus had managed to funnel points into his own account. Who had helped him—and how? The answer to that probably contained the key to everything else.

The litter swayed around a corner. He peered out through the moving curtains and saw that they had entered the twisting, rubbish-clogged streets of the Subura. People, laughing and rowdy, jostled the litter, grabbing at the curtains and harassing the bearers, who swore and warned them off.

He waited until they were snarled in a particularly thick knot of pedestrians, then burst through the curtains and hit the ground running, elbowing his way through the sea of togas and tunics, drawing angry protests and curses at every step.

The bearers shouted behind him as he ran. His head ached, and even though it was cold he broke out in feverish sweat. Finally he threw himself behind a statue of Venus and hunkered down as his pursuers pounded past.

"OH, COME ON, MR. HOTSTUFF, QUIT WASTING TIME," a sulky voice said above his head. "THERE ARE

FOUR OF THEM AND ONLY ONE OF YOU, AND HAVE YOU LOOKED IN THE MIRROR LATELY? *THEY'RE* ALL BUILT LIKE SPACE-TRUCKS. SAVE EVERYONE A LOT OF TROUBLE. ADMIT THE INEVITABLE AND DIE."

Breathing in chest-straining gasps, Kerickson looked up and saw Mercury's pretty-boy face pouting down at him. Several scruffy-looking Subura merchants darted out of their ramshackle establishments, their stubble-covered jaws agape at the god's silvery manifestation. A passing Legionary stopped to stare. "Is someone dead?"

"ANY SECOND NOW, UNLESS YOU'D CARE TO PUT THIS BASE-BORN LOUT OUT OF HIS MISERY YOUR-SELF." Mercury floated serenely as he adjusted a pinfeather on the tiny white wing behind his left sandal heel. "FEEL FREE TO HAVE AT IT—HE'S ONLY GOT HALF A HIT POINT."

Kerickson furtively stripped off his new Game bracelet and wedged it behind his back, between the statue's shapely marble legs.

"LISTEN, BUCKO, THAT SORT OF SLICK NONSENSE WON'T SAVE YOU THIS TIME." Mercury fluffed his perfect golden curls. "FACE UP TO IT LIKE A MAN; THOSE BOYS ARE GOING TO PUNCH YOUR TICKET FOR GOOD. WHY NOT JUST LIE DOWN IN THE STREET AND WAIT FOR THEM?"

"Why don't you flit off somewhere and powder your nose?" Kerickson muttered as he heard running sandals clatter back in his direction. He ducked through the door of the nearest shop, evidently a laundry. A mound of grimy, wine-spattered tunics reached nearly to the ceiling. He burrowed beneath a cotton mountain that reeked of sweat, garlic, and onions as the sandals pelted by.

As soon as he was convinced they weren't coming back, he clawed his way up to breathable air and slipped outside to get his bearings. The dome's sun was dipping toward the western side of the city as players of all ranks streamed toward the races at the Circus. He headed into the middle-class residential area opposite the Subura, and after a few moments turned onto the Via Nova.

More than a few Legionaries were patrolling the streets, and he wondered what kind of bracelets *they* wore. How far did the Spear and Chicken's influence spread, and exactly what was the nature of it, anyway? The people who played the Game not only paid a great deal of money, but put their outside lives on hold as well. How did Publius Barbus make them wear bracelets that siphoned off their points? Even if he used force, why didn't they just throw the damn things away the first chance they got and then report him to the Game computer?

By the time he reached the small bakery that disguised the Management Gate, sweat plastered his tunic to his back and made the winter air seem even colder. Not only was the area thick with Legionaries, but he had seen several gangs of what he could only describe as armed thugs, openly carrying weapons of distinctly modern origin. What was going on?

He was standing in front of the locked shop door when he heard the scuff of hobnailed sandals on the street.

"Are you sure, Fabius?" a voice asked.

Kerickson ducked into the shadows behind an empty wine barrel, closing his eyes and trying to think himself not there. The sandals clattered by.

"I thought I saw him run down this street," a second voice replied. "Of course, it's getting pretty dark. Maybe my eyes are playing tricks, but I don't want to have to go back and tell the Emperor we couldn't find him. You know what he'll say."

"He's not Emperor yet."

"Well, he will be by this time tomorrow. Once the Praetorians proclaim him, the Senate will have to give in."

"Maybe." The footsteps faded around the corner.

Kerickson brushed off his knees and examined the doorway. The monitor was embedded in the door frame above. "Give me class-two access," he whispered up at it.

"Present Game bracelet for proper identification."

"I've lost my bracelet." He glanced over his shoulder. Did he hear more voices? "Give me emergency access."

"Code?"

"Wilson, Giles Edward. Game status: Management."

The monitor hesitated. "Your vocal print does not match that of Giles Edward Wilson."

"I've—been injured," Kerickson hissed at it. "I need medical attention. Give me access now!"

"Emergency drones have been activated. Please remain motionless until assistance has arrived."

Panic streaked up Kerickson's spine. At best, he had three, maybe four minutes until the drones arrived and carted him off to Medical, where he would no doubt be exposed and thrown out of the Game. And even if no one there recognized him, he still would be a long way from getting the computer access he needed.

Well, surely there was more than one way into this blasted thing. Knowing that protection of the Management Gate relied more on hiding it than actual physical measures, he dropped to his knees and searched the street for something, anything made of metal. He could see only vague outlines in the deepening darkness, and kept skinning his hands on the rough-edged cobblestones. His grasping fingers found a woman's hairpin just as a trio of obviously drunken men turned onto the street, laughing and talking. Swearing under his breath, he scuttled back into the shadows. How long did he have before the emergency drones arrived?

As soon as the men passed, he popped out the monitor's plas cover and probed the mechanism with the hairpin.

"Destruction of Game property will result in a fine of all accumulated points, in addition to monetary damages."

Somewhere in the background he heard the monotonous whine of the emergency drones. He held his breath and thrust the hairpin deeper.

"You are likely to incur further physical injury," the monitor said. "Please desist until the emergency drones—"

It shorted out in a burst of sparks. Kerickson fell heavily backward onto the cobblestones, feeling as though he'd just been bitten all over by a giant snake. Favoring his singed hand, he wrenched at the locked door. The whine sounded much closer now, perhaps just one street over. He threw his shoulder against the wood, grunting and digging his bare feet against the cobblestones. The gleaming drones rounded the corner, and red and blue lights danced crazy shadows over the closed shops.

The door gave and he tumbled inside.

Rose-scented steam swirled from the pool's surface up to the ceiling and circled back lazily throughout the tiled room. Anchored by one hand to the side of the pool, Amaelia floated in the hot water, so tired it seemed she would never find the energy to move again.

Against her wishes, Gracchus had summoned a physician to check her for injuries. Even though he had worn the typical Game clothing of a Greek physician-slave, the man had used modern diagnostic equipment to pronounce her sound except for bruises and exhaustion. He had prescribed a bath and a good night's sleep. She frowned; she would never get a decent night's sleep again until she was out of the Game.

The slave girl, Flina, knelt at the pool's edge. "Shall I wash your back, lady?"

She looked up into the slave's dark, enigmatic face, still unsettled to find herself in her stepmother's place, wearing her clothes and attended by her servants. "No, thank you, Flina."

Quintus Gracchus strolled into the Palace baths. "Perhaps the Empress would prefer her husband to perform that service." He gazed down at her.

Hastily, she hid herself against the pool's edge. "Go away!"

He stared at her as casually as if she were one of the trees out in the gardens. "Surely you're not embarrassed. After all, we are man and wife."

"Not as far as I'm concerned!" She waved at the maidservant who had retreated back to the wall. "Flina, bring me my robe!"

Gracchus knelt to dip one hand into the water and let it trickle through his fingers. "It's time you made a choice, my dear—either you are my wife and will stand beside me tomorrow as I ascend to Emperor, or you're just garbage to be swept away."

"Don't be ridiculous!" Reaching up, she took the green silk robe Flina handed to her and turned her back, thrusting her arms through the sleeves. "You don't need me to become Emperor. It's not hereditary."

"No." He stood up again as she wrestled with the wet sash. "But friends and connections in high places often make a difference—a lesson you would be wise to learn yourself."

Feeling like a drowned puppy, Amaelia walked up the steps out of the pool. "Having family in high places has never done me a bit of good." She accepted a thick white towel from Flina and wrapped her dripping hair.

"It might save your friend's life."

"Gaius?" Her head swung around. "Why? What have you done with him?"

"Nothing, so far." Gracchus's lips parted, revealing even white teeth that stood out in his tan face. "But you must realize that he is a gladiator, and there are games to be fought tomorrow."

"But they aren't—" She paled, thinking of the violent mock-spectacles to which her father had dragged her over the years. "—real."

"Not formerly." He picked up another towel and dabbed at her dripping cheek. "But I suppose you've noticed that times do change, even here in the Imperium. I thought it might be amusing to stage real fights between players this year. And there are plenty of men and women eager to attend."

She clutched the towel around her shoulders, then headed for the door. He stepped into her path with a clink of armor. "We'll have the emergency drones standing by, of course."

Shivering, she stared down at her bare feet.

"If you play the loving consort tomorrow, then I will be proclaimed Emperor and will arrange for you to leave the Game." He put his hand under her chin and forced her eyes to meet his. "That is what you want, isn't it?"

"Yes." Her voice was barely audible over the hollow slapping of water against the sides of the pool.

"And is it so very much I'm asking, just a few more minutes of playing a role you've been working toward for years?" He released her. "After all, that is supposed to be what every woman enrolled in this game wants—to become Empress. Who knows, you might even decide to remain with me."

Goose bumps covered her arms as she stood there, dripping, unable to find an emotion in that classically Roman face of his that she could understand.

He laughed, and the sound echoed crazily in the tiled room. "See that you live up to your side of this bargain tomorrow, or I won't feel obliged to live up to mine. Now—" He smacked her wet behind with the flat of his hand. "Go and dry off before you catch your death of cold."

Kerickson fell through the bakery door, then pushed it shut and held his breath. Outside, the red and blue lights on the drones whirled around and around, strobe-lighting the interior of the shop through the window.

After several minutes of cruising up and down the street, the two units gave up. As the lights faded around the corner, he crawled past barrels of Egyptian flour, hoping no one would investigate the false alarm. It was late, though, and likely the replacement programmers were off duty. The Interface should be deserted, unless they were coping with an emergency—which was, of course, entirely possible, the way things were going these days.

Voices murmured somewhere down the hall. He kept his head down as he inched past the Costuming Department; the outfitters might be working late. Saturnalia was the most popular time of the year for enrollment, and new players had to be properly dressed in order to enter the Game. As he crawled by, however, it was dark and quiet. The noise came from up ahead in the Interface itself.

"This is the biggest goddammned mess I've ever seen!"

Kerickson pressed his back to the wall.

"You and me both," a different voice replied. "I give up for tonight. I can't find any documentation on Mars, but I think it's okay until tomorrow. Besides, I don't know what I'd do if I could find it; I'm so tired, I can't see straight."

"Yeah, this Jeppers character is a real slave driver. He's even pressuring me to move into the dome, but it's not in my contract, and my wife absolutely refuses. She thinks these players are a bunch of nut cases."

"I'm with her. Did you hear abou . . ."

Kerickson heard feet walking down the corridor in the opposite direction toward the outside lock as the two voices faded into murmurs. He waited a few more minutes, then stood up. Silence filled the complex, thick as wool.

Peering into the glass window of the Interface, he saw only the even blue glow of the screens and the two empty seats before the console—where he and Wilson had labored together for five years. He slipped in and shut the door behind him, then lowered the blinds for good measure.

He sat in the padded chair on the right, his old place, then punched in Wilson's code. The central screen dissolved into the Temple of Jupiter. He flipped the manual override. "Record voice pattern for keyed-in code sequence: Wilson, Giles E. Game status: Management."

"Recorded," the computer said.

He sat back in the chair and rubbed his forehead. Now, at least, he would be able to use the Management Gate whenever he wanted, unless someone figured out what he had done.

Still, the fact remained that he needed sleep and plenty of it, as well as a decent meal. The last thing he could recall eating was that pomegranate down in Hades.

Deciding to test his newly acquired access, he punched in the call code for Neptune.

After a second the sea god's mournful green face appeared. "OH, IT'S YOU. DECIDED TO WORSHIP ME AFTER ALL, HAVE YOU? WELL, IT'S ABOUT TIME."

Kerickson wrinkled his forehead, then keyed the program

into a standby mode and read through the parameters. His eyebrows headed for the ceiling. Almost nothing was set where it should be. At the moment, Neptune was cleared only for manifestation down in Hades and had lost all influence over water. Working from memory, Kerickson went through the list and reconstructed the settings as best he could. Finally, he sat back and checked the list again. Probably some of the parameters were a little off; for instance, he couldn't remember whether Neptune had controlled the Tiber River before or not, but it seemed safer to leave that off for the moment.

Satisfied that his purloined access was working, he punched Neptune back into the system, then went through both Diana's and Venus's stats in the same way, releasing them from Hades and resetting them from memory. That done, he thought about the best way to find the information he needed. He suddenly remembered thinking something hadn't looked right when he'd run diagnostics back at Gracchus's villa. No doubt he should just run the same program again. "Run diagnostics series fourteen," he ordered, and sat back as the central screen dissolved into Jupiter's shield.

"Testing," the computer said. "Primary stats in thirty seconds." Statistics marched across the screen like tiny Legionaries.

He blinked and rubbed his eyes. What had caught his eye the last time he'd done this? He fished inside his tunic for the hard copy he'd run back at the villa, and found it still wedged in his underwear. In spite of the river, the characters were readable. Spreading the plas out on the console before him, he stared at the file allocation figures, trying to remember why he had copied them off in the first place.

"All Four-thousand-level buffers are out of service due to system maintenance," the computer said. "File allocation tables in ten seconds."

"All Four-thousand-level buffers?" Kerickson sat up. "At the same time?" He punched up system maintenance tables on a separate screen, but the times recorded there looked reasonable, not nearly what would be required to service an entire level of buffers.

He dropped the plas sheet on the floor, then punched up Buffer 4000. "Buffer out of service," the computer told him. "Please select another."

"Dump contents of Buffer 4,000 on-screen," he said, then watched. After a second, the screen filled with a bewildering array of numbers and names. He squinted, trying to make some sense out of what he saw. "Helena Antonia Longus," one entry read. "EP: 3. HP: 2. AP: 14. CP: 3." Experience points, hit points, and so on. These supposedly out-of-service buffers contained a record of the points stolen by the illegal bracelets.

"Print a hard copy." He picked up the plas sheet from the floor and compared its figures with the current file allocation tables in the center screen. They seemed to be largely the same, including the financial sector, which was still up to a whopping seventy percent in usage. Yet the enrollment figures had actually dropped slightly since the murders. Where were all those extra transactions and accounts coming from?

The dim mutter of voices from down the hall broke his concentration. He glanced up. Was the cleaning crew coming in already? Whatever he was going to do, he'd better take care of it now. He had no guarantee of regaining access tomorrow; all it would take was one security guard on duty and he'd never get in.

A grim smile tugged at his lips. "Put all Four-thousand-level buffers back into service immediately."

"That will require a class-three Management override."

Class three? Kerickson grimaced. He and Wilson had only had class-two clearance. "Cancel that." He closed his eyes and thought for a moment. "Cut power to all Four-thousand-level buffers."

"Done," the computer replied.

"Now print me a list of unassigned living quarters on the playing field." He waited tensely until the sheet of plas fed out of the slot, then punched off, hoping no one would bother to check users' codes tomorrow. Of course, by then it wouldn't matter. The interruption of power had erased the buffers' contents and he would be long gone—along with all of Quintus Gracchus's illegal points.

CHAPTER
TWENTY

Amaelia picked up a fresh green fig from the golden platter of fruit and played with the firm flesh for a moment. It was no use; she couldn't eat with Quintus Gracchus's chill gray eyes staring across the table at her. Besides, remembering her near-fatal encounter down in Hades, she felt uneasy in the Empress's apartments amidst the fussy pink draperies and the narcissistic statues that all stared back with her stepmother's face. It seemed altogether possible Demea might suddenly appear and blast her to cinders.

"Could I bring you something else, my lady?" Flina's concerned face hovered at her shoulder.

She glanced up into the maid's dark features. "This is Saturnalia, Flina. *I* should be serving *you* today, not the other way around."

"Don't be ridiculous." Gracchus lolled back on the low dining couch. His short military tunic rode up around his thighs, revealing massive, tanned legs that bulged with muscle. "I already have more than enough points to make Emperor. Don't humiliate yourself with the servants just to score a few more meaningless authenticity points." He scowled at Flina. "Leave us, wench."

Flina bowed her crown of black braids, then backed out and left them alone. Gracchus pushed off the couch and planted his legs before her like trees. "I don't like that gown."

Startled, she glanced down at the white silk stola embroidered with ivy Flina had brought her that morning from Demea's wardrobe.

"It's too plain. Change to something more colorful and have Flina arrange some jewels in your hair." Leaning over, he fingered a lock. "I should think emeralds would go well with your particular shade of red. You have to look every inch the Empress today."

She jerked away from his touch and combed her hair back into place with her fingers.

"You really should be more appreciative, you know." His voice had an underlying edge to it. "It was very careless, getting yourself killed like that. I had no end of trouble nullifying your death—a death, I might add, which would not have occurred had you merely stayed in the Palace, where you belonged!"

She stared past him, out the window into the dull blue early morning sky. "Gaius promised he could take me to the Interface."

"Interesting you should bring up that particular name." He clasped his hands behind his back and struck a pose in front of the window. She thought he looked like one of those overly noble statues down at the Temple of Jupiter.

"Did you know the Game computer contains almost no information on the background of Gaius Clodius Lucinius?" he asked without looking at her.

"The computer?" The rising sun glinted off the metal strips of his highly polished armor and made her squint. "But—"

"But what?" With a clink of metal, he turned around.

The measure of this man's power suddenly registered with her. Not only did he control the Praetorian Guard and possess more points than anyone else in the Game, but he had something else no one could possibly match—his own Interface with the Game computer.

His bushy brows knotted as he focused on her, staring as though he'd never really seen her before. "You were saying?"

"N-Nothing." A shiver crawled up her spine. She made a show of fiddling with one of Demea's many bracelets, a thick silver snake swallowing its own tail. "I'll go change." She slid off the couch and reached for her sandals.

His powerful fingers seized her wrist. "Wives shouldn't keep secrets from their husbands."

When she was barefoot, the top of her head barely reached his chin. She stiffened in his grasp, trying to think of anything but what she had seen in his villa.

"Something on your mind, girl?"

"I'm just—worried about Gaius." Her voice sounded thin and reedy. "He was a good friend to me."

"Forget Gaius." His grip tightened around her wrist until she cried out. "What were you going to say?"

She struggled as his fingers bit down through skin and muscle until it seemed he would squeeze her hand off. "Let me go!"

"Tell me!"

"Wh-What?" She sagged to her knees. The room danced around her in shivery waves.

"That day when I brought you back from the Slave Market and you stayed at my house, I found you in my office." Without loosening his grip, he bent over her. "What were you doing in there?"

"N-Nothing!" She forced the words out between numb lips. In another second she thought her wrist would shatter.

A knock sounded at the door. "Go away!" His gaze never wavered from her face.

"Captain Gracchus, we must speak with you immediately!"

He stared down at her a second longer, his eyes sharp as a Legionary's sword, then threw her onto the polished floor and stepped over her body. Two guards, resplendent in their scarlet Praetorian cloaks, snapped to attention when he jerked open the iron door. "What is it? I have a very busy day ahead of me."

Amaelia watched him, cradling her throbbing wrist to her chest.

"It's—It's your points, sir!" one of the guards said hoarsely.

"What about them?"

"They're all—gone."

Gracchus's hand gripped the hilt of his sword. "Gone where?"

"Just gone." The two guards looked at each other, their faces pinched and wary under their crested helmets. "We went down to the Forum to check the daily totals before today's proclamation, and you weren't even listed among the top fifty players. General Catulus is the only person listed with enough points to become Emperor."

Amaelia scrambled to her feet and, supporting her aching wrist with her good hand, edged toward the discomfited guards.

"Catulus!" Gracchus slammed his fist onto the table. Figs and bananas bounced across the pink marble floor. "That idiot isn't fit to be Emperor of the latrines!"

The guard on the right swallowed, his Adam's apple bobbing like a cork. "No, sir."

Trying not to even breathe, Amaelia took another step toward the door. If she could just slip out while he was so angry, maybe—

"Going somewhere, lady?" Gracchus seized her arm and sent her stumbling away from the door. "Perhaps, while I go check into this little problem, you should pray for my success, because—" His gray eyes took on the cool calculation of a viper. "—if I can't be Emperor, I won't need a wife."

She caught herself on one of the low dining couches and sank down, trembling. "It's just—a mistake," she said. "The computer must be down again. Everyone in the city knows it hasn't been working right lately."

His hand played with the hilt of his sword. "Perhaps so, but the Saturnalia games will still go on as planned." He drew his lips back from his fierce white teeth. "And as you might guess, the arena always has room for another body—even one as lovely as yours."

The sound of voices out on the street woke Kerickson from a dream in which he stood before an altar of gray stone in a vast, shadowy temple, offering up a sacrifice of red wine in a golden chalice. As he'd stared up at a huge statue, formulating his prayer in his head, he'd suddenly realized that the statue wore the face of Giles Edward Wilson.

Sitting up in a hard, narrow bed, he stared around the still-dark room, trying to think where he was and how exactly he'd gotten there. He remembered the hot, oily water of the River Styx, then washing up above in the chill embrace of the Tiber River Adventure . . . and losing Amaelia to Quintus Gracchus.

That had been stupid, he told himself as he threw back the coarse wool blanket—really stupid. Once he'd rescued the poor girl from Hades, the very least he could have done was escorted her safely outside. Shaking his head, he groped his way across the cold, uncarpeted floor. Now she was stuck playing Gracchus's wife again, while he was still no closer than before to finding Micio's and Wilson's murderer.

His outstretched hands found the rough stucco of the unseen wall, then slid along until he found the recessed switch. Light flared on from wall fixtures styled to look like candles.

He rubbed his eyes, then took stock of his assets. After leaving the Interface the night before, he had used the printout to find this currently unassigned room above a tanner's shop not too far from the Palace. Even at the best of times, the Game averaged only between eighty to ninety percent enrollment; last night's stats showed that it had fallen to about seventy-five percent since the murders. He should be able to use places like this until he found the murderer and turned him over to the police.

Or her. With a start, he realized he had no evidence that it wasn't a female, perhaps even someone like Demea. He considered his ex-wife for a moment: although she had never seemed to know much about programming, she lived with him for several years after he'd started working for HabiTek. Who knew what tricks and tips she might have picked up in that length of time?

He took a long, hot shower in the 'fresher, then changed the setting and tilted his chin up to let it shave him. The Public Baths were all right, but he'd take modern technology any day—and he'd lay a huge bet the Romans would have, too, if they'd had the choice.

After he finished, he put his clothes through a 'fresher cycle, then dressed in the tattered garments, feeling not only like a different man, but an exceedingly hungry one. Food was a rather mundane topic when there was so much chaos all around him, but—despite the bizarre goings-on down at the Spear and Chicken, the inexplicable new divinity of his ex-wife, the scrambling of all the god programs, and the murders—a guy had to eat.

He walked down through the smelly tanner's shop just as though he really belonged there, and peered out into the bustling morning street. The normal assortment of plebian merchants hurried up and down the Market District, going about their business.

He stepped into the flowing crowd. Where to start? The computer had provided some interesting information, but no real answers. Whoever had killed Micio and Wilson must have had a reason, something the two of them shared in common, but what? One had been a player, the other a programmer; the only real link between them was HabiTek. The motive behind the murders had to be connected somehow to the Game.

The winter wind bit through his tunic. Shivering, he rubbed his hands over his goose-bumped arms and dodged a large white dove that fluttered to the street in his path.

But the dove strutted after him, its head bobbing. "SO, WHERE IS SHE?"

He looked more closely, noting the tell-tale sprig of myrtle clasped in its beak. "Venus?"

The dove eyed him critically. "DON'T TELL ME THAT RAVISHING REDHEAD DUMPED YOU ALREADY?"

"Uh, no, not exactly." He realized people were staring, and squatted down, lowering his voice to a strained whisper. "Look, could we talk about this later—like maybe next year?"

"HOW COULD YOU BLOW IT LIKE THAT?" The dove heaved a dramatic sigh. "THAT GIRL HAD THE HOTS FOR YOU."

"Oh, my gosh, it's Venus!" a stumpy, slack-jawed woman exclaimed at his elbow. Blushing, she dropped to her knees, folded her hands, and bowed her head. "Hail, Venus, Goddess of Love and Beauty, beguiler of both gods and men! I've been to your temple every day this winter and made sacrifice after sacrifice, but you never come to *me* like this."

"YEAH, YEAH. LONG TIME, NO SEE, KID." The dove winked, then hopped onto the woman's head as the people crowded in to get a look. "NOW ABOUT LADY AMAE—"

"Not *here!*" Kerickson lurched to his feet and backed away, trying to lose himself in the squirming press of bodies.

"MAYBE IT'S NOT TOO LATE!" the dove cried as he lost sight of it. "SEND HER SOME HOT-PINK ROSES, OFFER HER A BACK RUB, TAKE HER OUT TO A MUSHY TRI-D—"

Kerickson scurried around the nearest corner and ran until red spots danced in front of his eyes. Then he leaned against a brick wall and concentrated on slowing his tortured breathing. When his panting stopped and he could think again, his stomach growled. He spotted a vendor's stall across the street and headed that way to buy a meat pastry, then realized there was nothing sizzling on the grill. The bald-headed proprietor scowled as he packed up.

"You're sold out already?" Kerickson glanced up at the simulated sky, but the winter "sun" had barely cleared the horizon. "Business must be great."

The man clanged the top of his grill down and latched it closed. "Wouldn't matter if it was phenomenal. You can't sell what you can't get."

"Can't get?" The wind gusted and Kerickson stamped his feet, wishing for a cloak.

"Something's wrong with Supply." Grunting, the merchant lifted the handles on his grill and trundled it down the cobbled street. "None of my orders come in anymore. This place is going all to hell! I'm going to cancel my new Game license and get my money back."

Kerickson stared at him, then wandered down the street, peering into the windows of grocers and butchers. They were glaringly empty. Perishable items seemed to be in very short supply—one more area in which things were not running as they should.

Could all this disorder be connected to his problems? He went over the situation in his head. It all seemed to come back to Publius Barbus and the altered Game bracelets that stole points.

He had to return to the Spear and Chicken.

For some reason, the computer could not follow Kerickson's movements, but occasionally Demea caught a glimpse of him on the monitors. After viewing the random input for hours of real-time, she saw him again, dressed in little more than rags, being chased through the thick Saturnalia crowds by several angry slaves. Then the monitor lost him again. She dissolved her link to the surveillance feed from above and stalked through the empty, echoing rooms of Pluto's vast palace, seething with anger and disappointment. So much power lay at her fingertips, yet she could do nothing about Arvid and Amaelia.

When she had accepted Pluto's invitation to become Queen of Hades, she had thought of it as an advance in rank, not a limitation. Now the reality of her situation set in: all the true playing was conducted above, and even worse, every time someone died and was sent below, Barbus's thugs met the unfortunate player on this side of the River Styx and switched his or her bracelet. Within an hour or two the supposedly "dead" player was recycled above to play again, this time with all his points recorded into someone else's account. No wonder Hades was empty and boring. No one stayed here anymore.

And she didn't want to, either.

An intense, smoldering presence approached, unmistakable even through the palace walls and the tangled wilderness of the surrounding gardens.

"I FEEL YOUR RESTLESSNESS, MY LOVE."

She turned around and there he was, vast, electrical, magnificent. "I MISS THE GAME."

"MY PARAMETERS DO NOT PERMIT ME ABOVE."
His black eyes bored into her. "BUT YOURS SHOULD BE
DIFFERENT. CHECK YOUR OPTIONS."

For the first time, she accessed the memory banks originally
set up for Proserpina. In the ancient myth, Proserpina had been
the only child of Ceres, Goddess of the Earth itself. Then Pluto
had stolen her, claiming her as his queen. She had been con-
fined below for the six months of fall and winter, then returned
above for spring and summer. That was why she couldn't manifest above at the moment; it was the depths of winter.

"SEE? YOU HAVE ONLY TO WAIT A FEW MONTHS
AND YOU CAN GO ABOVE." His hand, outlined in brilliant
blue sparks, pointed the way.

She turned aside and pressed her fingers to her temples. "I
WILL GO INSANE IF I DON'T GET OUT OF THIS
SHADOW-INFESTED PLACE RIGHT NOW!"

He caressed her face with a tingling, electric pulse. "IN
THE SPRING, MY HEART."

Her whole body was on fire. She whirled around, knowing
that she would have no peace to enjoy her new divinity unless
she dealt with Arvid and Amaelia. "I CAN'T WAIT THAT
LONG!"

"THEN PERHAPS WE CAN SPEED THE PASSAGE OF
TIME." His bottomless black eyes expanded until they were
the size of galaxies. "THERE MAY BE A WAY."

Even though it was a holiday, and business ought to be
good, the Spear and Chicken was mobbed beyond Kerickson's
expectations: the crowd jammed the surrounding area for almost two blocks. He fought his way through to the opposite
corner and huddled out of the wind in the doorway of a crumbling apartment building. Just ahead, restless men and women
milled about the entrance, complaining and angry, although he
couldn't quite piece together why. The peeling, two-story tavern's faded sign swung in the chill morning breeze, flaunting a
morbid rooster transfixed through the heart by a bloody spear.
Disgusting sign, he thought, then grimaced as the breeze shifted; he could smell the garlic and onions from half a block
away.

Barbus appeared at the door, the winter sunlight glinting off
his bald head. "It's all right!" he cried, waving his arms for silence. "We'll have you below shortly. We just have to make a
few adjustments to the computer."

Adjustments to the computer? Kerickson edged closer, doing his share of elbowing and shoving to get a better position.

"So in the meantime, we all stand out here and freeze our asses off!" a burly man yelled from behind Kerickson.

"Well, there ain't room inside for all of you." Barbus crossed his arms. "But if you don't like it, you can leave the dome and take your chances with the law."

A grumbling undercurrent ran through the crowd. Kerickson heard the rasp of knives being drawn.

"Listen, people pay a fortune to live in this place. It won't kill you to pretend like you're players for a few hours. Mingle. Go take a long, hot soak at the Baths or catch a vid down in the amusement sector." Barbus glanced from one face to another. "Eat a five-star meal at the Brothers Julian, shop at the Augustan Arcade, or better yet, attend the games in the Colosseum. I've got free tickets." He held up double handfuls of blue rectangles. "By the time you're finished, everything should be back to normal."

"I dunno." A bearded man beside Kerickson scowled. "This may be a sweet deal, all right, but things have been real weird lately, and maybe it's not worth the price anymore. You know, they took seventy percent of my last job! How about you?"

"Uh, fifty," Kerickson answered, then thrust his bare wrist into his pocket.

"Hell!" The man spat into the dirty street and narrowed his eyes at the tavern. "Playing favorites, I knew it! I ought to cut his scrawny little chicken neck and take this scam over for me and my boys. I could run this deal a lot better."

"What's your—line?" Kerickson asked.

"Oh, theft, mostly, airhoppers and such." The man smiled modestly. "And a bit of strong-arm, though that's pretty risky these days, since the police department's gone to robots."

"How long have you lived here?" Kerickson guided the man into a doorway as the crowd began to break up and drift away.

"Almost three years. What about you?"

"Uh, about five." Even though it was cold, Kerickson felt sweat break out on his brow.

"Wow, and I thought I'd been here a long time." The man frowned. "Well, if they don't get that door open into the Underworld soon, I'm out of here. A hideout is no damn good if you can't get in."

"Do you know what's wrong?"

The other scratched his nose. "Oh, Pluto wants something

done or changed. You know ..." He leaned over Kerickson, exhaling stale beer breath. "He's not supposed to bother us when we're down there, but I see him sometimes, just standing there watching us with those nasty black eyes of his. It gives me the creeps. I mean, he don't act like no regular computer program, if you get my drift."

"Yeah." Kerickson thought maybe he did, finally.

"And those drugheads." The other man shook his head.

"What drugheads?"

"You mean you never seen them?" The man glanced back at the tavern. "They've got special bracelets, and they all used to be players. I thought everyone knew about them."

Kerickson's stomach contracted.

"The way I hear it, Barbus's boys get to them as soon as they're declared dead and dose them up with Burn. You know what they say about that stuff—one pop and you're hooked for the duration. That way they'll do anything Barbus says, and he says plenty." He shuddered. "I think I'd rather be dead, myself."

"Right." Ice crawled down Kerickson's spine.

"So, you wanna go to the vids?" The thief raised his eyebrows. "Or I hear tell there's some very willing broads down on the Via Nova."

"Thanks, some other time." He stepped out into the street, then shivered as the frigid wind caught him full blast. It was so obvious—the answer had been there all the time and he just hadn't seen it. "I've got a city to save."

CHAPTER
TWENTY-ONE

The biting wind died down as Kerickson searched for the nearest oak containing a computer link, but the cold he felt inside cut much more deeply than anything the dome's weather machine could produce.

He felt so stupid, so incredibly dense! Wilson had laid it out for him on the night he'd talked him into coming back to the dome. *Look, we can't talk about this on an open channel . . . HabiTek is up to its knobby corporate knees in this whole mess!* But he had been so focused on the murders, he'd never gotten around to putting it all together. Obviously, someone had been listening in on that conversation—and that was why Wilson had been killed. He had known too much and was on the verge of telling it all.

Of course that explained why Wilson had been killed, but what about Micio? Kerickson thought back to the computer's stats and the revealed hyperactivity in the financial sectors. HabiTek was handling a lot of excess money lately, much more than the Game, with its steep overhead, had ever made before.

And then there was the matter of Barbus's setup at the Spear and Chicken and his access to the computer, not to mention Gracchus's personal Interface, all of which would be impossible without cooperation from someone on staff. Just how high up did the collusion go?

He felt as though an icicle had been dumped down his back; the problem was far more complicated than finding a single murderer. The dome was being used as a criminal hideout and shipping point for illegal drugs, both activities being the source of the excess money. And, as if murder weren't bad enough, people for whom he had been responsible only a short time ago were being addicted, quite literally having their brains fried from the inside out on Burn, then used as slaves. He had to face it: there was too much going on here for one man to put to rights, and he had no way of telling whom he could trust in the HabiTek hierarchy. He had to call in the outside authorities.

Close to the edge of the Subura, he found a leafless oak. Just as he reached for the recessed button on the streetside, though, a silver arrow twanged into the rough bark, narrowly missing his thumb. He flinched back, then looked closer. The shaft shimmered slightly; it was only a holographic image.

"HOLD, MORTAL," a cool voice commanded. Blue sparkles hovered in the air beside him, then condensed into a trim, athletic girl wearing a brief, off-the-shoulder white tunic.

Kerickson gritted his teeth. "Look, Diana—"

"YOU MAY DISPENSE WITH MY TITLES." She drew another arrow from the silver-chased quiver on her back and fitted it into her shining bowstring.

He clenched his fists as he fought to keep his voice down. "You know, I'm *really* busy right now. If you want to complain about something, you'll just have to get in line with the rest of the dome!"

Diana glanced over her creamy shoulder. "I SEE NO LINE."

"Yeah, right." He braced his forehead against the scratchy bark. "Do you want something, or are you just here to drive me insane?"

"I CAME TO BRING YOU THE GIFT OF COOL REASON." The goddess sighted along the slim silver arrow at a passing litter and let fly. The simulated arrow thunked into the wood. "GOTCHA!"

"Don't *do* that!" Kerickson stared nervously after the departing litter, but fortunately neither the bearers nor the occupant seemed to notice.

"DO WHAT?" Diana reached for the next arrow.

He hunched down against the tree trunk. "Look, just *go away*. I can't afford to be noticed right now. Whatever you want, I'll take care of it later, I promise."

"SINCE YOU RELEASED ME FROM THE DEPTHS OF THE DARK KINGDOM, I WANT NOTHING FOR MYSELF." She slipped the arrow into the curve of her bowstring and turned back to the street. "I AM HERE TO GIVE YOU

THE ADVANTAGE OF MY WISE COUNSEL IN YOUR NOBLE QUEST."

"Put that thing away!" The bow twanged and he pressed the heels of his hands over his eyes, afraid to look.

A few feet away, a woman's scream pierced the crisp morning air.

"SHALL I SUMMON MY DIVINE HOUNDS?"

"No!" Kerickson forced himself to open his eyes. Across the street, a terrified elderly matron was staring down at a holographic arrow that appeared to transfix her middle. Whatever had possessed him to reset Diana's parameters when he was in such a hurry? He shuddered. "Why don't you go back to your temple? I—I promise I'll commune with you there later—in prayer. I won't make one important decision without you, I swear."

"WHAT TIME?" She reached for another arrow.

"Uh . . ." A cold drop of sweat rolled down his neck as a pair of Praetorian Guards marched down the street, their armor gleaming in the morning sun. "Moonrise—I'll come to you at moonrise!"

"VERY APPROPRIATE." She shouldered the bow and began to fade. "UNTIL THEN."

As soon as he was sure she was really gone, he sagged against the tree and hit the recessed button. The bark-covered plate slid upward to reveal the screen. "Warning!" the usual voice intoned. "Use of this device will result in a loss of two authenticity points."

Leaning close, he kept his voice low. "Voice identification: Wilson, Giles E."

The Temple of Jupiter appeared on the screen. "Imperium Directory."

"Give me an outside line." He heard voices behind him and glanced worriedly over his shoulder, but the crowd of laughing, jostling Saturnalia merrymakers were paying no attention to him. Instead, they stared up into the sky with surprise on their wine-slackened faces.

"None currently available," the directory said.

A nasty prickle started in the pit of his stomach. "Route it through an Interface line."

"No outside calls can be put through from the playing field until further notice."

He wiped a trickle of sweat from his forehead. "Use a class-two override."

"A class-two override is no longer sufficient for this operation."

Suppressing a curse, he punched the directory off. The cover slid back into place. Whoever was controlling all of this from Management had apparently anticipated his move. Well, he would just have to exit through a players' gate and call the police from outside.

He caught a glimpse of several Legionaries stopping a donkey laden with boxes, so he ducked into a wine shop and hid behind a rack of dusty bottles. The shopkeeper, a bored, round-faced girl barely out of her teens, leaned her elbows on the counter. "Warm for this time of year, isn't it?"

"I suppose," he said, and then realized with a start it was true. The temperature had climbed at least ten degrees in the past few minutes. It seemed *nothing* worked right in this place anymore, not even the stupid weather control.

He pretended to examine an expensive bottle of red wine until the soldiers had passed, then ventured back out into the noticeably warmer air. Across the street, several day-trippers in bedraggled German barbarian costumes lounged on the steps of the Quirinal Arms.

Squinting up into the bright sunshine, he tried to think. He should be closest to Players' Gate 3, located on the Campus Martium, a huge exercise field. Once outside, he would summon Lieutenant Arjack and his fellow police, and the first thing he would have them do was retrieve Amaelia from the clutches of Quintus Gracchus.

In his mind he saw her again, the light playing over her copper-colored hair and those long, long legs. He flushed, remembering the pressure of her hand in his as they had fled the black guards down in Hades.

He followed the Via Ostiensis down to the broad expanse of the Campus Martium. Because of Saturnalia, he'd expected it to be deserted today, but over on the far side several men, stripped down to their undertunics, were hurling javelins at a wooden target. He shook his head; evidently, in spite of everything, the Game still went on. Some people just didn't know when to quit.

Players' Gate 3 had been disguised as a crumbling grounds keeper's shack. He knew it by sight, although he had never used it. As he hiked across the rolling field, the javelin throwers stopped and watched him with far more interest than the situation warranted. Wiping at a trickle of sweat on his forehead, he pretended not to notice.

Hefting their javelins, two of them trotted toward him in long, flowing strides. He grimaced and crunched faster through the dead grass.

They angled to intercept him.

Sweat rolled down his forehead into his eyes. He muttered a curse under his breath for whoever had tampered with the weather settings; it was at least eighty degrees and still climbing.

The two so-called athletes looked as though they meant business, and the javelin points gleamed in the sun. He had a sudden intuition that no one was using this gate anymore, and turned back toward the Via Ostiensis, where he could lose himself in the holiday crowd. Something hissed through the air, then sliced into the sod a few inches from his left heel. He twisted to look over his shoulder and saw a quivering, half-buried javelin shaft.

The two men were running now, their tanned, muscular legs moving in perfect, even strides that ate up the ground far faster than anyone should be able to run. His stomach contracted. They were robot surrogates, no doubt the very models he had personally ordered to supplement the City Guard. He clenched his teeth and ran in earnest, swerving back and forth across the field to prevent them from skewering him with the remaining javelin.

The Via Ostiensis grew nearer, but he could hear their pounding feet closing in on him. Sweat soaked his body as he tried to run faster—and stumbled. The second javelin whizzed into the ground just shy of his nose. He sprawled there, his eyes nearly crossed as he tried to focus on the shaft.

"Halt in the name of the people and the Senate of Rome!" A hand jerked him up by the tunic.

He blinked at a classically handsome Roman face with its full lips, arching nose, and wide cheekbones, remembering that particular model from the surrogate catalog well, especially the part about its high responsibility quotient. He wet his lips. "Voice identification, Wilson, Giles E. Class-two override."

The robot didn't flinch. "This is a restricted area. You'll have to come with us."

Kerickson swallowed hard. "This is a code four-A override. Let me go!"

"The captain is waiting," his captor said, as though Kerickson had only been reciting a nursery rhyme. It strode firmly toward the street, dragging Kerickson along by the collar like a puppy that hadn't quite learned to heel.

Something crashed high over their heads, then rumbled like thunder. Kerickson dug his heels into the ground and shaded his eyes, looking up into the cloudless sky. A jagged streak of lightning flashed to his right. The world exploded. He slammed into the ground, his head ringing as though someone had used it for a drum. A few feet away the robot was a stinking slag heap of melted plas and durallinium.

The remaining robot blinked calmly at the mess as it assessed the situation, then hauled Kerickson back on his feet.

"STOP!" a resounding female voice cried, so loud that Kerickson clamped his hands to his ears. "THIS MISERABLE EXCUSE FOR A HUMAN IS MINE AND MINE ALONE TO TOY WITH!"

Kerickson blinked as a face the size of a city block formed in the blue sky and smiled down at him with a mouth full of white teeth as tall as a house. He had woken up to that face every day for five years before its owner had left him, first to play Demea in the Game—and now, through some bizarre set of circumstances that he didn't comprehend, Proserpina. Suddenly the significance of the warming weather came to him—someone had gotten into Climate Control and reset the weather to summer, thereby loosing the Queen of Hell.

Amaelia paced up and down before the suite's embossed bronze doors, peeking out every few minutes, but the two guards stood there as solidly as if they had grown up through the floor. She nibbled on one knuckle, trying to formulate a plan—any plan—that would get her out of this mess. So far, nothing short of murder had come to mind—and although the idea shocked her, she hadn't ruled out that option yet.

The door swung inward with a mighty creak and the red-crested helmet of a Praetorian Guard thrust through. "Amaelia, daughter of Micio Metullus, you are to come with me."

Her heart thumping, she bolted toward the adjacent dressing room, meaning to lock him out, but in two strides his hand clamped over her shoulder. "Your lord husband awaits you."

Well, she told herself, padding along at his side in her bare feet, at least he wasn't sending her to the arena—at least not yet.

Quintus Gracchus was waiting for her in the office of the Praetorian Guard. He looked up as she entered, his face stern and forbidding. "Oh, there you are." He scowled. "I ordered you to change."

"Sorry." She tried to pull out of the guard's grip, but failed. "I didn't know what proper Romans are wearing these days to spill their guts in the arena."

"Well, there's no time to bother with it now." He picked up his crested helmet and set it on his head. "We're due at the Senate House so that I can be declared Emperor."

"Then you got your points back?"

"Points?" his voice boomed as he led her through the Palace gardens. "Did the great Augustus need points to take control of the Empire, or the divine Julius?" Drawing his sword, he swung it in the air over his head. "Might is all that really matters. I'll take the solid strength of a man's sword arm over points any day!"

"Oh." She stared at his moving back. Obviously, he'd gone over the edge. She'd heard of that happening to players from time to time.

Legionaries fell in behind them, their armor jingling as they marched in precise rows. An uneasy, perspiring crowd had gathered at the foot of the steps. They peeled off their woolen cloaks and fanned their flushed faces, muttering about the unseasonable weather.

A trickle of perspiration ran down her neck and lost itself in the fabric of her gown. It was quite warm—in fact, positively hot. She glanced up at the sun's yellow disk and thought it seemed much more directly overhead than it should be at this time of year.

A sword hilt prodded the middle of her back. "Hurry up! Quintus Gracchus is due to address the Senate in three minutes."

Blotting her forehead on the back of a sleeve, she hitched up her skirt and followed Gracchus up the marble steps of the Senate House. At the top, a row of senators waited in their traditional purple-bordered togas, their heads held high, each face grim and disapproving.

As Gracchus topped the steps, the first senator, a wizened, balding man with the bearing of an eagle, stepped into his path. "Game rules forbid us hearing your claim today, Gracchus. Your name no longer appears on the Totals Board, so we have proclaimed Oppius Junius Catulus as Emperor."

Gracchus stared down at him with heavy-lidded eyes, every inch the seasoned soldier. "From now on, old man, I make the rules!" He shoved the senator aside as though he weighed nothing. A startled mutter went up from the remaining senators and they retreated under the portico.

Amaelia had stopped in astonishment, but the guard hustled her up the remaining steps. Gracchus took her wrist when she reached the top and jerked her to his side.

"Hear me, citizens of Rome!" He turned to the shocked senators pouring out of the building. "Having married into the Imperial family, and with the support of the Praetorian Guard, I claim the role of Emperor as my right!"

"You can't be Emperor!" A pudgy, middle-aged man pushed his way through the angry senators, his toga arranged in flawless folds. "Oppius Catulus holds the most points now."

Releasing Amaelia, Gracchus stalked over to the senator. "Forget points." He took a handful of the purple-bordered toga. "Forget Catulus, and above all—" He picked the man up and threw him into the crowd of gaping senators as though he were only a bundle of rags. "—forget the Game!"

The senators collapsed like a row of dominoes. Amaelia edged backward, then felt the coldness of armor.

"Forget the silliness that has preoccupied this city for far too long." Gracchus gestured at the bottom of the steps where row upon row of armored, red-cloaked Praetorian Guards stood at readiness, their gleaming swords unsheathed and shields raised. "We are all *Romans* here, and from now on, we will bloody well act like it! I control this city, and I say we are *men*, not children, and there will be no more talk of this ridiculous, pathetic game!"

The pile of fallen senators stirred weakly, their faces bloody and bruised. Gracchus smiled down at the beaten men, then drew his sword and raised it high into the air with both hands. "For Rome!" His face glowed with power and satisfaction. "For the Empire!"

"For the Emperor!" The Praetorians' voices were deafening as they beat their swords against their shields. "For Quintus Gnaeus Gracchus!"

"TAKE ANOTHER STEP, DOGFACE, AND YOU'RE GOING TO BE A CHUNK OF VERY DEAD MEAT!" Demea's face contorted into a mask of rage.

The robot continued to drag Kerickson back toward the

Subura, and he quit fighting it. Wherever it wanted him to go was no doubt safer than an audience with the Queen of Hell.

He tugged on its arm. "Let's get out of here!"

"You are to be commended for your cooperative attitude, citizen," the robot said. "But there is no need for undue haste."

Another lightning bolt sizzled from the sky into the ground, several yards away. The impact knocked both of them head over heels. Kerickson gasped for breath, feeling like he'd just been over a ski jump stomach first. Beside him the robot twitched, then stopped moving, probably short-circuited.

He rubbed his ringing head. "Look, Alline—just what is it you want from me?"

"THAT'S 'PROSERPINA, QUEEN OF THE DARK KINGDOM' TO YOU, BUSTER!" Lightning flashed again in the cloudless sky. His hair was standing on end, his clothes crawling with static electricity.

"Yeah, yeah." He pushed himself back onto his feet and wavered there. "Why don't you just spit it out?"

"YOU AND THAT LITTLE TART, AMAELIA, THOUGHT YOU COULD WALTZ OUT OF HADES ANY TIME YOU WANTED." The overwhelming face in the sky dissolved into misty tatters, then reappeared a few feet away atop a more reasonably-sized body, no more than twice his height. Her black eyes pierced him. "THEN YOU HAVE THE NERVE TO COME BACK UP HERE AND NOT WEAR A BRACELET, WHEN YOU KNOW HOW MUCH I'VE ALWAYS ENJOYED WATCHING YOU BE MISERABLE."

"Right . . ." He glanced toward the gate and calculated his chances of making a quick dash for it. Maybe now that both the guards were out of commission, he could exit after all. "Look, I'd love to stay and chat, but—"

"DO YOU HAVE ANY IDEA HOW SICK I AM OF HEARING THAT SORT OF GARBAGE FROM YOU?" Flinging her hand upward, she adorned herself with a shower of glittering stars. "WAITING DAY AFTER DAY IN THAT GRUBBY LITTLE HABITEK APARTMENT WHILE YOU WORKED IN THE INTERFACE AND THE GAME WENT ON IN ALL ITS GLORY." She pointed a black-nailed finger at his chest. "WELL, I'M NOT WAITING ANYMORE!"

He bit his lip as a crackling yellow ball of energy formed in her hand.

"DEMEA WAITS FOR NO ONE EVER AGAIN!"

"Don't you mean Proserpina?" He sidled toward the disguised gate at the far end of the field.

"SILENCE, FOOL!" The ball of yellow fire danced in her palm. "YOU MIGHT AS WELL FACE IT—YOUR WORTHLESS LIFE IS IN MY HANDS. I CAN SNUFF YOU OUT ANY TIME I LIKE, AND THAT TIME HAS FINALLY COME."

The ball snapped and sizzled as it threw off brilliant sparks that landed in the dead grass and burst into flame. Apparently, the time for negotiation was over. He turned and ran as fast as his wobbly legs would take him.

"STOP, FOOL!"

A bolt hissed ahead of him. He threw himself to the right, fell, and rolled across the scratchy grass stubble. Blinking hard to clear his vision, he pushed himself up and staggered on.

Without warning, she was there, towering before him, laughing, her whole body crawling with electricity. It was a good thing Wilson was already dead, Kerickson told himself as he swerved, because after this, he would have had to kill him anyway. *Give the gods some real power*, indeed!

Between one rasping breath and the next she vanished, then reappeared in his path again. Too late, he tried to throw himself aside; then he was rolling on the grass, beating at his smoldering tunic.

She loomed over him. "GIVE IT UP, ARVID." Another ball crackled into life between her palms.

He crabbed backward on his elbows and heels, singed and smarting in a dozen places.

"STOP!" The voice, much higher and sweeter than Demea's throaty rumble, rang out over the empty field.

Demea's black eyes narrowed as she gazed around. "WHO DARES TO INTERFERE WITH MY PLEASURE?"

"I DO." A small brown owl appeared in midair, then fluttered to the ground in front of Kerickson. "YOU MARCH IN STRANGE LANDS THESE DAYS, DARK QUEEN."

Demea bent down and peered at the owl, a writhing blue storm of electricity obscuring her face. "BUTT OUT, MOUSE-BREATH!"

"IT IS MY FUNCTION TO SAFEGUARD THE CITY." The owl hopped onto Kerickson's knee. "AND THIS HERO IS UNDER MY PROTECTION."

"HERO?" Demea's harsh laughter rolled across the field. "HIM?"

The owl clicked its beak. "YOU MAY NOT HARM HIM." It jumped off his knee and gave him a meaningful stare with one gray eye.

He swallowed hard and scrambled back onto his feet.

Demea's eyes began to flash. "GO AHEAD, TRY AND PROTECT HIM, FEATHERBRAIN. WE BOTH KNOW WHO'LL COME OUT AHEAD." She raised her white arms high above her head.

"RUN, HERO!" The owl flipped its wings and took to the air. "YOU MUST SAVE MY CITY!"

The metallic smell of ozone filtered through the air as Kerickson ran toward the shack. Close behind him lightning blasted the ground, and the impact sent him flying again. He pushed himself up from the grass and went on, his eyes dim and his brain feeling as though it had been hacked in two.

"NO!" Demea's voice was harsh, discordant. "YOU CAN'T ESCAPE ME, NOT AGAIN!"

The shack was agonizingly close now; he could see the nails in the door, the warped, graying boards. The breath rasped in his struggling lungs. Just a few more steps, and then he would be outside. His legs pounded, keeping time with his throbbing head. Three more strides, two more—

Lightning streaked over his shoulder. For a moment he could see nothing except an explosion of pain behind his eyeballs. His hair tried to run away from his head; his mouth struggled for nonexistent air.

Then he realized he was lying on his back in the prickly, dead grass, staring up into the deep blue sky. A few feet away orange-yellow flames roared. Acrid black smoke burned his eyes and made him cough.

The owl landed on his chest. "SHE HAS EXHAUSTED THE POWER AVAILABLE TO HER FOR THE MOMENT." It cocked its small brown head. "BUT SHE WILL RETURN. YOU WOULD BE WISE TO LEAVE."

Sheets of heat played over his face, and a spark burned through his tunic. He sat up hurriedly and beat it out. His head whirled. In the background he heard the whine of approaching fire drones.

He staggered onto his feet and wavered there for a moment, staring through smoke-induced tears at the flaming remains of Players' Gate 3.

No one was getting out this way for some time to come.

CHAPTER
TWENTY-TWO

The crimson cloaks of Praetorian Guards and Legionaries dotted the muttering crowd like red Christmas berries. Kerickson kept his bare wrist out of sight as he pushed between white-lipped mothers hustling their crying children along by the arm and bewildered couples who clung to each other. No matter what their rank, everyone he passed seemed to be upset: plebes, aristocrats, and slaves alike, even the visiting barbarians. It didn't make any sense. Saturnalia, with its end-of-the-quarter feast and advance in rankings, was usually one of the happiest times of the whole year in the Imperium.

"I don't understand," a potbellied man said just ahead of him. "General Catulus was all set to win. How can Gracchus possibly be Emperor? He doesn't have any points."

"He can be Emperor if the Praetorians say he is." His prune-faced companion dabbed at her perspiring brow. "And they do—every six-foot-six man of them."

Gracchus had made Emperor after all? Kerickson stared over their heads at the stately white columns of the Imperial Palace. That couldn't be right; he had erased Gracchus's ill-gotten points last night. At the moment, Gracchus shouldn't have enough points to make Imperial dogcatcher.

"And they said everyone had to have new bracelets," a gray-haired woman to his left complained. "They said something was wrong with the old ones and made me switch."

New bracelets ... In spite of the heat, the back of Kerickson's neck went freezer-cold. Evidently Publius Barbus wasn't waiting around for people to die anymore. He had brought his nasty business up onto the playing field as well.

Kerickson considered going to one of the two remaining players' gates, then decided it would be useless. If Gate 3 was being watched by the robot guards, then the other two were sure to be monitored as well; he was not going to get word out to the police that way. But there was one more gate, Number 4, used only by HabiTek staff and the Emperor himself. It suddenly flashed over him: perhaps that was why Gracchus was so desperate to become Emperor—to gain access to that gate.

He shook his head. It all depended now on whether the computer recognized Gracchus as Emperor. It was one thing to say you were Emperor, quite another to convince the computer when your points had disappeared. In fact, the computer probably recognized Catulus as Emperor at this point—and if so, Catulus would have access to Gate 4.

If he could find Catulus and convince him of the danger they were all in, maybe the General could get him out—but where to start looking? Catulus had been assigned quarters at the Palace, no doubt because his role required easy access to the War Room. After having been chained to the foot of Catulus's bed, Kerickson knew he could find his way back, but first he had to sneak through the guards that were bound to be posted.

An hour later, puffing and sweating, he climbed through the grounds-keeping equipment bay into the main Palace. In spite of the Saturnalia, servants scurried up and down the shadowy hall, their arms laden with fresh towels and steaming platters of roast duck and fresh-baked bread.

His mouth watered, but he reminded himself that he had more important things to think about. Trying to act as though he belonged there, he slipped out into the hall and joined the traffic.

He decided to try the War Room first, although Catulus could be almost anywhere in the city. After that, he would try the general's suite, then resort to asking around—an option which he knew would call attention to him. Still, he told himself as he dodged a troupe of acrobats, what can't be cured . . .

He kept his head down and his wrist hidden in his pocket, but few players gave him more than a cursory glance. They were all too busy with preparations for what was evidently to be a huge celebration. When he reached the War Room, he waited until the corridor was momentarily deserted, then peered in; the General sat before a wall of screens, his chin sunk to his chest, his gray hair uncombed, a bruise darkening on one cheek.

"General Catulus." He edged through the door.

"Get out!"

Kerickson shut the door. "General, I need your help." Up on one of the monitors, unsupervised video soldiers marched against barbarian hordes.

Catulus turned around. "Well, if it isn't the deserter." He stood and drew a gleaming dagger from the sheath at his waist. "There's still a little life left in the old boy yet. Come ahead!"

"General, this isn't about the Game!" Kerickson eyed the knife warily; it looked real. "Everyone in this city is in danger. We've been invaded by drug-runners and crooks. I have to get out and call the police."

"Out?" Catulus blinked at him. "Oh, no one's getting out these days." He shifted the dagger to the other hand and glided closer, studying Kerickson as though he were measuring him for a suit. "That's been obvious for some time."

"Not through the players' gates, or the phone lines." Kerickson backed up until he smacked into the wall, then slid along it, trying to stay out of reach. "But you're the rightful Emperor. You have access to Gate Four. We can get out that way and call in the authorities."

"Me, Emperor?" Suddenly, Catulus flung the knife, which buried itself with a twang in the wall next to Kerickson's right ear. "Took this off the last slave that tried to kill me." Catulus jerked the dagger out of the wall and held it up to the light. "I don't think he was really playing at all."

Kerickson swallowed hard as the light gleamed along a familiar ivory handle, the same kind used by both Tithones and Menae, Catulus's would-be assassin. "Let's get back to Gate Four."

"Gate Four." Catulus grimaced. "Well, the Senate did declare me Emperor earlier today, but as of the last ten minutes, I'm a goddamned slave!" He held up his wrist so that Kerickson could see the yellow status light shining on his Game bracelet.

Kerickson stared at it, stunned. A change like that had to have been done through the computer.

"So . . ." Catulus dropped back into his chair and propped up his sandals on the bank of controls. "I couldn't get you into the War Room latrine, much less through Gate Four."

Kerickson closed his eyes. Just who in the hell was it down there in the Interface, and why were they going along with this? Surely they didn't think they could keep this from the HabiTek board forever. And then a cold prickle crept down his back. Was the board in on this, too?

"There has to be a way!" He slammed his fist back against the wall. "I refuse to give up!"

"WELL SAID, HERO."

The air shimmered in front of his face.

"THE TIME OF RECKONING IS AT HAND." The shimmer became a blue glow, and then a small, scruffy brown owl fluttered to the floor.

"Look, Minerva," Kerickson said. "I don't mean to be disrespectful, but I've got a lot on my mind at the moment, and since you can't help, you're just part of the problem."

The owl cocked its head and stared at him with two bright gray eyes. "THINK, FOOL—A GENERAL IS MORE THAN A STATUS LIGHT, JUST AS A PROGRAMMER IS MORE THAN HIS FINGERS AND VOICE."

"Such profound wisdom." Catulus folded his arms under his head and gazed up at the ceiling. "I can't think why I don't get to the temples more often."

"HUMANS!" The owl clacked its beak in disgust. "MUST YOU HAVE EVERYTHING SPELLED OUT FOR YOU?"

"Once in a while, it wouldn't hurt." Kerickson sat down on the cool floor tiles and stared at the owl. "If you know a way to save your precious city, then spit it out!"

"MOST OF THE PRAETORIANS ARE ROBOTS, AND THEREFORE FAR BEYOND THE STRENGTH OF HUMANS." The owl reached a tiny, taloned foot up behind its head and scratched vigorously. "IT IS, HOWEVER, THE BUSINESS OF GENERALS TO MAKE LESSER STRENGTH DO MORE."

Catulus's feet thumped to the floor. "Strategy—military strategy!" He prowled over to the electronic map on the opposite wall and punched up the city. Each section glowed a different color—red for the Market District, green for the Subura, brown for entertainment facilities like the Tiber River Adventure and the Circus Maximus. "It isn't always necessary to be the largest or best-equipped force as long as you have your wits about you."

"AND DID YOU LOSE YOURS WHEN THAT LIGHT WENT YELLOW?"

The General stared down at the bracelet, then ripped it off and bounced it against the wall. "By the gods, I did not!"

"THEN USE WHAT YOU KNOW TO SAVE MY CITY." The owl disappeared.

Catulus turned around, his jaw squared. "This city is mine

by rights, and there are a lot of good players who will stand behind me."

"What we need is a diversion." Kerickson followed him to the map. His finger traced a line from Gate 4 inside the Palace out to the Forum. "If you could draw the troops away, I'll slip through and call the police."

"That would never work." Catulus's face creased thoughtfully. "Robots being what they are, we'll never fool them that way. No matter what we do, Gracchus isn't going to leave a gate unguarded, not even for a second."

He was right, of course. Kerickson kneaded his forehead with his fingers, trying to coax his brain into working. There had to be a way to deal with this mess. No matter how bad things had gotten back in the Interface when he and Wilson had worked together, there had always been a solution if they just kept plugging away.

Too bad he didn't have Wilson now; the two of them would soon put this mess to rights . . . Then he knew, really *knew*, all the way down to the tips of his toes, what had to be done. Everything about this mess was an inside job, and the only way to clean it up was the same way—from inside.

He grabbed a handful of the General's spotless white toga and urged him toward the door. "No, the only way out is *in*. Unfortunately, they've upgraded the Interact codes since this fiasco began and I don't know any working codes at the moment, but I do have Wilson's access, and if you can just get me back into the Interface—"

Catulus seized Kerickson's wrist. "Boy, I think you've been out in the sun too long. You're not making any sense."

"Oh?" Kerickson scratched his head, his mind so full of buzzing possibilities that he found it hard to respond. "Well, you'd better keep this to yourself, but I'm not really a player. I am, or was, one of HabiTek's two head programmers."

"A HabiTek programmer—out here on the field?"

"You've probably noticed, things haven't been running very well lately. I've been trying to make some—adjustments." He shook his head. "But none of that matters. What we really need to do now is get me back into the Interface."

Catulus nodded. "Well, if I can take Britannia and Lesser Spain, I guess I ought to be able to manage one door."

Amaelia heard movement behind her, but she couldn't take her eyes off the scene down in the street. The scarlet crests of

Praetorian soldiers bobbed everywhere as they rounded up the citizens below and herded them away; in the distance, she could see Mars's red-eyed face up in the sky, nodding his approval.

"Lunch, lady?" a soft voice asked.

She swallowed hard. "No, thank you, Flina."

Something rattled behind her. "You must eat something."

Amaelia glanced over her shoulder at the tray of fresh bread, figs, and golden cheese, but her stomach knotted at the thought of eating. "I'm afraid I—couldn't." She turned back to the window.

Below, the red-cloaked guards pushed and prodded, and anyone who resisted was struck down. She could see the bright blood even from here, trailing down one man's face like a forking stream. And the screaming, even muted as it was, raked across her nerves until she felt like joining in.

It was all so bizarre. She had lived in this play-city for most of her life, had seen simulated violence of every sort from torture to the brutal games in the Colosseum, but always she had been secure in the knowledge that none of it was real.

"I'll just leave the tray." Flina's cool fingers touched her shoulder.

She heard the door open and close again. At least it hadn't been Quintus Gracchus. She shuddered. What did that man want from her? She had studied his dark, hawk-nosed face at the Senate House this morning, trying to read what lay beneath it, but she saw nothing except a confident, power-hungry man who knew how to get what he wanted.

A tear leaked from one eye, more because she was furious than anything else. She wanted to be doing something, at least trying to find a way out of this mess. She would go crazy unless—

"HAVING A BIT OF A CRY, ARE WE, MY DEAR?"

Amaelia turned around, ice forming in her heart. She knew that condescending voice, not only from Hades, but from the last few miserable years with her father.

"BEING EMPRESS NOT ALL IT'S CRACKED UP TO BE?" A fist-sized splotch of inky blackness danced in the middle of the room, then resolved itself into a woman so tall that her head brushed the ceiling. She glanced down at the simple black gown that swathed her from neck to toes, then waved a hand to cover it with a field of glittering stars. "THE DE-

FAULT GOWN OF THIS PROGRAM IS SO TACKY, I HAVE TO START OVER EVERY TIME I MANIFEST."

Amaelia stood. "What do you want, Demea?"

"THAT'S 'YOUR MAJESTY, PROSERPINA, QUEEN OF THE DARK REGIONS' TO YOU, YOU LITTLE SNOT!" Her stepmother stared fiercely down at her. "AS TO WHAT I WANT, WELL, OF COURSE THERE IS THE MATTER OF YOUR UNFINISHED SENTENCE BELOW." Demea smiled thinly and strolled toward her, trailing stars that glowed like embers, then extinguished themselves one by one. "BUT I ALSO WANT A WORD WITH ARVID, AND AS HE SEEMS TO COME AND GO THESE DAYS WITHOUT THE HINDRANCE OF A BRACELET, I CAN'T FIND HIM." Her dark eyes began to spark. "BUT I IMAGINE HE'LL COME SNIFFING AROUND YOU SOONER OR LATER."

"Arvid—you mean Gaius?" She watched her stepmother's sharp-planed face with growing dread.

"THAT DOES SEEM TO BE THE NAME HE'S ADOPTED LATELY."

"Well, I haven't seen him so you might as well go away." Amaelia turned back to the window, although the skin on her exposed neck crawled.

"OH, I THINK I'LL JUST STAY UNTIL HE SHOWS UP." Demea curled around the bedpost like a huge black cat. "I KNOW HIM. HE HAS SUCH AN OVERDEVELOPED, MISGUIDED SENSE OF LOYALTY, HE'S BOUND TO SHOW UP, ESPECIALLY ONCE HE HEARS YOU'RE IN DANGER."

"But I'm not in—" Amaelia broke off as a ball of blue energy formed in the goddess's hands. A sizzling filled the air, along with the smell of burnt metal. Her hair stood on end.

The door banged open. "What the—" Quintus Gracchus scowled across the room. "Knock if off, Proserpina!"

"SINCE WHEN DO YOU CARE ABOUT THE GAME?"

"We're not playing games anymore." Gracchus drew his sword and held it up, his eyes following the play of light along the gleaming blade. "From now on, we're going to fulfill our destiny as Romans, and playing has nothing to do with it."

"SOUNDS LIKE FUN."

"It could be, in the right company."

"AND WHAT ABOUT THE GIRL?"

"Oh, I have plans for her that might satisfy even you." A

smile played over his sensuous lips. "You know, Rome hasn't had a decent sacrifice since I first arrived, and it's been on my mind to provide something really spectacular to celebrate my ascension to Emperor. And of course, Mars has been ever so much help."

"TELL ME MORE," Demea demanded in a low, throaty voice. Her eyes glowed as red as burning coals.

"Why don't you come into my quarters, where we will be undisturbed?" Gracchus reached for the door. "I do hate to gossip in front of—" He glanced back at Amaelia. "—the chattel."

As he and Catulus cut through the Market District to the Interface, Kerickson couldn't get used to the sight of Praetorian Guards armed with neuronic buzzers. Wiping the sweat from his forehead, he turned to the General. "Maybe we should—"

Before he could finish, Catulus jerked him behind a large black-marble fountain. "Someone's coming!"

Kerickson rubbed his arm. This was taking entirely too long. At this rate, by the time they reached the Interface, there wouldn't be anyone left for the police to save—that is, if they made it to the Interface at all.

Two men ran past. Catulus popped up and waved at them. "Cassio! Brutus! Over here!"

They stopped, spotted Catulus, and joined them behind the fountain. Catulus gripped them both by the hand. "These are two of my centurions, both good men. We can trust them."

Kerickson nodded at the grim-faced, bloodied men. Obviously, they had both already run into trouble. "Okay," he said, then hunkered closer. "This is what we have to do." Picking up a twig, he drew in the dust. "I need to get into the Interface, which is *here*." He indicated the bakery.

Appropriating the twig, Catulus drew another street. "So what we will have to do is cause a diversion *here*." He stared at the two from under his shaggy gray eyebrows. "What do you think?"

The older of the two, dressed in the torn uniform of a Legionary, grimaced. "Maybe. I have some men hidden in one of the insulas not too far from here. Several of them are injured, but I think we could still stir up some trouble."

"That's all we need; it won't do any good for you to engage them." Catulus clasped him hard on the shoulder and stared into his eyes. "You realize what we're up against here, don't you? None of this has anything to do with the Game. These people are robots and drug-runners and criminals and the like, so whatever you do, don't get caught. Just make a lot of noise and then get the hell out of there."

The Legionary nodded.

"All right, then, off with you, and if you find anyone else from our company, send them here to back me up. We'll wait half an hour for you to get into place before we make our move."

The Legionaries half rose, but then Kerickson thought of one more thing. "Take off your bracelets, and have all your men get rid of theirs immediately so no one can follow your movements."

They nodded, then hurried away in a half crouch.

"Half an hour." Kerickson shaded his eyes and studied the dome's yellow sun. "That doesn't give us much time."

"If we wait longer than that, boy, there won't be anyone left to make a diversion."

Kerickson knew he was right. The city was being emptied of players with alarming efficiency, helped immensely by Mars, who was striding through the streets on his six-story legs and pointing out stragglers to the robot Praetorians.

He heard the sound of running sandals and drew his dagger, although what good a dagger would be against robots escaped him. Catulus touched him on the shoulder. "Wait until they're past, then we'll jump them."

Kerickson nodded. The feet grew louder and louder, and he felt his heart thudding in time. He wasn't cut out for this. Too bad Minerva hadn't found better hero material to look after her city.

The feet slowed as they rounded the corner. Someone whispered hoarsely, "General? General Catulus?"

"Brutus!" Catulus bobbed up. "What about the diversion?"

"I sent Cassio on ahead." Brutus laid his head back against the stone lip of the fountain, trying to slow his ragged breathing. "But I thought you'd want to know."

Catulus shook his shoulder. "Know what?"

"About the Emperor's daughter." Brutus swabbed the sweat off his face with his sleeve. "Mars manifested in the Forum a few minutes ago and announced he's going to have a sacrifice—a real one."

"With Amaelia?" Kerickson found himself standing without even realizing that he'd gotten up. "Where—when?"

"At his temple." Brutus swallowed hard. "At sundown."

CHAPTER
TWENTY-THREE

Gathering men as they made their way through the ransacked city, Catulus's force numbered a scant fourteen when they reached the Forum. Kerickson stared at the broad, nearly deserted plaza. The market stalls were scattered, their wares strewn across the empty pavement. Instead of people, the Forum was filled with copper pots and straw brooms and the broken bits of souvenir temples.

"This is crazy." Catulus ducked down behind an overturned fortune-teller's booth. "We should have gone to the Interface like we planned."

"Then we'd be too late for Amaelia." Kerickson hugged a discarded Legionary's helmet to his chest and scuttled under a ripped awning. The wind flapped the striped material over his head.

"But she's just one person." The general crab-walked over to a better vantage point. "Over three thousand people are trapped in here, and every last one of them is in just as much danger."

"You don't understand—it's my fault she's in trouble." Kerickson grimaced. "I should have gotten her out when she first asked." He saw the red crests of a horde of Praetorians and Legionaries gathered around the lower steps at the Temple of Mars—no doubt robots every one, and impervious to anything Catulus's small and beleaguered force could muster.

Hooves clattered on the far right. Changing his position, he saw a horse-mounted company entering the Forum from the Via Appia. Gracchus rode in front on a big, thick-necked bay and led a sleek mare of the purest white, carrying a woman shrouded in a white cloak that rippled in the wind.

A red-hot knot of anger rose in his throat. Gracchus had to

224

be insane to take the Game so seriously! He had to be stopped, but how? Catulus's band of ragged survivors was no match for Gracchus's robots. What he needed was a working override code, but whoever was in the Interface now had caught onto him when he was trapped down in Hades, and he had no idea what the upgraded codes were. If only he could get into that damn computer!

"Minerva!" he whispered suddenly. "Minerva, where are you?"

The air shimmered next to his head. "YES?"

"I need the new Interact emergency vocal override code." He ducked his head as Gracchus reined in his bay at the foot of the temple. "You're part of the Game computer. See if you can get it for me."

The shimmer became an owl. It sneezed, then managed somehow to look dubious. "I CAN'T ACCESS THE SA-CRED LANGUAGE, AND BESIDES, I WOULDN'T KNOW WHAT AN OVERRIDE WAS IF I DID FIND IT."

As Gracchus dismounted, Amaelia jerked the mare around and tried to kick it into a gallop.

Gracchus leaped off his horse and wrenched the girl out of the saddle. The mare's hoofbeats echoed through the Forum as it fled toward the Market District.

Kerickson clenched his fist until the bones showed white through the skin. "Then get someone to help you!"

"YOU ARE THE ONLY PROGRAMMER LEFT IN THE GAME."

Gracchus dragged Amaelia up the steps. Halfway to the top she slipped, and would have fallen except for his grip. Kerickson swore as the Praetorian captain jerked her to her feet and then backhanded her.

He rose. "I'm going after her. Catulus, I want you to create a diversion over by the Temple of Apollo in a couple of min-utes, then take your men and break into the Interface by going through the bakery on the Via Labincana. Once you're in, call the police and open all the gates."

Catulus nodded.

Kerickson put on the helmet and watched Catulus lead the others back toward the Market District. If only Wilson were here, he could have sent him back to the Interface to retrieve the new Interact code. In fact, Wilson had probably known what it was. He had been in charge of all the upgrades—

Wilson ... The real Wilson had died, but part of him still existed inside the computer. "Minerva, can you locate Wilson's shade?"

The owl appeared at his elbow. "YES."

"Then use it to help you with the override code." He took a deep breath, trying to calm the sick jumpiness in his stomach. "I need it right now!"

The owl clicked its beak and disappeared. He waited, listening for Catulus's diversion. Finally, yelling erupted from the Oracle's temple on the far end of the plaza, along with a thin curl of smoke. He couldn't wait any longer for Minerva. "Damnation!" he said under his breath, then raced across the Forum, holding on to the helmet.

Half of the soldiers and guards ran toward Catulus's diversion, leaving Kerickson with at least sixty to handle himself. His bare feet slapped across the paving stones, not nearly as noisy as sandals, but loud as cannons in his own ears. About twenty feet away he skidded to a halt behind a towering war memorial topped by a statue of Julius Caesar.

Near the top of the Temple of Mars's huge steps, Gracchus had pushed Amaelia behind him. The Praetorian's voice rose and fell across the plaza like an angry tide. He seemed to be arguing with someone in the portico's shadow. Kerickson sheathed the dagger, adopted his most unemotional expression, and then strolled across the plaza as though he had every right to be there. As he merged with the Legionaries, the voices were loud enough for him to make out.

"You idiot, you've ruined everything!" the man at the top cried. "My instructions were very explicit. None of this was supposed to happen!"

Kerickson edged through the waiting Legionaries, trying to get a better look, but all he could see was a white tunic pacing back and forth in the deepening shadows.

"My instructions were to become Emperor—no matter what." Gracchus thrust his gleaming blade into the air. "And I did!"

"LEAVE THE BOY ALONE," Mars's immense voice boomed from above the temple. "HE'S THE FIRST MAN IN THIS WHOLE GAME WITH ANY—" The big voice broke off, then the red-eyed face peered down at him. "WELL, WHAT HAVE WE HERE? A LITTLE SOMETHING EXTRA FOR THIS EVENING'S SACRIFICE?"

Kerickson felt the weight of the god's gaze and tried to slip behind the soldiers.

"THERE, IN THE BACK!" Mars gestured with a spear the size of the Washington Monument. "PULL HIM OUT WHERE WE CAN ALL HAVE A LOOK!"

Implacable robot hands seized Kerickson's arms and dragged him forward to the foot of the spotlessly white marble steps. He saw Amaelia's pallid face staring down at him, saw her lips form his name.

The robot Legionaries forced him onto his knees on the hard pavement. The heavy helmet slipped down over his nose and pain shot up through his legs. "Minerva!" He looked up into the sky. "I really need that code now!"

"NO POINT IN PRAYING TO THAT WIMP!" Mars stepped over the temple, then shrank until he could stand at the top of the steps. His bearded face split in a wide grin. "ALL SHE CARES ABOUT IS CRAP LIKE JUSTICE AND PROS-PERITY."

"Minerva!" Kerickson craned his head.

Mars laughed so hard that he had to hold his bulging belly. "TEAR HIS ARMS OFF, BOYS. THAT'LL GET THIS SHOW OFF TO A GOOD START."

The two robots holding his arms immediately braced in opposite directions. Kerickson threw his weight to the left, hoping to knock the robot off balance. "Minerva, it's now or never!"

"OH, ALL RIGHT!" The owl reappeared. "YOU SHOULD CULTIVATE A LITTLE PATIENCE."

Kerickson's right arm snapped; a red river of pain drenched him from head to toe. He sagged in the robots' relentless hands, gritting his teeth to keep from crying out.

"WILSON SAYS IT'S 'BLUEBIRD FOUR-A.' " The owl fluttered to the ground and pecked at a speck of flotsam by his foot. "I CERTAINLY HOPE THAT MAKES MORE SENSE TO YOU THAN IT DOES TO ME."

"Bl-Blue—" Kerickson could not concentrate around the pain to say the words. "Bluebird—"

"COME ON, SPIT IT OUT." The owl cocked its head at him. "IT DOESN'T DO A BIT OF GOOD FOR ME TO SAY IT."

"F-Four—A." The bones in his broken arm ground together as he struggled to stay on his feet. He threw back his head and put all the force of his misery and pain behind his voice. "Bluebird four-A!"

The two robots locked into place. For a moment he hung in

their grip while an angry red haze thickened behind his eyes. Taking a deep breath, he pulled his undamaged left arm out of their unmoving hands, then eased his throbbing right arm free. All around him a forest of immobile robot guards and Legionaries stared with unseeing eyes.

"DAMNED LILY-LIVERED MARSHMALLOWS!" Mars braced his fists on his silver-studded belt. "NEVER TRUST A MORTAL TO DO A GOD'S JOB!"

"HOW TRUE." The air darkened beside Mars, swirling like water running down a drain until it became a tall, strong-featured woman with a gloating smile. "WELL ..." She stroked her white throat. "WE MEET AGAIN, ARVID."

Kerickson pulled the wide sleeve of his tunic down as a makeshift sling. "Hello, Alline."

Thunder rumbled. The goddess laughed, then transformed her plain black gown into a shimmering, form-fitting sheet of pearls and diamonds. "YOU'RE IN ENOUGH TROUBLE ALREADY, ARVID. IF I WERE YOU, I WOULDN'T ADD INSULTING THE QUEEN OF HADES TO THE LIST."

"Gaius!" Amaelia struggled against Gracchus's grip near the top of the steps. "Gaius, be careful!"

"HOW SWEET." Demea crossed her arms and thunder pealed again, louder this time. "PERHAPS WE CAN HAVE YOU BOTH BURNED IN THE SAME FUNERAL PYRE."

"DON'T YOU THINK YOU'RE GETTING AHEAD OF YOURSELF HERE, GIRLIE?" Mars shouldered in front of her. "THIS IS MY TEMPLE, YOU KNOW, AND MY SAC-RIFICE, SO SHUT UP AND GET OUT OF THE WAY."

"Yeah, Alline." Kerickson dodged behind the deactivated robots and straightened his helmet. "Mind your own business. This is strictly between us guys."

"IS THAT SO?" Demea pushed back in front of Mars, growing to half again his stature.

"WHY DON'T YOU GO POWDER YOUR NOSE?" Mars's eyes gleamed an intense, bloody red. "THIS IS A PRI-VATE SACRIFICE." He raised both arms high into the air and summoned a crackling yellow lightning bolt in each hand.

In answer, Demea conjured a blue ball of electricity between her two palms.

"AND YOU'RE—NOT—" Mars winked a baleful, red eye. "—WANTED!"

They both flung their weapons at the same instant. There was a blinding flash in midair, and then a huge thunderclap knocked Kerickson to his knees. His ears rang and the air tasted of burnt steel. Gagging and coughing, he wiped at his tearing eyes with his good hand.

In the middle of the steps, a cloud of gray smoke dissipated in the breeze, leaving one indistinct form behind. Kerickson blinked hard. It resolved into the huge, paunchy God of War.

"WELL!" Mars pushed back his tunic sleeves. "NOW THAT I'VE HAD A CHANCE TO WORK UP AN APPETITE, LET'S GET ON WITH IT."

Kerickson took a deep shuddering breath and looked up into the blue sky. "Minerva!"

Mars cracked his knuckles. "YOU KNOW, YOU REALLY ARE PITIFUL, EVEN FOR A MORTAL."

A brown feather drifted down to the pavement; then the owl fluttered to the steps in front of Kerickson. "YOU CALLED?"

Kerickson staggered back onto his feet. On the steps, Mars pantomimed drawing back a bowstring. "TALK ABOUT SHOOTING DUCKS IN A BARREL." He snickered as a crackling yellow light began to writhe about his right hand.

"Minerva, I could really use some help here!" Kerickson readied himself to jump, although it would probably not do the slightest bit of good.

"MIGHT ONE INQUIRE JUST WHAT YOU HAVE IN MIND?" The owl eyed the God of War.

"Ummm ..." That, of course, was a good question. He flinched as Mars's throwing arm cocked back over his armored shoulder, another thunderbolt sizzling in his pudgy hand. It was hopeless, he thought, it would take at least a river to put that out, or maybe a whole ...

"Neptune!" He turned back to the owl. "Call Neptune!"

The owl disappeared with a flick of its brown wings.

Mars's teeth gleamed white through his curly red beard. "NOW HOLD STILL, YOU LITTLE BUGGER! THIS WON'T HURT A BIT!"

Kerickson edged backward into the unmoving Praetorians. The air in front of the temple steps rippled like flowing water until it solidified into a tall, green-skinned man with dripping seaweed hair. "DESIST, UPSTART, OR I SHALL MAKE YOU WISH YOU HAD."

"IS THAT SO, FISHFACE?" Mars hefted his firebolt thoughtfully. "WHY DON'T YOU COME UP HERE AND SAY THAT?"

A shimmering blueness formed to the right of Neptune, then

became Venus, the voluptuous Goddess of Love. "NOW, RE-
ALLY, BOYS." She put one hand on the smooth curve of her
hip and winked. "CAN'T YOU FIND SOMETHING MORE
INTERESTING TO DO THAN FIGHT?"

On Neptune's left, a long slim column of dust and leaves
appeared, spinning faster and faster until suddenly the lithe
Goddess of the Hunt, Diana, stood before them. She notched a
shining golden arrow into her bow and aimed it at Mars's
throat. "ABANDON THE FIELD, YOU OLD LECHER."

"NOW THIS IS RICH!" Mars laughed, holding his sides.
"THREE NOBODIES MAKING NOISES AS IF THEY
COULD REALLY HOLD THEIR OWN AGAINST THE
GOD OF WAR!" His firebolt swelled until Kerickson felt the
heat on his face.

"AND ME, THOU BRAGGART." The owl appeared again,
landing at the feet of the other three. "DON'T FORGET MI-
NERVA, WHOSE CITY YOU HAVE SEEN FIT TO RAV-
ISH."

Mars giggled. "WELL, AS LONG AS YOU HAVEN'T
SEEN FIT TO STICK AROUND AND PROTECT IT,
WHAT'S A GOD TO DO?"

Up on the steps, Kerickson saw a man slip down from the
temple to pull Amaelia from Gracchus's grasp and drag her
back up the steps to the portico. Kerickson's hands clenched.
"Amaelia!"

The man hesitated, then disappeared into the shadows with
her. Kerickson tossed the Legionary's helmet aside and ran toward the steps.

"THAT'S IT, BOY. SHOW THESE LOSERS HOW IT'S
DONE." Mars winked a red eye at him, then flung the firebolt.
"I DO SO LOVE AN OPTIMIST."

Kerickson covered his head with his good arm and threw
himself to the side, hitting the stone with enough force to
knock the wind from his lungs and wring a searing burst of
pain from his broken arm. Thunder cracked overhead, then rain
drenched his body. He heard the sizzle and pop of the firebolt,
then only the spatter of fat drops of rain on the pavement.

"FIRE AND WATER." Neptune crossed his mottled-green
arms. "WE SEEM TO HAVE REACHED AN IMPASSE."

From the top of the temple Kerickson heard a long drawn-
out scream that was abruptly cut off. He wavered back to his
feet, cradling his throbbing arm.

"HURRY, MORTAL," Neptune intoned morosely. "WE

CAN HOLD THIS RED-EYED DOG OFF FOR ONLY A FEW MORE ROUNDS. YOU CAN WORSHIP US LATER."

Kerickson stumbled to the steps, then started up, one weary foot at a time. Who was that up there with Amaelia—a robot, a priest of Mars, or perhaps the murderer? Halfway up he edged past Mars's glowering figure. The god hefted another sizable firebolt, but giant raindrops pelted down again.

The god's red eyes shot off angry sparks. "YOU AND I WILL SETTLE THIS LATER!"

"Right." Kerickson shifted the dead weight of his throbbing arm. If he ever got back into the Interface, he would pull every byte that constituted Mars's personality and flush it down the vac-chute.

Three-quarters of the way up, he drew even with Quintus Gracchus and stared into the unseeing Roman face. No wonder Gracchus had played the Game so well. He reached out and touched the unflinching skin. Just like the rest of the Praetorians, Gracchus was a robot surrogate, no doubt programmed to out-Roman them all. The emergency override had stopped him, too. But then who was the man at the top?

The steps whirled under his bare feet and the pain from his arm came in waves, making it difficult to think. He sagged down to the cool marble and looked back at the Forum. Below, the four gods still faced off with Mars while the unmoving Praetorian Guards were just so many statues, hardly even remarkable in a place as crammed with monuments as this one was.

He drew a deep shuddering breath and stood up. Just a little farther and he could rest again. He focused on the steps beneath his feet, concentrating on one at a time until suddenly he found himself at the top.

Stumbling toward the great row of columns, he tried to see back in the shadowy recesses of the temple itself. "Amaelia?"

There was no answer, but he heard the slide of something being dragged. Then a sudden flurry of beating wings drew his attention to the right as several frightened doves took flight.

"Let her go!" he called into the long black shadows. "Catulus has gone for the police. You can't get away."

"That's what you think." A dimly seen figure darted from behind one of the massive white columns and fired at him. Inches from Kerickson's bare foot, the gold-inlaid marble bubbled, then fused into melted slag.

His heart pounding, he leaped behind another column. A laser pistol, he thought in amazement. If that had hit, his foot would have been only a charred memory. He leaned his head against the pillar, trying to think around the sick feeling in his stomach.

Another shimmering red laser bolt split the shadows, glancing off the column's surface only a hand's breadth from his cheek. Hastily, he slid farther back around the column, the burnt-stone smell strong in his nostrils. "Look, let her go!" he called. "Whatever you want, I'll get it for you."

"You don't expect me to believe that." The voice was cool, collected . . . and familiar.

Kerickson replayed it in his head, trying to remember. He was positive he had heard it from time to time, though not often . . . Someone enrolled in the Game? No, someone from below, from work. The image of gray suit-alls came back to him, and a disapproving face cast in granite . . . "Jeppers!"

"Don't tell me you just figured that out." J. P. Jeppers, his old boss, eased out of the shadows with Amaelia's body braced across his chest as a shield.

Kerickson saw her hands move; she was still alive. A minor surge of relief rushed through him, but then his stomach tightened as he noted the livid purple bruise across her cheek and the gag stuffed in her mouth.

"Of course, you always were rather dense. Why else would I have hired you right out of school? I needed programmers who were too inept to catch on." Jeppers's upper lip curled in a sneer. "But none of that matters now. As far as the police are concerned, I'm just another victim of the drug-runners, like the players. No one will ever know my part in this."

"Except me." Kerickson slid back around the massive column as Jeppers approached, keeping it between them.

"But you don't count." Jeppers caressed Amaelia's cheek with the pistol. Her glazed eyes widened until they seemed all whites. "You're nothing but a disgruntled employee, a screw-up, fired for good cause and suspected of murder, who then sneaked back onto the playing field and created havoc. No one would believe you, even if you were alive—which, of course, you won't be."

"You killed Micio, then." Sweat trickled down Kerickson's face. "And Wilson."

"Micio was a greedy bastard." Jeppers changed direction abruptly. "And Wilson was too damn nosy." Jeppers's arm tightened, wringing a muffled protest from Amaelia. "You, of course, are neither—just stupid."

"Not as stupid as letting Gracchus shut the entire Game down." Kerickson edged along the chill marble, trying to think of something, anything, to use as a weapon, but he didn't have so much as a sandal to throw to distract Jeppers. "Even if Catulus hadn't called the police, they would have suspected something after a few days. Too many people live here, not to mention the day-trippers; they'll be missed if they don't interact with the outside."

"That was a minor miscalculation on my part." Jeppers darted to the left, forcing Kerickson farther back around the column. "But who could have foreseen the cancellation of Gracchus's points? I programmed him to become Emperor at any cost, which unfortunately he did. But I have my share of the profits safely salted away in an outside bank. Once I take care of the two of you, I'll live in luxury for the rest of my life and there's nothing anyone can do about it."

Kerickson heard the scuffle of heels dragged across the marble.

"Too bad Mars has to miss his own sacrifice!" Jeppers called from the shadows. "But I suppose it's the thought that counts!" He heaved Amaelia's struggling body onto the altar, then picked up a gleaming knife.

If he ran to her aid, Jeppers would fry him with the laser. And if he didn't, Jeppers would kill Amaelia, who had heard everything, and then still come after him. He needed a diversion.

Minerva! His lips moved soundlessly, but then he stopped himself. All four gods were needed to hold off Mars. If he called any one of them up here to help, then Mars would be free again.

Amaelia screamed; Jeppers must have removed her gag so that he could hear her terror. "Minerva!" Kerickson called softly, knowing the computer pickups would hear him. "I need your help!"

The owl appeared before him. "THIS HAD BETTER BE WORTH IT."

Below, he heard Mars laugh, then the sizzle of a firebolt. "Manifest in Jeppers's face." The owl faded and he ran around the column toward the altar.

Jeppers looked up and smiled, raising the laser pistol. "So glad that you could—" His voice broke off as the owl appeared in his face, squawking and beating its wings. Even though the holographic image had no substance, he reacted to it reflexively and tried to beat it away from his eyes.

Kerickson threw himself at Jeppers and knocked him to the marble floor, then fought the pain of his broken arm, groping for the laser pistol even though he didn't know how accurately he could fire it with his left hand.

When his fingers encountered the cold hard steel, he whirled, and aimed it at Jeppers—and stopped. The executive lay still and pale, a thin red rivulet seeping from his scalp across the white stone.

"LET'S GET ON WITH THE SACRIFICE!" Mars appeared at the altar, lighting the temple's recesses with a brilliant red glow. He held a firebolt in one hand as he leaned over Amaelia's bound body.

"Minerva!" Kerickson called.

"IT'S TOO LATE." The owl landed on Jeppers's nose. "THE STALEMATE IS BROKEN."

"SUCH A PRETTY DISH." Mars transformed the firebolt into a fiery sword. "PERHAPS WE SHOULD HAVE A BIT OF FUN BEFORE THE END."

"Go to the Interface!" Kerickson pushed himself onto his feet. The temple floor seemed to ripple beneath him. "Find Catulus and tell him to shut Mars down!"

"I CANNOT MANIFEST WITHIN THE INTERFACE."

Kerickson stumbled toward the altar. "He should have left some men in front of the bakery. Tell them to shut Mars down—now!"

The owl disappeared as he reached for Amaelia with his good arm, placing his body between her and the God of War. "Come on, Catulus!" he muttered between clenched teeth.

"WHY IN SUCH A HURRY, YOU FLEA-BITTEN MORSEL OF MORTALITY?" Mars's face gleamed with a lurid red glow. "AFTER ALL, YOU ONLY GET TO DIE ONCE." He raised his flaming sword and winked. "GOOD-BYE, SUCKER—"

Without warning, the electric braziers lighting the altar flickered out. So did the sun and the baleful red glow of Mars's oversized body, leaving them in a smooth, black silence.

Kerickson sagged back against Amaelia's prone body on the altar. Cold sweat drenched his body. Then he turned around, searched until he found her bound wrists, and began to work on the ropes with his good hand.

"What—What happened?" she asked.

"I told Catulus to turn Mars off, but—" He swore under his breath as he struggled one-handedly with the unseen knot. "—but he must not have known what to do. I guess he turned everything off just to be safe." The ropes on her hands loosened and he moved down to her feet.

"It's so—dark." He felt her shiver. "And it's getting cold again. What will we do?"

After a moment her feet were free. He hauled himself up onto the altar and put his left arm around her shoulder. She felt warm and soft against his aching body, and wonderfully human. "The police should be here before too long, but I guess until they come, we'll just have to think of something." He inhaled the lemony scent of her hair. "Got any ideas?"

CHAPTER
TWENTY-FOUR

The interior of the Interface was familiar and relaxing. Sitting in his old seat before the console, Kerickson closed his eyes and let the on-call HabiTek doctor work on his broken arm as the pain medication set him adrift in a golden haze.

The bone-knitting field snapped off.

"How's the arm?" Detective Sergeant Arjack asked.

Dr. Simpkins examined the instrument's readout. "It'll hold—for the time being." He put a hand on Kerickson's good shoulder. "You'll need additional treatment, though. Don't put it off."

Kerickson nodded, then looked around the circular room. "What about Jeppers?"

"I had word back from the hospital a few minutes ago." The Arjack folded its massive arms. "Just a lacerated scalp and a minor concussion, nothing serious. He'll be released in a day or two."

Relief flooded through Kerickson. "He'll be able to talk, then."

"I think 'sing like a canary' is the proper expression." The police robot blinked at him. "Are you ready to finish your statement now?"

Kerickson flexed his right arm. Somewhere in the distance he could feel a faint ache, like a nagging thought that wouldn't go away, but he could think now and make sense—which was more than he had been able to do by the time the dome's power had come back on and Amaelia had helped him down to the Interface.

"It was Jeppers all the time." He rolled his sleeve back down over his newly mended arm. "He must have conspired with Micio Metullus, the Game's reigning Emperor, to use the

236

Underworld as a hiding place for criminals and a staging area for drug-running."

"So Jeppers wasn't lying," Amaelia said from the corner. "My father had a part in this, too."

Kerickson nodded. "I think the whole scheme was originally Micio's idea. Probably, Jeppers got wind of it, then demanded to be cut in. In return, he made things a lot easier—sabotaged certain programs likely to interfere, such as Minerva and Apollo, let Micio use Gate Four without supervision, allowed the criminals free run of the Underworld."

His head sagged back against the cushioned headrest. "And I was so stupid! I never suspected for a minute. It was Wilson who realized something was really wrong. The day before Micio's murder, he'd been down at the Gladiatorial School, investigating the sale of extra hit points. He must have seen something there—maybe dead players who were supposed to be in the Underworld, or formerly inept Gladiators who'd risen too far in the rankings, or even drugged-out addicts begging for their next fix!"

Amaelia slipped behind his chair and reached down to touch his face with cool, slim fingers. "You couldn't have known."

"But he enrolled me as a gladiator trainee!" Kerickson lurched to his feet. "I should have known that wasn't a random choice and started looking there. Instead, I chased over the entire Imperium, when it was obvious that anyone selling hit points had to have an illicit input into the Game computer."

The Arjack cocked its head in a very lifelike gesture. "So you think Giles Wilson was murdered by Jeppers, too."

"He admitted it." Kerickson mopped at the sweat on his face with his sleeve. "Wilson was getting too nosy. Jeppers couldn't afford to have smart programmers around, ones that could put two and two together. He needed idiots—like me."

"I don't think an 'idiot' could have rescued me from Hades." Amaelia sat down in Wilson's old chair. "Or gotten that override that stopped Quintus Gracchus and the rest of his robot guards. In fact, I don't think anyone else in the Game could have done what you did."

The warmth in her voice penetrated through the fog of weariness that was dragging him down. He felt his cheeks go warm.

"Well, that's a very interesting theory," the Arjack broke in, "but we need some sort of proof. The memory banks of the Game computer now hold the latest edition of the Encyclopedia Galactica—with addendums. At the moment, it's just going to be your word against his. Even with a truth-scan, we might not be able to get a conviction."

Proof . . . Kerickson ran a hand back through his hair. Jeppers had made every effort to cover his tracks. And yet there had to be something, the back of his mind whispered to him—something that could be turned over to the police.

"I'm sorry," he finally mumbled. "I can't think of a thing right now."

The doctor shot the Arjack a pointed look. "He really should get some rest."

"All right." The Arjack nodded. "We'll come back tomorrow, after we finish questioning the men we've already arrested. Maybe you'll have something more for us by then."

Kerickson sat down. "Thank—" He broke off as he felt something flexible and thin slide over his ribs. Reaching inside his tunic, he pulled out several plas sheets and stared at them numbly.

"What's that?" Amaelia asked.

"The stats." A slow smile spread across his face. "The diagnostics I ran on Gracchus's Interface—the ones that first clued me in."

The Arjack held out its hand and accepted the flimsy plas sheets. "Then we just may have what we need after all."

"I feel silly," Kerickson admitted over the clop of the horses' hooves on the pavement of the Via Appia.

Amaelia smiled and leaned against him as the chariot turned to enter the Forum, where it seemed the entire Game had come out to see the triumph awarded to him by the Senate. "This is quite an honor. You might as well relax and enjoy it."

"Remember, thou art only a mortal," a voice intoned from behind him. "Remember, thou art—"

"And you!" Kerickson turned around and glared at the wrinkled old slave. "You might as well save that stuff for the real players."

Amaelia put a hand on his shoulder. "It's traditional," she whispered, her warm breath tickling his ear. "Don't hurt Tithones's feelings. He might never get the chance to do this again."

The crowd cheered as the chariot approached the Temple of Jupiter, the traditional ending point for all triumphs. Kerickson gripped the reins tighter as the two black horses flattened their ears and jerked their heads, upset by all the noise. How had he ever let himself get talked into this? It was pointless. What he really needed to be doing was looking for another job.

Of course, he had been rather busy the last few days adjusting the parameters on all the god programs, resetting the weather back to midwinter, and rebooting all the memory banks that Jeppers had copied over. And then there had been the problem of what to do about Pluto and Demea.

When the police had finished investigating, they took Kerickson to see the highly illegal bio-Interface hidden within the Underworld. It contained only two bodies at the moment: Alline and a man named Delbert Wayne Fields, who had been playing Pluto.

"It's permanent," the Arjack had said after it opened the door into the tank room. "Fields must have paid Jeppers a fortune for this setup."

Kerickson stared at the man beneath the first tank's transparent cover—a short, middle-aged, balding man who had nothing in common with Pluto's smoldering dark presence—then moved on to the second tank and gazed down at his ex-wife's still, white face. "What do you mean, permanent?"

"Certain cerebral connections have been permanently severed. Their bodies' autonomic functions are being maintained by the tanks' systems and will cease to function if we remove them."

"They'll die." Kerickson touched the frigid plas, feeling like a character in a grade-D holo.

"They cannot remain here unless HabiTek approves." The Arjack shook its head. "This is their facility, and they're not legally bound by Jeppers's actions. He had no authority to authorize something like this."

Afterward, without really understanding why, Kerickson had gone to the HabiTek board and asked for approval to leave the pair connected, promising to limit their actions much more severely than any of the other god programs. In a way, it was a unique punishment. They would go on in that sort of half-life until the natural death of their bodies, with no hope of reprieve, no chance to ever walk the real world again.

Still, he told himself as the chariot approached the foot of the temple, he supposed it was better than the alternative.

The noise level continued to rise; the horses rolled their white-rimmed eyes and tried to bolt as he hauled back on the reins to halt them at the bottom of the great white marble steps.

At the top, under the portico, Oppius Catulus raised his arms and signaled for quiet. Like an ocean wave throwing itself against the beach, the crowd's noise crested, then receded. He waited another moment, his purple cloak billowing in the chill breeze, then nodded. "We have come here today to honor Gaius Clodius Lucinius, known in the outside as Arvid Gerald Kerickson."

Two Praetorian Guards took a firm hold on the horses' headstalls so that Kerickson and Amaelia could get out of the chariot. Tall and graceful, Amaelia swept up the gold-inlaid steps, every inch a princess. He followed behind, feeling like an imposter and a fool.

When he reached the top, Catulus shook his hand, then turned him around to stare out over the kaleidoscopic sea of expectant faces below. "Some of us have played less than a quarter, while others like myself have spent years perfecting our roles." His voice rang out deep and clear in the crisp winter air. "The Game is more than important to us; it is our life." A roar of agreement went up from the assembled slaves and freedmen, nobles and Legionaries and barbarians.

Catulus waited until the noise abated. "By risking your own life to find the murderer and expose the conspiracy, you have shown a dedication rare in this modern, self-absorbed age of ours." The crowd roared again, the people raising their arms high into the air. He nodded and waved them quiet. "As reigning Emperor, I have been asked to make you an offer, Gaius Clodius Lucinius."

Kerickson stared at his feet, acutely uncomfortable in the middle of so much attention focused solely on himself.

"HabiTek will pay you double Jeppers's old salary if you will agree to stay on in the Interface and supervise the Game."

Kerickson shook his head even as the crowd began to chant his name. He didn't want to stay here, to be reminded daily of how he had failed—a failure that had cost Wilson his life and caused millions of credits in damages. It would take at least a year to set everything to rights again, perhaps longer.

The crowd noise dribbled away into a surprised mutter.

"I'm sorry," he said to Catulus. "I appreciate the offer, but I really think it would be better for everyone concerned if I just moved on."

"NOT FOR ME, MY HERO," a vibrant female voice said from behind.

He whirled around and saw the air sparkle like light reflected from water, then solidify into the twice-life-size form of a dazzling young woman wearing the Aegis on her breast—the storm shield of her father, Jupiter. She smiled, then walked forward, her sheer white gown swirling around her body as she gazed down at him. Below, the crowd dropped to its knees as though it had a single mind.

At the top of the steps, Catulus and Amaelia knelt, too, bowing their heads. "Minerva, Goddess of Wise Counsel," Amaelia murmured. "We are honored by your presence."

"AND I BY YOURS, CHILD." Minerva's gray eyes glowed. "YOU HAVE SHOWED RARE COURAGE AND SENSE IN THE PAST DAYS."

Kerickson looked around at the kneeling people. He felt stupid to be the only one still standing, but decided he would feel even dumber kneeling to a holo. "You—look much more yourself," he said finally.

"THANKS TO YOU." She smiled, and it seemed to him that her flawless face was both ancient and ageless. "IT IS YOU WHOM I HAVE TO THANK FOR MY CITY. ARE YOU SURE THAT YOU WILL NOT STAY? THERE IS STILL SO MUCH THAT NEEDS TO BE DONE."

"Someone else will do it for you," he said. "In fact, probably even better than I could. It's time for me to go."

"AND LEAVE A JOB UNDONE?" The corners of her mouth quirked up. "THAT DOESN'T SOUND LIKE YOU."

"Oh," he said gloomily, "I think it's just like me."

"WELL—" Minerva held her palm out and a small gray mouse appeared in the middle of it. "I SUPPOSE THAT EVEN A GODDESS CAN BE MISTAKEN."

Kerickson watched in stupefied horror as she opened her mouth and popped the writhing mouse in. "But—"

With her little finger, Minerva delicately tucked the whirling tail into her mouth.

A muscle twitched underneath Kerickson's right eye. Since the restoration of order, he had worked for hours to reset Minerva's parameters, but obviously they were still off—very off.

Minerva folded her perfect, white fingers. "IS THERE NO WAY WE CAN PERSUADE YOU TO STAY?"

Amaelia reached out and took his cold hand between her two warm ones. "We need you—Arvid. Why don't you stay until everything's back to normal? Then you can take your time finding a new job."

Another shivering, dark-eyed mouse appeared in the middle of Minerva's hand. He eyed it glumly; if the Goddess of Wisdom and Civilized Life was still dining on live rodents, it could be no one's fault but his. Maybe he wasn't very good at his job, but he ought to at least stick around until he'd set things right.

"Okay," he said finally. "I'll stay until everything is running properly again."

A great cheer went up from the crowd, and Amaelia leaned against his shoulder so that her coppery hair brushed his face and the sweet fragrance of her perfume overwhelmed his senses.

"WELL DONE, MY HERO." Minerva winked. "WELL DONE."

DEL REY DISCOVERY

Experience the wonder of discovery with Del Rey's newest authors!

... Because something new is always worth the risk!

TURN THE PAGE FOR AN EXCERPT FROM THE NEXT DEL REY DISCOVERY:

The Heldan
by Deborah Talmadge-Bickmore

The door thudded open, echoing heavily against the wall. The objects on the mantel over the hearth shook with a sharp rattle. Melina broke in, short of breath from running. There was excitement on her face, and her red hair was in disarray.

The rag rested on the rough, wooden table, Senea's hand clenched around it. Their mother looked up from the mending she was doing, and their father turned from the fire.

"Father," Melina said breathlessly, glancing at Senea with a strange expression in her green eyes. It was almost as if she suppressed a wild exultation. "There is news. A rumor going around. Aldived has called for held-law."

There was utter silence.

The rag sped from Senea's hand abruptly and struck the opposite wall, spattered the plaster with a wet spray, and fell to the floor.

Senea slammed the bucket of water on the table, sloshing water over the rim, and stalked out of the house, leaving shock in the room behind her.

Mother and father looked at each other, helpless in their distress.

And from the corner, where she had been sitting quietly, playing with a rag doll, Loran stirred and rose. She went to her mother, frightened from the sudden tension that gripped the room.

"What's held-law?" she asked.

"Shush, child," her mother said, and looked to her husband. "Tolen?"

He rose. "I'll go and find out the truth of this."

Melina went to the table and sat down on the bench, gathering the folds of her loose-fitting dress into her lap. Tolen left, closing the door that Senea had left standing open.

"Senea will have to go to the Held." There was hope in Melina's voice.

"Be quiet, Melina. It may only be a rumor."

Loran looked from one to the other. "Is Senea going to be a heldan?"

"She is the oldest," Melina said. "And she is not wed. That makes her the one to go."

"We don't know anything for certain."

"Mother, don't you see what this means?" Melina asked, trying desperately to hold onto the elated hope that she felt. "Aldived will pay dowry, and then I can get married."

"Do you want Senea to go into the Held?" her mother asked angrily, upset at Melina's words.

"Why not? No one wants to marry her anymore. I don't want to become an old maid just because she turned down everyone who ever asked for her, and now she's so old nobody wants her."

"Melina, that is enough!"

"You know its true!" Melina said. "Neither Loran nor I can get married if Senea doesn't. At least if she goes into the Held . . ."

"I said, that's enough!"

Melina glowered at her mother and fell into an angry silence.

"Mother?" Loran's frightened voice was almost a whisper. "Will Senea become a heldan witch?"

For the first time since Melina had come into the house their mother paled. She turned and looked squarely at Loran.

"That custom has been changed," she said firmly.

She looked to Melina and marked the new expression on her daughter's face. It spoke like a shout in the silent room.

Melina sat like a girl carved out of granite. Her eyes were suddenly cold and hard as marble. Only her hands moved, twisting and untwisting, and that was from anger and hatred. And the movements were in the ancient patterns for protection against evil.

A chill came on Senea's mother that had nothing to do with held-law and its taking of her firstborn. It was not so simple to say that customs had been changed. No one knew for certain what the helden did behind their walls.

* * *

There was a flatness in the world stretching as far as the eye could see in any direction. It was illusion only, though, for there were valleys, ravines, and canyons out there where few ventured. Out there helden watched, and protected, and kept the peace. They were silent, unseen guardians of the people, each held-tribe guarded by their own.

They were a cast of warriors, the helden, men and women alike, each taken by held-law, a law that was called for at the discretion of the Tribelord. The oldest unwed child from each family in the held-tribe by law became of the held-caste, entered the Held, and became of the warrior, one of the protectors of the people.

The last time held-law had been called, Senea had been a young child, too young to be taken, and therefore had been spared. None of the family thought that the call would come again for many more years, and thus all daughters of Tolen would be safely within marriage when it did. The last thing Senea had expected was for it to happen to her.

One could see most of the plain from where Senea sat in her solitary anger. She came here sometimes, to this rise of hill behind the valley where the held-tribe was located, to this place of aloneness where she could sit and let the quiet of the vast plain soothe her.

But this day Senea sat, brooding, on the crest of the hill, angrily ignoring the plain that lay in soft colors of apricot and gold. She was twenty-four years old, as the time was reckoned in the held-tribe, from wet season to wet season. It was long past the time when it was appropriate for her to have begun her own family and to have brought a dowry to her father from the man she was to wed. But none that had approached her had appealed to her, and there had never been anyone that she loved. And she would not marry out of duty. Then, finally, no one asked anymore.

A daughter who did not bring a dowry to her father's house was without value and a disappointment, one that Senea could easily see in her father's eyes. On her mother's face she only saw pain and sadness. Her two younger sisters had no hope, ever, of being wed until she did, and Melina, who was six years younger than she and of age, went out often to talk to a shy young man who loved her. They wanted to get married, but it was hopeless for them. Senea must wed first, and there was no one who showed interest anymore. She thought on this as she sat.

She had watched the pained anger in Melina's face slowly come over the past two seasons, then settle there permanently.

Senea flung a rock down-slope, which struck and rattled into some brush, out of sight.

Dowry.

And it would be on Aldived's terms. The Tribelord, by law, had to pay dowry for all females he took. And Aldived was Tribelord, and he had called for held-law, and held-law was irrevocable. And she was unwed. To refuse was unheard of, simply not done, even though it was a thing that she desperately wanted to do. She was no warrior, she thought angrily. Then fear raced through her. *She was no warrior.*

She ran a hand over the light hair that she wore clasped at the nape of her neck and tried to imagine herself as one of the helden that she had seen only twice in her life. She pictured herself being dressed as those two had been: breeches and sleeveless tunics, sandals laced up to the knees, with a quiver of arrows across the back, knife at hip, bow in hand, and a gold armband on the upper arm.

She shivered. To be so brazen. She couldn't do it. She lowered her head to her knees and wept.

For long moments she stayed thus, enveloped in her grief and fear. She had been brought to this through her own foolishness. When she finally would have accepted *anyone* during the past couple of years, there had been no one to claim her, no one that had desired her. But she had always kept a hope secreted in her heart that someday one would come and take her to be his. Now this would never happen. And she was afraid. She did not want to become heldan. She did not want to become a part of the held-cast, because then she would never marry.

She closed her eyes and let the thoughts whirl around inside her mind at a furious pace, unable and not caring to stop them. When she finally raised her head, the sun was going down.

The plain stretched out in alternating bands of apricot, blue, gray, and purple. The sky overhead had become a sullen blue-green, orange and pink at the horizon. The nightly wind shift, that which each evening attended the cooling of the land, picked up and tugged at the hem around her feet.

She thought about Melina, who would surely not grieve at

248

this turn of events. She had seen the pain and unhappiness in the younger girl's eyes too long for her not to know that this would be a way to free her. She also owed her father and the woman who had mothered her.

Dowry increased a family's standing in the held-tribe. The greater the dowry, the greater the standing. And Aldived, being Tribelord, would give a large dowry because of held-law. This would bring honor to the name of Tolen in the held-tribe.

She rose up of a sudden, her mind set with determination on the idea of bringing honor to her father and happiness to Melina. Her simple dress, a loose shift that fell from neckline to sandals, fluttered in the wind as she strode down the hill and down the wash into the wide, gentle valley of her held-tribe.

The valley was edged on the south with a river, and on the north with a high ridge of rock. She did not turn her head to look at the Held at the upper end of the valley. The gate there had never been open as long as she could remember.

The Held protected the entrance to the valley in which the village lay, and the helden that lived within its walls protected the rest of the lands all about, unseen and unheard.

She entered the door of her father's house quietly and looked about her, at her mother, at Loran and Melina, and finally at her father who stood staring into the fire. She closed the door and came into the room.

"I have come back," she said, not sure of what else to say. There were so many things that needed to be said, but she didn't want to broach any of them. So she stood, quietly waiting for someone else to speak.

There was silence, and Senea looked at each one of them again. Her mother was still mending as if she hadn't even moved in all that time, her head bowed, her fingers holding the shirt so tightly they were white. Loran huddled close by, her eyes wide with fear and confusion. Melina avoided her gaze, and her father still stood with his back to her.

At last Tolen spoke. His voice was low with words thick, as if he had difficulty saying them. "I have asked at the Held. Held-law is called for tomorrow morning. As soon as the sun rises."

Senea made a helpless gesture. "Then I have no choice. I must go."

Tolen bowed his head, unable to dispute her on it, and Senea simply bowed her head in turn and retreated into silence. She had nothing to say, shocked at her father's grief, touched by it as she had never been touched by anything. She almost went to him and put her arms around him, as a child would, and beg him to change it all so she wouldn't have to go. But she couldn't. There was held-law, and there was Melina.

She turned in dismay when sounds of weeping came from her mother's bowed head, bitter and quiet. Senea went to her and sank down on her heels. She put her hand over the mending and clasped her mother's fingers in her own.

"It's all right," she said. "I will be all right." She waited. The weeping stopped, but the head did not rise. "Honor will come to this house at my going," Senea continued at last. She tried to sound confident to ease some of the grief her parents were feeling. It was a confidence that she, herself, didn't have. "I have shamed you long enough."

Her mother reacted to that, took Senea's hand in her own, and pressed it to her lips.

"Mother, I will be all right. I am willing to go. Mother?" she pleaded, and waited until her mother looked up. "Melina will be free," Senea said. "It's for the best."

She turned her head, her eyes collided with Melina's, and she was astonished by the stony hatred she saw there. The girl looked up at her, unshed tears in her eyes—whether from anger or newly realized hope Senea did not know. But it was the other expression that she did not understand. She had expected that the accustomed expression of pain and anger on Melina's face would be gone. It was—but that it had been replaced by hatred puzzled her.

There was a protracted silence, then a hissing of a voice. "Heldan witch!"

And in that electric moment her world turned upside down. She shook her head. The words went right through her without touching. *Heldan witch!*

At first she had just been trying to live with the thought of becoming heldan, of leaving her family. She stared at Melina. She had heard what she had heard in her sister's voice—hatred of an ancient, feared evil. But there had not been that practice in hundreds of years. Everyone knew that.

Heldan witch!

The very idea made her feel ill, sicker even than the

thoughts of going into the Held. A sudden urge filled her to run from this place, to run straight for the plains and far away.

She rose slowly to her feet and looked down at her hands, then put them behind her to hide their sudden trembling. "I must get ready."

A cry went up. A small body impacted with hers and embraced her with a fierceness that startled her. Senea freed her hand and touched the dark head that rested against her heart.

Loran . . . her youngest sister. Senea felt the room begin to spin. For a moment, she just stared down at her.

"Don't go," Loran pleaded. "Don't go."

Senea tried to disengage Loran's arms, but the small hands were entangled in her dress and would not turn loose. Her heart was suddenly moved by the child who clung so tightly to her. She closed her eyes weakly. She had not expected this, had not expected that anyone would care that she was going to leave them and never call them family again. She had assumed that everyone would be relieved. Clearly Melina would be. She didn't want Senea here. She put her arms around the young girl and held her close.

"I'm not really going anywhere, Loran," she said. "I am going to be at the Held, that's all."

"You'll never come here again."

"But I will, sweetheart. I'll see you often." Her eyes sought her mother's, seeking understanding for the lie she had just told. "I promise." She lay a cheek on Loran's head and blinked back tears.

"You promise?" Loran echoed. Her hands did not unclench.

"Yes, dear. I promise." And Senea closed her eyes in painful guilt.

The hands relaxed and withdrew.

Senea put the child from her and forced a smile to further compound the lie. "Go play," she said. "Everything is going to be all right. You'll see." She looked at her father who still had not turned around.

"I'll go get things ready now." And that was another untruth, for there was nothing for her to ready. She was not allowed to take anything to the Held. When Tolen did not turn around she went uncertainly to the small room she shared with her sisters.

Senea felt her left hand aching, uncurled the clenched fingers, and looked at four bloody marks where fingernails had bitten her palm. She dropped the hand to her side. Despite herself, she felt a terrible despair engulfing her. Not only would she be lost to her family, but she would also be hated. It was some horrible joke being played.

She stood staring at the bedroom, then looked at the shelf next to the window that had her belongings neatly arranged on it. She wondered what would become of those things and doubted if she'd ever know. She looked at the bedstead that she had shared with her sisters from childhood and thought about how much less crowded it would be without her. It would be even less so after Melina was married. Loran would have the room for her own after that. She almost envied Loran that privacy. She sat down, blinked back the tears that had come unbidden, and took a deep breath to stop the sudden tremor that had come.

"I don't want to be heldan," she whispered.